I JONATHAN

A CHARLESTON TALE
OF THE REBELLION

A Novel
by
George WB Scott

Archetype Imprints
an imprint of
Southern Rocket and Fountain City Publishing

PRAISE FOR I JONATHAN

"An engaging narrative that draws you into the story with geographical and historical accuracy and maintains its grip to the final word."

—Stephen Scruggs, U.S.M.A. and U.S. Army Veteran, Civil War Reenactor - 1st U.S.C.H.A.

"I know lots of people who call themselves writers who aren't as good...Civil War Charleston, was a complex place of fiery secessionists and perplexed immigrants, African Americans both enslaved and free, sailors, soldiers, musicians and drunks, old veterans and young secessionists knew nothing of war but would learn about its horrors all too soon."

—Jack Neely, Executive Director of Knoxville History Project, journalist and author of numerous books on East Tennessee history and heritage

"An impressive work of art!...Writing skills are superior, as is his knowledge of the time period...Replete with fine details...First class!"

—Rick Crary, writer for Indian River Magazine, author of A Treasure We Call Home

"The literary world has just about exhausted the moving of red and blue lines across the landscape. Languishing Lost Cause belles and beaus are likewise about "played out." It is time to look at the war through some different eyes...Charleston itself is the unsung "main character" of this story...It is my pleasure to review and recommend your 'I Jonathan: A Charleston Tale of the Rebellion.'"

—Meg Groeling, writer for the blog Emerging Civil War and author of Aftermath of Battle and the upcoming First Fallen: The Life of Colonel Elmer Ellsworth, the North's First Civil War Hero

"The high moment for me in 'I Jonathan' was the trip on the blockade runner. That segment was crafted with passion and intensity and attention to detail. I enjoyed those pages immensely. Great description of action and unique characters."
—*Steve Dean, Knoxville Civil War Round Table and creator of WBIR's award-winning Heartland Series*

"The writer is quite gifted...The descriptions are excellent...The characters are alive..."
—*Patricia Benton, Charleston, SC, Native and Knoxville writer*

"Scott's novel offers a spellbinding glimpse into Civil War Charleston, reminding us that the war touched those far removed from the battlefield even as the more routine aspects of life continued...I did enjoy it!!"
—*Caroline E. Janney, author of Remembering the Civil War: Reunion and the Limits of Reconciliation and John L. Nau III Professor in the History of the American Civil War at the University of Virginia*

"A real pro, obviously. Compelling work..."
—*Dan Pope, writer for Shenandoah, Gettysburg Review, author of Housebreaking and In the Cherry Tree*

"Seen through eyes rich and poor, black and white, the epic path of the Civil War is brought to life. A great read and marvelous contribution to understanding one of the formative periods of America."
—*Dr. Milton Russell, Professor Emeritus, University of Tennessee*

"The imagery, imagination, and detail are astounding... What a gift!"
—*Nancy Millar, former Director of the McAllen Convention and Visitors' Bureau, author of Birding the Border: Tales of the Rio Grande Valley*

Archetype Imprints
is an imprint of

Southern Rocket and George Scott Creative Enterprise

ARCHETYPE
IMPRINTS

SOUTHERN
ROCKET
PRODUCTIONS

Published by George WB Scott and Fountain City Publishing

Cover Art: Photograph by George Brock Scott

Library of Congress Control Number: 2020908932
ISBN for Print: 978-0-9760867-5-8
ISBN for ebook: 978-0-9760867-6-5
BISAC Code : FIC014060 Fiction/Historical/Civil War Era

Also by George WB Scott:

Growing Up In Eden, a Memoir

Dedication

To Jack Thomson of Charleston, who was my guide,
even though he never knew it

To Mary Boykin Chesnut, who blessed us with her
diaries and journals

To my wife Mary, who has been a great help
in this book's preparation, and
without whom my own life
would be meaningless

A NOTE FROM THE AUTHOR

I do not represent this book as anything but fiction, though I have verified many elements as to time and place.

Several years ago, I received a query letter and a box of old but readable papers from a Mrs. Taylor of Greensboro. I have not published anything under the business referred to in her letter in more than a decade, but was fascinated when I read a few pages of the documents.

It purports to be a story of a resident of Charleston, SC, living there during the Civil War, as told to his great-great nephew in 1941.

Because of my interest in history and the intriguing nature of this work, I eventually decided to format it into an actual manuscript for publication.

Wording of the times, which may be offensive to some, has been eliminated or limited to a minimum while making an attempt to retain enough to be true to time and place. To any who may be offended I apologize.

I have made some changes such as paragraph formatting and altering proper surnames to avoid concerns of descendants of actual people. I have also reworked some of the archaic terms, phrasing and/or misapplied grammar. Much of the wording and sentence structure I have not altered, as it may have been created for emphasis or other valid artistic reasons.

I have since tried to contact Mrs. Taylor, but can find no record of her since receipt of the papers. I suspect she has moved on, in whatever form that may mean.

Thank you for your interest in this story.

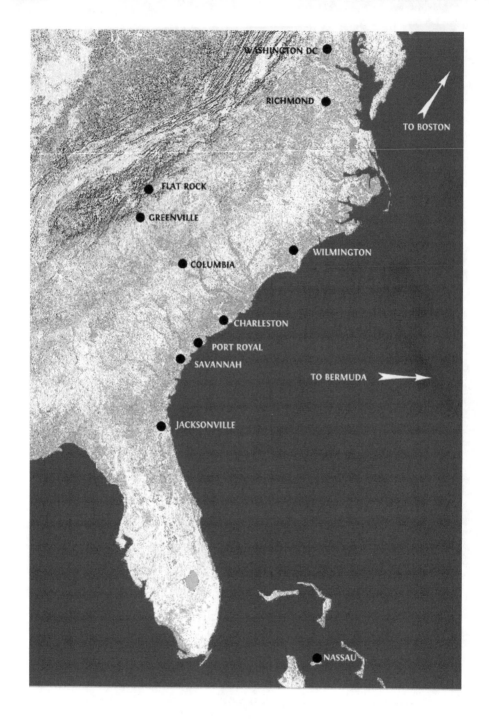

SOUTHEAST COAST OF
AMERICA

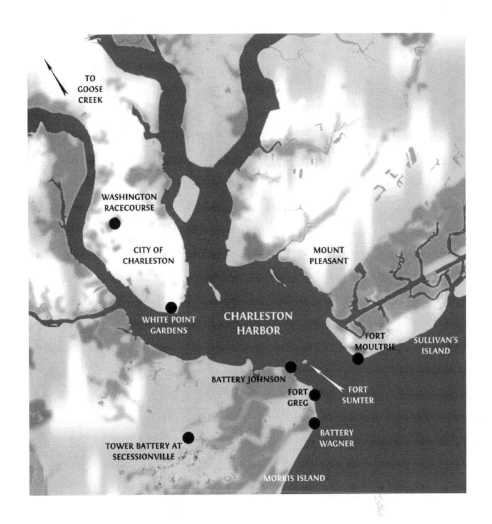

CHARLESTON HARBOR

GEOGRAPHIC FEATURES AND ELEMENTS OF ITS DEFENSE

The night had been misting rain.

Gullah was up early, combing the shore for whatever had washed up, whatever God would send him this day.

Brother Dolphin was sporting with his fellows in the waves, and came close to shore to speak to Gullah of the impending storm.

The sky was black with cloud, but no storm would follow this, no storm of nature.

Gullah looked across the waters and heard distant clanking of metal and shouted orders of men.

He watched the light, and Dolphin spoke again of the storm to come.

It was beginning.

I JONATHAN

A CHARLESTON TALE OF THE REBELLION

INTRODUCTION

My great-great uncle was turning one hundred.

My name is Ralph Bennett, and I barely remembered even meeting Great Uncle Jonathan when I was a young child. My great aunt, the sister of my mother's mother, sent me a letter and told me I should attend his birthday party. She was not up to the trip, and she said our side of the family should be represented. I was finishing up my second year of undergraduate work in the Department of Commerce at the university in Chapel Hill in early June, and had just been told by Gloria, the young lady I had been seeing, that we "weren't right for each other."

I was eager to get out of town and a trip to the mountains would be a welcome break.

I left on the early train and had to change lines three times before finally reaching Hendersonville just about six that evening. There weren't any soldiers or sailors on the trains yet; the Japs didn't bomb Pearl Harbor until later that year. Things would change fast after that.

The stories in the papers reported that the French government, bullied by the Germans, directed its own army and navy to defend itself against the British in Africa. What a world!

The evening air was cooler in Hendersonville than in the Piedmont; summer came into the mountains slowly.

I checked in to the guest home I had arranged earlier, ate the supper the owner had saved for me, and walked up the street past the old folk's home where Great Uncle Jonathan was staying. It was close to mid-town, a very large older home now used to house about ten pensioners – Uncle Jon included. Some of the tenants, all very pale and white, were sitting on the front porch with blankets on their laps. Some looked like they had passed away already. But they were tended by nurses, so I guess they still breathed. I rather dreaded seeing the vital uncle I remembered in the same condition.

I suppose I'll end up in a house like that some day, or die before I do.

A light in an upper room went dark as I passed by.

I returned to the guest house for the night. I'd already read several newspapers on my ride – grim reading about what was happening in Europe. Mussolini was telling his people that the United States was already in a de facto war with Italy.

In the parlor Duffy's Tavern was on the radio, followed by Ed Sullivan's show, and I listened for a while but I was beat and made an early night of it.

The birthday party was set for lunch the next day, a Saturday.

Next morning I ate scrambled eggs and biscuits at the house and walked toward Uncle Jon's place.

The kindly people let me in and took me to the too-warm dining room where places were set and a cake was ready for us. There was a large upright piano against a wall, a Chickering, and the linoleum flooring glared sunlight's reflection banking in from the row of windows.

My mother had died three years earlier, and my father was not interested in leaving his banking business to make the trip so I wondered who other of my relatives would be there.

Our family was not large. Uncle Jon was the father of my grandmother's sister-in-law. Mine was a distant and watery kinship. But I had felt the need to get out of town.

Cousin Alice was there, Great Uncle Jonathan's granddaughter who I had not seen in more than ten years. She was my mother's cousin from Raleigh, about forty-five years old, widowed from the first war, no kids. We tried to make some conversation, but we had little in common and fell into talking about the latest Hope and Crosby "Road" picture that I had seen with Gloria a few weeks

3

earlier.

Noon came and I expected to see a cadaverous figure rolled in on a chair, but my great uncle strode in, a steady walk, smiling broadly, accompanied by a colored nurse. He was not a large man. His hair was not snow-white as I had expected but yet had a dash of brown. His wrinkled face was alert and smiling. He went to the appointed chair and sat.

The crowd was not large. Most of his friends had passed on, and his wife had died decades ago. I had never met her.

Cousin Alice, myself, and several of the more alert house residents were the only people sitting at the table, though there were another six or eight colored people near the door. A man named Hiram was representing the Methodist church affiliated with the house and was the master of ceremonies.

Before the celebration got underway the older of the colored group, a white-haired woman named Flora who must have been over seventy, came over and spoke to Uncle Jon. They were obviously very familiar with each other, and as he listened and smiled at her, she brought her other relatives over and one at a time introduced or re-introduced them to him. Later I would get a better understanding of who they were and why they were here.

As the cake was brought in, we all sang "Happy Birthday," accompanied by Hiram at the ringing piano. Then Hiram stood and addressed the people gathered. "Everyone, we're here to celebrate the 100th birthday of our brother in Christ, Jonathan Vander. This morning he rose to another beautiful day by the grace of God, and it brought to mind this hymn, 'It Is Morning In My Heart.'" He then played and sang that lively hymn – so nice to hear a song of a morning for a centenarian instead of a sunset.

As the minister sang that song Alice leaned to me and said, "Ralph, you should hear some of the stories your great uncle has told me. See if you can get him to share some with you a little later."

That little whispered suggestion by my mother's cousin led me to hear the most moving tale claiming to be fact that I have ever heard.

SECTION ONE

FROM BOSTON TO OBLIVION

1

ROGUE

Later that day I sat with my Uncle Jonathan and began to hear his story. He had napped and washed and was ready to receive me in the little parlor beside his room, his attendant Mrs. McKay within call.

He named me "Nephew Ralph," a label I treasure.

Each person's life story grows and grows until it ends, often without it being revealed to anyone.

I captured his before it was lost to the ages. This is what he told me.

* * *

My life perhaps really began when my mother died. She named me Jonathan after the author of one of her favorite books, the tale of a man who travelled to strange lands. I was only 14 years old in 1855, and until then she and I were so close that my life was just a part of hers, God bless her gentle soul.

I had no siblings, and her tender love for me was the cocoon in which I was raised. I guess now I could see this as selfish of her, as I was left unprepared for life. Suddenly at the age of fifteen I faced the world alone, or at least with only my father, which was much the same thing.

I was in my later years of secondary school, and including the boys there and the people I knew at our Congregationalist church my circle of friends was small. Mother was protective of me, careful of the company I kept; perhaps too much so, though I did not realize it at the time. She had seen some of what bad influences can do to the young, and in those streets of Boston there were rough immigrant children from Ireland that she kept me from, and even some families of German Jews were beginning to move to our city, people of a religion Boston had prohibited in the past. I thought it odd that these landless people were despised by Americans though they are the tribe from which the Savior had sprung.

Mother's family was from a farm in southern New Hampshire, two brothers and parents who wore out their lives toiling in an unforgiving land. Agents from Boston visited their church one Sunday, and like the other girls of the town Mother was offered a position as a worker at a new factory in Lowell, Massachusetts where young rural girls were hired for the spinning and weaving machines. Her parents were glad of the chance for her to better herself as they saw it, perhaps beyond the chances of an early marriage to one of the local fellows of little prospect and less education like her brothers.

The young women were offered a life with many benefits unknown in the countryside, such as dependable meals, a safe and managed heated dormitory, regular religious services, and instruction in literature and mathematics. Libraries were provided with a wealth of books of many topics, and she embraced knowledge of the classics and an appreciation of art along with the monetary benefit of her employment.

As with many of the workers at Lowell she met suitable gentlemen at supervised teas arranged by the dormitory chaperons and it was at one of these she met my father, a rising attorney in need of a domesticated wife. Mother had worked at the loom for more than two years, and it had become clear that the unwholesome airs carrying cotton lint and dust were causing her to cough more than she should. My father, seven years her senior and third son of a third son of an old family from New York, offered my mother a respectable position as his wife, and rooms of her own in his Boston home in an exchange for the dormitory room she had been sharing with nine other women.

She had always been slim and of a youthful comeliness, if not beauty.

Her brothers had taken over the farm from her aging parents and there was no place for her in New Hampshire. So she married, leaving her bosom roommates of the factory dormitory, though she kept correspondence with one named Ellen, who later married and had a son about my age named Edward. I knew him remotely through her and we exchanged notes a time or two, and once shared a shopping holiday with our two mothers. Even now I vividly recall a small restaurant where Edward and I experienced the magic of frozen iced cream.

My father was a man not unlike myself in his selfish needs as I later came to see. He believed that he had, as he stated to my mother more than once in my childish memory, "married beneath his station" in taking a poor factory girl as his wife.

Mother bore me within a year of their marriage and devoted her life to pleasing me, feeding me, keeping me warm and clothed, and protecting me from the world. I didn't see this at the time; it was just the way I grew up, and was my normal universe. Mother found in me the replacement for her friends, and for her family.

She was never in robust health and often suffered from difficulties of the lungs. In the last year of her life she spent more time abed, finally gasping, and finally failing.

I spent my days after school-time sitting by her side, reading to her the works of popular writers like Scott and Cooper, as well as Shakespeare, and scripture which promised a better home with Jesus after she died. She finally drifted from this earth to Another, where one day I may see her again. So our minister told us.

The doctor said there was nothing to be done, he had seen this many times in former loom workers. I will never forget the last weeks at her side, the oppressive dread of the knowledge that my world would soon be without her. So sad.

She shed her life in gasping fits of agony.

My father was quite ready and prepared to be single again, and after a few weeks of appropriate mourning found himself in the sights of an impoverished New Jersey widow of ancient name and little fortune. Though he was not wealthy, his legal practice had grown enough to provide a comfortable life for my new mother and her daughters.

The wedding service was brief, and I found myself suddenly living in close proximity to two lively and pretty young women, one older and one younger than myself. The careful nurturing by my judicious and wise mother was completely swept away with fiery compulsions and unexpected drives of impending manhood.

Fanny was two years my senior. She often dressed in white with lacework about her neck, and had a glorious curving figure that would require a casual observer to give copious thought to the handiwork of God. She would carelessly brush against me in passing in the hall, her chestnut hair trailing an aroma of musky jasmine – and some indefinable woman-scent. I would catch my breath and turn to watch her, wondering what spirit had possessed me. She would continue on her way, briefly glancing back at the discomfort she had caused and perhaps noticing the arousal I was at a loss to conceal.

The younger girl, Laura, still deceptively clothed as a child, crept behind me on one such occasion and leaned to whisper in my ear, her warm breath pricking the hairs on my neck, "Come with me. I want to show you something." My mood at this moment prevented me from doing otherwise.

The careful and tender care of Mother who kept me under her gentle protection did not prepare me for the disruption which so easily and carelessly devastated my life.

What she "showed" me was, in review, a childish exploration of something that could generate a reaction in an adolescent, though the surprising experience elicited an emotion that went beyond the simple physical euphoria of sensation.

Four times over the next weeks this wide-eyed child of soft hair and teasing smile led me to a deserted room to explore my response to her caresses. This experience generated in me such a nervousness that I was constantly desperate, in hopeful anticipation of the look from her, a small beckoning, a breathless walk to the darkened room, and a complete submission to this young girl with the soft hands and smiling lips.

Laura was the spark of my humiliation, my hope, and my downfall.

On my new mother's discovery of us together one afternoon in the empty darkened chamber Father was quickly persuaded to send me to Europe, where I was to live in Paris with a distant unmarried aunt of my father's, and to study architecture at the School of Beaux-Arts in hopes of my developing a talent along those lines. But mainly to get me out of the way for his wife to better establish herself in our house.

9

I was rapidly packed and sent to the docks where I embarked on a merchantman from America to the Old World.

Before leaving I secretly met a last time with young Laura, now wearing adult clothes better fitted to her blooming figure, and I swore I would be faithful to her forever. I elicited the same promise from the very young woman, and we imagined how our lives would permanently be entwined and we would live happily together the years of our future.

I was a callow seventeen then, still idealistic.

My time in Europe was instructive on one level, less so on another. My aunt kept me sheltered from the more free culture of France. I'll tell you about that sometime, but I want to get back to my coming to South Carolina.

Charleston, you see, was not my intended destination.

I spent the summer and winter in Paris, an ocean and half-year away from my Boston home and the woman I knew I loved, into whom I had poured all my anticipation of life. Then we toured Italy with my aunt and her mature female companions. I sent Laura many letters expressing my continued faithfulness and longing, but got none in return. I had planned to stay another year in Europe, but my sojourn was cut short when a letter reached me while in Belgium, I the grieving and lonely lovesick fool. I was missing two women, Mother and Laura, the only two women in my world.

My father was ill, and he wanted to see me as soon as could be. Included was a bank draft for the money to travel back home to Boston.

As rapidly as I could manage, I booked a cabin on a sail-steamer and left Le Havre in mid-summer of 1860.

My passage was not an easy one.

The first days were placid as the wheels of the steamer plied the dark waters when the wind was against us, and the sails carried us when it was fair. The vast unmarked waste loomed as background in my tumultuous mind.

My hours spent on deck when the sun was out were periods of reverie and dreams of my impending marriage to Laura, standing before her mother to declare our love and taking my inheritance to establish our home. I could find work as a tutor at first, until I found an apprenticeship at an engineering house where I would continue my studies in structure design. We would live on what my father left me, and on love, and build our world.

I was in one such ponderous daydream as I gazed at the regular rippling waves of six feet in height spreading into the distance, finally to be lost as they flowed over the curvature of the world, when I saw far to the south a strange and shocking vision.

Without apparent cause, at about a mile distant the water had shifted. A deep trench in the sea reversed itself and a dune of rolling ocean had lifted to an enormous height in a freakish wave. It arose from the bottomless void below and advanced, moving and growing, a monster shifting the waters and approaching our vessel obliquely.

Some of the crew saw it and called to the captain who was below decks. He jumped onto the deck and urgently ordered the ship's sails trimmed and the bow turned toward the freak wave. All hatches were quickly sealed.

The fluid ridge did not tarry but grew to more than a hundred feet above its neighbor waves in a great rush of water. I knew not what it was, and thought it might portend the end of the world. But then it began to slump and recede back into the deep.

It sent a rushing hump of water out and lifted our ship at an alarming angle, raising the bow and nearly putting our stern below the sea as the stricken sailors gripped the gunwales and lines until it passed away toward the horizon.

The men were mute as they ceased their sailor-work. They removed their caps and some of them prayed as the captain turned the ship westward again to resume its rocking course to America.

The captain clamped his pipe in his teeth, stood tall again, and called on the men to go about their work. With wide-eyed stares the men took up their ropes and wrenches, collected their tar-pots and tarpaulins, and resumed their labors in awed silence.

I later heard from some of the sailors that the wave was called a rogue, and they had heard tales of them before, though few men lived to tell of one.

Some speculated that it was a sign of a change of current in mid-ocean, and in the confusion the water built up on itself.

Some believed it was a ghost of a lost ship that struggled to lift itself from the bottom, but the hungry sea would not let it crest the surface.

Electrical or magnetic attraction was another theory, though I saw no evidence of anything electric that day save our own attention.

One whispered it was Poseidon himself, reaching from his world to that of his brother on high.

Some murmured that they come in threes.

Many were silent; all were thoughtful on the matter.

Personally, I believe that it was a harmonic resonance of wave action, perhaps several of their nexus lines meeting at a vertex in random fashion, a coincidence of nature. That makes sense, right? But highly unlikely, rarely seen, at least by those who were not swept forever below the surface.

In any case, this striking event did portend something tragic, some unexpected consequence in my own life. I am still in the echoes of that divination.

We continued our course. The captain read the skies well, and in mid-Atlantic he steered us south to avoid a fierce storm. We did not escape all of the rough weather. I spent three days wishing the ship would run aground on an island, or even sink and end the misery that my stomach brought to my whole being.

We did not sink but were blown so far off course that we eventually made landfall in southern Florida, that new American state of swamps and reptiles, oranges and cotton.

Now short of coal, the crew, still awe-struck from that giant wave after more than a week, adjusted sails as the captain took his bearings toward the small port of Jacksonville where we put in to re-supply. A new course was plotted to the port of Charleston, South Carolina to properly repair and refuel.

The weather had calmed to a good sailing breeze, and one day and one night's sail brought up the low sandy coasts of South Carolina. At sight of the entrance to the bay, the captain lit the boiler and fired the last of the coal to drive us into the harbor.

As the windy wash of our ship's progress was replaced with engine power, steam began to drive the ship. Sails were drawn down and the throb of the turning wheels awakened the boat to a direct purpose with a force of its own making.

Fishing boats and ships of cargo were streaming from the inlet out to sea as we drew into sight of land that dawning day. My excitement grew. I noted the smaller boats haloed with white sales burdened under a freshening breeze. The larger ships were mostly square or sloop rigged, but three large steamers lofted black coal smoke and sounded their horns as they released their pilot guides from their service and headed into blue water.

Many were piled high with white bales of cotton headed for the mills of England, and to New England as well. To Boston, my home, where I knew Laura was awaiting me.

Oh, that all we knew for sure were truths!

I had not seen Charleston nor anything of the American South before this day. As we neared the low swampy shore we engaged a small pilot steamboat which guided us through the labyrinthine channels among the sandbars into the harbor bay.

2

MEETING STREET

We passed into the embrace of the guarding headlands and neared a small island with a brick fort a-building.

For decades since the wars of separation from England, plans had been made to protect that harbor. An artificial island was created by dumping New England granite brought from Massachusetts onto an existing (though transient) sand bar, and over the decades a solid foundation rose from the inlet waters, large and firm enough to sustain a powerful battery of cannon. This was expected to effectively seal the port from any ship or armada which attempted to force entry, and now the shape looming large in the open water was nearly complete: a fortress.

In a short time it would prove most effective.

Workers labored on the hot walls. Scores of black figures pushed barrows and carried hods of mortar up scaffolding to set brick on brick as the tops of the walls rose.

I had not ever before seen this many Negroes together at one time, though I had seen free blacks in Boston, and more in Paris.

We passed under the ominous shadow of where the guns would be mounted in the strengthening citadel.

One of the masons clad in white work clothes with a red kerchief tied around his head was supervising a team of workers while laying brick. He lifted his eyes from his work and gazed on us as we passed. I was giddy with joy at our reaching shore at last and

14

waved at what I assumed was a friendly face. He paused, then slowly waved his glistening adamantine arm. He turned his eyes from us and shifted his view out through the harbor as if seeking what would come next to his city.

The ship was using the very last of its coal to control its progress following the pilot boat toward the docks as I viewed this ancient walled village of Charles Town.

"The Holy City they call themselves," said the second officer, a stocky sailor from Connecticut. He spat. He disapproved of slavery, and this city was built mostly on the labor of slaves. Yet each man of the crew spent that evening in one of the churches of this city and thanked God for preserving his life from the leviathan wave that had towered over him but a dozen days earlier.

The next time I traveled blue water the world would be a most dangerous place, and my place in it an enigma.

The city's buildings rose before us, many gleaming white and new. Prosperous and fair and modern, this city. Not to compare with Boston in size, yet of a good harbor and good prospects.

The partially completed yet imposing Custom House greeted us. Its bold assertion of commerce together with the city's high white steeples defined the nature of this Christian community, and a glance from the harbor displayed God's blessing on the wealthy port. The sun shined brilliantly on the spires, on the fleet of commerce at the dock, on the massive rooftops of the warehouses, and on the cranes lading the bales of cotton high onto waiting ships.

We were to spend two days in port. As I stepped from the gangway onto the weathered planks of the city docks and passed by the warehouses, I felt the unsteady shore of American soil, and though distant from New England, my own.

The docks were similar to those in Boston. Men brought goods to and from, and called to each other in English, though with a different accent from that of Boston. Horse-drawn trucks and carts rattled this way and that. Dogs and boys, both black and white, romped about among the draft animals and warehouses.

Whether coming to this port or leaving from it, these barrels of turpentine, skeins of cordage, the sustenance of marine commerce, all were familiar in sight and scent to what I had seen in Le Havre and Boston. Large quantities of bags of rice were piled under great warehouse roofs, and the enormous masses of cotton piled inside looked like great drifts of snow in the shadows. High wagonloads of cotton were drawn to the steam-driven machine which would compress them into heavy bales.

An errant thought came into my head from my childhood: had the cotton been snow, I would have sledded.

I was concerned about the health of my father of course, but what eased my step was my knowledge that my beloved Laura would soon be in my arms forever and there would be no end of my delight. I hurried to the telegraph office by the tracks on Broad Street near the hotel where I would spend the night. This was in the heart of commercial lifeblood of a vital city, with mules and horses towing their loads, barrows, bearers, and businessmen.

At times I could see only black men, and I imagined it a city of Africa.

There was something more, though, something exciting and lively, youthful and growing. There was an obvious military flavor to the city, with uniforms much in evidence. Teams of Irish dock workers loaded or unloaded cargoes, except for the massive bales of cotton and the casks and bags of rice. These were loaded by colored workers, the slaves I had read of as a child back home.

As I entered the telegraph office the tall clerk smoking a pipe and looking stern and bored was transcribing a message coming from the mysterious nether-land at the end of the wire. A man was near him, busily scribbling.

The scribbling man was about thirty years old and wore a new gray suit, and in some indeterminate way made it look comfortable. He reached a paragraph and rapidly glanced up at me. "Hello," he flashed a quick smile. Swiftly his eyes returned to his task.

"Oh, ah, um…" I pontificated. I was caught off of my guard by his greeting. "Good morning sir."

"Quiet!" He held up his hand, raised his eyebrow to an astonishing height, then pointed to the telegraph, "What was that last?"

16

I JONATHAN

"They say three hundred should suffice," replied the telegraph-man in clipped monotone.

Three hundred what, I wondered.

The gray-clad man who had silenced me nodded as he listened to the tapping. This scribbling went on for quite a few minutes. My patience was suffering from anxious delay. My trip to Europe was a great education, but my life was entering a new chapter and I was growing restive to relay my current location to Laura.

The gray man began whistling. No tune, just a slightly rhythmical pattern of noise to accompany the tapping. I considered repeating his command of "Quiet!" but quickly considered other options as my business with the telegraphy may be awhile waiting. On my way to the office I had noticed a shop selling soda water drinks flavored with a selection of syrups and juices. I was not familiar with anything quite like this being served in Paris and resolved to sample local flavors while awaiting my time with the key man at the office.

I found a chair about three blocks from the doorway between Cumberland and Queen Streets and sat in the warm shade of the canopy. The traffic of the bustling roadways and sidewalks was a pleasant change from the monotony of the voyage. I ordered one of the sweet bubbly beverages from the waiter and observed the citizens of Charleston drifting up and down Market Street and also those seated around me.

The accent there was a delightful contrast with the normal English spoken in Boston, bringing to mind the difference between the accents of Brussels versus that of Paris. I fancied myself able to recognize these subtle differences, but then I fancied many things about myself those days.

Men were talking about the growing differences they held with the city's main trading partners in the North. Two ladies in day shopping dresses sipped from their unalcoholic tumblers and shared what new fashion items were being advertised in the magazines they were holding.

At another table two older gentlemen in business attire were working out a deal apparently about bird droppings, which was a novel subject to me. The elder and less prosperous-looking one, short with reddish hair, noted my attention and gave me a quick smile and nod, perhaps gauging my credit worthiness.

My attention returned to the door of the signal office when the disheveled whistler came to the threshold. I stood to go there but he turned back in, apparently recalling some spectral message he must send to the other end of the wire. I reclaimed my seat as my order arrived, sweet and cool.

Conversation I overheard under the shade of the canopy ranged deeper into politics.

Many in attendance felt Vice President Breckinridge, the staunch Southerner from Kentucky, had a chance to win the American presidency. Others thought Douglas would eke out a victory. Few believed that an unknown former one-term congressman from a frontier state under the standard of a new third political party would have a chance, even with the Democratic Party split between Breckenridge and Douglas, and with Bell drawing votes for remnants of the old Whig party. Others did not care.

Some were determined to draw South Carolina out of the Union and continue its undeniable economic success. Independence and freedom! Their interpretation of these goals was somewhat different from that of their northern brothers living in "free states."

I sampled the sweet and spicy drink and from around the corner appeared a brace of young women of this climate, fully turned out in social dress for their class, the planter class. My drink was surprising and even distracting, but these two young women were a sight to see, and a vision to be enjoyed, more compelling than the soda-water.

One was bright brunette, her hair a hard color of black, like midnight in a coal mine. Perhaps darker. Indeed, its depth might swallow up all the light of a man's resolve and send him tumbling if he were not wary. The other had hair of soft brown, minding one of fine brandy, and their voices were certainly drunkening. Each carried a parasol against the sun which matched the trim on their skirts. And each was followed by a female servant bearing the spoils of a day's shopping, one with three bundles, one with a basket jammed to overflowing. The Negro women were both slim and simply clad in

18

shifts. Sandals or light shoes held their feet and they looked happy as they chatted quietly to each other.

"Jenny! You've bankrupted me!" exclaimed the wealthier looking of the two businessmen.

"No, Father," said Jenny Haywood. "I've spent only my allowance." The guano salesman stood as the young ladies approached.

"Jenny, Carla, you are two visions from Heaven. The gardens of Charleston wilt as you pass." Hyperbole with an Irish accent.

"Mr. Tyrone, I've bought all the pink silk you have!" claimed Carla, "at least of the shade I want. Your sly compliments cannot increase your profits from me this week."

"Ladies, my comments are heartfelt, and leap from my throat unbidden, and with all sincerity."

"Mr. Tyrone, I believe our business is done for the day," stated the planter.

"All right, Thomas. I'll have two tons of that manure delivered by Saturday."

"Hold on, Jack. At your price, I'll take half a ton."

From there the conversation passed again into negotiation, and the ladies grew bored. "Eppie, go call the carriage," said Carla behind her black locks. As her servant left bearing her bundles, two tall young men in a neat gray uniform appeared, and both bowed from the waist. I had seen courtly bows in my time in Europe, and had practiced one myself at a gathering in Brussels, but this sort of behavior was quite out of fashion in Boston, at least in the circles I had known. Young men saw it as a silly ancient behavior, and older men found it too painful. Here it appeared it was not passé.

"Ladies, you are two visions," said one.

"Oh, Martin," scolded Jenny of the brandy hair. "Mr. Tyrone has already used that compliment. Don't we deserve something original?"

Martin was a robust and bright sandy blonde just shy of six feet. Sunlight flashed off his curls and bright buttons, a striking sight. He appeared about my age, as did the other who was taller and had a commanding presence. I later learned his name was William.

"I am abashed," said Martin. "I will dedicate my free evenings for the next month in composing compliments to match the beauty you bring to my world."

Carla looked at Jenny and arched an eyebrow. "That's pretty good, Jen."

"I beg your pardon," said a voice behind me. The disheveled gray man. I had forgotten about him.

He nodded to the gathering who appeared to know him, then turned to me. "I'm Charles Gallard. I did not intend rudeness." He held out his hand.

Realizing the telegraph was available, I quickly shook his hand and said, "It was not a problem sir. Good day." I took a last sip and dashed to the wire station. Overhearing the silly chatter between two lovesick Southerners reminded me of my own heart's desire, and quickened my steps.

As I entered, the clerk rose and took my order. Thinking back on the message now, I see no reason why I had spent so much money, emotion, effort to get every word right. It wasn't elegant, and it led to a rapid realization of my doom.

I had spent the previous two days en route from Jacksonville composing and reconstructing the brief message for which I would pay the outrageous fee to send:

> lauramyloveiamreturningtoyouatlasttocomplet
> emypromiseandbeginmynewlifeofdevotiontoyouf
> oreveriawaityourreplyexpectedarrivalsixdayslov
> ejonathanincharlestonsc

Why are those rates so high? It's not like you are feeding a horse to pull a coach to carry a letter to Boston. It's just a magnetic clacking.

I expected a reply the following morning.

It was perhaps an extravagance, but I had a porter carry my trunk to the Pavilion Hotel and checked in. I was eager to spend the night in a real bed, and clean myself up from my days at sea.

The money from my father's stipend for my travels was nearly gone, but I could afford a good meal and a nice rest.

20

After dining I took my ease on the porch overlooking the flow of humanity and horses parading on Meeting Street, just a few blocks from the telegraph office.

From my trunk I had pulled some drawings and sketches I had made of the ruins of Roman architecture I had seen in France and Italy, and began to enhance them with details of my own fancy.

I noticed the trees in Charleston are not the elms and sycamores of Boston, but palms, like those in the south of France, and a type of evergreen oak which can grow very large. These are live oaks, as were used to build the American heavy frigates for the Second War of American Independence fought forty-five years earlier.

There are other trees as well, but these were strange and notable to me at the time.

As I pondered the botany of the South, carts and carriages of the city wended their ways of commerce. One passing cart carrying six Negro workers was driven by that same mason foreman I saw on the island fort that morning as we sailed into the harbor. At least he wore the red kerchief on his head. He noticed my glance and nodded, and I returned the silent greeting.

"There you are!" cried the gray disheveled man I had met at the soda water bar. He climbed the stairs up to the veranda of the hotel.

"Oh, yes," I said. "Sorry about dashing off like that, but I needed to get a telegraph message to my family." Family? Yes, at that point Laura was the closest to family I had save my failing father, and I expected was soon to be the closest I could ever have.

He again proffered his hand. "Charles Gallard," he stated again. We shook and he sat.

"Jonathan Vander, Boston."

His eyebrows went up. "Welcome to Charleston, Mr. Vander."

Charles was interested in my travels and I indulged him, telling him something of my stay in Paris, including seeing the flying man, the Louisiana chess genius, the Roman limestone caves where sparkling wine was aged, some of the arts, cathedrals, and inventions I had seen, and the lively and athletic dancing known as the "Can-

21

Can" by men and women on public streets. I also shared with him my study of architecture. He was delighted at my rough sketches and asked about the aqueducts, the Roman gates, terraced vineyards, capitals, columns and buttresses. It seemed there was nothing in which Charles was not interested.

Charles was of a patrician family of the Charleston area with lands, slaves, homes in nearby Summerville, and a small estate of sixty acres or so in the North Carolina western mountains. I later discovered this was not unusual for wealthy families from the Low Country, as the coastal area of South Carolina was called. That mountainous region was even then known as "Little Charleston."

He was the fourth son of a second son and was not in line to inherit the majority of the family property, but a comfortable allowance let him explore his interests in botany, engineering, chemistry, and other obscure studies.

"If I might offer some advice, Jonathan, I suggest you not speak too freely of your hometown. It appears that there is a growing effort to draw my country away from yours."

I was aware of the political differences.

In Paris at every opportunity I would slip my aunt's carelessly watchful eye and leave her with her female friends to find a cafe where political discussions were enjoyed and argued.

I shared thoughts of the issues with Americans I would encounter, often in the wee hours over brandies and once, wormwood. Though I hadn't been attentive to the issues in detail, I had heard of a minister named Beecher in New York and his sister who had written the popular newspaper serial, which became a book, "Uncle Tom's Cabin." I hadn't read it, deeming its subject matter too depressing to include among the books I read to my dying mother, and my own interests quickly turned to the nature of the arch and the vault. And then in France there was the dazzling variety of activity, food, art.

Charles and I shared a final glass of Madeira, that rich fortified wine that Charleston seems to have always loved, and I bade him goodnight.

Farewell, with no hint our future adventures.

3

MISSIVE

That next morning despite a slight heaviness from the wine the night before, I broke my fast with some bread and bacon, and with a hot and bland porridge of coarse Indian meal which I learned was locally referred to as "grits." Instead of sweetening, a bit of salt and bacon make it a delicious bowl.

I dressed and packed my small valise, paid my bill with most of my remaining funds, and arranged to pick up my bag and trunk a bit later. I walked back to the telegraph office and found several citizens there ahead of me.

Two women were speaking about the telegram one had received. She had just learned that her son was coming home from the United States Military Academy in New York, and she was not entirely happy.

"Do you think this means he has given up a military career?" she asked her friend. She later learned he had not, though he would see service in a different army.

An older man was with his son who was reading to him what must have been a phonetic telegram apparently from New York in a strange language. The young man was pronouncing the sounds, which the older one was striving to comprehend. Apparently the older man was new to Charleston and his brother up north only spoke the Jewish language of Yiddish. I later leaned that not all Jews speak Yiddish. Many speak a Southern dialect of English.

Another youth dressed in the uniform of a Citadel cadet was dictating his message to the coolly smoking telegraph operator. "I am not returning to Philadelphia. Stop. I am staying with my friends and preparing to train with the Palmetto Rifles." He would later learn all that decision could mean. He would be marching, yes, and not just in parades, but in a bloody killing war against his childhood friends.

At a table were two men doing business. One was a salesman from New Jersey and one represented a local firm. I overheard enough to know that the one from Charleston wanted to order a large number of rifles to outfit a local company, and the salesman from New Jersey was eager to sell what he asked, as well as bullets and powder.

Business is business.

Eventually the people in line ahead of me were through and I asked if there was a return message from my transmission of yesterday.

In a slot in a pigeonhole on the wall the cloud-wreathed clerk drew a paper and passed it to me.

I eagerly took it and stepped outside to read it in better light.

Images of Laura's sweet face with that lively, mischievous spark in her eye thrilled me. I hungered for what she had written me.

But it was not from Laura, but from my childhood friend Edward:

> Jonathanmyfriendyourfatherpassedthreeweekslau
> rapregnantmarriedfiveweekssafejourneyedward

I reread the note several times trying to combine the letters into an alternative message but could not. Sixteen words which I felt ended my life. Only sixteen to draw from that one long horrible word!

The enormity of this great rogue wave rose, and then thundered down upon me.

4

FELLOWSHIP

I left the telegraph office porch in an unworldly daze. I held this precious paper from Boston, a reply from the woman I love, but it was made up of another man's words, then another man's handwriting. And yet another man's child was growing inside Laura. She was to be mine!

The sky was a clear blue, the birds sang their careless songs of love. Brilliant sun dappled the shade of the oaks as I wandered past Washington Park and drifted back to my hotel. Yet the bright July day for me was dark and foggy. I thoughtlessly gathered and packed my valise and let my feet take me to the waterfront. I passed two lovers walking hand in hand toward the town Market, and I wanted to curse their joy and knock them from each other.

Have you ever been in love? Sometimes there is no controlling what it makes you do.

I let myself drift down Broad, to East Bay beside the quays. I passed my ship, now loading, but did not see it.

On I walked in profound anguish and tried to square my own life with the new reality which had struck me. I continued in my dull haze, westward past wharves, the line of grocers, past warehouses, past German alehouses and bowling alleys, up Washington Street beyond rail yards and along the shore to the marshy end of the city.

Behind the docks and warehouses were low grog shops, some little more than lean-to sheds and a bench. Irish songs were already being belted out by impromptu trios and quartets, lively songs of innuendo, or wailing tones of tenors singing of their homes, their mothers, their lost loves.

I sat on a rotten crate by a pier and gazed on the grassy edges of the Cooper River as the sun lifted to afternoon and faded into evening. In the distance to the south I saw the loading of ships on the quay.

I felt no hunger, but there was a gnawing of my stomach's flesh from the distress of my heart. One of those ships was mine, the ship bound for Boston, the town where my father had been buried three weeks ago. Where my step-mother and her daughters lived in the house he built for her, and where my towering shame abided.

Seagulls swept and dipped, calling to each other, "Laura! Laura!"

The faint distant bells of St. Michael's Church tolled the hour as the sky grew dim, and were joined by the Huguenot church, St. Philip's, and other churches. Don't they all use the same clocks? What is the time in Boston? It didn't matter, I knew it was too late.

Too late.

Is Laura hearing bells? Laura and her husband!

The ship's loading was complete and the tide was nearly at its high mark. My ship would be outward bound soon. Already the boilers were fired and heating. Laura would be warm at home with her husband.

Waves lapped near my feet in the grassy mud shore. Market stalls and carts were packed up and the horses pulled goods back to their storage areas for the night. In the distance I saw the gas street lights being lit one by one.

As I sat, a crew of workers walked by on the road out of town alongside a cart. The driver was the mason in white I had waved to as my ship came to harbor two days previously. A different reality was upon me now. He stared and waved once again. He and his crew disappeared up the sandy pike.

In the distance a bell from the ship was calling all passengers. Calling me.

The lapping waves drew a mesmerizing power over my brain. A few yards offshore a dolphin swept by, followed by another. A few splashes and they were gone. I looked up and saw my ship was also gone.

Like Laura.

As a deeper dusk gathered about me a tribe of Irishmen came near carrying flasks and bottles. They were singing and approaching in the gloom. Theirs was a slow progress from the dock area, and their harmonies could have been improved. I did not recognize the slow song they were lowing. One of them had a gentle voice in the higher range, and the besotted chorus could occasionally pull together surprisingly well.

I suppose it was Friday evening, and having just gotten off work they were gathering in the fellowship of the common worker.

One began a sad song of home across the sea as they slowly came near. Despite the sad song, these men could not keep the sadness inside. They passed the bottle and each in his turn spoke.

One of the men said to the other, "I got a note from my sister that our aunt has died."

Another one said, "Did she say anything before she died?"

The man said, "Oh, yes! She spoke non-stop for more than fifty years!"

Because of the sadness of the previous song I was a bit stunned to find them sharing humor. This experience confirmed to me that the Irish are of a mercurial temperament.

They began "The Jolly Ploughman," and as they drank and sang, one started a small fire of some driftwood in a screen of bushes.

At the end of the song, they all yelled, "May your ploughshare never rust!"

I came near, and they silently welcomed me while carrying on their own entertainment. They began a ballad of Cork.

The bottles made their rounds again.

"One night me father and his brother were walking through Derry and they noticed a severed head on the street. My father picked it up and looked into the dead face. 'It looks like Seamus O'Brien,' says Da. 'Oh, no,' says his brother. 'Seamus was much taller!'"

The jokes were not particularly funny, or perhaps it was my state of mind. The Irish accents made them strangely macabre.

It came to be my turn to tell a joke, and they all looked at me expectantly.

"My fiancée' got pregnant while I was out of the country, and married somebody else."

The men grinned and waited for the punch line.

After about half a minute, these jovial fellows turned to another and he said, "Why can you never borrow money from a leprechaun? Because they're always a little short!"

That got their evening back on track. I kept silent as the bottle was passed, songs were again sung, and they eventually left me and the remains of the smoldering fire to find their homes, or further entertainment.

As they left, one named Denis, smallish and dark, came to me and set a mostly-filled bottle in my hands, put his hand on my shoulder and somberly nodded, then disappeared into the night. Perhaps he had experienced a similar tragedy to mine, or perhaps he could simply imagine.

I couldn't.

The sad melodies and the fiery liquid in the bottles they freely shared led me deeper into sadness and self-pity until my senses left me altogether.

5

OVERSIGHT

When I awoke in the gray morning I found ashy remnants of the night's fire, two empty bottles, and a foul taste in my mouth. I had slept on the shore, though Denis or another one of his fellows had placed my coat over me or at least within reach before he left. A simple kindness to one's fellow man.

The dew lay heavily on my face and some movements from the corner of my crusty eye drew me to notice some crabs which had come to pick about their neighborhood by the sea in the early hours before dawn. One had crawled into the cuff of my trousers, which spurred me to jump to my feet and shake a jig to rid myself of the interloper. I fell to a seat in the sandy soil.

My eyes slowly focused and the world around me stopped its wavering long enough for me to realize my plight. My only blood relative had died and his widow, who was no friend of mine, may have by now arranged inheritance of all his goods and debts, sold his house and decamped to her family home in New Jersey with the funds from the sale. My name was dismally sullied with shame by my former fiancée, soon to be a mother of another man's child. I was nearly penniless in a strange land, my ship had sailed, all my worldly possessions were entombed in my trunk in a hotel room I could not pay for. I had no money, food, shelter, nor prospects for any.

I staggered to my feet and walked out of the wild break of shrub where I had sheltered and looked down the road toward the city, then back the other way to a group of poorer houses. A wagon pulled by an enormous mule slowly made its way toward me, heading toward the quay.

As the wagon drew nearer, I could see in the early light it held three men and a boy, and several other workers walking beside it. The mule glanced unconcernedly at me as he approached. All were Negroes, though one was a lighter shade, referred to in Charleston as "yellow," who apparently had a white ancestor. I learned that this was not uncommon.

I recognized the rider beside the driver as the man in white with the red bandanna from yesterday and from Sumter, and on the hotel porch taking my ease with Charles. He apparently recognized me too, and noticed I was not at the hotel.

With a word to the others in the cart the man told the driver to stop the wagon. He lithely stepped from the cart.

"Good mornin', suh," he said as his wagon stood by. His eyes scanned the weeds I had slept in, and the remnants of my "camp."

"You been here all night?"

Strangers in this town apparently become familiar with one quite quickly.

"I missed my ship."

He pulled a small parcel from the back of the cart and told the young boy to drive on to work with the others. "Go on ahead. I'll be 'long directly."

The lad, black as a moonless night, glanced at me then at my questioner, and brushed his whip across the rump of the mule, who did not wait for a more emphatic command. He leaned into his traces to pull the cart ahead on the sandy road.

I looked at the sturdy African before me. He was not as tall as I, about five feet six inches, and built like a brick mason – stout and firm. His skin was startling in its darkness, darker than anyone I had ever spoken with before. He again wore white, a bright linen, newly laundered. He looked me up and down and seemed to make up his mind.

"Suh, the city don't like people sleepin' out doors like this. Don't you got friends to stay with?"

Well, no, of course they wouldn't, and no, I didn't.

I suspect he had seen people in desperate straits before, as both of us certainly would in the future.

My silence spoke more than anything I might have said. I believe he could read the sudden change in my fortunes.

"It looks to me like you' in a bad way right now. If you want to

30

walk with me a while, I might can help you get someplace."

I didn't know what to say to that. "How can you do that? Doesn't your…" I hesitated at using the word. "Doesn't your owner care that you aren't working?"

He didn't flinch at my question, but looked me in the eye and replied. "Suh, I am my own master. I'm free."

I didn't know there were free blacks in this city or in the South, though I had seen a few in Boston, mostly by the wharf. I fancied myself as educated and "of the world," at least for a nineteen-year-old, yet there was much in this life to learn.

"I know where you could sleep for a night or two while you get yourself situated." I had no option apparently, and the day was lightening. He and I began walking to the quays.

"I don't 'spect you had any breakfast." He opened the small parcel he had taken from the wagon. "Biscuit and ham. Don't worry, I ate good this mornin', and I'll eat good for lunch." I was not sure what to say or do, but the aroma of the still-warm biscuits decided me in short order, queasy as my stomach was. I chewed slowly.

This black freeman, a common worker, was showing Christian charity to a hapless traveler. Perhaps he was from the tribe of Samaria, in his own family's exile in America. Or perhaps he was simply a good man behaving toward travelers the way Jesus, Homer, and other philosophers and teachers taught us.

I walked the sandy trail to Charleston docks with my new black benefactor, eating the food he had given me and listening to his short-term plan for my suddenly planless life.

His name was Jacob Johnson. He was born a slave near Savannah, and trained as an apprentice mason. He married a valued house servant who bore him a son on the plantation where grew up, but Jacob was sold to a very wealthy planter near Mount Pleasant who was building a large house. That was just before his 20th birthday. He saw his wife only rarely for the next six years.

His new owner had lost his two sisters – one to yellow fever and the other from an infection from a cut – and his wife and infant son in childbirth. As he grew older, the lonely man became more reliant on his servants, who were then the only close human relationships he had. When he died, his will stated that his property should be sold, and ownership of his slaves would be transferred to the slaves themselves.

That was fifteen years earlier, and since that time Jacob had worked and saved money and "bought free" his wife, who bore him another son soon after her move to Charleston, the first free born child of his line in generations. He was purchasing his older son as he could, and meanwhile "rented" him from his Savanah owner.

The "high yellow" laborer and the other workers in the wagon were other rented slaves for projects his business was contracted for. He was their overseer and paid their contracted wages to their masters, and some to each of the workers themselves, which no one else need know about.

Hundreds of free blacks lived in Charleston and worked for wages or ran their own businesses as carpenters, masons, mechanics, even hoteliers. A lumber yard was owned by a free black who even hired some white workers. Several fine hotels on Broad Street by St. Michael's church were owned by free blacks, serving only whites. Some freemen were themselves slaveowners, buying them to use as laborers.

Because of the excitement about the current 1860 presidential election and the possibilities of what might happen afterward there was a great demand for labor, both slave and free. The U.S. government was increasing the pace of construction of Fort Sumter where I had first seen Jacob when I entered the harbor.

The fort dominates the entrance to Charleston Harbor, conceived and begun nearly thirty years earlier as a means of preventing a hostile country (Great Britain was thought the most likely at the time) from sending an armed fleet against the city.

What eventually happened might be called ironic.

Scores of slaves and free workers labored to complete the fort as a strong point for U.S. forces, and the strength of the structure was not lost on the people of South Carolina.

The state was rapidly talking itself into separating from the United States of America, a country younger than some of its own citizens, and not yet fully formed. Other states of the South had been largely influenced by Charleston and its sister cities in the Palmetto State. The state's culture had spread from the South Carolina Low Country to Alabama, Mississippi, and Louisiana, which contained New Orleans, the largest city in the South. This culture of slave plantations spread to Florida, Kentucky, Tennessee, even Texas. That new state was now growing on its own Gulf shores the desirable Sea

Island long-fiber cotton developed at plantations on Edisto and other South Carolina islands.

The highly profitable performance of the plantation system ensured vast sums for well-run plantations of size, and was driven by profits to expand the system into the new territories across the West. The great wealth provided comfortable, even extravagant living for the ruling class and a guaranteed bright future for its descendants.

It also guaranteed a permanent class of slaves. These cheap laborers were mostly forever denied the possibility of ever rising to the wealth which the high classes saw as their birthright. And of course it guaranteed within some in the North a jealousy and resentment of the wealth and inherited privilege of their Southern brothers and the unfair competition of a slave labor force.

So the South was preparing to separate from the country it was so vital in founding. It was gathering its forces, building its defenses. Thousands of hands bearing spades, trowels, hammers, and harnesses were needed, as were seamstresses and tailors, engineers and farriers, sea captains, cooks, metal smiths, and accountants. And of course, an army.

Draymen were also needed.

Jacob told me a friend of his needed a captain for his delivery crews. This was none other than Tyrone, the merchant I had seen my first day in Charleston at the soda water shop promising a plantation owner a load of South Seas guano at a bargain rate.

The Irish handled most of the local freight trade except for rice and cotton, but Tyrone, an Irishman himself, had determined to use black labor, though he needed a white overseer for some deliveries within and outside the city. In fact he was "Scots-Irish," and many in the Irish community would not work with him.

After curfew unsupervised slaves were not permitted about town – one of the residual rules resulting from a slave uprising nearly forty years before. No whites had been harmed in that time but the fear of repeating such deadly uprisings as were seen in Virginia and some islands in the Caribbean scared the ruling class into executing those charged. A strict and tight reign was kept on the travel of slaves and even free blacks ever since.

The Charleston City Guard was established to enforce the rules on unsupervised slaves and had only recently expanded to become a real police force which patrolled for suspicious characters and slaves out past curfew. Soon most city policemen would, like their brothers and cousins, join the marching societies, the shooting clubs, the killing societies, all uniformed, ordered in lines, and would turn their faces and march north.

Jacob had an agreement with Tyrone that he would furnish one or two workers for such trucking work and he knew Tyrone could use me to manage the laborers.

A deal was struck that morning between Jacob and me that I would be hired as Tyrone's occasional overseer. He would use me as needed. I would retain the passes for the slaves used, and keep such accounts as required on a daily basis, though I was not ever good with finances. Jacob would send Tyrone the men when needed.

Tyrone made arrangements to retrieve my trunk from the hotel and held it for me in a shed next to his office, near a warehouse where I found a space for a cot, my new lodgings.

So, I found gainful manual employment for the summer and into the fall of 1860 from the charity of this kind freeman Jacob who saw my need. Social caste in Charleston was not as fluid as in some other cities, but certainly allowed a friendship between me and the men I oversaw, and with Jacob Johnson and his family.

He became my guide and trusted mentor.

6

DELUSION

Charlestonians grew up with the institution of slavery and mostly didn't see it as bad or as good. It was just the way their world was.

Most Charlestonians recognized free blacks as beneficial citizens (though not allowed to vote, and enduring other restrictions which varied from state to state throughout the South). I say recognized, but they were really just part of everyone's life, like seagulls, horses, sunshine, government taxes, rain, and everything else each of us lives with in our individual worlds.

Slaves certainly made rice production possible, as no free man with a choice would spend ten hours a day in the humid hundred-degree swamps cutting irrigation channels through muck tangled in jungly roots. Plantation owners made lots of money from rice. So slavery to them was good.

I suppose, if they called themselves Christians (or at least good people), they could convince themselves that it wasn't bad for the slaves. I guess you can fool yourself into believing just about anything if it is in your own interest.

Jacob was respected as an accomplished mason and contractor for building jobs. He was often hired to build walls and walks.

One day in early fall I had delivered a cartload of lime to a country plantation worksite where Jacob had a crew working. I agreed to carry the four back to their downtown lodgings, two in a tightly-packed warren of a dormitory where slaves and free blacks were housed on Clifford Alley off King Street. They had their papers and passes, though we would not be questioned as I, a white man, was obviously managing them. Later when the war came everyone needed a pass to travel.

Two of these men were Jacob's sons and I would take them to his house. They had worked hard in the Southern heat all day, and had the fragrant aura of the working man about them, as I suppose I did.

The oldest of the three, Esau Johnson, climbed up front with me on the buckboard, which surprised me somewhat. The slaves and free blacks I had observed until then were generally so subdued that one generally would not have ridden alongside a white stranger, and without invitation it could be seen as an insolent and even aggressive act. He sullenly climbed onto the board and looked straight ahead, his jaw clenched. Having come from another world of Boston where I better understood social norms, I did not wish to challenge his preference. The others climbed into the back.

We sat mutely as I brushed the crop against the flank of the mules and clucked them to begin with a slow start. I experienced my neighbor's scent, and realized how I, who had driven long miles in sun and shade and manhandled my weighty deliveries must have been my own veritable bouquet. His smell, mine, the mules. The gentle breeze was welcome.

The beasts did not mind the weight of the men riding in the cart as the land was flat and they were certainly used to hauling loads of sand, guano, stones, bricks, shells, and other more refined goods. They had their lives of pulling weighted carts and they seemed at least as satisfied with theirs as I was with mine. More, I think.

As a gregarious soul when not in that dark pit of self-pity, I began to slowly question the young man. He was a very dark-skinned fellow not prone to verbal expression, at least not to a stranger.

The cart squeaked along the sandy trail to the main road through the tunnel-like canopy of wild Southern jungle trees. I commented on how different the vegetation is down here, so different from my home in Massachusetts. At this statement, the demeanor of the young man became a bit less grim. He expressed that he would like to see my home state. He could read, and had read that there were people in and around Boston who were working toward the freedom of all men: "abolitionists."

This language in this tone I had not heard in my time in Charleston. The "Abolition Movement" was roundly and routinely condemned and dismissed among everyone I heard speak of it there, all white of course. Many whites realized that they were on the wrong side of history, that slavery was a dying institution left over from a more primitive time, not justifiable by literate Christians. Yet the world in which they were born and in which they lived supposed that state-supported slavery was not only acceptable but the ordained will of God. Multiple references within his own Book justified it, such as:

> *And if a man smite his servant, or his maid, with a rod, and he die under his hand; he shall be surely punished.*
> *Notwithstanding, if he continue a day or two, he shall not be punished: for he is his money.*

from Exodus, and from the New Testament:

> *Let every soul be subject unto the higher powers. For there is no power but of God: the powers that be are ordained of God.*
> *Whosoever therefore resisteth the power, resisteth the ordinance of God: and they that resist shall receive to themselves damnation.*

Damnation is a scary thought among Boston Congregationalists and must have been the very terror to a Baptist slave. Such language made me uncomfortable, and I was not alone in any crowd who heard this.

Yet this young man struck me as one not to sit quietly and accept his continuing an inherited fate. He realized that doctrine written thousands of years ago might not exactly apply in later ages.

For in these moments as the mules shuffled along and the slight warm breeze brought us the swampy smells of the forest, we could discuss the simple desire of all slaves: to live like free white men and women. It would probably require the apocalyptic ruin of their overlords and their families, a new "French Terror." The younger boys in the back of the cart were silent, only listening.

After a half-hour or so we joined the main road with its traffic of walkers, riders, carriages, and cattle. Our discussion lagged and stalled as we passed stern-faced white men riding to their homes and we wondered if they could sense our recent conversation. They passed on to their destinations and on to their fates, as we did to ours.

I dropped the workers at the street where they were to sleep, and Jacob's sons to his house. I hoped that Esau, having perhaps no right to a great inheritance, would at least that night find himself possessor of a good mess of pottage.

Political speeches had all been made, it was time to vote. I didn't attempt to, and would not know who to vote for anyway. Vice President Breckinridge seemed to be the favorite around town. He spoke of Southern rights, and certainly had the experience and background for higher office, but some thought him a secret abolitionist.

Well anyway, he lost.

The candidate of the new Republican Party won, or at least came in first, as no candidate had a majority. The Democratic vote was split in three parts.

Because the elected candidate did not support expansion of slavery into America's new Western states, Charleston's sidewalk orators now called the South to secede from the United States.

And it did.

7

A JOYFUL DISPLAY

In the next few weeks parties were held all over South Carolina. Even the birds and beasts were excited, especially the horses who were receiving more of the curry brush than usual.

A great convention, the Provisional Confederate Congress, was held in Charleston in mid-December, 1860. A smallpox scare in Columbia drove the meeting to St. Andrew's Hall in Charleston, then to the larger Institute Hall, quickly renamed "Secession Hall," where the pronouncement was proclaimed on the 20th.

A year later neither St. Andrews Hall nor Secession Hall would be standing.

Regular demonstrations of public statehood bravado were followed by impromptu speeches about the city, followed by drunken celebration and then recovery far into the following morning.

The city was awash with politicians and would-be such, their admirers, hangers-on, supplicants, sycophants, siblings, servants and chaperons.

Parades were held in Charleston with brass bands, cockaded cavalry, drum corps, and fire companies (in which I never marched), as each new edition of the Mercury or the Courier newspapers carried stories of other Southern states vowing to withdraw from the Union and join a new Confederate Republic. Our fragile Union seemed torn asunder.

During one great parade the pride of the Low Country rode their brilliant mounts and reminded me of nothing so much as the reviews I had seen in Paris of the cavalry. Each soldier wore a new frock and sported a glorious plume on his hat, rivaling the leopard-skin-draped helmets of the French in their shining breastplates. Bands played the tunes known to all American military bands, though I admit I was a bit surprised to hear "Yankee Doodle" coming from a column bent on leaving my northern countrymen by any and all means, including infliction of death.

Also in step were the Palmetto Rifles, or Jager. This contingent were almost all Germans, by blood at least, some of whom spoke little English. Others had lived in Charleston for three generations and had grown up speaking with the Low Country lilt, which I was practicing myself. In fact, if I kept my Boston-accented mouth shut and wore my regular clothing, I looked more Charlestonian than these Teutonic soldiers in their pointed, plumed helmets and waxed military mustaches.

The crowd cheered the Palmetto Jager, and I could only imagine the reaction if they had been marching through Parisian streets instead of in this city.

The smartly dressed and tasseled Citadel cadets, musket-armed or with shining blades, stepped in time to their band. They were followed by row upon row of new recruits. Volunteers from all over the area were enlisting for their expected year of service. These men had joined to be trained, but weren't quite yet. They could mostly march in step which seemed to have been the first goal of the officers they elected. Some companies led by various flags of no similar designs were in uniforms, though many companies were dressed in civilian farm clothes. Some carried muskets, some hunting rifles, and many carried pikes or lances. I feared for the chances of any man who would be sent into battle with sharp sticks against professional riflemen from my state, though I later heard that this in fact had happened. I caught myself at this thought. Did I wish that they were armed better to harm my fellow Bostonians? What foolishness. How foolish to march at all!

Yet the music was stirring.

The faces of the crowd cheering the parade were joyful. Women and older men would point and cheer if they recognized one of their family or a neighbor. What a festival! They did not believe in the impending war. A simple show of force to those they termed "Yankees" would be enough to ensure their independence. No one would die. In fact, one prominent leader swore to drink all the blood

40

which may be spilled in any war with the North. In retrospect that macabre thought became hideous beyond conception.

The fire engines with their crews marched with military-like precision though their duty was not to kill, but protect. Not as glorious nor cheered as the knights which passed earlier; a shame! Their fire engines were polished and smart, with curried and liveried horses that seemed to like the crowds and attention. They knew they looked good. The crews marched neatly, still in their firemen's uniforms, soon to be exchanged for those of the army. The German company showed off its new steamer, a gleaming brass job from Philadelphia, with proud black geldings in full parade dress, the fire crew themselves in black coats with flashing silver buttons. Next came the Irish Fire Brigade with puffing chests, swaggering in their resplendent finery, bright red and green, with tall plumed hats, and shouldering axes.

At the end of the parade marched the Ethiopian Fire Brigade. The older pumping wagon they manned had been burnished and shined and glittered like lightning flashes. The men, mostly black but with some mulattoes as well, were freemen of Charleston: barbers, carpenters, masons, and smiths. As the Ethiopians passed, I recognized my friend Jacob Johnson in the group. I caught his eye and he briefly grinned and gave me a large nod as he strode on.

They walked beside their mule-drawn wagon. The mules didn't seem to care about the honor they were part of as they simply drew their load in that splendid parade of Southern Independence and Victory. The firemen, on the other hand, marched in a cadent step, in bright white shirts and caps with heads high.

The sun had broken through the clouds and they blazed. What this crew lacked in expensive clothing they compensated for in attitudes of competency and pride. This show of the Ethiopians left me with no doubt of their desire to appear able and willing to ensure safety of the houses of Charleston. Better than Germans? Well, certainly not worse. The Germans had looked good, too.

I had paused on my mission to carry a new shipment of shirts, socks, under drawers, and belts which Tyrone had sold to the army for its use in the coming year. I clicked to the mule and we continued our way through the streets.

I felt at home with the mules. It seemed we were three of a

kind, perhaps never to rise above our present station, never to know joy. Simply workers. Never to have a family.

What family I had about me at that time was the company of fellows I would meet at an alehouse near the Cooper River docks at the east end of Calhoun Street by Wharf, a simple shack run by an Irishman named Murphy.

He catered to the working class, though occasionally businessmen showed up if they were in the area. Murphy did his best to make his bar safe and comfortable within the limits of what one can do under such rough circumstances. The main room was about forty feet by thirty, with an anteroom which served stews and simple fare at a low price. There was a piano against the east wall, surprisingly in pretty good tune, which would get use from time to time. The mirror behind the bar increased the illumination of the turpentine lamps, but when I looked at it my reflection served as a reminder of my sorry state.

This was to be my grand parlor; the warehouse my bed chamber.

On the night of the last Wednesday of 1860, the Federal garrison stationed at Fort Moultrie on Sullivan's Island moved by stealth to occupy the newly armed island fort of Sumter in the middle of the entrance to Charleston Harbor.

This ominous occupation by Charleston's new enemy of a heavily armed fortress with cannon that could range on the city caused excitement for the citizens, the merchants, the cadets, and for society.

There were cheering crowds, heady celebrations and bonfires in the streets when secession was ratified. And more than a few felt the South was in a runaway train racing toward disaster.

8

STRAWBERRY TEA

On an evening of the last weekend of 1860 I was piloting Tyrone's cart, rolling and bumping along St. Phillips Street, then up Archdale to Queen. The cobbles of the street were showing stone as the sand which normally covered them had mostly washed away in recent rains.

Though this delivery was in a respectable section of the city, I had armed myself at Tyrone's suggestion and expense with a large knife of a design named after the famous Louisianian-turned-Texan Jim Bowie. I never had to use it other than to cut cordage, canvas, or leather strapping, or even to display it as a weapon, but it gave me some comfort when I travelled less secure neighborhoods, and would again do so in more turbulent days.

I drove along East Bay toward the Battery and past the great houses. At that time the homes were still in their prime, oil lights glinting and with holiday wreaths on doorways. Matrons and their daughters were taking their ease in the cool night on the piazzas and in their gardens, or preparing for evening events.

The house where I was delivering my last load of the day was owned by a family with a plantation on John's Island and hosting a holiday party for some of the young society men and women. Everyone was still flushed with the bravado shown by declaring independence. The shocking news that the Federal army garrison and their families had secretly moved from their station to occupy Fort Sumter three nights previously had everyone in a high state of excitement, and rumors abounded about the guns of Sumter aimed at downtown Charleston, perhaps this very house!

Young men were flocking into town from nearby plantations and further upstate to witness or join in the coming confrontation between the Militia and the Federal troops, who seemed determined to hold the strong point in the harbor. Columns of cadets and new recruits had spent the afternoon marching, marching on the Citadel Green parade grounds, perhaps more to burn off youthful energy for many of them than anything ominous.

The air was cool but not cold compared to the Decembers of Boston or Paris, the cloudy sky dimming to dark. I rolled up Queen and pulled the team to a halt in the alley, tied the horses and knocked at the rear door. When it opened the fragrance of baking bread and ginger cakes wafted toward me reminding me of my last meal, or rather lack of it. I was greeted by a slim woman in her late twenties. She was wearing a simple shift with a ruffled apron and sturdy work shoes, apparently a white serving maid in the large house. Her expression was not happy, not depressed exactly, but more like she was living without joy.

Her name was Isabella.

As with any first meeting, I had no inkling of how this person would influence my life and my view of the world. And of myself.

"I'll get the servants to unload," she stated, and motioned me inside. "You can sit here." I placed my hat on the kitchen chair she indicated, and after leading the two dark-skinned young men to the cart I sat in the kitchen. The maid brought me a cup of tea, a small pitcher of cream, a tiny cup of white lumps of sugar.

"Will you join me?" I asked, unsure of how I should address the woman. My appearance, though cleaner than my worst, was certainly not up to the standard of the suit-clad party-goers.

Her hair was a dark brown, rather stiff. I recognized her accent as different from Charleston. She had a slight build unexpected for one who did manual labor – washing and loading and scullery. Her face was regular, with a short pug nose, a long jaw, stern eyes, not showing rouge or powder on her cheek. Not smiling, but not unpleasant for all that. A smile could have made all the difference.

"I am working." She turned and left to tend and serve the party. My suggestion was dismissed, but with cause, so perhaps not "dismissive."

I heard the sounds of a piano from the parlor as guests began to arrive, the young debutantes and their beaux.

I sweetened and milked my tea and briefly thought of how I, a dispossessed refugee without home, friends, family or position, was seen as deserving of tea. Bondsmen attached to this house where they had worked for years unloaded my cart and could not take this small pleasure of refreshment. Yet they who knew the warm companionship of family and friends, who were likely known throughout the community were – solely because of their heritage – viewed as less than me. I, an unworthy character as I then saw myself, sat in my chair and drank from my cup.

Perhaps the workers will have tea with their families at the end of their day.

I was surprised that my drink had a surprising hint of a strawberry flavor, pleasant in its sweetness.

As I took my tea the house was a bit disrupted by the arrival of some new guests at the front. Excited voices of young men were greeted by the higher tones of the women of the house as they welcomed the guests into the parlor. A decorated Christmas tree still stood in these waning hours of 1860.

As the music permeated the house servants were drawn into listening as well and I, after carefully placing my cup on its saucer, moved into the back edge of the audience as the men began to speak.

"He's done it now! We all hoped Major Anderson would just pack up and go, or even join us. He is from Kentucky, and has a Southern wife!"

"He is friends with General Beauregard!" said another. "He was Beauregard's artillery instructor at West Point!"

There was some discussion in the little groups, with the girls flirting with their fans and young men in uniform or waistcoats striking heroic poses. Among the men in uniform was a cadet I remembered from my first day in Charleston named William. He stood tall and brilliant. He was surrounded by young women and seemed comfortable in his place at the center of attention.

I kept my place in the shadows as the pianist began a stirring interpretation of "La Marseillaise," and the men stood tall in self-congratulatory grandeur. The music was such that it made even me tap my foot, enticing even me to march off to battle.

One of the young men named Timmy, brother of William, too young for arms at fifteen, seemed amazed by the pianist. His gaze never left the musician that evening, fascinated by his digital dexterity and mostly by the dynamism of his body in motion – and of his face.

The music washed over us all. I have always found it intriguing that a tune can generate moods and emotions sometimes not appropriate to the time.

When the pianist had completed his work he was roundly applauded by his audience, and he accepted a glass of claret. Then all glasses were charged and a toast was called, "Damnation to the Yankees!"

There was an immediate apology for allowing profanity to fall upon the assumed innocence of the women. Some blushed, most grinned and sipped their glass. The high spirits and good feelings of the evening were too strong to be upset by that simple breach of etiquette.

Again, I heard the term "Yankee" as if it referred to disparaged foreigners from another land, not Americans. I had grown up thinking it a term of honor.

The chaperons, mostly matrons with an elder spouse or two, were seated against a wall near the fireplace and nodded approvingly as the different young men approached and greeted the women visiting their house. The promises of new configurations of planter dynasties were forming in the giddy air.

One of the older men suggested a reading. There was a quick response and the favorite recitist, young Timmy, gave forth with a popular Tennyson poem. Many of these men had by now memorized the work, and it was not unknown to me from my readings to my dying mother.

Tim's slight figure and gentle posture transformed into something martial and strong. His high voice took on a timbre and resonance which demanded attention. He spoke with authority, this child, and before our eyes became a captain:

> *Half a league, half a league,*
> *Half a league onward*
> *All in the valley of death*
> *Rode the six hundred….*

The group stayed silent, rapt by the cadence, the imagery, themselves believing how these very young men in the room around me would, when called, demonstrate a heroism as great as the doomed Englishmen on that battlefield at the end of the world.

> *...Theirs not to make reply,*
> *Theirs not to reason why,*
> *Theirs but to do and die.*
> *Into the valley of Death*
> *Rode the six hundred....*

Every young man there imagined himself on that field, achieving the glory he knows is within him, soon if needed, to chase the Federals out of Sumter and build their new nation. This small, gentle and effeminate youth reciting the tale of the great deeds of that Crimean afternoon became a stern vessel of Truth, of Gallantry, pouring the fire of brazen manhood of the martyrs into his speech:

> *...Flashed all their sabres bare,*
> *Flashed as they turned in air*
> *Sabring the gunners there,*
> *Charging an army, while*
> *All the world wondered....*

We in Massachusetts had learned this poem in school, and there is no denying its effect on young men who in their northern climes were perhaps reciting it themselves in those days before the war.

Now, as I understand such things, a light cavalry brigade conducting a frontal attack on emplaced canon is usually not the most rewarding military maneuver.

But that is not the point of the poem, nor the reason for its popularity.

> *...When can their glory fade?*
> *O the wild charge they made!*
> *All the world wondered.*
> *Honour the charge they made!*
> *Honour the Light Brigade,*
> *Noble six hundred!*

Noble six hundred! This is the sort of thing that channels youthful high spirits into the organized, state-sponsored murder of other young men identical to themselves! Honor! Ha! How little they knew of the trials ahead. And many of them indeed lived up to the standards of those light cavalry warriors, though unsung and many dying far away in a dark forest, beside a bridge, in a wheat field, a peach orchard, a river bank, a nameless road.

The audience stood in humble ardor of the words and the moving delivery of little Timmy in his verbal valor. The eventual fate of this child none of us could have imagined, this youth so smitten with the piano player.

"Please, give us another, Abe!" cried a cadet, and the pianist again took his seat at the instrument to the enchantment of his enraptured admirer, now shrunk again to youthful innocence.

Yet Abe seemed to share my thoughts.

He played a Christmas hymn, a plaintive tune of thoughtful melancholy.

9

RUMBLE AND POP

In the early days of 1861, the entire town was busy sewing, building, smelting, smithing, doing the work of preparing for war. Though at the time it was expected to be a war of parades, parties, speeches, and treaties – not bullets and blood.

I was at Murphy's saloon again late that night. Everyone was excited about the movement of the troops and siege trains of cannon about the city. Each ship and train which came in brought newspapers transcribing great speeches of war by the powers in capitals and colleges around the South and up North, or in Europe. The air was electric, though as the evening progressed to night, words became more bellicose, declamations by emotional workmen became louder. A few remained silent.

Men who voiced beliefs other than those proclaiming the rights of slavery and of Southern independence had mostly been driven from the city in short order.

My fellow countrymen from the harbors of Philadelphia or New York or New England silently paid their bills to the barkeeps and inns and slipped out of the city, seeking their own company and a way back to their homelands.

I had not found occasion to express myself on these matters.

I saw Charles, the disheveled gray-suited man from the telegraph office with whom I had shared memory and Madeira on the porch of the Pavilion Hotel in July. He was on one of his visits to Murphy's discussing some business matter in a corner, sipping his particular brand of liquor, Cognac brandy I believe.

Murphy's Ale House was always smoky, even when it was

largely vacant. Some serious young men who wished to affect maturity would smoke pipes, but most everyone else had cigars, often called "segars" back then. I was not ready to wander up Washington Street and to my warehouse pallet, so I grasped my tankard and journeyed through the blue cloud, closer to Charles's corner seeking whatever intelligent companionship I might find.

Some of the conversation I overheard: "The issue with your import service is that when South Carolina begins licensing trading import companies, the regulations on what is allowed in will be wide open at first, then become more restrictive. There will be a war you know, and it may last several months, even years."

A war which lasts for years! What fools!

I leaned against the wall in the shadows and listened as my thoughts took a short journey to the west, to Citadel Square.

I had seen fresh companies of men drilling and marching with shining steel pikes and swords flashing as they saluted their ladies, who had fixed satin favors on their arms as if to render them invulnerable. Bands played martial music and the strutting soon-to-be heroes smiled, stroked their mustachios, swore their oaths, and accepted glorification from friends and families.

Then they gathered in their clubs and taverns and praised themselves over what a grand display they had made.

Charles' business was completed. His companion from the Trenholm Company shook his hand and unsteadily walked away. Charles stood with him and saw me. It took him more than a moment to place me. My clothing and facial grooming (or lack of it) were changed from the evening when we shared wine on the porch of my hotel.

He came to me and extended a hand, yet another hand extended me in this "holy city" now plummeting toward its doom.

Why he suffered the presence of such a wretch as myself I do not know, but it was a comfort to me. I was not challenging to him I suppose, yet could carry on a conversation of classical literature or global politics, and I could hold my drink as well as could he. Almost as well. Perhaps not.

I have seen Charles down a full quart of fine Scotch whisky in less than three hours, win ten dollars in a game of darts, drive his losing friend home, and then return for another drink to discuss the finer points of engineering with his partners.

On this evening Charles seemed gregarious and lively. Perhaps discussion of the vagaries of import law left him looking for different conversation, even with the likes of a homeless itinerant carter like myself.

We spoke for a time of the chances of France and England joining with South Carolina in a coalition against the government in Washington City, and how many other Southern states would join the confederacy of states now brewing.

Many had thought that South Carolina would sulk for awhile, alone or nearly so, then decide to rejoin the United States. Others thought there would be a firm declaration of independence, and the forces of the republic to the north would withdraw and set up regular diplomatic relations with her sister republic to the south. Most thought there would be no war, or just didn't think about it. But some wanted war, and worked to start one.

Some wanted it to begin that very night.

The government in Washington dithered and hadn't gotten around to issuing clear orders for their troops on Sumter through the fall and winter of 1860, now turned 1861.

There had been some back and forth about when Anderson's command would surrender, as there was really no alternative as things were. The U. S. Government had failed to supply their troops with food and reinforcements and even to reply to urgent telegrams while the fort still had access to that service, nor to the messages hand delivered to their commanders in the capital. Little wonder that many in Charleston believed there would be no war. The Washington government would not even answer its own commander as to whether he should evacuate or fight.

Charles and I were deep in late foggy hours of velvet, where free thoughts can surface or be hotly expressed, then forgotten. We plumbed the depths of a bottle of spirits across the table. Smoke from cigars and pipes created a pervasive and comforting glow of thick blue atmosphere in the lamplight and humid air. It was like being in a grotto of fortune-tellers.

A cold light rain began to fall.

The barmaid passed quietly by our table and on to the dwindling number of other customers. As she passed, we paused in our discussion of, as I recall, of the superior virtues of Belgian undergarments for women – that is, lace over simple satin. I did not reveal that my shy and virtuous life sequestered by my aunt while in Europe (and my childish oath to my lost Laura) had prevented me from actual experience in such subject matter. Yet my imagination told me that there is something about lace on a woman's form which is more enticing and arousing than garments lacking it. I'm sure there is much to be said for simple satin as well. Charles was disputing my view, something about the purity of form. He often had his own contrary views.

Charles was often contrary to the general opinion of just about anything.

He thought the South should not break free, but should work toward an eventual release of the slaves, a purchase by the U.S. Government and repatriation to Africa. I think he may have missed the thought that after several generations many slaves may have considered themselves American, too. And those who can read may want some of the rights stated in our sacred documents.

I think at that point I bade Charles farewell, and wandered back in a growing dank shower to my pallet in the back of Tyrone's warehouse beside the Wilmington and Orangeburg tracks. Dawn was breaking, closing a late night even for me.

Riders dashed through the streets with news that shots had been fired.

The cannon's distant rumble disturbed my preparation to find my bed.

Despite the rain, the streets became more lively with sound. People of the city came out of their homes and gathered on the wharves. Some were attended by their house servants. A silent and apprehensive party of citizens awaited what would come next.

The harbor lights were extinguished through the night to prevent supplies and reinforcements for the Federal garrison from easily finding their way into the harbor to the occupied fort. There was still a signal light visible from the island, but the heavy guns were not firing from Sumter, not replying to the cannon firing in the distance. Some among the scattered crowd voiced the fear that an attack on the fort or its relief ships would provoke canon fire from them.

These first salvos were thankfully aimed away from the city. Just two years further along there would be other shots, and many thousands of them that would arc into the city.

Rumble and pop, distant artillery fired on a ghostly form, real or imagined across the water. Practice cannon fire was not that rare those days in Charleston, but these sounds were the first of many blasts heard by the citizens shot in anger.

As exciting as this news may have been, my condition was such after a forlorn liquid competition with Charles that I realized sleep was my goal and I returned into the shadows of my warehouse corner and to my rest.

The next day during my crude luncheon in a cotton warehouse where I had overseen cargo for delivery, I heard a report of the action. I had arrived late that morning, about 9, and not in good form. Tyrone handed me a cursory note, and I went to harness the mules.

New deliveries were more of fabric these days as factories and families prepared martial clothing for their young men. Gray and blue cloths by the bolt, buttons, braid, and leather.

"We were asleep on the dunes," said a gregarious cadet that noon as I took a respite from my deliveries in the damp city.

The young cadet presented a contradiction of himself in his uniform, buttons and collar neat in the light by the stove as he revealed his mystery of the early morning to the workmen. Yet he reclined in a careless unmilitary manner. The men were silent, and I wondered if the slaves listened for the same reason as the white workers.

"The ship cruised toward the harbor. It was there to supply the troops on Sumter in the early gloom, like a thief in the night! A signal rocket was sent up by a guard boat, and that got our attention. We awoke our commander!"

The stout young man paused for effect, and all leaned a bit closer.

"We Citadel cadets had established a series of batteries on Morris Island along the channel leading to the harbor entrance." The midnight rocket glare from the guard boat caught the eye of a lone sentry on watch, and this young man of sixteen realized that he had seen what many regard as the first signal of belligerent activities in the tragic contest to follow.

"Might I beg a sip of water?" the speaker implored.

The host, foreman of the cotton press, was abashed and immediately drew from his beer bucket a brimming mug.

The cadet brushed back his hair and eagerly took a long draw. All awaited his next words. He smacked his lips.

"We had been on watch for weeks. Our commanders heard from New York news reports that a mission was coming." He took another draw. "Those papers in New York love to print what the Navy was doing.

"Our artillery crew had drilled and drilled, and we were like a fine timepiece in our movements. My duty was to ram home the powder and shot." He seemed pleased by his duty, loading the gun with the charge that given a true aim would land on the ship.

"We saw the shadow move toward us, creeping northeast up the Main Channel."

He paused, a lunchtime ominence.

"The cadet on watch roused his fellows in camp among their cannon. With excellent precision," he told, "we manned their stations and awaited the orders of their commander.

"Yet the major hesitated to give the order.

"He understood that firing on a ship bearing the flag of the United States of America would be an extraordinary act. This would be the first officially consummated act of war to separate from the federal government!"

That government was established by Southerners and Northerners together just a few decades before. That government was now led by a nobody lawyer from a frontier state who had won only forty percent of the vote. Many even in the North considered his victory illegitimate.

"But the cadet captain gave his command. He smartly turned and did his duty. 'Number one, fire!'"

His eyebrows lifted as he quietly stated, "We fired."

He leaned forward and began more lively as he described the first blow.

The challenging warning shot ricocheted atop the water well in front of the steamer, the signal to halt. The only reaction from the ship was to release a large garrison flag on its foremast in challenge. The boat proceeded slowly up the coast.

When the ship did not stop, the next shots were in earnest from the cannons and their crews on Morris Island. Several succeeded in striking that boat, filled with soldier reinforcements, supplies, and newspaper correspondents.

The storyteller highlighted his cannon crew's efforts and the extreme importance of his job as the sponger who also rammed the shot.

Like automatons the crews had loaded, aimed, fired, sponged, loaded, and repeated until the balls flew, as he described it, like a blizzard of iron whirling about the ship.

I had witnessed cadets at practice, and could imagine the methodical precision as they worked their weapons. I had seen them moving with precise motion like the mechanical clock figures I had seen in Bruges two years earlier, each movement carefully planned and timed to optimize efficiency.

Other batteries and forts in the area heard the cadets firing, and they opened up on the distant shadow target themselves. Though enthusiastic their aim was high, so they depressed their guns for better effect. Finally, a shot disabled the steerage. The ship was halted, and used its sidewheels as means of changing direction, and turned away.

A great victory for South Carolina! Victory for the cadets of the Citadel!

The youth's mug was refilled, and the teller accepted the congratulations of his audience of ten or so. A few sidled away from the small gathering, wondering what would follow the attack on the flag of the United States of America.

Major Anderson at Fort Sumter had read of the approach of the supply ship in a local paper but had received no official notice of it and didn't believe it. The official dispatch sent to him never reached his command. On Fort Sumter when alerted by the sound of cannon firing, Major Anderson had his guns run out and readied as a show of force, but was hesitant to open fire in the confusion. Some of his garrison wanted to fire on the surrounding batteries to suppress their fire. Others did not, but the army was apparently not a democracy and the commander decided to withhold fire. A wife of one of the soldiers was not so reticent and had to be physically restrained from pulling the lanyard on a readied gun when she assumed a supply ship's approach.

Imagine a battle being fought simultaneously with the enemy and with your own wives!

In the end, the unruly behavior of the rudder and the activities of the shore batteries caused the *Star of the West* to turn and make way back to New York. Anderson wrote a letter of complaint to the Governor that he was unaware of war's declaration, and was disappointed that South Carolina would fire on a U.S. vessel without provocation.

And so, the city's relations with the forces at Sumter irrevocably changed.

10

RACE

The city was alert with the possibilities of what might come next. But first there was a society event.

Besides guano, fabrics, and foodstuffs, Tyrone dealt in luxury items and wines – really whatever he thought he could make a profit on, often things that weren't sold by his competitors.

One day in February, Race Week, we loaded the larger of his carts with tea cookies, jams and marmalades, flaky pastry cakes wrapped in oiled paper, tins of fish paste, goose liver pate' and boxes of crunchy biscuits, twenty boxes of bottled wine, seven casks of ale, and a berry-flavored syrup to dissolve in water to make a kind of punch.

All of this and bundles of white and blue serviettes were settled in the cart and covered with an oiled canvas tarp to protect from rain, of which there was none, and from dust, of which there were clouds. The mules stood carelessly stoic awaiting the driver's command. Tyrone elected to use mules that day, as his horses would not compare favorably with some of the equine flesh showing at the track. His strong mules looked competent and did not invite comparison.

He also handed me a folded paper holding fifty dollars to place on the nose of the local favorite.

Washington Race Track was a mile oval on a broad field next to farms on the upper peninsula north of the city, the "neck," where it narrows due to swampy land to the east and west. For years it was a field of contest for horses as well as the occasional duel between men.

Traffic was brisk on the road that sunny morning, with many

carriages and their liveried drivers carrying gentry in their finery, as well as with common working-class people white and black, riding and walking to the track.

This was to be a great race from what I heard, a challenge from the owner of a $20,000 purse winner against the best horse of South Carolina, quite different from the race I first had seen as a child, with both my parents. As I guided the team toward the track I reflected on my earliest experience with horse racing.

That contest was at a county fair outside of Lowell, Massachusetts. There had been rain the night before. The grass on the field was wet and there was mud all about. My mother kept me close as we strove to keep up with Father. His quick steps led us to a row of benches to view the parade. He had bought me a roasted ear of Indian on which I nibbled as the riders passed by to line up at the starting ribbon.

I remember not being very impressed as an eight-year old, not at first. The horses mostly were not as fine as the better carriage horses in our town; not all were thoroughbreds. The jockeys were mostly farmers' sons, though there were a couple of riders in colors atop beasts that stood out as superior animals – no-nonsense riders on small light saddles.

A shot was fired and the ten or so animals were spurred and whipt into wild flight. The grass was slick and two horses went down in the first stretch before the turn.

This got my attention.

Watching a half-ton and more of horse fall and struggle in this rough, casual race was pitiful to see, and one of the men did not rise. His horse had turned its leg badly, struggled to its hooves and stood wide-eyed, twitching its withers but not even trying to walk away.

The racers pounded the wet turf in the distance and were nearing the tree at the end of the pasture, where they would slow and make their turn before the run to the finish.

At the turn, taken wide by the two thoroughbreds, several animals bumped each other, and another horse went down. One animal having made the turn decided he'd had enough, and ran at right angles to the others, and despite the efforts of his rider to thrash him back into the herd, he left the field for the road home.

The remaining competitors were determined to cross the line first, and it became evident that the two thoroughbreds would be the only debate that day. The farmers' sons gamely competed among themselves to see who would show.

One of the two won, the other placed, and I was too young to care which. I had a kernel of corn stuck in my teeth that was taking my attention. The audience cheered, with some profanities expressed by some. My sweet mother did her best to cover my ears at the sound.

My father was quite pleased as he had placed a small wager on the winner's nose. We made our way to the transport as my father collected his winnings. The horse with the turned leg was slowly led staggering from the field, and I heard a shot from that direction.

I don't think these races are legal anymore, or at least not officially permitted. Too dangerous for rider and horse.

The next race I saw was when my father took me to a harness track in Franklin Park in northern Massachusetts also near Lowell, where Mother had managed the company looms. This was the year before my trip to Europe. That outing was somber, as I was already in the bad graces of my father's new wife. This was an escape for just the two of us, and both of us recalled silently with solemn glances that race of years earlier when my mother accompanied us.

That gray day my father lost every bet. We left with no glad feelings between us, nor for the future.

Charleston was sunny that day though, and people were smiling. All sorts of excitement were in the air both from the impending match race and the possible military contests with U.S. forces, somewhere to the north at some unknown date. Many, perhaps most, still held that the two countries would never come to blows. The very field of this event would prove a sad statement of the opposite in less than three years' time when it became a military prison camp.

As I drove past the Grove farm to the Washington Track, the Palmetto Rifles had assembled and were marching to and fro, creating a stellar display of Germanic military precision for the gathering crowd. These fine young men in dashing colors and bright buttons, spiked helmets and plumes struck me as the epitome of martial discipline.

At the finale of their display they marched in formation, broke into two lines, turned at twenty yards between them, and as one, shouldered their armed muskets – aimed at high angles – and fired!

The report sounded as one blast toward the sky, and a plume

of blue smoke ballooned above their sparkling bayonets.

Perhaps more of a circus act than a martial demonstration. But they would show later on a field far away that their abilities were more than show.

The grounds were bustling with visitors from all strata of the Charleston area and beyond. Servants and groomsmen were scurrying to and from the grandstand bringing refreshment to the fine women and their men in the high seats. There were many Africans in the audience in their own areas, some well-to-do, most simple house servants or free tradesmen.

The grandstand faced south on the north side of the track, ensuring the warming rays of February sun would comfort the gentry ensconced on cushioned chairs, some under lap blankets. Old and young were in attendance at this highest social event of the season. I recognized the two young women sitting together, Carla and Jenny, from my first day in Charleston as I waited at the tee-totaler shop to send a telegram to Boston. They were engaged in animated conversation, the subject probably more masculine than equine, and I doubt they would have recognized me that day, dressed as I was.

Male spectators smoked and chewed and spat into cuspidors placed where they did the most good, which was not much.

Numerous "side shows" and food stands lined the track. Some were in permanent buildings rented out for the occasion; others in portable structures or even tents brought there for the quick money to be made.

Many shacks dealt in fine wines and liquors, some in "teetotalling" beverages, and not a few selling side-bets on the races themselves. I conveyed Tyrone's envelope of cash to one of these bookmakers and received his receipt.

Among the distractions for the crowd was a counting horse, a trained pig, a juggler, a man who could guess your weight, height, and age, and there were the usual dog tricks, shell deception games, and card tricks.

As always at such tracks, numerous shady characters were doing their best to swindle and cut purses and pick pockets. My ragged appearance precluded me from being a prime target for such fellows, but I kept my wits about me, and my knife.

I saw Charles in woolen waistcoat and top hat mingling with some plantation gentry. I would not have countenanced a recognizing nod if I were he, nor would I have even had I been my previous self. Yet he did afford me a brief wave.

I expect they were discussing the recent events regarding *Star of the West*, possible resupply of Fort Sumter, the impending actions the U.S. Government must take, or perhaps the political structure and foreign positioning of the new Southern Confederacy.

Further missions for supply and reinforcement to Sumter were postponed and the soldiers garrisoning that lonely outpost had grown more desperate, hungry, cold, and resolute. Their friends in Charleston had tried to send boatloads of food to the troops and to their wives, all now reduced to eating old bread and dried salt pork and finally to only mostly rice. Anderson and the garrison proudly refused gifts of food from town, even from those at whose homes they had dined in months previous.

I delivered my wares to the man in the building Tyrone had rented and led my mules to the watering area with the grooms. As Tyrone's mules drank, I scanned the competing horses now lining up for the first heat.

These were to be "flat races" as opposed to hurdles in which other horses would race later in the day.

The celebrated entrant from Virginia was named Planet, a six-year-old which had won races all over the South including at that same Charleston track, and also which had taken a $20,000 purse the year before at a track in New York.

Planet was known as a four-miler, though he was a champion in all lengths. This was to be a four-mile race. He was a tall and beautiful chestnut stallion, a sterling example of a thoroughbred, standing nearly sixteen hands, long in body, thoroughly sound. He was a heavy favorite, and betting was lively.

South Carolina presented its entry, Abilene, a fine five-year chestnut mare with a streak of white on her face. She had contested with the famous Congaree, the wonderful horse beaten just the previous year by this same Planet she now challenged.

The air was filled with the chatter of the crowd, the barking of the dealers of ale, cider, biscuits, neighing and snorting of horses. Colorful flags on poles rustled in the breeze.

The horses were led up to the line, alert but not lathered.

The crowd hushed, paused in anticipation.

A tap struck on the head of a drum – they were off!

The competitors leapt forward, and it was a joy to see the two powerful animals matching each other stride for stride. Their sinews and legs stretched and pounded the dirt, their jockeys rocking in time with the power beneath them.

Now these were two fast horses, and each jockey thought he had the faster ride. They got up to speed and rode easily, not seeming to strain around the oval for the first mile. Planet jumped to an early lead with Abilene keeping pace and biding her time a few lengths in the rear.

Alongside the track, boys on their own mounts rode along testing their horses against the speed of the race. The crowd was in rapt attention following the action.

As they neared the grandstand and the audience the crowd cheered above the thumping of hooves and the rush of the wind. This was a thrill!

The riders crouched atop the undulating horses.

In the second mile, Abilene closed the gap.

The horses increased speed.

Abilene continued to gain on the favorite, and had drawn nearly even with a mile and a half still to run.

Half a league.

Both horses were still running "within themselves," as the expression goes, quickening the pace but not straining, not yet. Each had a reservoir of strength to draw upon.

It looked like their speed increased with each stride, building the thrill, displaying beauty of this creation of God and man.

As the beasts turned the post marking the beginning of the final mile, Planet remained about a length ahead, but now Abilene with her rider made her move.

Visible for a half-minute across the oval the two horses appeared side by side, shoulder to shoulder with each step. It was a vision of dance, like orchestrated choreography of eight legs pumping and placing, matching their steps on the field, driving a quickening tempo to measure the swelling chorale of the watchers' voices.

Now the jockeys employed their crops and made the horses work.

This was what these beasts were bred for, lived for, these few minutes of speed.

The South Carolina mare pulled away, showing her fine head

leading as she streaked across the straightway and came into the final turn.

When horses like these thoroughbreds race, the motivation seems to be more their own than in the nearly irrelevant rider. There is a natural desire to run with the opponent, to outrun, to compete, to challenge. The victor glories. The opponent either is heartbroken or, like men in contest with each other, wants to retry the bid on another field, until finally there are no more energies to challenge, no more forces to marshal, no more cannon, no more armies.

No more hope.

On this day there was hope! On this day the gold braid on uniforms shone in the sun. Everyone here knew the situation at Sumter could lead to one short demonstration of troops in the field. But the war, if it came, would be over before it began and heroes would return home in a parade of triumph to bands, banners, cheering women in their finery. The braid would still shine.

Or perhaps after years of deathly struggle and loss, privation and injury, the braid would fade from years in mud and rain, in blood. Maybe the faces above the gilded collar would be sallow and wizened by the witness of man's great folly.

Perhaps the sleeve would be empty.

But on this day the clothes were fine and bright, the faces well-fed, the laughter free, the air festive, and the hurtling horses on the track displayed all that is good and fine in the world.

Planet increased his speed; Abilene matched him.

Planet strove. Abilene advanced.

Noble Planet gave his last, but the mare's blood was up and would not be denied. Tyrone's wager seemed assured.

As they neared the pole Planet flagged and relinquished the race as the pride of South Carolina charged on to win!

The horses slowed to cool down, the jockeys each waving congratulations to the other, and a great sigh went up from the crowd, some in despair and some in victory. Winners and losers.

The favored was a great champion, but even the best champion when tried often enough can be beaten. Southern armies would learn this in a very few years, but those lessons were in the future.

The sun lit the field and the crowds knew joy.

This was Charleston's last best day.

11

JOLLY FAREWELL

After the horse race and my trip back to the stable I was standing near the docks, waiting to see if Tyrone would give me a schedule for the next day. I was not eager to work, but needed a means of paying my share of the food in the warehouse space I shared with some other itinerate workers.

We cooked communal stew-pots when we ate in the warehouse – stews of fish some of us caught, rice of course, and vegetables we would "find" among the crates and bushels of the warehouse traffic.

Some of the men who slept in the warehouse had paused there on their ways traveling home, catching rides in the railroad cars as space was found, some fleeing creditors most likely, or wives.

In any case, we would huddle about the bubbling pot when we cooked together, but I would often spend time at Murphy's or one of the German beer houses when I had a spare shilling or two.

On my last visit to a bier haus I overheard several Germans still speaking in accents of Hanover or Prussia. The men were conflicted as to what was expected of them as American Southerners, as Charlestonians. Most of them did not own slaves and didn't approve of it, and now found they were expected to work or even fight and die for it, and to be free of the government to which they had just sworn allegiance!

Many did join the army; many died for a government which did not exist when they had arrived in America.

On this night I planned to choose the less conflicted company of the alehouse.

1 JONATHAN

I waited by the pier but Tyrone was not to be seen this evening. As the sky darkened, a small pilot steamer approached the docks from the bay. The open boat held eight passengers, six of whom had been offloaded from a passing ship just outside the harbor inlet.

Some of the men were returning from the North, from schools and from business trips in New York or Philadelphia. Two were in West Point greatcoats, with footlocker trunks in tow. One man was older, swarthy-skinned, with dark gold embroidery on his elaborate jacket. He had a trimmed mustache and a fine leather valise.

I scanned the docks again for Tyrone or his messenger. Shadows under the eaves of the warehouses were fading as sunlight left the amber sky.

Somewhere to the north Laura and her new family were preparing to eat dinner, perhaps laughing at my state. Damn her.

I was already damned, and unable to release my mind from my fantasy of that young woman with whom I had shared just a brief adolescent rapture.

The mustachioed man with the broad brimmed hat and fancy jacket announced to his boat companions that he would stand all of them to a round of ale at the first good house of drink. Several agreed; others were eager to see family or had other goals that evening. After a last quick glance for Tyrone I fell into step with the men guiding our expected host to one of the finer taverns on Meeting Street connected to a small hotel, several blocks from my usual grog shop habitats.

The man's accent was Latin – not Italian, but Spanish I thought. This benevolent soul was a Mexican, named Ricardo.

Free drink was an incentive I would not pass by this night. It was cool, and I was without a coat. A good pot of beer would be a fine start to another evening of mourning.

We entered the smoky light of the Cork Inn, a hotel and restaurant and not a real competitor with a casual establishment like Murphy's Alehouse, and one I usually did not frequent. The name was a non-sequitur, as surely people entered to take a cork out.

Bright but not cool was the inside of the inn, lit by whale oil. As at Murphy's, the main room held the bar and billiard tables; a smaller room the dining tables covered with cloths, much finer that my regular tavern. Groups of men were clustered about discussing the horse race and Anderson's presence at Fort Sumter. Some felt the relocation of Federal troops was an aggressive act and demanded retaliation against the "foreign occupation" of Charleston's most vital defensive point.

As long as U.S. troops held Fort Sumter the threat of the North was real. Many wondered what that new year of 1861 would bring, but most didn't, caring more about their own businesses.

One strange element of the situation in the harbor was that Colonel Anderson was really a Southerner. Many in Charleston liked him and he had regularly attended social events in the city, both public and private. As a professional soldier in the employ of the Federal government he chose (and many in Charleston thought properly) to obey his orders and do his duty as he understood it. His secret move to the fort in December had surprised the town, and the discussion was ongoing concerning what next he might do.

"My friends," called the Mexican, "join with me in celebration. This day has brought me to a city I have never known, to friends I have never met. Let us enjoy this night, for I am not long in this world." With that cryptic phrase the gentleman put on the bar a gold Spanish doubloon, enough and more to fill the flagons of the sixty or so men and the five women in the house.

A barkeep carried two great ewers of his goods to the cups of the congregation. "Ale in this one, grog in this," he stated as he made his rounds.

"Ale," I said, and watched the foamy tide rise in my schooner. I never had a taste for grog.

I drained it in quick order, and accepted another from the deep urns of the bar man. The Mexican was leading some of the men in a song of whom few understood the words, but the melody was haunting and easy to follow. The language of Spain was never one of my studies. I had studied Italian at school, and I had more than a bit of French from Paris, so I could pick out a word here and there – something of a maid who spurned her lover.

I didn't need another reminder.

An unintelligible chorus backed up the singer whose high tenor wailed of love and of loss, this unknown brother of mine in the usual sad state of mankind. As the singer finished each song, the barkeeper would make his rounds again, nodding to the Mexican when it was time for another coin, though in fact I think he may have been less than honest with the foreigner after the third coin. At this rate the purveyor could retire soon to his own plantation.

I carried my refilled vessel near a billiard table, where a tall and gangly man in uniform was making a delicate shot. His opponent was small, dressed in a dark suit, and had a worried look on his face. "I don't know if I should continue at this game. My wife expects me home soon."

The soldier, his kepi cocked to the side as he leant over the table replied, "Wives are wonderfully forgiving creatures." His stroke put the end to the game, and as he was collecting from the small worried man, the loser of the game said, "Yes, but she will worry. I have time for only one more game."

Soldier boy grinned broadly and accepted one more game from the poorly playing husband. "But I really shouldn't stay for more than one last game, so let's increase the stakes on this one," said the worried man. And so, playing to pride, the small pool sharp with the anxious expression allowed the cocky soldier to risk and lose his month's wages.

My flagon dry, I returned to hear yet higher notes coming from the Mexican circus. There was a growing throng gathered about this seemingly bottomless cache of wealth and song.

Mexican hospitality is excessive, or so I believe from this experience. Ricardo began giving away his very possessions. He turned to a stout fellow next to him and exclaimed, "You have no watch? You must have mine." He pulled his fine watch all scribed with design from his vest pocket and handed it to an astonished working bog Irishman, who had never in his life earned enough for so fine a piece. Ricardo began passing out rings, silk handkerchiefs, his knife. He lifted his embroidered coat from a nearby peg and his eye lighted on me. "You have no coat, and must have mine. I am in a great mood for giving tonight."

I took the coat, as I had lost mine the evening before while sitting for a friendly game of cards. I tried it on and found it to reek of a strong herbal perfume. It was snug but was cut very well. I could not move freely in it but I know that for that style, it fit me fine. Indeed, it seemed to have been possessed of a bit of witching.

Immediately as I put it on, from a doorway of the restaurant toddled a young cherub perhaps five years of age, in a wonderful light-yellow frilled dress fit to her tiny figure. She had a rosy face, bright golden curls, and was pursued by who appeared to be her twin sister, though five years her senior, also frocked in pale gold and lace.

They joyously skipped across the room toward the opposite door. As the elder chased the younger, a young woman of about seventeen years entered the doorway, similarly dressed, of a striking figure and hat following those who must be her nieces. She had the bearing of the planter class, and a clean and glowing complexion, slightly rouged lips, arching eyebrows and blonde curled hair, and was followed by one who might be her older sister. She was of more maturity, of calmer disposition.

This woman was Mother, and directed her servant to gather the two errant children outside the fine tavern to their carriage. She was a bit imperious, and had an air of command and genteel order, and was perhaps the most wonderful sight I saw that day.

This glorious woman, about thirty-three and at the height of her feminine powers, struck me dumb by her grace and silent charm. She gazed about the room as if searching for someone, her husband? As her eyes swept the room, all talk, all song ceased. Her countenance fell on each of us, on me as well. The Mexican gave her a brief bow, which she ignored and continued her probe.

Through the doorway following the magnificent woman was yet another of the family, still in the pale gold fabric. This woman was of fifty years or more, a matron in regal hat above greying locks, a shawl of knitted cotton, a laced dress. She smiled at the view of her daughters and the children as she and the others passed through the tables of diners and out the doorway. She seemed satisfied by the sight as they danced ahead of her, the fruits of her life.

And yet another woman, older, helped in her infirmity by a cane and an older hand-servant, stepped slowly through the doorway.

She must have been over seventy, dressed in a stately manner yet of a similar pale gold. She walked deliberately through the room to the doorway. As the last of the women of this family passed, I realized I had witnessed the great truth of mankind. It was a parade of the human condition, the most successful life a woman can have. From giggling infant to beguiling youth, to blooming feminine flawlessness, to the paragon of satisfied mother, then happy grandmother, at last to aging woman, spent and awaiting the grave.

This coat was magic, and had taken me as witness through seventy-five years of life in but a few minutes.

The bartender made his rounds again, "Ale or grog! Present your cup," and again I accepted a great measure of ale.

French with a Spanish accent: "Brandy, M'sieur!" cried the Mexican, who everyone now called Ricardo. "Brandy, wine, whatever anyone wants!" The innkeeper accepted yet another coin and filled a tray of tumblers with brandy from two new green white-labeled bottles. This was drinking a bit rich for the regular clientele of working American, Irish and German workers, and several had had their fill and exited after thanking Ricardo for his generosity.

But those men missed the grand entertainment of the evening.

I lifted a glass before a light and gazed into the rich brown of the clear distillate, my generous portion enough to slow the mind of a sober man. The amber depths drew me in. The color minded me of the hair of the young woman I had seen at the racetrack the previous day, Jenny, first seen that day in Charleston, the day before lightning leapt from the telegraph wire to strike and splinter my soul.

My hand was not yet shaking, but the ale had brought my sight to waver a bit. Or perhaps it was my hand, the hand which had caressed Laura, whose love she had pledged to me. The shadows of the room shimmered in the lamp light and in the distortion I saw through the glass, and I imagined seeing her face when it was full of what I imagined was love. I lifted the glass of brandy to her as she was that evening so many centuries ago, in that other world, the one lost when I left for Europe.

The Mexican had given everything of his but his shirt, clothes, and his valise. He turned to one of his original companions who had crewed the pilot launch, now wearing Ricardo's fine tie, and told him the leather grip, finely tooled and set with silver, was his. "But first I must retrieve something from it, a gift from my father."

As I brought the tumbler to my lips, I whispered a silent toast of farewell to my past hope, and a prayer to be rid of the pain of my lost Laura. "My beloved Laura, my beloved, my life." I heard a loud clap beside me. As I gazed into the cloying amber depths of my glass, a tiny splash disturbed its surface, a droplet of crimson. I turned toward the Mexican and saw him collapse, with a hole through his head and droplets of blood spattered onto my new jacket and around the room. A pistol lay in his hand, and gun smoke stank the room.

I looked again at my glass, and saw a tiny ball of tissue suspended, and blood on the surface beginning to dissolve and spread into the brandy, a toast to my Laura, our lost future together.

I drank deeply the sweet burning liquids.

I shared a communion of despair with brother Richard.

12

ADRIFT

I don't recall most of the rest of the evening. I remember a fuss about getting the body out of the ale house and where to put it. Someone suggested the jail, at least for the evening.

A Sergeant Kerry from the City Police arrived and directed some of us to lift the body, so recently a singing, generous bonhomme, now an unwieldy dripping waste of a man.

When the leg of the Mexican slipped from my grasp the sergeant turned a disapproving glance at me. He recognized with disdain my rapidly deteriorating state of inebriation and had another carry out poor Ricardo, to the Second District lock-up. It usually held overnight unaccompanied slaves, or black-skinned sailors from foreign ships who knew no better than to walk King's Street without a white companion.

The stunning event quickly changed the tenor of the evening. Most diners and those of our party immediately went home, but those of us who stayed quickly emptied the full pitchers purchased by the cooling Ricardo.

It solves not their cares, but drink is a balm for many men.

One of the crewmen from the launch named Bertrand asked me where he had left his boat, and I have a vague memory of staggering under most of his weight toward the waterfront. It was late, and the weather that cool night was blurry and spinny. Bertrand and I apparently succeeded in finding the small craft, or at least the waterfront, because I awoke later that evening disturbed that my ingestions that night had caused the ground beneath me to become very unsteady. I felt I could not arise from my reclining position, but that I should attempt it. When I did so I discovered that though my stomach and brain were not on the same corporate plane, the floor itself was shifting and moving. And rather curved in places. I grasped a wooden rail to look beyond it and saw nothing but water. On the other side also was water.

I was apparently adrift in a dingy.

I felt in no mood at all to remedy my location, and felt it would be safer to recuperate in my present situation than risk swimming.

The crescent moon was smudgy and low on the horizon. The sky that night was mostly cloudy, with starry breaks in between. How like life is this sky, largely obscured, with unreachable visions of heaven between the clouds.

I lay in the boat rather soggy and heavy-headed, listening to the small lapping waves as I drifted in the bay, tasting bile in my mouth, the bile of my life.

A large fish swam by, and revealed itself to be a curious porpoise. His head crested the surface, and through his exposed eye he gazed at me. I shrunk from his curiosity, not wanting to represent mankind in my present condition to this creature of the other world. I think he understood. He returned to the deep with a small slap of his tail on the water.

Charleston lay dark against the low horizon. The streetlights had been doused hours ago, though a very few windows revealed late-night studies by the sleepless, writing in their diaries the wonderful days they have had, or perhaps love letters to someone.

Fools!

Perhaps soon the earliest risers would begin to ready themselves for the day ahead. I had no mind of the time, as I had no watch. Ricardo had given that to someone else. But I had the perfumed and embroidered jacket of the suicide, blood spattered and vomit tinged, not quite enough against the cool of the open bay in these first weeks of the year. Perhaps in the morning, more warmed by the sun, I might rouse myself to employ the oars near my hand.

"Ahoy, who goes there?" came a sharp voice from the distance. I painfully sat up and turned my melon head toward the sound. A dark mass of rock appeared on the water, perhaps seventy yards away. The solid shadow seemed to slip upward into the night, but I righted myself and emptied a bit more from my stomach, and spat. The rock wavered in the gloom. I shrunk down in the boat. Maybe the voice would decide I was just a piece of floating debris, which seemed appropriate to me. I was not ready to be rescued.

"Who goes there! Craft, identify yourself!" I heard far-off splashes, the sound of oars. My constitution had not yet righted itself, and I felt not up to the challenge. My desire to steady my stomach outweighed my fear of drifting off into the Atlantic.

The splashes came nearer, and finally our boats bumped together. I turned my eyes to the launch and saw four men at oars, and six more men in black. They were armed with fearful looking rifles aimed at my belly, the source of my agony, and the men were not smiling.

"You there, who are you? What are you doing out here?" The armed men looked about them for other boats, perhaps filled with men armed with their own killing weapons.

My gaze was unsteady and surely not threatening. The sergeant turned in disgust. "Tow him back to the fort."

This is how I first came to the man-created island of Fort Sumter. Immediately upon setting foot upon it I set two knees there, and hands, and vomited up the last sour remains of Ricardo's generosity. In my wretched reverie I had a passing thought. How many of us, like Ricardo, get to sing at our own wakes?

Morning dawned gray and cold. I lay in a sandy pit, covered by a coarse wool blanket, my head against a brick wall. Was I in prison?

Yes, one of my own making. Or simply fate? There's an easy excuse!

My current residence was, it turns out, a simple store room empty of any stores excepting my forlorn soul. Morning light, "rosy-fingered dawn," crept in around the door frame. As I was making my third attempt at sitting up, a harsh knock came on the door.

"OK in there, we're coming in."

The light from the opening streamed in and was welcome, though harsh. I was able to grasp it with my mind as a point of triangulation with the floor and my eyes. The world had three dimensions, though unsteady ones.

"Get up. Smith, get him up and bring him out."

"Aye, Sir."

A sergeant and a private lifted me none too gently from the

sand. I was helped out into the blinding sun of the greensward, the great courtyard. There was a body of soldiers being addressed by the famous Major Anderson, commander of the U.S. Army garrison of Fort Sumter. My view of the curious sea birds on the parapet was a strange counterpoint to the harsh faces and fierce weapons held by the soldiers.

I realized then that the uniforms were of course blue, not black as they had seemed the night before. Eyes of the men turned toward me as I staggered out into the sunshine. My legs were growing more steady though the cold had left stiffness in my joints.

"Eyes front!" barked a sergeant to the twenty or so soldiers in formation.

Anderson continued, "I know there is some lack of comfort, and eventually perhaps some danger." His voice was not loud, not even strong, but he had the resolve of a career soldier. "I have heard of the complaints. I understand, believe me.

"Despite your country of origin, I expect you each and all to do your duty as you have sworn, to uphold the laws of the United States of America. Whatever each of you may feel in your heart, that is between you and God. Your actions are between you and me, and will be judged based on your oath to the army you serve."

He was not a large man, and appeared kind, but this was not a time for kindness, surrounded by a wealthy city of armed and hostile citizens. These were soldiers following orders of what Charleston now saw as a foreign power.

"Our government has been notified of our situation and will send reinforcements and supplies in good time. Our duty is to hold this fort until that time, when we will receive new orders. Until then you will continue our daily drills. Act like the soldiers you are. I want no more complaints!"

Salutes and commands dismissed the men. Anderson had a brief discussion with his officers, glanced toward me, then entered one of the doorways across the yard.

Each of these soldiers under Anderson, himself a former slave-owner, resolved to do their duty to the uniform they wore, perhaps partly because of the example set by their commander. This small force played its current part in the looming national tragedy. When these soldiers eventually returned to New York, some resigned and returned south to join the forces seeking independence.

But on this day they grimly obeyed orders and prepared for defense.

I looked about and noticed other soldiers were on the high walls surrounding the courtyard gazing toward the new and threatening batteries to the north on Sullivan's Island and to the south on Morris. Some stared at Charleston, where they had friends or perhaps even lovers. A few peered through glasses out to sea seeking a rescuing fleet.

The lieutenant came to me and my guards and ordered us to the office of the major for interrogation.

One of the guards from the wall called, "Lieutenant Doubleday! A boat is approaching."

The lieutenant's eyes snapped toward me. "Heaven and hell!" Doubleday snapped. "This rock is becoming a major port of call!"

He turned toward the guard on the wall. "Thank you, sergeant. Report to me and the major when the craft is identified. Do not fire without orders."

The three of us marched to an anteroom of the major's office and sat on the bench.

"Are you hungry?" asked my sergeant, more kindly than I expected this day.

The lieutenant spoke, "We will not feed every Charlestonian who paddles his little boat to our fortress!" This Doubleday fellow was apparently not good in the morning. "We have enough to do in feeding ourselves." Actually, I wasn't hungry. My stomach had not nearly yet settled.

Lieutenant Doubleday knocked and entered Major Anderson's office. The door was closed. "I'll get you a biscuit when we leave here," said the sergeant. "Old Abner is concerned we won't get supplies and will have to beg from the city, and he's not one for begging."

The lieutenant returned and ordered me in to see the major.

Major Anderson glanced at the brocade on my soiled jacket.

"Mr. Jonathan Vander," said the major in measured tones, "it seems you have arrived by accident, from what my men tell me." He lifted a pen from his desk in an absent manner and pointed it at some papers before him. He had something of the school master about him. "Some of my men are concerned that you are a spy, come to report on our state of affairs to those who wish us gone from here."

That would be everyone in Charleston, as well as every man under Anderson's command.

"Well, I think no one who cares about us is in any doubt of our state. We have virtually no food, but we do possess powerful cannon and plenty of ammunition. We have enough men to properly man many of our guns, and those here are resolute in our determination to follow orders and protect the government we serve, to the last extremity."

I didn't care about this. I wanted to go home and get in my own bed.

"I have no desire to detain you." That sounded good to me so far. "I will release you upon your oath that you will not use your observances here against us, though I believe that there is nothing you could say which could damage our position. Do I have your word?"

At that low point in my life I was under no illusions of what he thought my word was worth, nor even what I thought it was worth. There was a time when I had held my oath at great value. Eventually I would again.

"I swear."

Lieutenant Doubleday's eyes informed me we shared a common estimation of the value of my compact.

A knock on the door of the chamber announced a visitor.

The small boat approaching that morning held a black-clad man of rather short stature and rosy complexion who stood at the door until he was invited in. I was waved out, accompanied by the sergeant who left me with a young private. He eyed my jacket with curiosity. Its magic was active still.

The passenger entered the major's chamber with a servant carrying a large black photographic device with legs.

The private and I sat on a bench and watched the wheeling gulls overhead as the kind sergeant went to find me a biscuit. "Do you think the people will let our relief come to us?"

How could I tell the young man his relief would never arrive?

"I don't know, maybe."

I had seen the Citadel artillery crews readying their positions against just such a thing.

Batteries had been set up all along the approaches to Fort Sumter. No United States ship could come through unscathed, and unless they were prepared to run such a toothy gauntlet and accept their losses, there would be no succor for these men marooned on an artificial island with nothing to eat but gunpowder and lead.

My sergeant arrived with two hard biscuits and a small fist of salt pork. In my state of quease I could nibble at one of the biscuits but the pork was completely out of the question. I couldn't look at it. The sergeant, who may have at one time in his life felt a similar way understood. He wrapped it in a newspaper and pocketed it.

The breeze from the sea blew the United States flag stiffly and was cool, so the three of us went into a room on the barracks level. A single candle illuminated the room, and around us I saw shadowy bunks and some decks of cards. Stacked against one wall were rifles, ready for use. An oil lamp hung from the rafter but was dark due, I assumed, to a shortage of oil.

Sumter confiscated the dingy I arrived in which bothered me not at all. I didn't know who owned it, and if I didn't know, then it didn't matter. I'm not sure this is good philosophy but I accepted it at the time.

Doubleday found us and directed the sergeant to have me brought to the steam launch which had brought the daguerreotypist to the island. I was to return with him.

His name was Cook, and he had a photographic shop in downtown Charleston. I had seen him about on my deliveries but had had no occasion to meet him to that point. The photographic portrait he had requested from Major Anderson would become famous. That gentle and kind schoolmaster's image brandishing his sword was captured by a shadow of silver on the glass plate and silently stated to all that he was prepared to use the weapons at his disposal for the purposes of his government.

The boat ride in the mild chop of the water back to the city was uneventful. The eyes of the black boatmen looked at me when I was not focused on them. That was a bit unnerving.

Smoke and steam from the boiler blew away quickly in the fresh breeze, and as the screw propelled the launch toward the now-familiar steeples of the city my dulled senses looked ahead to another day of dismal labor and survival.

Life can be just living.

The success Mr. Cook had selling his image encouraged him to order additional supplies, and when Tyrone received them, I delivered them.

I visited the armed island again under different conditions. I'll tell you about that later.

As we drew near the quay, I shucked off the blanket and straightened myself in my brocaded jacket, which had lost the gentle bouquet of the night before and now smelled more like the rest of my clothes. As I brushed the sand off and pulled it taut to button, I found an inner pocket. Within this pocket was a small cache of four shiny U.S. silver dollars, a gold Spanish doubloon, and a mysterious key. I held up the key and wondered what room or chest it would unlock. Perhaps a lover's bedchamber?

The metal tender served me well. I kept the key as a talisman, a reminder of Ricardo in his despair, poor man. He never unlocked the door he sought, whatever and wherever it was.

It would take me three years to find what the key would unlock for me.

13

LAMENT

As the garrison's plight at Fort Sumter became more desperate, letters were passed to the fort nearly begging the major to surrender under the most gracious terms. They could keep their weapons. They could salute their flag. They would be provided safe transport.

All terms were rejected.

Each night fire barges lit by nervous coastal defense forces scattered their ominous light across the harbor. Each night sentries on the shore watched for the feared landing of thousands of U.S. troops. Each night the sentinels at the fort in the harbor grew more fearful of the enemy regiments surrounding them. They had used the last of their oil and could no longer provide a guiding light for ships they still hoped would try to resupply them. Finally, Major Anderson estimated that they could retain control of that vital post for five more days, the last three with no food at all.

General Beauregard was soon to put his cannonading studies to test against his mentor and dear friend.

On one afternoon I delivered my goods to the warehouse, collected the receipt, and went into Murphy's for a draft. It was late in the day and I knew Tyrone would not be upset. He had received a large shipment of goods from Liverpool and was gleefully opening crates and bundles of fabric, leather goods, and a special order of fine china. Along with the order he had received some fine cut crystal stemware and punch bowls, just in time for the parties. I could relax with an ale before returning to my pallet at his warehouse. I was in a secure job now that his other workers, the white ones at least, were joining the army. Labor was at a premium.

As I walked into the pub, I noticed five or six soldiers gathered around a grizzly sergeant who was telling them of his own first sergeant when he was a young recruit. They listened to his story of the veteran of the Seminole Wars who taught him the ways of the army. At the end of his tale, one of the privates raised his glass and toasted his sergeant. The others raised their glasses, and the sergeant stood and yelled, "HOO-HAH!"

It was years later that I learned the expression was from a Seminole Indian chief who was at a meeting with speech-giving white soldiers. When it was his turn to orate, he simply stood and yelled, "HOO-HAH!" and since then the phrase has been a statement of exuberance among enlisted men and officers in the American military.

I sat at the bar and the maid came to serve me.

"Bonjour Mademoiselle," I remarked in Parisian.

"Bonjour. Puis-je vous servir, Monsieur?"

She spoke French! "Certainement, une bière dorée s'il vous plait. Merci."

Her eyes didn't change from the half-lidded view she had of her shadowy world. Her dress was stained and missing a button. Her hair was unkempt.

I had heard her speak enough to know that she was not French, or at least not from any part of France I had visited, but that she was educated in the language surprised me a bit. Most of her speech was in monosyllables.

She turned and brought me the brimming cup and placed it before me. She looked down at the bar for payment.

"I've seen you here before," I said. "That's not the same as meeting, is it?"

No answer.

"Where are you from, mademoiselle?"

"Baton Rouge, Louisiana." Her deep voice was valueless, seeming to care nothing for me, for the world, for life. What brings a person to such a relationship with the world? Oh, I am not the one to

80

query this. Love, without doubt.

"Louisiana? I've not been there yet, but hear it's a city of great beauty." I had hoped to get a reaction, to make her correct me about Louisiana, but no.

She looked coolly into my eyes and turned away. She walked into the back room and began stocking shelves. I glanced at my reflection in the mirror behind the bar. So much for new romance.

In the corner at the upright piano a man took a seat and began to sing and play an Irish air, slow and reflective, which made each eye in that pub weep: "The Lament of the Irish Immigrant."

> *I'm sittin' on the stile, Mary*
> *Where we once sat side by side*
> *On a bright May mornin' long ago*
> *When first you were my bride;*

The plaintive chords filled each corner of the room.

> *For you were all I had, Mary*
> *My blessing and my pride:*
> *And I've nothin' left to care for now*
> *Since my poor Mary died*

"For the love of God, Abe!" cried Murphy from behind the bar.

The pianist gave me a wry smile. "I love to play that one for them," he whispered.

The pianist was Abe, of the Christmas party where I had met the serving girl Isabella and heard the "Light Brigade" poem recited.

Seeing him in this humble setting made me feel I could speak to him. I approached him and introduced myself and congratulated him on the evening's entertainment at that holiday party.

We shook hands, his long and firm. He looked into my eyes.

"I am pleased you like it, Jon."

I offered to purchase for him an ale, to spend a portion of my day's earnings, but he waved to the serving maid and told me, "They let me drink for free if I give them a little music."

He began a lively rendition of "The Blue Juniata,"

This humble tavern was a sometimes-haven for Abe. That afternoon we shared some conversation between or even during his playing. Some of his music was so lively he seemed to be swimming in it up to his elbows. More were sweet and sad.

In a humble dark pub, sometimes confidences are shared between strangers which could never be told to a friend in daylight. I spoke to him of my present condition, my city of origin, and how I had traveled the world and lost that which I had most sought. He listened well, without dismissing my simple childish yearning of that which could never be.

I told him I was working for Tyrone.

"Yes, Mr. Tyrone. A gentleman in most all he does."

This seemed slightly shy of an absolute endorsement.

"Oh, do you know Tyrone? I have found him most agreeable and of an enterprising nature."

"Don't let him sell you any hair dye," said Abe with a raised eyebrow. I knew to what he was referring.

Then he told me of the demon he was wrestling. He had a love of his own, a woman out of his reach for some undisclosed reason, who was as bright and talented in her way as he apparently was. Refined, not wealthy, a creative and beautiful woman. Not married, but somehow not attainable.

Mysterious, like much of life.

He went into a reverie of his own sadness, and played and sang "Open Thy Lattice, Love," as I took my exit.

As I left the tavern I nodded to Murphy and waved to the dull French girl. The lyrics spun in my head as I left the shadows.

...Then open thy lattice, love, listen to me!
While the moon's in the sky and the breeze on the sea!

14

AN ENTERTAINMENT

The stagnant Sumter situation had become ever more explosive as winter warmed to early spring. In desperation, early one morning an unauthorized small boat sailed to a parley with the garrison in an attempt to save lives and prevent the impending catalytic incident. As the small steam launch approached the island, those aboard the launch were immediately held at gunpoint. The fort's commander was advised. He dressed and awaited them in his office.

While Anderson and the emissaries of South Carolina negotiated in the next room, one of the men, a lieutenant I think, saw a jug on a tabletop and poured himself a drink of whiskey.

As soon as he had swallowed the dram it became apparent that whiskey it was not!

The surgeon had been treating himself with a small drop of iodide of potassium, and the officer had swallowed enough to kill ten men.

There then ensued a debate among the garrison whether the surgeon should pump the poison from the stomach or if, in the thoughts of the irascible Lieutenant Doubleday, they should not allow an enemy to poison himself.

The surgeon did not hesitate to pump the offending liquid from the imbiber, with the excuse that he was not about to allow US. medical property to be stolen from his command by any subterfuge.

As I recall, everyone survived the incident.

My acquaintance Charles Gallard could be expansive in conversation.

In the dubious environment of Murphy's Alehouse, one night long after more reputable public houses were closed and dark, he led me to suspect his enthusiasm might have been generated from an artificial stimulant. His usual beverage was cognac.

While in Paris I encountered a drink called the Green Fairy in some of the smaller coffee houses. It was not a regular bottle of spirits. I was told it could generate a series of thought processes which came with such rapidity that no rest was possible until the creations of your secret mind found egress through verbalizations, or through artistic works. I only sampled it once in those years.

I had no knowledge that Charles had imbibed this or other drug, but I suspected his drum roll of discussion was not entirely natural.

It was late. I was weary but carried along the stream of thought with him as I listened to the fantasies of this eloquent and perhaps slightly mad Southerner. He spoke of the oneness of God, and of God's many faces, how he must indeed be within every grain of sand on the beach, in the very gnats and flies in the air, and in the moonbeams which fall on our graves in the night. If God is in the moonbeams and flies, is it a sin to swat at a fly? Is He not in us as well? If He is in each of us, do we not have divine rights to do whatever we wish? Charles went on to recite line after line of "The Lady of the Lake" by Scott, then elements of what he claimed was the Magna Carta itself, which I think he rather made up. But I didn't care, the night continued, and the bright eye of the man was captivating.

The times I spent with Charles let me grow out of myself for an hour or two, when I could travel the paths of our conversation as on a sunlit turnpike.

Several shadowy characters in a dark corner grew restive and began speaking in high voices. Finally, one Irishman picked up another and in the struggle they both fell onto their own table, crushing it to the floor. Each sat up, bloodied, each put their hand on the other's shoulder, and they bawled, crying like babies, and declared they loved the other like a brother, and each would buy the next round.

The crash had broken Charles's train of thought, and the barkeeper appeared with a large club over the weeping Irishmen, and called that the bar was now closed. Charles and I left. I tried to keep up with him, but his pace was quick and sure; mine slower and less steady.

The cool night air was misting rain, and it revived me. It was not many hours before dawn, and yet the streets were not completely deserted. Charles led, and we drifted south down King Street toward the Battery where a generation earlier cannon had fended off the might of the British Navy. We approached the Battery which was indeed armed. I became aware of a restiveness in the community. As we neared the water, I saw the cannon there were staffed with alert crews.

We mounted the stairs and stood on large flat stones of the water walk. We gazed toward the dark sea which on this late night was not dark.

For weeks fire barges had been towed near Fort Sumter ready to light up the area around it for observation if a relief ship should approach. Tonight there was much more light.

The sky split with sunlight, shifting beams of white. But the light came from the earth, not the heavens. This light was manmade, brilliant, and directed at the new brick structure on the island in the inlet. The blaze of mighty lamps flooded the harbor. Drummond lights use lime and flame to shoot reflected rays of brilliance. We could easily see Castle Pinkney as well as the form of Fort Sumter, clearly visible in the distance. The wives had long since evacuated from that sandbar where men starved in the dark and cold, waiting for fiery death because of a promise they made to their country.

I had learned promises could mean nothing. Later I would learn that they can mean everything.

As we looked, Charles continued his rattle about the theories that made the big lights work and how they would change the way cities would feel, creating safe and magical streets for all mankind. Businesses could now operate night as well as…

In mid-sentence a sparking object dashed an elegant arc across the overcast sky. I had seen meteors, of course, but this one was less steady in its path curved at a much greater angle. As the meteor passed directly over Fort Sumter it exploded in a brilliant flash. A cheer went up from the men at the guns, and a gruff voice ordered us to clear the walk.

"Well, it looks like we've started a war tonight," proclaimed Charles, who then became, for an unrepeated time, speechless.

In the lull of our conversation we heard the report of the mortar that fired the signal shell over the fort. As we looked out to sea, we saw flashes of light, obviously cannon fire, coming from Sullivan's Island, and Morris Island, Castle Pinkney, and from where we knew there to be a metal raft fitted with cannon termed the Floating Battery.

The cannon at the Battery where we stood did not fire as the target of Sumter exceeded the range for these guns, but soldiers and their commanders cheered on their comrades. Scores of cannon across the estuary bay fired. We saw the beginning of what would come to be known as the War for Southern Independence, though I have heard many other names for it as well. To those who started the war, that is what it was.

Charles and I watched the spectacle in the distant glow of the Drummond lights amid the chatter of the cannon crews and the delighted screams and cheers of the Citizens of Charleston, now awake and on their piazzas and rooftops, viewing the national debacle as if it were an entertainment for their amusement.

In my soft condition of inebriation I sat back and watched the show. This great demonstration of the firepower of a wealthy and well-armed city against a forlorn and paupered military post was bravado with no good purpose.

What if a force of fifty burly Irishmen had surrounded a work party of three exhausted field hands after a day's work and set to beat them with shillelaghs? Is this something to be cheered, even by the wives of the Irishmen?

The lights were entertaining, and I reclined against a stone step to watch, and must have drifted into sleep, even as the furor of war was birthing.

Gray light crept beneath my eyelids and a chill swept through my body. I could see several figures against the lightening mist, gazing toward the target in the gloaming.

I stirred my stiffening limbs to arise and stood leaning against a stanchion nearby. Many citizens were milling about, seeming to try to decide where to take their country now that it was independent.

*　　*　　*

I JONATHAN

My great-great uncle Jonathan was alert and strong, but the evening was late.

When he paused, Mrs. McKay stepped in and I knew it was time to call it a night, so I asked and he agreed that I would come again the next morning.

When I returned to my guest house the innkeeper reminded me of the hours. I apologized and made arrangements to stay another night. I had time, no reason to return immediately, and my father has always been generous in my allowance of money, if not of his time.

And Gloria was not waiting for me.

I returned the next morning after breakfast and we began again, his eyes closing for a moment, then brightly looking at me as he took up his story.

*   *   *

15

SWEET LION

Tyrone was a queer man, but not unkind, not unChristian. He continued his attempt at my rehabilitation, hiring me to accompany shipments out to the country where the air was more pure, the mind more clear, the sun more hot, the mosquitoes more hungry, and sometimes I thought that perhaps this was not charitable after all.

He placed the occasional advertisement in the Charleston Mercury or the Courier newspapers for hair loss remedies or wigs, and he seemed to believe lots of them. He had actually tried to reverse his impending baldness. On more than one occasion I noticed such hair he retained had changed color overnight.

The previous year Tyrone had eagerly accepted me at Jacob's suggestion and put me to work while helping me improve myself. Well, he tried, but I didn't want to be improved, and frankly I didn't want to work, either. I was used as a means of keeping cheap labor from getting held by the constables, and that is about it.

But the orders came and so did the shilling or two which I needed to survive in whatever shelter I could find for a pittance. I was saving the coins from the Mexican jacket for my return voyage to… where?

My benefactor Jacob assigned me one of the "darkies," as they were often called by their owners or the plantation overseers, his older son Esau, still owned by another master. He was a serious young man of eighteen years, tall and strong. He was thoughtful and would occasionally let loose a spate of Sea Island philosophy worthy of the cafes of Paris, which I had enjoyed only a year prior. Now I was in the employ of Tyrone's International Southern Shipping and Trading

Company.

Esau, his younger brother Eli, or one of his rented slaves and I shared many hours on the trail to Mount Pleasant, James Island, Kiowa Island, even to Georgetown and Edisto Island. Once I was sent on a delivery to Port Royal. That is a story for another afternoon.

Usually the cargo we transported was humble. I oversaw his draymen carrying tons of bird guano harvested from the South Sea Islands to enrich the depleting soil of South Carolina plantations. The Irish carters at competing houses did not much care for this work, though they would take it if there was none better. The mules knew the familiar tracks and were quite easily handled, so one black worker, slave or free, would accompany me with the wagons of fertilizer from the far end of the planet to the farms of America.

Was I just wasting my youth, my life seeping out with my sweat? What is the point?

My wagon of guano rolled on.

Several of our customer plantations were too far away for easy travel so the planters would arrange their own shipments. When they came to pick up their guano, they often brought their families into Charleston in their carriage for the week. While the planters made their arrangements their wives and daughters shopped for the latest goods from Europe and from up North. The blockade had not yet plugged the channels of commerce. "Servants" would be sent ahead to return with their loads of soil improvement, and the ladies would follow a day or so later with their own burdens: sweets from France, cloth and lace from Belgium, silver from Spain, books from The Netherlands and London, magazine publications from New York and Philadelphia. And Boston.

One spring day I was given a charge of delivery to two plantations near Summerville, a town with fewer mosquitoes and bad airs, where many wealthy families would spend the most oppressive months of the year. It was just a bit cooler than Charleston, about thirty miles from the city. One planter was to host a week-long gathering of families of society. This was soon following the success, if that is what it could be called, of occupying Fort Sumter.

The trip to Summerville was a short ride by rail, and I arrived before noon. A hand from my destination named Cato met me at the station. We loaded the goods onto two carts, one Tyrone had hired and one Cato had brought from Pond Spring Plantation. I was to make the second delivery that afternoon and return the following day.

The main event of the party was to be a four-day gala with music and feasting, and the foods were to be exotic. One of the two wagons was full of tinned and dried delicacies from Colombia, Portugal, wine from Italy, and Madeira, brandy from the Cognac region of France, exploding fire toys from Nice, fantastic sugary creations from Sorrento, French tinned goose liver pate', and a wealth of preserved mushrooms, brandied plums, and a very well-packed mysterious cask, which I later would find held the candied carving, entombed in powdered sugar, of a three-foot golden lion specially made in Paris at the express commission of the plantation owner.

How many bushels of rice did it cost? Or bales of cotton, or hours of slave labor? Or, even, how many slaves? Souls of men used in commerce.

As we drew near the entrance lane of the main house of the plantation we passed lines of field workers bending to their daily tasks of cultivating the rows of cotton bushes. The bolls were just beginning to crack, and if the weather was good a profitable harvest would come soon. The cycle of labor and profit would continue, with the owners gaining more wealth, purchasing new gilt furniture or bright watches, shimmery satins for their women, books of heroic poetry for their sons. Perhaps pleasure voyages to Europe. The workers would grow their families, continue their work, and perhaps get new shoes and new work clothes each year if the profits were good enough. If not, last year's shoes would have to do, if there were shoes at all. Rags would suffice until another harvest. If profits were too low, their children might be sold away to keep up the style of the owner.

And it was the hope of the plantation owners who supported independence that this cycle would continue forever.

These men and women and their families were called "darkies," or "niggers" in less polite company. If they were to be called black men, that would designate them as a form of "men," and may require them to have rights that creatures which were not men could lack. Best for them to be designated something other, so one's conscience would not be easily bothered using them as beasts and selling them when cash was needed. It wasn't intentionally hateful, just business.

But who could not see it as a hateful business?

As Cato and I turned into the lane near the house a servant met us and directed us to the delivery behind the mansion. We drove past the homes of the field workers, a row of small rude houses big enough to sleep four, no bigger, though many housed families of six or eight.

It was about noon when we arrived, and plans had been made for me to deliver to the other plantation and spend the night there, returning to Pond Spring Plantation the next day. The kitchen workers unloaded the goods from one wagon and Cato went to his cabin. I went to the white worker's mess where the overseer and the carpenter ate, though both were busy at their duties.

As I noticed the next day's party getting set up in the plantation owner's home, I recalled the times I had attended such glittering celebrations in Boston, Brussels, Paris, Rheims; not for me to enjoy that night, I thought.

I ate a quick bite and walked to Cato's hut, carrying a demijohn of corn. I would share an hour of comradeship with these inhabitants of a simple slave's shack before taking my second delivery farther north. So low had I sunk.

Cato brought me to the cabin of one of the plantation's grooms named Brutus. He had just arrived from the stables where he worked. A senior groom, had worked early and would work late, so was giving himself a long lunchbreak this day.

His wife had set a lunch for him and his children. These workers were not used to a social visit by a white guest, and were not at ease. I nearly turned to leave, but Cato hailed me. "Hey, what's in that bottle you're holding?"

Cato salved their feelings, letting me share this contraband liquor with the slave and father. And so, I was able to ingratiate myself in this foreign and forbidden culture back of the big house.

Cato was so gregarious and story-filled that his light repartee soon put them and me more at ease. My host, somber and sinewy, a rather small man with chestnut features bade me sit by his hearth. He and his wife and child sat on the crude bed at the end of the cabin as she braided the stiff curls of the daughter.

Cato told a story of his childhood, of how one Sunday his mother had threatened him with disaster if he did not sit still in church. As she led her children home through the cobble-stoned streets of Charleston, she pointed to the round pavement stones peeking through their sandy surface and told him what they really were: the bleached skulls of bad children who wouldn't sit still for the preacher's sermon!

"And ever since then, I have walked very respectfully over the headbones of my brothers!"

Brutus and his family laughed at this one. Then the master of the house, master at least for these few hours of separation from his overseer, told his tale.

It was an old story of a rabbit who fooled the other animals of the forest into doing things they would not otherwise do. This clever and devious rabbit, who he called "brother," succeeded in fooling a bear into harvesting a large load of sweet potatoes from the field of Brother Fox. Fox was fooled into blaming the theft on Brother Wolf, whose honor was offended when he heard the slanderous lie. He burned down the house of Fox and chased him into the next county. The rabbit meanwhile cooked the stolen sweet potatoes in the embers of Brother Fox's house and made his feast. This was an entertaining tale, and the corn liquor had made the teller a bit more enthusiastic than he might have otherwise been. I'm not sure of the moral lesson of this tale, nor the value of it to civilized society. The concept of someone happily eating stolen yams baked in the embers of another's burned house was not a tale that disclosed a useful lesson – at least not to me. I heard a variation of this story again years later.

Cato indicated I should tell a tale next. I pondered the tales to tell. My education, largely at mother's knee, had filled me with stories of Homer's Ulysses, of Arthur, of Ivanhoe, and Hector. Could these humble folk relate to a tale of the Green Knight? What of the story of Washington's attack at Trenton? Would a tale of Socrates or Perseus entertain this shack of enslaved Helots? Maybe Leatherstockings, or Rip Van Winkle, or Sleepy Hollow…

As I silently debated my options, the musicians tuning up for the party in the big house drifted our way, and I commented that it had been nearly two years since I had attended my last party like that one.

I must admit that I had fallen to a low state indeed, and my present appearance, unshaven for days and with a mop of long and tangled greasy hair, dressed in grime of the gutter and slop houses I shared would lead anyone to doubt my ability to share company with the local royalty at the mansion across the lawn.

"Oh, Mr. Jonathan, you never danced at a do like that," said Cato. "I mean, just because you're white don't mean you can go to those doin's."

"Yes, I have danced with the local royalty of Boston. And even of Belgium, once." She was a daughter of a minor noble, and used me to show herself on the floor to another man of the nobility. This is not important to the story.

The host and his wife smiled, but didn't believe me. Cato was more challenging. "I'll bet you could not go in there and fool those rich folks."

Whatever I have been, I have never been a liar. Had I? Oh, well yes, certainly. "Yes, I could do it, but I couldn't do it looking like this."

"If I get you a coat and help you clean up, I'll bet you my pony's saddle to two silver dollars you can't fool any body in there."

A wager! "Done! Now get me a good coat that will fit me." I knew he had no means of doing this, so this challenge was all hypothetical. Cato took a good pull from the corn jug and with a great grin, dashed from the house. This startled me, and I had a growing sense of dread of his actions, and what he might return with.

And so it was that I was fooled by degrees into making good on a feeble boast of a time I really cared to forget. On the other hand, it precluded my delivering a tale of Antigone, or perhaps of an incestuous union of a Greek king and his own mother, which on reflection may have confused the audience and even caused them to ask me to remove myself from the slave shanty.

I found my escape from unwanted attention through the subterfuge of agreeing to masquerade in the appearance of myself, at least as I had appeared but a year or so earlier; a self I no longer recognized as real.

I went back to my delivery duties.

By sundown I arrived at the next plantation farther north toward Ridgeville and delivered the small order of machine tools.

My delivery went without incident, and I unloaded my shipment. After a hearty meal of ham and cabbage I slept in a room provided by the overseer, a German who ruled the cotton plantation when the owner was away, in this case at the party. He spoke good

English and apparently had a slave as a common-law wife, or perhaps concubine. She seemed comfortable with her position, perhaps as good as a she could reasonably hope for in the present social structure. She was kept warm and fed and her duties were more domestic than farm-related. What of love?

Henry was the name he used; Americanized from Heinrich I suppose. He could read well enough to comprehend that his tenure was in jeopardy due to the possibility of impending hostilities, but we did not share much discussion in the way of politics, or of society either.

He mentioned his dream of his own farm someday, and spoke of the unbounded fields awaiting hard-working men in the Plains to the west. Some of his cousins had moved to Chicago and then to Wisconsin. I don't know that he didn't eventually make his way there, and whether he took his woman I can't say.

The next morning I delayed the journey back to the party location, and took my time on the road. I dreaded facing the challenge of becoming myself again at a lavish party, if indeed Cato had success in finding my costume.

This entire expedition would have taken me out of Charleston for four days, and I did not relish returning to the city, but I had no real alternative to hand. That day I feared the trial of lights and music, yet it also held a beguiling dream-like allure, a visit to a past self where things were right in the world and a happy future was nearly in sight.

In those days and especially later after the war had really begun, extended deliveries away from Charleston helped me evade the occasional inquiry of my not being in uniform. Often when I returned from such a delivery the sergeant or corporal who had earlier inquired of me being out of uniform had been sent away to march into glory to the north and I never heard more of them.

I passed again through the gates of the estate in late afternoon, left the cart with the grooms and went to the dormitory where I was to sleep.

Cato found me, a large grin on his face, and bade me follow him back to the household of the slave family. I came with an excitement and trepidation that trembled my steps.

Under his arm was carefully folded a fine formal jacket,

probably worth more than any three slave huts on this row together. "One of the Graves boys had too much whisky too early, got mad, and challenged one of the cadets to a duel. That cadet was smart and chose his weapon, which was his own arms, and they wrestled. The Graves boy got beat and ran off home without his coat. I found it back of the kitchen. Ramona, she's the cook's daughter and she's kind of sweet on me, she cleaned it up and give it me when I told her what you were going to try."

As the household helped me in my reluctant escapade I grew apprehensive of my reception. As the old grime was washed from my body, Brutus stropped and honed a razor to blaze the stubble from my face and found me a clean shirt and other garments to wear in my masquerade. I imagined myself as a Montague about to intrude on a private party of Capulets.

I tried on the jacket, and as my run of bad luck ran, it fit very well, just a little long in the sleeve, which helped to cover the cuff of the white shirt the slave had provided. The blouse was too grand and fancy for a field worker, with ruffles, flourishes – nearly a fanfare – and a formal collar. It was in good shape but for a little wear and that cuff, likely torn by its original owner in an unknown incident long ago, and since given to the worker for Sunday dress. The cuff had been well mended. This garment fit me a bit better, though cut too full in the breast. The original owner obviously enjoyed his comestibles.

A surprisingly clean and shiny pair of shoes was brought forth from under the bed of the household. They were too large, so cotton in the toe must do for that, and their soles had worn out completely, but their appearance was impressive from above. Comfort was not the point tonight. This family, impoverished by tradition and the law of the land, gave me all of their most prized male clothing for the lark of the evening – or perhaps the nightingale.

The family stood about me and as I put on the coat and the tie from its pocket, and as I stood and brushed my hair with my fingers, the Africans drew back from me, as if by wearing the clothes of a gentleman I became one of the class they were taught to respect, admire, and honor. And mostly to fear.

The clothes had an effect on me, also. I stood tall, and reviewed myself in the small looking-glass of the house. Yes, I appeared to be that other person again, the one I used to refer to as "me."

Now, the evening's challenge was becoming important: to prove myself to myself.

"Cato, I will enter with the help of your paramour in the kitchen. Please lead me." I really used that term "paramour."

It was just past dinner time so I hoped that I needn't fear too confining a conversation.

Cato was a bit more respectful than usual to me. Not that I deserved it. "Yes sir, Mister Jonathan." He silently turned and opened the door for me to pass through. As I stepped over the threshold he said to the inhabitants, "I'll bring him back so's you can get your things off his dead body." He flashed a wide grin and slipped out.

We walked past the kitchen gardens of the slaves, past their stinking privy house, moving carefully across a dirt roadway to protect the gleam of my shoes, then up to the herb garden beside the kitchen door. The night had turned cool, the stars creamy against the sable of heaven, or whatever substance of matter that holds those lights that glitter above.

Cato approached the door and called for Ramona. She appeared smiling brightly to Cato until she saw me. Her grin faded and she gave a brief curtsey, probably by reflexive action. Or perhaps my earlier self was wearing me, now.

We entered the warm kitchen full of steamy smells and lit brightly with oil lamps and a blaze from a cooking oven. To our right was the scullery, with piles of trays and roasting pans soaking or awaiting their foamy baths.

To our left working at a table was a small black figure dressed all in white with a white turban on his head. He was quick and short, putting the final touches on a truly magnificent cake of ivory flecked with blue candy chips, a green palmetto of crystal sugar standing a foot tall above its highest tier. The crescent moon was ensconced above the fronds of the tree, the symbol of South Carolina in its greatest glory. Like the state itself, it awaited its heaviest doom: to be eaten.

The elfin gnome glanced up at me from his labors, looked me head to toe, and returned to his craft. This lord of the kitchen staff, for all his artisanship, his skill and subtle method, would never wear the suit I wore, would never enter the world of sparkle and light beyond the kitchen door. He was not white. He was not free.

During my sojourn in Paris studying art and architectural pieces at museums and craftsmen's shops I had briefly been shown into the shop of a sculptor named Charles. He was creating a bust of the most remarkable figure, a Nubian or Sudan Negro King. He was carving it out of what I think was onyx and white marble. But the striking feature was the visage of the king. Though the figure was made of black and white stone, the artist had formed a living man who could, it appeared, command armies.

And here in this steaming kitchen was a man just as black, this slave, and with a commanding face worthy of a Caesar. And because of the conditions of his parents' birth and no other reason, he would never command. One dark figure was of stone and the other, unfortunately for him, only of flesh.

My own situation now took my attention. I lifted a flute of sparkling wine from a nearby tray and sipped, composed myself. I passed Cato, who was no longer smiling.

I ventured forth through the kitchen passage.

My entrance into the Enchanted Hall was quiet. I slipped along the wall, unseen by the revelers whose attention was turned to the master of the house. He was speaking to a group of expensively dressed men, some with their wives.

The party was as beautiful as any I have seen on this side of the Atlantic. I slid to the outer fringes of a group of men discussing Sumter and turned to see the matron of the house clad in pink silk, bows, and sashes.

I have never been quite able to comprehend what makes a woman's gown fashionable or stylish. I think it's the woman who makes the gown beautiful, and her belief that it enhances her own form, or presence.

I can usually detect those considered daring.

The twelve-piece orchestra played a lively waltz on violas and oboes. The players were all black save the conductor, a young man of about twenty-four dressed in full tails, that same Abe from the Christmas party in Charleston who I spoke with at Murphy's Ale House. A piano stood to the side of the dais.

Fifty pairs of gentry, men in black and grey or in the sleek uniforms of the Citadel college or the Edisto Rifles, and women in pastel gowns with voluminous skirts whirled about the polished floor.

An enormous chandelier flashed and sparkled with candlelight and cast a halo about the room – so very different from the dank and shadowy warehouse where I slept.

One side of the room opening onto the piazza was flanked by somber dark sentinels armed with tongs and serving spoons. About them was a florid display of candies, glowing candles, puddings, decorated fruits and punches, all presided over by the great Parisian sugar lion I had transported earlier. He was ferocious looking, with one raised clawed arm of golden crystal candy and a curling and breezing mane that framed his great muzzle, ablaze with deadly teeth. This fell beast of a lion, so fearsome, was in essence sweetness, and would eventually be eaten, or ground to powder and dissolved in tea.

On this night it appeared marvelous and fierce like the young men in this assembly.

As I surveyed the table and the items I had carted from Tyrone's storage, I noticed the white servant from the Christmas party I had delivered to months ago, Isabella, serving punch. She was dressed in livery this evening, a white serving-girl being a sign of refinement and wealth in some circles.

"Would you like some punch, sir?" she asked, arching her eyebrow in amused recognition.

I placed my flute on a nearby tray and replied, "Thank you, yes," and marched boldly up to her to accept the glass cup. "Not rose tea?"

We said no more to each other, but our gazes revealed a book of tales.

I sipped the milky concoction, smiled again and turned away.

The strains of the European composition climaxed in a flourish, followed by gentle applause, and the master of the house tapped a bell held by a servant dressed in white.

"My friends, we take this time in our lives to refrain from discussing the price of cotton or rice, of how we are going to improve our servants next month, of wind and storm, of the rates of exchange. Tonight we gather to celebrate the good life in our Southern land, the beauty of our women, the benevolence of the Maker who provides us with the wealth of our farms." The speaker was the master of the plantation, Mr. Moray. His high forehead and dark brown hair gave him a patrician appearance, though his narrow mouth and long thin nose made him look as if he would rather be elsewhere, in some Elysian field among his own kind better even than these, his guests.

That was just my interpretation.

He went on for a while about what a wonderful country it was, before he finally introduced the chorus we were apparently about to hear. They filtered from the crowd of dancers, seven young women and five cadets, proud and erect in their martial dress.

As the host pontificated, the members of the choir shuffled into position and exchanged glances with each other and with some in the crowd. The singers arrayed themselves on the wide steps of the sweeping staircase which curved gracefully above them. They looked like they were carved of Grecian marble, each poised, self-aware, graceful. The men were young, strong and clean-shaven, except for the side whiskers some of them sported. Many were in military academy uniforms and shone in martial resplendence.

The young women were clad in the lacy work of hundreds of hours of skilled hands. Their forms, feminine curves enhanced by the hoops of their bell-shaped skirts, were reflected in the lacquered balusters of the stairway: a line of a hundred womanly shapes arising to the house's sleeping quarters.

Among the choir were young ladies I first observed at the soda-water café my first day in town. There was brandy-haired Jenny and her friend of the black, black hair, Carla, and Citadel cadets William and Martin. Apparently Jenny and Martin were more harmonious now.

Among the listeners was Timmy Ledger who had recited the "Light Brigade" poem with such impact that night last December.

The orchestra conductor sat at the piano below the curving balustrade, attentive yet not preparing to play. He knew there were yet words to come.

The host introduced the minister to bless the evening.

Reverend Poste, a man I would meet later on my Southern odyssey, closed his eyes and raised his right hand. He was dressed in evening wear but with a simple church stole over his shoulders.

He spoke with a deep accent of Tennessee, or perhaps northern Alabama.

"Heavenly Father, we ask You to bless this assembly, gathered to enjoy the bounty You in Your beneficence have given us, and we ask You to lead us through the trials ahead.

"You have graced our lives and this land with Your love and Your generous hand.

"We thank You, and we beg that You hear our prayers for continued peace.

"We dedicate our songs to You and Your people.

"In the name of Your blessed Son Jesus Christ we beg You, Amen."

The chorus began its presentation with a lively old Negro spiritual.

I'm going to pray when the spirit says pray,
I'm going to pray when the spirit says pray,
I'm going to pray when the spirit says pray,
And obey the spirit of the Lord!

I'm going to sing when the spirit says sing,
I'm going to sing when the spirit says sing,
I'm going to sing when the spirit says sing,
And obey the spirit of the Lord!

Those harmonies were not refined but joyous and in full voice. William's booming baritone was notable. This rendition got everyone in the mood for song.

The next was more formal, a delicately intoned Stephen Foster song, "My Old Kentucky Home," with Abe at the piano. There was still hope in those days that Kentucky would join its slave-holding neighbors in the Confederacy.

This gentle and happy song was performed with elaborate harmonies of young voices. Among other gracious elements the lyrics claim that the "darkies are gay."

So much to salve the feelings of the slaveholders.

I know from experience that this was often true despite the hardships of their lives, but what is not in the song were the wishes that their lives could be more hopeful, as good as any white person's could be, which in that society was impossible.

Next was "Lorena," the sad song of a past love never consummated, followed by "Aura Lee," then "Come Where My Love Lies Dreaming," "Kathleen Mavourneen," and "Shenandoah," the last sung acappella.

When the final song's echo had faded, many in the crowd were in tears, and indeed it was moving.

The conductor returned to the piano and began the Beethoven movement from his Ninth Symphony, "Ode to Joy."

I had never heard this played as a solo piece on piano before, and the effect was thrilling. The evening's music progressed from the choral performance to uplifting piano music and to the dance tunes that were to follow.

Abe's performance had a close audience of young men and women, and once again Timmy stood enraptured by the piano despite the persistent attentions of a girl by his side who was nearer his age.

I saw that Jenny noticed me, though it was obvious she could not place me as the traveler patron at the tea-totaling shop from the previous summer. She and her beau stood close to me when the keyboard became the focus of the room with the Beethoven piece.

As the composition passed its climax, she turned to me.

"Good evening, Sir. I am so glad you could join us tonight."

The pianist ranged through several classical and popular tunes as a background for lively conversation. He played a piece by Johann Sebastian Bach which came like a smooth breeze blowing through the assembly.

'May I present Martin Tenate of Castle Oak Plantation, currently attending the Citadel."

I extended my hand and looked at the smiling yet strangely stern face of the cadet. "I am pleased to make your acquaintance, Sir. Jonathan Vander, lately of Paris."

His eyes were steady and I think he realized my hidden accent may be from a city most opposing Charleston.

"I trust you are enjoying your foray into the Southland. Where are you staying?"

Here was the challenge I had accepted in the slave quarters. Here is where I must convince these people that I am more like they than I am like those they do not respect. And I felt I must do this without actually lying.

"I am in Charleston on business with one of the local trading houses, a Mr. Tyrone, and learned of this party through a mutual friend." There was not much information in that, so I plowed on. "Yes, I am greatly enjoying the climate here, and such a beautiful plantation must be a great source of joy and pride to its owners. I congratulate you on your excellent rendition tonight of the choral works. The host's table is also quite extensive. His wine cellar has some of the finest wines I have seen this side of the Atlantic." Better to get them thinking of where I have been than where I am from, or where I may sleep now. "The champagnes especially are excellent. The labels chosen include the most respected houses in the region."

"Do you know wines, Sir?" asked the cadet.

"I have a small appreciation of them. I have toured the chalk caves of Reims and enjoyed a champagne festival in Eperney. But even there I have seen nothing to compare with this presentation. What a magnificent lion! Is it glass?" Time to end this conversation and move on.

"Candy, Sir," explained the girl. "Spun sugar. Its fierce appearance belies its true nature, which is quite sweet." She grinned and turned toward her beau, and he smiled at her.

The pianist had finished the Bach, and we all turned to applaud.

"I hope you will excuse me, Mademoiselle, Monsieur. I must speak with the conductor. He has performed magnificently." With a bow I discreetly walked toward the piano and its artist. A woman was taking his place at the pianoforte. She appeared about sixty years old and dressed neatly but in older clothes, once fine, now a bit out of time. Her presence was warm, and the conductor presented her with the music for her to play. I approached the maestro as the piano began some lighter music, polkas and waltzes.

"Hello," I loudly stated, as if to introduce myself. "My name is Jonathan Vander. I want you to know how much I enjoyed your work. Your performance was exciting for us all."

"Thank you, you are too kind." The artist quickly looked me over and with recognition from our earlier meetings discovered my secret. "Please join me in a glass of Madeira." This vintage is not my favorite, but the invitation for private conversation was welcome, and I nodded to Jenny and Martin, and exited with Abe.

He was a cool character, and did not hint that he suspected me of audacious deception.

At this point we had come to the drinks table and punchbowl near the magnificent confectionary. Isabella quietly observed the black liveried attendant as he served each of us a tall stem of the dark and fragrant fortified wine from the Portugal colony. In the years ahead this would become an even greater favorite among Charlestonians, a reminder of sunny hills of islands beyond the blockading fleet, beyond their ill-fated city, even then becoming my own.

Abe and I toasted Ludwig von Beethoven and observed the room filled with candles and light.

An older woman with a most elaborate gown and head covering sat on a large chair and looked like nothing so much as a queen holding court, or a duchess receiving obeisance from her tenants. Several older black-clad petitioners were greeting her and paying respects. About her were white-coated servants keeping the candles about her lit and her glass full.

At her feet was a large white dog, a poodle. I had seen these beasts while in Paris. They were used in the German and French country for retrieving waterfowl. They were popular among the fashion elite, especially when shorn in a pattern of large fluffy cushions. This made them look rather effete, perhaps even silly on a dog that stood nearly waist-high. I wondered how the animals felt about their preening and brushing. Poodles were, I was told, as smart as a terrier and as strong as a hound, and very loyal.

Abe noticed my gaze. "The dog's name is Pierre, like our general."

General Beauregard was Cajun from Louisiana but had been adopted by Charleston.

A tall, slender young man approached us. His eyes were dark as was his hair, but his skin was fair, and he had a long Frenchman's face. He was clad in an exquisite black suit.

"Abe! A wonderful performance! That Beethoven piece was truly excellent. Please join me in a segar." He found in his slim waistcoat a pair of fine hand-rolled specimens and gave one to Abe. He turned toward me with the other and found a third for himself. "Who is your friend?" he asked Abe as we drifted toward the piazza's doors.

I knew that Abe could expose me if he wished. I guessed he understood my being there was not quite right. But Abe paused and turned toward the piano which was emitting a delightful sound, subtle and lively. I did not recognize the composer. Abe smiled a beatific grin.

"Oh, yes, that is Mrs. Daphne Barringer," said Abe. "Quite a musical talent, isn't she? She is newly returned from Savannah, and is offering lessons in pianoforte. She has taken a house directly across from my own, just a few blocks north of White Point Gardens. You must come see me, and we will give you a private performance in duet."

It seems that Abe had given me a route to escape, but I decided I was in for the game.

"Good evening, Sir. I am Jonathan Vander, recently from Paris. I fear I have not had the pleasure."

The tall gentleman gave a quick glance at Abe, then extended his hand to me. "Welcome to Pond Spring. My name is Francis Moray, this the home of my father Carroll Moray. I trust you are finding the entertainment acceptable?"

"Enthralling and delightful. I had just sought out Abe here to thank him for the evening. Where does such talent come from?"

"Jehovah, I'd say." He raised a wry eyebrow, and Abe smiled and gave a slight bow.

"Abe is our secret weapon. If he can be enticed to entertain, the affair is a certain success! Abe, when is your next engagement?"

Abe replied, "I will be playing some Bach for the Sunday service at St. Luke's. I hope you and your family can attend."

"I look forward to it. If we cannot attend this week, perhaps you can be encouraged to play at our church soon, if we may work you so hard after your own day of worship."

So Abe was of the Israeli faith! I hadn't realized, despite his name. Yet the new President of the United States shared the name and was no Jew.

"We have a newly installed organ from Germany which I am sure you will find to be nearly a match in quality to a performer like yourself."

Even though a Hebrew, he was welcome in the homes of these Christian Southerners. He was not what I was taught to expect of Jews, which were much disparaged in Boston at the time, reflecting on the Shylock of Shakespeare and the moneylenders of Paris, where Jews had only recently been granted equal rights to Christians.

"I've heard of this organ," said Abe, "and also hope that Mrs. Barringer will have the opportunity to put it through its paces. Speaking of which, how is your stable for the races this coming year?"

The conversation devolved to the race of last February and the prospects for future races, though none imagined that the track would be relegated to housing Federal prisoners before long. The time was right for me now to break away and find a less high-profile conversationalist.

"Excellent to meet you. I must go check on my friend," I lied, and with that I took my leave and walked farther out on the veranda, where small groups of men discussed politics and smoked red-glowing cigars. The rich smoke was heady, a scent of manhood.

This house had a view of a grass pond beyond the tended gardens, filled with all manner of flowering shrubs – azaleas, yellow trumpets of Carolina Jasmine, flowers whose scent filled the night. I'd delivered to several plantations which had no gardens, being solely focused on profit.

Chinese lanterns suspended from wires illuminated the lawn just below the house where couples walked manicured trails within their glow. The buttons of the men's uniforms flashed an occasional shine, and the white, pink or yellow voluminous skirts of the women glowed almost like lanterns themselves in the lights and moonlight. The moon was nearly round, high among the occasional drifting cloud, and reflected in the water.

In the distance the windbreak of trees showed a black line which blotted out the stars in the distance. Miles beyond those trees lay the beach, the ocean. Beyond that, Boston, or Paris. Or Timbuktu.

I drained the last of the sweet wine in my glass and observed men leaving the veranda from time to time. I saw the trail to the urinal booths and privy houses which I realized I could avail myself of. I drew a last time from my segar, dropped it in a handy cuspidor and walked down the flag-stoned path. As I approached the booth, in lantern's light I recognized Francis Moray by the entrance, holding a towel. "Hello, Francis we meet again."

The light was bright, but shone yellow from the Chinese paper. Francis looked at me silently with his dark eyes. His hair was more curly than I had noticed earlier, and he had changed into a white coat.

The door to the nearest privy opened, and as a portly man in a gray coat exited, Francis picked up a pitcher from a stand and poured it over the man's proffered hands. Then the man took the towel from Francis's arm.

"Thank you, Alexander. How is Carroll treating you these days? Feeding you enough? If not, you tell him I will buy you at a price you are worth! Ha ha!" The fat man wiped his hands and threw the towel back to the slave as he waddled up to the house.

I was taken aback, as I realized this was not Francis. In this light he was his twin. I noticed some differences now that I looked, such as his lips being a bit more full, and his complexion was at least a shade darker, though difficult to discern in the stark and soft light from the lantern.

I walked quickly away to the opposite end of the lawn but I felt the hot eyes of Alexander on me as I walked. I could take my chances making my water in the shadows of the bushes beyond the garden, and could puzzle out much too quickly how the slave of a plantation owner could be the mirror image of the man's own blood son.

The path I trod was worn, but not a formal trail. It wended through some informal plantings of exotic flowering shrubs I was told were planted some years earlier by a man from Georgia named Beckman or something like that.

I sidled around a bush and completed my business, then noticed a glimmer through the shrubbery and went a bit further down the starlit path. It opened into a dew-laden meadow. The moon was now lower on the horizon and the Milky Way was sparkling bright against heaven. In the distance I saw three figures beneath an enormous live oak. The huge tree was itself silhouetted against the starry mass, with its branches spread to the skies like the wings of a gigantic angel draped in raiment of Spanish moss. A lantern on the ground illuminated the three uniformed men as they spoke among each other.

The cadets did not see me, so I came a bit closer. At a distance I could hear their oaths.

"By the blood of our fathers, on our holy honor, we will not wash, nor cut our hair, nor taste liquor, nor court a woman until our arms have guaranteed the success of our cause!" This was spoken by the smaller of the three, not that he was very small, but the others overtopped him. I later found their names to be Kit and Louis. I already knew of William, the cousin of Francis Moray who had welcomed me to his plantation.

106

"Kit, that is too much. I don't mind the hair, and I guess the washing and liquor are all right, but not to court a woman? This war could take months to win!" This was spoken by Louis, tall and lanky, apparently enamored of some maiden, who I later found was the black-haired Carla I had seen with Jenny on my first day in Charleston. He spoke slowly and deliberately.

"These are the oaths sworn by knights on their way to the Crusades!" rejoined Kit.

"You're both right," William said in his baritone. He was a commanding figure in the light and shadow. "But we must make the oath one we can bear.

"I propose this: 'I swear by the blood of my fathers, by the names of my family, by the heritage I hold dear, to never boast; to cherish loyalty; to honor and respect all women; to live with charity, courtesy, and humility, and to grant mercy to those deserving it. I swear never to let grooming blade touch my person until the field is swept of our enemies and our final victory is won, and the South stands a free and independent nation!'"

At this Louis and Kit enthusiastically agreed, and all three drew their blades and held them in the lamplight, beneath the stars, pointed to heaven.

Together they shouted, "I so swear!"

"And men," spoke the leader, "Let us also swear that when our time is done, we be buried beneath our holy soil, here, on this sacred spot where our souls declared their fealty to our oath, to our land, homes, and families!"

Louis took a small bottle from his pocket and uncorked it. He held it high. "To our oath, and our everlasting loyalty!"

The three of them then shouted, "HOO-HAH!"

Each nascent hero beginning with William took a draw from the flask.

Then following William's lead, each one took a dagger from his waistband and cut a shallow wound on the palm of his right hand and on the back of his right wrist. Then they grasped the neighbor's bleeding right wrist with the cut hand and shared their blood in a triangle of honor.

I had never seen nor heard of this ritual before. Perhaps it was just another example of William's innovative leadership. From wherever that blood ritual had originated, along with the words, the swords, and the drink, the vow did seem a strong oath. It was one that could only be fulfilled by the creation of that new nation by force of arms on the battlefield, or alternately by the death of all three. How could these men live with themselves otherwise?

I had seen enough of that heroic silliness for the evening and left the meadow the way I had come.

As I walked carefully along the path nearer the house, I overheard two lovers in the shadows speaking in whispers.

"I must have you. We will share no shame, as long as we have one another!"

"You know how I feel about you. I want you, and you will be my lifelong love. We will build a life together, but we must wait."

The rustle of a hoop-skirt left to my imagination the movement of the two lovers. I froze in my tracks and pondered how ethical it was to eavesdrop on such a private conversation. I weighed whether I cared about ethics any more, even relating to men swearing oaths to each other, or whether in my present state of masquerade I should also ape being a gentleman in my private behavior.

From a distance came a woman's voice: "Jenny! Time to come in for your goodbyes."

Whispers: "That's Aunt Peggy. I must return."

"One more kiss."

I stepped backwards and broke a twig on the trail. The snapping sound brought the cadet out of the shadows, ready to defend. "You! Jonathan?"

I was embarrassed at their discovery of me. "The men's booths were too crowded and I had to find other arrangements. I beg your pardon."

Aunt Peggy again, "Jenny! Come here now!"

Jenny stepped out from the canopy of trees, and she and Martin walked toward the house, he with a stern look back at me.

"I'm coming, Aunt Peggy. Martin and I were just looking at the constellations."

As they neared the house, Aunt Peggy was in a state. "Oh, no, Jenny. If it becomes known that you and Martin were out alone in the dark, oh dear. Your reputation! Your family!" She began to hyperventilate and cry.

"Wait for me, Martin," I cried a bit louder than necessary, and hurried up the trail into the lights. "Your eyes will adjust themselves to the lantern light faster than they did when I was showing you the belt of Orion." I recognized Aunt Peggy as the Duchess I had seen earlier with the poodle.

Aunt Peggy was surprised to see me. "Who…"

I quickly spoke in the best and most refined South Carolina accent I could affect, "Jonathan Vander, at your service, Madam."

Jenny quickly added, "Jonathan Vander, please meet Margaret Moray, my mother's cousin. Mr. Vander is an associate of Mr. Tyrone and is visiting Charleston for a while."

"Indeed," Aunt Peggy replied, cool yet relieved.

Martin chimed in, "Mr. Vander was very kind to demonstrate a navigation technique he had learned…."

"On my recent voyage to Paris," I continued, hoping to distract the woman from where I might be from to another cosmopolitan city. "I followed the same technique used when Lafayette sailed to join General Washington to fight the British." I hoped an appeal to patriotism and two hallowed names would deflect any investigation as to my city of origin, and from what might have been happening among the jasmine trellises beyond the lantern light.

This was a bit too much information for the spinster to grasp in one sentence. "Mr. Vander, ah, I am pleased to make your acquaintance. Thank you for accompanying my niece and her friend on this, ah, this scientific observation."

While Peggy was catching her breath, I reached down to pat the white mop on the head of her dog Pierre. He accepted my caress, but was wary, and growled. Then I quickly looked at Martin and Jenny and saw them exchange a glance mixed with relief, embarrassment, and perhaps a secret promise of a later meeting.

"Thank you, Jonathan, your explanations of the meteor and how it affects our weather was most enlightening." Martin should be careful when he improvises excuses.

"Of course. Always a pleasure. Good evening, Madame, Miss, and Sir."

As I walked away I noticed Martin walk to the cadets who had sworn under the oak and began to speak to William. The three had just stepped up to the side porch, and each of their right hands were tied in a white bandage.

The orchestra finished its final piece and the conductor dismissed the musicians who silently folded their music stands, put away their instruments, and left in a body with great dignity. I suspect they had their own after-party elsewhere, and what a time that would have been! I can only imagine the music they played for themselves on those instruments.

Inside, the event was breaking up. On the porch a few of the cadets, perhaps a bit too deep in their cups, were well into a rousing verse of "Vive la Compagnie."

The social people who lived nearby were lining up and taking their leave of the host and hostess. Servants waited on them with their coats and hats, and others summoned their carriages. Even saying goodbye was done in timed progression.

As the chorus of the song of camaraderie faded, Abe began playing the haunting song of "The Bloom is On the Rye." A duet of young women sang the words.

> *My pretty Jane! my pretty Jane!*
> *Ah! never, never look so shy.*
> *But meet me, meet me in the Ev'ning,*
> *While the bloom is on the Rye...*

The goodbyes were paused as the melancholy song recalled memories to the older couples who drew nearer each other.

> *The Spring is waning fast, my Love,*
> *The corn is in the ear.*
> *The Summer nights are coming, Love,*
> *The moon shines bright and clear...*

Many held hands together, and not a few turned their faces to their spouses and enjoyed a silent reflection of life, of youth, of the hope of a young man or woman, and the memory of an older one. I have no doubt that each old man looked at his septuagenarian wife and saw the shining face of their first meeting, as she saw his.

The two sopranos sang, their soaring harmonies sweet in the lyrics:

> *But name the day, the wedding day,*
> *And I will buy the ring,*
> *The Lads and Maids in favours white,*
> *And village bells, the village bells shall ring.*

The Spring is waning fast, my Love,
The corn is in the ear.
The Summer nights are coming, Love,
The moon shines bright and clear;

Then pretty Jane, my dearest Jane,
Ah! never look so shy,
But meet me, meet me in the Ev'ning,
While the bloom is on the Rye.

No eyes were free of emotion.

I assessed the gathering and observed this sampling of the plantation class, educated, gracious in manner, mostly gentle and genteel. They were as admirable as any group I had witnessed in Boston, Paris or Brussels. I didn't know what their futures would be, but I felt that except for the one damning fault of the society into which they were born, this proud Southern peerage of loving families and friends was as able, accomplished and worthy as any group on earth.

And I was not fit to be in the room.

I edged my way toward the kitchen where Cato was awaiting my exit and would escort me through the rear. As I neared my escape, Jenny, accompanied by the Duchess, neared me. Aunt Peggy was discussing the pedigree of Pierre with a man about her age. The dog kept a watchful eye on him and occasionally turned his canine attention upon me.

Jenny placed her hand on my arm. A sudden warmth filled me.

"Mr. Vander, I am glad I get the chance to thank you for your assistance this evening. Martin and I will one day be married, but until things are more settled, we are expected to be chaperoned. We appreciate your rescue."

That was the first time an American woman of social quality had touched me since my voyage to Europe. Or, as Laura's behavior showed, maybe the first touch ever of an American woman of quality. Save Dear Mother.

Long months had passed since I had looked on a woman of her class at such close quarters. Often it is easier if there is not a

111

common verbal language between a man and a woman; the best communication need not be verbal, and in my experience in France and Belgium, shy as I was, often is better so. Paris was far away as was my former life, but that night I played the part I had fashioned for myself.

"Miss, it was my duty and pleasure to help you. I wish you all the happiness possible, and I am at your service if ever I can be of help of any kind in the future." I wondered at the irony I felt leaking into my voice. "It is only a matter of time before you and Martin can share in the wonderful future I know both and each of you will have."

Any more of this and I would burst! Yet what was to eventually happen to Martin, Jenny and myself was beyond ironic.

Her touch on my arm drew heat from my body, and a trickle of sweat on this cool evening ran down my side. She did not leave, and the Duchess continued her conversation with her own elderly beau. I did not want her to leave, but I realized what a low beast man is, to covet another's woman, while I could offer her nothing. She would want nothing of me if she knew who I was, where I was living – who I really was.

The young men's impromptu chorus from the side porch again began, this time with the rather ribald "Billy Boy," and stanzas which should best be sung in segregated company, if at all.

"A lovely gown, Miss Jenny. I believe I recognize a lace pattern from Antwerp." I had seen her servant carrying that silk at the soda-water shop nearly a year ago on my first day in Charleston.

"Thank you, yes." She stopped short and looked at me, as if trying to place me. "Mr. Vander, that is a lovely shirt you are wearing. My father had one similar to it at one time. It was his favorite dress blouse, until he tore the cuff while calming a horse. I think he gave it to the groom. Who is your tailor?"

"Oh," I lied, "an Italian man in Boston. I'm sure you have never heard of the man. He has a little shop near Beacon Hill." Her eyes flickered at the name of the city where my father had patronized such a shop. I should stop speaking to her, but didn't want to leave her company.

The line of guests moved ever closer to the two Mr. Morays and the wife and daughter of the estate. I felt I must flee from the light of this woman Jenny, lest I be drawn in like a moth.

"I must congratulate the chef on his fine presentation tonight. If I do not see you again this evening, thank you for your company, and good luck to you and your beau. I grasped her hand in the French manner to kiss it, and as I did the mended shirt cuff was exposed from my stolen coat.

I did not miss a beat of the performance, but the eye of Jenny saw the cuff of her father's favorite shirt, now repaired, and her eyes widened. I turned from her gaze and felt her raised eyebrow follow me as I bade farewell to Aunt Peggy and her companion. Pierre gave me the slightest quiet growl as I approached to pet him so with a wave, I went into the kitchen.

An older man was seated at the piano and was gamely playing a version of "Old Rosin the Beau" as I entered the kitchen and its steamy haven of anonymity.

Pots and pans were being cleaned amid steam the rhythmical movements of one of the scullery crew. He was a slender black man of medium height and build, but when he turned his turbaned head toward me, he nodded, then stopped and looked right through me. I had seen him before.

He was one of the men in the cart Jacob was carrying to work that first day after I had marooned myself in Charleston. His name was Tommy.

He would scrub pots. He would follow orders to lay brick on brick, or dig ditches, hoe cotton, pick rice, and die owning nothing, not even himself.

Yet the man was obviously not propertyless.

This man owned a thing, a natural affinity to music which lived in every component of his body. I saw him from time to time, and no matter the conditions he always was singing, usually an inner song, but often making songs out of the common language he spoke in his daily work.

He would create natural rhymes and rhythms from his speech, his work, even that night as he was cleaning pots there was a cadence of his work, magnified by the resonance of the pans.

He looked at me and smiled, a wide toothy smile, and nodded again before returning to his labor, rattling the pots and swishing the water in a rhythmical music created from his own being. This happy wretch had made peace with his world, and so was no wretch at all.

I know the difference!

I turned from the captive musician and saw the two pianists Abe and Mrs. Barringer sharing a small table and two glasses of Champagne. I recognized the brand Ruinart as being one of the best, rare on this side of the Atlantic. The bottle was in a silver pail filled with chipped ice, and the two pianists were laughing like young lovers as they toasted each other with the sparkling intoxicant. Though there must have been nearly forty years difference in their ages, Abe at about twenty-five years and she much older, their conversation was lively and quick. I caught not a word.

The best communication is not always verbal.

I thought then that I recognized the essence of the love-sickness Abe had told me of that day in Murphy's.

The serving girl Isabella entered the kitchen carrying some serving pitchers, and after placing them near the sink to be washed, she gave me a glance of wry admonishment as she returned to her serving station in the great hall. We would meet again.

Cato and young Ramona were in an alcove behind the storeroom. His face was flushed with as big a smile as I have ever witnessed, and her own was smiling in angelic calm, a satisfaction perhaps borne of having been told a great secret, or having been given a great promise. Perhaps both. I doubt if much of that communication was verbal.

Young Cato saw me and gave the girl a brief kiss. The pretty creature resisted letting go his hand as he came with me, but in the end she waved him goodbye and we made our escape.

I brought the slave household a stolen piece of the foot of that sugar lion wrapped in a napkin.

I did not seek to collect my wager, but returned to the life I was living.

16

TOO LATE

Of the earlier days in my life, the time I felt most free was when I walked the streets of Paris. I had a stipend from my father and would greet strangers on the sidewalk with a happy "bonjour!" I spent my days in the museums, the cafes, the parks, the cathedrals while my aunt entertained her women friends.

How different now!

My days were structured at the whim of my employer, who followed the wishes of his customers. Mine was the end of a chain of desires.

After a day of overseeing the loading and unloading of two carts of goods for Tyrone's store and presenting and signing bills of lading, I drove the empty cart through the streets of the city with my workers riding in back. I say "my workers," though indeed they weren't mine, or Tyrone's who rented them, or even their own. These men were slaves, the property of faceless others.

The men were tired, and I let them ride. I would pass by their quarters on the way to that of the mules, and to my own.

After the unfortunate incident when Major Anderson's former artillery student supervised the attack on his former instructor, if "supervised" is the proper term, bellicose newspaper editorials and speeches were thrust upon the public regarding the rapidly declared independence and confederation of various states of the Union.

One state after another declared: Mississippi, Florida, Alabama joined the new republic, then Georgia, Louisiana with its large and bustling harbor, Texas – the land of Sam Houston, who himself strongly cautioned against leaving the Union – and even Virginia, the home of Washington and Jefferson, Madison, Monroe and Tyler, when it was told that Federal troops would march through the Old Dominion to suppress unruly separatist states. Virginians decided to stand with their slave-holding brethren than follow a path they saw as unconstitutional and un-American. Arkansas and North Carolina declared in May. At last even Tennessee overwhelmed pro-Union farmers and Hillmen in its eastern regions and voted to join the new Confederacy. Its strongest voices were based in its cotton growing western regions and the slave markets in Memphis. The railroad trading interests in Nashville and Chattanooga tipped the balance.

The leaders of the rebellious states, all propertied and affluent, justified the righteousness of their war to protect their families and "their way of life." Can anyone justify killing their fellow men to keep themselves owners of others? But men would feel the need to defend their homes from invaders, even men who had no slaves.

Of the remaining slave states, Kentucky's voting was suspect and conveniently not recognized by Washington. Despite a pro-Confederate governor, Missouri voted to remain in the Union; Maryland dithered, was threatened, and soon occupied by Federal troops; Delaware voted to remain with its major trading partners in the North.

The new President in Washington called for 75,000 recruits in the U.S. Army to chastise the wayward children of America's South, and bring them back into the Union.

Lines were drawn, and the "recreational" rifle and artillery companies I had witnessed in Charleston began marching in earnest. They saw and believed threats in the blusters and broadsides of the Northern newspapers flowing from the pens of abolitionists and those they called "Black Republicans."

And the ranks of the U.S. Army did swell with new recruits.

There was no question in the minds of the United States government that this was a relatively small matter, that a few wealthy and rabid plantation owners had whipped up a crowd of the local people enough to fire on Fort Sumter and chase the lawful garrison out. A quick summer's campaign would put things right.

There was no dispute among leaders of the South (and many Northern scholars) that plantation owners had the Constitutional right to own slaves, and no question for many that the individual states had the right to separate and form their own association if they wished. There was also assurance in the South that if the various states were indeed threatened by invasion, the superior fighting qualities of Southern men would rapidly straighten things out and establish their rights for all time.

So, the forces of the United States prepared themselves to quickly correct the Southern states. Washington expected the whole enterprise to last about three months.

Defenders always have stronger incentive than those invading someone else's home ground. The South with its well-trained army led by graduates of the U.S. Military Academy (as was the Federal army), its own academies, and veteran generals of the Mexican War would shut the door on the Northern troops and then go home to their plantations and farms. The whole affair would be over by fall.

One side thought its strength of supply and manpower were irresistible. The other believed its fighting abilities and resolution were unmovable.

Both were right, to the woe of this nation of brothers.

A few relatively small incidents in Missouri and Virginia began to get the blood up of the opposing camps, but the battle fought in July at Manassas Junction and Bull Run Creek near Washington was expected to end the matter. Washington believed the Southern forces would be soundly whipped by the cannon and blades of the U.S. Army, and reconciliation would begin.

The same day as that battle the U.S. House of Representatives passed the War Aims Resolution which stated that the war was being fought solely to preserve the Union, not to end slavery. Three days later the resolution passed the Senate as well.

But it was too late.

That battle was expected by both sides to be the first and last of the war and was a disaster for the North. The Southern forces handled themselves well, and the overconfident men of the North were surprised with defeat. Citizens of Washington brought picnics to watch the Southern forces humiliated, but instead fled with their army back into the city in fear of their lives. Alarm spread, and there was fear of an invasion and loss of the U.S. capital. But Southern forces withheld their advance, and the North retired to lick its wounds and gird for a longer war.

Newspaper reports of the glorious Southern victory near Washington City were met with joyous celebration in the streets of Charleston. Their troops played a major and pivotal role in the victory, some a part of the instantly famous Stone Wall Brigade. Details were found in the Courier and Mercury, and repeated on the street for weeks.

It was commonly thought that this shaming of Federal troops while defending their own capital would lead to terms of peace, or else the Southern Army would march into the capital itself!

From my perspective it seemed that it would indeed be the end of the dispute, and if I stayed in Charleston, I would find myself in a foreign country within a few weeks.

The cafes were bustling, the docks loading and unloading for transport to England and France. All was good. The city's people had little fear of a determined resistance from Washington, and I had seen the splendid armies of Southern soldiers trained and sent north.

Carloads of heroic legions returned from the northern field of battle a bit the worse for the fighting and some few with injuries. There were some missing comrades who had actually fallen in the resounding victory.

The few families who would never again see their sons would not believe it was only a few. For them it was The End. Anything later was nothing to the experience of losing their family's best, their heirs, their family princes, the ends of their lines.

But for most it was a tale of resolute bravery, of defending the homeland from invaders who would force their foreign ways upon them.

118

There were a few bodies returned. There were funerals. There was sadness. No one wanted war. Well, almost no one.

Church services prayed for the souls of the glorious young men who must be sacrificed to save the South's way of life. I wondered what sort of Christian would sacrifice their own blood for the state-sanctioned bondage of other men and their families.

There were celebrations of victory! A triumphal parade was held at each arrival of soldiers. Bands, sweets, dances, dinners.

One of these triumphal celebrations included the three young men, Kit, Louis and William, who had sworn the oath under the live oak. They were briefly back from service under General Bonham. Their force had participated in a victory under the great Virginian general named Jackson, becoming known as the commander of the Stone Wall Brigade.

The three comrades were bound by blood. Each now sported longer hair and beards, had sworn by their holy honor under that magnificent live oak the night of the plantation party at Pond Spring Plantation, and had succeeded in their Iliad.

It was a sight to see those who had pledged themselves to never rest in defense of their homeland, and who had prevailed on the field. They allowed themselves to be triumphed, with a carriage ride through Charleston down Bay Street to the Battery, and up King, enjoying the shaded ride and waving to pedestrians who may or may not have known them individually, but knew these uniformed soldiers were their heroes.

William, Louis, and Kit took their tour of glory and eventually retired to the lavish house of a friend where they allowed drinks to be brought to them by wealthy patrons, and took their ease that night before returning to their individual homes in the morning.

They perhaps thought the war was over and they would be forever heroes.

They would learn that dreams of men can fail.

Outreach to Washington to calm the storms of war was not accepted. It would have involved recognition of an independent Confederate government.

There were soon more calamities on both sides of the conflict.

Northern papers proclaimed the need for more soldiers, more ships to send south.

The blockade, which the Northern government proposed and soon began, was considered by everyone to be an impossibility. The U.S. Navy had only a few score ships, mostly coastal sail boats, and there were three thousand five hundred miles of coastline to patrol.

Charleston was now under the command of a new general named Lee who later became famous. Beauregard was busy elsewhere, so they sent this smallish graying officer to prepare against the invasion of the army to which he had but lately held allegiance. He had served that army well, including service in the war with Mexico, and had commanded the troops who captured the notorious abolitionist murderer John Brown.

This new commander once rode past me in the street and tipped his hat, which surprised me. He rode a dappled grey, and sat his saddle with an air of command and competence. His expression was calm and thoughtful, not exactly the fierce visage of an Agrippa.

He and his escorts exchanged comments on the city as they slowly walked their mounts through town toward their quarters at Mills House hotel.

In those anxious days of the early war there was a high level of braggadocio. Plantation owners provided fetes and gatherings, and Tyrone did his best to provide the finest delicacies for the refined Southern palate.

I was sent one fine and clear blustery day with Tommy, the rhythmical pot-washer from the plantation party, to another plantation to the south with a cartload of tinned pate', marmalades, fine cookie biscuits, and seven cases of Bordeaux wine.

We passed lush cotton and rice plantations being worked by fewer slaves now, as labor was needed for digging defensive earthworks, and the workers left to labor were often older men and women with children.

At first the journey was uneventful other than the observation of a beast I'd not seen before, not of this continent, being used to

120

work rice paddies. It was as large as a bull, yet had a cap of curving horns that gave it a very exotic look, as if it were wearing a warrior's helmet from Viking days. But it seemed docile enough and quite at home in a watery field of rice. Water buffalo, perhaps, and not related to our western buffalo, I think.

I expect soldiers from one army or another eventually butchered and ate them when fresh beef rations were not available.

A large Federal fleet was preparing for an invasion of the South. It was suspected and feared it would head directly to Charleston Harbor. It would force its way to the city with guns blazing and reduce docks, warehouses and homes to cinders. A stout defense from Forts Sumter, Johnson, Moultrie – even the battery by White Point Gardens itself might stop it – or not.

New York newspapers wrote of the fleet, and the story was relayed via telegraph throughout the country. Charlestonians prayed that it would not reach their harbor, and with a combination of relief and dread we learned that the great armada was sent to take the large and mostly undeveloped harbor at Port Royal to the south, not Charleston.

Throughout the countryside surrounding the port and Hilton Head the owners of plantations with sons serving with the army had no one to defend against the expected arrival of Federal troops. These worthies, lately so flush with crops of rice and cotton, fled with their most prized furniture, china, and silver to Columbia, to Atlanta, to their mountain homes, and to Charleston.

As "Rhythm Tommy and I drove south, we encountered carts, carriages and field slaves driving pigs and other livestock along the roadway. They crowded out other traffic. We turned off the highway onto a road leading to a field planted in cotton, never to be further tended nor harvested. Great profits wasted.

I parked the cart and we tended the mules as the river of wealth and the wealthy flooded north.

As we waited for the human and animal train to abate to continue our journey, Tommy and I ate our packed lunches and finally decided to camp for the night. He seemed agitated just sitting still. Such inaction was at odds with his natural tendency for motion.

"Mr. Jonathan, we ain't got no call to sit this place with no destination, can't get to where we need to be, just waitin' here for the folks to pass. Just don't seem right to stay here now, when abolition soldiers is headin' our way..." he spoke his words in a sing-song cadence, expressing the same thoughts as I was thinking, though my thinking was less eloquent and without the entertainment factor.

As we had no other food for our suppers, we sampled the paté and the biscuits. These delicacies may have been fine for a party, but for a real meal liver paté and meringue candy get old quickly. I did enjoy a bottle of the Bordeaux, and we slept soundly, sheltering beneath the tarp.

It was luck for us that the weather was breezy and not stormy. We found later there was a great storm out to sea.

We repeated our disgusting meal for breakfast, and I decided the way south was obviously not a proper direction for us. We reversed our course back to the city, joining the flow of travelers fleeing from my invading countrymen.

The fleet arrived in South Carolina after their trial by storm.

As it left its northern port, winds rose and waves rolled and a mighty storm smote the ships as if the prayers of Charleston were answered by a sympathetic and wrathful God. Their war of separation must be sanctioned by the Almighty, who obviously would use His power to aid His chosen Southern people.

Three Federal ships were lost beneath the waves. Others were damaged and forced to return to home port. Many were scattered across the surface of the sea and straggled to their rendezvous point.

A sufficient force survived to meet at the entrance to Port Royal where they began a circular course of attack on the two forts.

Reinforced batteries had been built in preparation and were armed with various sizes of cannon, both smoothbore and rifled, but they were no match for the fleet. Ship after ship passed its broad side toward the batteries, and hundredweight after hundredweight of exploding shells pounded the defenders, upending guns, scattering sand.

When the naval forces of the United States occupied the site there was so little left of the human defenders that human remains were described as fragments of bloody rags, where once stood beings God had created in His own image.

The good harbor of Port Royal Sound, a mere seventy or so miles from Charleston, was then in the possession of a powerful enemy. Now the Federals had a fine base of operations from which to train their troops and stage their navy for blockading and shelling of what I had come to accept as my city.

As the supply and troop ships landed and disembarked their various cargoes, U.S. forces prepared for the closure of the ports of Charleston and Savannah.

Once established, the army conducted raids on the plantations around the area. The few remaining people lived in fear of having their homes sacked or burned, so they fled too. The nearest city of any size was Charleston. Refugees all, from rice and cotton millionaires and their servants and slaves to the poorest white families.

Thousands of slaves were left behind or walked away from their homes, and many followed in the wake of the uniformed Federal troops. Eventually special fatigue units were formed of the newly freed Negroes.

Hundreds crowded the streets of Charleston.

The wealthy booked rooms in hotels and stayed with friends or in their city homes, while the poorer classes slept where they could in sheds, warehouses, store rooms, anywhere they could find shelter from the cooling November weather. Some stayed in town near the waterfront near the window sash factory.

Charleston was set for its single greatest catastrophe.

17

LUMINOUS CITY

Christmas was not far off. Streets that a year earlier had been packed with early shoppers and holiday revelers were now jammed with marching recruits, merchants, and suppliers carrying their wares to depots and docks. There were hundreds and hundreds of escapees from the threatened farms to the south.

Until now the greatest challenges for these people had been either harsh labor in the fields, or boredom at their plantation homes. Now all sought places to sleep, cook, to just survive in a world so different from life on a quiet farm. There were fears of invasion or worse, and very shortly worse was to come.

There were many fire crews in Charleston before the War. They held monthly or even weekly meetings where they gathered in social fraternity to toast each other's exploits, tell tales of their adventures, model their uniforms. In holiday parades the crews would burnish and paint their engines and pumps, brush their horses, shine their helmets, and display their brilliance.

Most crews were all white. They were praised for their heroic work as well as their fancy uniforms. A few crews were free blacks, who also displayed well in parades. Occasionally when needed, a black crew had a white member, or a white crew had a black member, though this had not been the norm before the war. Now in the last months of 1861 most of the young men of the white crews were serving as infantry in Virginia.

The town was alive with people early that night. The glow from the gas streetlights silhouetted the shops and houses; rays of light shot through the smoke and vapors rising from the city. A breeze was beginning to stir from the bay.

Things were looking up for me. Well, the bottom of a cesspit would perhaps look like up for the poor soul I fancied myself then.

I was awake early that day and retired early that evening. I had spent the day delivering ice, which we could still get then, and other goods to the Mills House and the Pavilion Hotel. I had slept there my first evening in the city. After delivering bills of payment to some of the ships along the wharf I was nearly in bed when I heard the bell. I ignored it and prepared to sleep, but the bells didn't stop. I went out and saw a glow in the sky.

I turned to look at the steeples of this "holy city," with its self-satisfied airs, its churches and cathedrals, its calm, gracious gentility and sanctimonious view of itself. One of the steeples, St. Michael's, had a red lantern suspended from a pole on its northern side, a sign to fire crews that told them what section of town the fire was in.

People who visited Charleston after that war said it looked like a holocaust site because of artillery bombardment, and true, that was bad enough. But the real destruction was from that fire.

An evening cooking fire started by displaced slaves from Edisto or somewhere had started with the crisp smoky scent of ham that rapidly turned to woodsmoke as sparks escaped into an outbuilding used to store hay. The tinder flashed and flames rapidly leapt up the walls of the old building, and from there the city of wood-roofed structures was open to the fire's appetite.

Flame swiftly climbed up the walls the rising breeze fanned the embers. The fire grew hotter. Bells rang and fire companies jumped to their wagons.

General Lee staying at the Mills House surveyed the growing inferno from the balcony. He directed his men to soak the hotel's bedclothes in water and hang them from the balconies and windows. This prevented flying sparks from igniting the dry wood siding of the building, and it was largely because of this action that this structure survived.

Many, many buildings were lost.

I heard people shouting in the distance, grabbed a jacket, and walked toward the disturbance.

Then I ran.

I arrived at Bay Street and saw the flames rising like brilliant

125

glowing sheets being blown in the stiff wind. One fire crew was on the scene and another was pulling up, bell frantically clanging. The horses weren't smartly brushed like in the parades, but were alarmed, lathered, eyes wide and rolling, yet still followed the guidance of the drivers.

Fire companies and volunteers from the onlooking crowd helped residents move themselves and their property from approaching windblown flames to safer places, which often also caught fire. Despite moving their goods more than once, many citizens lost everything.

I helped move goods from a threatened townhouse, a friend of Tyrone's, and as I carried them to a cart, I was accosted by Jenny Haywood of the brandy hair, wildly calling me by name.

"Jonathan! Jonathan!"

She recognized me, even with my face and hands covered with dust, even without the mended shirt sleeve cuff. Indeed, I had inadvertently grabbed my Mexican jacket and found that it yet retained its magic powers. They were needed that night.

I was a worker in the fire, and could have been gentry or peasant, it didn't matter.

She was dressed in clothes for the theatre that had become disheveled in the frantic flight from the blazes. She pleaded with me to help move her parents out of the way of the flames, as the roadway was blocked by crowds of those seeking to put out fires, or move properties, or just to observe.

Without trying to explain anything I ran with her to the carriage of her parents. The coachman was only a boy, and Mr. Haywood and he were trying to calm their horse who was stamping and rearing, in fear of fire and the rapidly moving crowds around him.

I don't consider myself any better with horses than the next man, but I could calm one, or at least hoped I could.

I removed my enchanted coat and with some effort placed it over his head, covering his eyes. He stood more still, though lathering and still stamping and shifting his feet. I grasped the bridle and led him away, talking and then singing quietly to him. The only song to come to mind was the Foster song, "Camptown Races," though when I reached the part about "run all night," I changed the lyrics to a slow and soothing, "doo-dah, doo-dah," repeated over and over to him.

126

We slowly moved northward on Meeting Street to about George Street, blocks away from the growing disaster. Squads of cadets from the Citadel marched in the other direction to give what aid they could.

As I lifted the Mexican jacket, which would see other use that night, Mr. Haywood took my hand and looked into my eyes. "Son, I thank you." He then turned to calm his excitable wife who was still in the coach, and helped his coachman lead the still skittish horse farther away from harm.

Jenny was tearful in her thanks, and before she followed her father, turned her streaming face back to look at the burning city. I left her there, the yellow flames lighting her features as if she were on a theater stage.

There is something thrilling about a fire. For a while a building looks like it is bothered, irritated by the flame. As it grows, the fire envelops the house, which wears it like a brilliant, flowing cloak. Its shape is swathed in a bright, dancing, dreamy glow and the building seems to grow in size, sweeping in and out of dazzling form. Its luminance dominates the attention of all about it. Heat from the blaze is not unpleasant at first, especially in December. But the relentless radiation becomes uncomfortable and worrying, the skin of one's face and arms feels beaten, drying.

Crowds of people are held rapt, staring at a new form of nature, or rather its perversion.

Fire changes a structure built by the labor of men into dazzling heat and light, finally falling bit by bit, either leaving its skeleton ablaze, or in a sudden collapse, walls and roof failing and tumbling, blowing a billow of sparking smoke and burning dust into a spreading spiral of flying coals, like the down of a dandelion blowing across a field, its seeds seeking other places to root and grow.

Building after building fell prey to the brightness. More bells rang.

Civilians, soldiers, and members of the City Police could not contain the blaze.

The ocean tide was low at that hour and the hoses from the pumps could not reach to pull and shoot water from the harbor to the sash factory, which was lost, nor to the buildings downwind, now in full fiery array. Great waves of flame spread high into the night. The

127

faces of the people were masks of astonished wonder – some fearful, some prayerful, all in the thrall of the mighty event.

Horses neighed, the inferno roared; bells rang, and the people gasped and cried.

As I returned to the roaring and tumultuous scene a third fire wagon appeared, pulled by mules and carrying Jacob Johnson and his sons. There were only the three of them, and I called and ran to help. Jacob handed me an axe, to what purpose I knew not.

The fire spread.

A military officer arrived and began calling out orders. Soldiers and cadets from the crowd began moving, running ahead of the striding blaze.

Mothers gathered their children as the crowd stepped back from the heat. I was sunburned that dark, cold, damp night.

I joined the running men and obeyed the orders of the officer to remove people from the houses in the path of the hot wind and sparks.

There was confusion at first, and resistance, though finally families and servants grasped that they were in danger and in a frenzy began clutching what they could to move out of their doomed homes.

Then the wind faded and a light misting rain began to fall. Many of us hoped the calamity was over. We slowed long enough for a brief prayerful rest. But immediately the rain stopped and the wind grew rising to nearly a gale, and fanned the dancing blaze.

Fire bells rang and now church bells joined them.

The fire leapt to new buildings, ravenous.

The roar of the combustion sounded like the very breath of the Devil.

We worked all night, sometimes moving families, furniture, and goods more than once, fleeing the pursuing beast.

The rolling apocalypse reached the gas works. Great green jets of even hotter fire spewed up against the dark city, illuminating everyone with an unearthly sheen that could have heralded the end of the world.

The fire marched on.

Churches fell, venerable houses of wealthy men, factories which the South relied on to pursue the war, storehouses jammed with canon, arms, goods, and food, all fell to the rampaging light.

Other homes would catch aflame from the sparks and would

either have its fire extinguished by men climbing roofs with water and wet sheets, or would be engulfed and terrifically destroyed.

To my left toward Logan Street, I heard a horrific scream. A small house in the rear of a larger home was burning, but the fire was mostly inside. The structure was not a flaming mass like other houses lost in the light.

The screaming continued, and I guessed it was a child. I ran to the door – locked! – and swung the axe. I broke the door and as I opened it air rushed into the room and fed the flaming walls. A figure was writhing on the floor near a broken window. The air feeding the fire brought the low roar of the flames to a crescendo as it whistled through the doorway and swept me into the room.

I don't know how the fire made its way inside that wooden building before the outside caught. I can only guess a flaming brand blew in through an open window. That may not be the cause at all.

The wretched figure on the floor was beyond thought in painful and reflexive shuddering, shaking in the hot air about it, thrashing against a still-dark wall. Sparks of flame spat and landed on the blanket over its head, spotted with flame, and its cry was like that of a demon. In that instant I wondered what additional hellish curse was being laid on me – a fleeting thought.

My skin felt thrilling flashes of heat as I dashed toward the person and carried/dragged it from the house through the door, against the streaming wind. I stumbled onto the street and continued to crawl and drag the hopeless victim from the now collapsing house, into the dark alley.

When we were far enough away, I beat the small bits of glowing crumbs from the blanket and smothered its remaining flames with my own now-ruined jacket, completing its final charm –salvation of a life.

The figure moaned and cried, and I may have cried too.

I lifted the charred blanket and saw an elderly woman with eyes clamped shut, desperately gasping, and grasping what was left of my shirt.

A City Police officer arrived at a reckless run, and as he tried to push me away from the cowering and choking wretch, strong hands gripped me from beneath the blanket and did not let go.

"Mammy, oh, Mahir," the big policeman cried. Over and over, "Mahir, Mammy, oh, Mother."

129

Slowly the woman released me and transferred her grip to her son.

He drew his whistle, blew and hollered to a man carrying a water bucket and brought him over. The policeman removed his coat and tore his uniform shirt into rags which he dipped into the bucket and gently wiped the burns on his mother's face and arms.

Others gathered around, and I backed away from the pair, still on the ground and catching my breath and coughing up ash.

The policeman's face was more visible as my vision cleared, and I recognized him as Kerry, the sergeant who directed me to carry poor Ricardo out the night of his suicide nearly a year ago.

The large Irishman fretted and whimpered as he tended his dear mother, who began to whisper consoling words in Irish to her frantic son. The two simply hugged and comforted each other until Doctor Jinkins arrived. Each comforted the other, one of wounds, the other of anguish.

"Jonathan!" A call from Jacob.

I slowly came to my feet and found I was sound, though scalded by the heat. Later when near a mirror I would find that my facial hair had burnt off, and much the hair of my head was frazzled to cinders. My arms were completely naked of hair beneath my charred shirtsleeves.

And the fire marched on.

I rejoined my fire crew, now without an axe and no longer under the protection of Ricardo's enchanted jacket.

At one point we heard large explosions. A military officer had ordered several buildings blown to pieces to arrest the fire's progress, and this worked! This firebreak was made by reducing family homes to atoms, by throwing the dust and fragments of a family's possessions into the air, a sacrifice. The act isolated the area and held the devastation of the great city within boundaries. But the absolute destruction of the heart of Charleston was visible in the downtown for decades and cast a permanent pall on the city.

In fact, few people were injured due to the rapid orders of the general who took control, but the sight was disheartening, gloomy, a blow to the pride of the city. If the Romans had wrought their anger on Charleston as they had on Corinth, the desolation of these hundred or more acres could have been no more complete.

130

As early sunlight began to crawl into the city, I rejoined Jacob and his crew with a replacement axe and we went home to home, moving charred beams to search basements and hollows for survivors. We found a few.

We also found a few who didn't survive.

As we cleared the homes one at a time in the growing dusty dawn, our faces smeared with ash, our lungs coughing up dust and smoke of the smoldering city, the world in my view was Sodom and Gomorrah, as if God's wrath had smitten this city, this "holy city."

Some of the churches tolled the hour, and these bells, unlike the frantic ringing of the night before from fire wagons sounded like a dismal dirge for the stricken community.

We moved like spectres in those lightening gray hours as we shifted hot charcoal members of structures, seeking the unfortunates who may yet have survived. The entire wasteland crawled with those like us, searching for people or digging through the blasted remains of their homes to salvage some small item, some treasured bit of their lives.

I came to the remnants of the home of the Christmas party of a year ago, where "The Charge of the Light Brigade" had been recited.

Someone had blundered.

As we carefully worked toward the back of the house with Jacob and his sons, we lifted a blackened beam and uncovered a burnt hand, a smoking blanket, and finally the burnt face of the serving girl Isabella.

She coughed, opened her eyes, and lived.

131

SECTION TWO

TRANSIENT SALVATION

18

BLESSING

After that big fire there was plenty of cleanup work for anyone who could supervise workers. With Tyrone's approval I was put to work by Jacob, largely to keep track of his hirelings and to appear actively busy and therefore not required to serve in uniform.

Tommy was in the crew, rhythmically calling the workers to lift and haul together. Working with him we kept up a regular meter, cadence and rhyme in our motion, the way a troop of soldiers marches to the music of a band.

In those first weeks of 1862 we cleared roadways and helped move stones and burnt material. The army was taking most of the horses, but we still had Tyrone's mules. They were deemed important for the war effort in loading and unloading trains to and from the warehouses, often containing food and supplies to be sent to Virginia.

I reflected that the ruins about me resembled some of the sketches I had made of fallen Imperial Roman columns I saw in Italy.

As our crew cleared some of the burned beams from the smoke-stained foundation of the Circular Church, two city policemen walked toward us. One paused about thirty feet away and the other addressed me at close quarters. He was Kerry, the son of the burning victim, the policeman who took dead Ricardo to the lockup.

"Jacob Johnson told me I would find you here." By his accent I guessed he came to America from Ireland in his early teen years. I have always had something of a talent for gauging accents. Or maybe I'm kidding myself.

I wondered whether he was here to arrest me as an undesirable from up north, or to direct me to report to an army recruiter.

"Are you the man who saved my mother in the fire?" I relaxed a bit at this.

"Yes, Officer. How is she?" This was about three weeks after the fire.

"She's alive, and for that I'm grateful."

He was a large man with sandy brown hair, about thirty-two years old. His jaw was square and his gaze was stern, but his eyes were wet with tears. "She is pained, but recovering. The doctor is giving her laudanum and she is resting, healing."

I remained silent as he regained his composure.

"She believes you were sent from God to save her."

Sent from God!

"She was praying to St. Michael, and believed she was lost to death before you broke the door in."

I recalled the thrashing of her figure as if possessed by, well, I don't know what, demon or angel. But that night only mortal fear and pain.

"She wants to thank you personally, but wanted to get better first." The big officer held out his hand, and I grasped it. As I did, he forcefully pulled me to him and hugged me, and expressed a sob.

He quickly broke the embrace and wiped his eye. His partner in the near distance had turned partly away and pretended not to watch us.

"Jonathan, me lad, if ever I can be of service in any way, please do me the favor of letting me help you." Then he said in a low voice with eyes closed, "Go raibh míle maith agat!" or something like that, an Irish blessing, I suppose.

He turned and quickly marched to his mate, and they walked up the street through the black dust.

He was another in the mosaic of relationships that would direct my life to, well, eventually to where I went, even to here.

There was some rebuilding, but mostly the ghastly stone

skeletons of devastated homes, churches, and businesses stood as a testament to the drastic change in all our lives. Their shadows made the barren streets a macabre museum.

Citizens who had lived in houses that survived stayed, but others began to flee the city in an orderly migration inland, even to the mountains.

I noticed that among those who stayed was Jenny's Aunt Peggy who I had met along with her poodle at the plantation party. Her city house was south on the Charleston peninsula and escaped the fire. She still had faith that the cause would prevail and their world would maintain the graceful style she had known her whole life. She and her maid servant would still walk her neighborhood streets with her large white dog Pierre as if there were no war, no unpleasantness.

The city continued to work, to bring rice and produce and men in from the countryside, to process them, and to send them north to feed the ever-demanding war.

In February there was a great celebration of the birth of President Washington, that slave-owning Virginia general who made an independent America possible. I wonder what he would have thought of it then, the country having grown to the Pacific Ocean, his progeny, now pulling itself into pieces.

Would he have approved another independence movement?

Would he have fought to keep his slaves?

The blockade the U.S. Navy had promised was beginning to tell. Ports of the South from Virginia to Texas were patrolled and stifled somewhat, though generally the effort was considered impossible both in the North and South. In fact, the "Anaconda Plan," named after that constrictor snake and meant to strangle commerce, was very porous. "Blockade runners" had little trouble, at least at first, in evading Federal warships that could not usually compete in speed or seamanship with the cotton-laden transports. They bore the "white gold" to the world, and returned arms-laden, to feed the machine of the Southern military.

Later in the war the blockade became more effective, yet the runners became faster with new custom Liverpool-built ships, and grew ever more adept at evasion and deception. I'll tell you more about that later.

In late February the sad news came that President Lincoln's son Willie had died, apparently from infected water, which was a problem in many cities, including Charleston and Boston.

Boston had fixed its problem earlier than most cities. I recall the Boston event my mother took me to when I was about seven years old, really a chance for me to hear the band play. It was the occasion of the public water works dedication.

Though at the time I was eager to hear the music and see the parade of cadets with their flags and muskets, the important part of the day was that the city would now have a regular source of clean water! If you can believe it, some people opposed the idea. It took decades to overcome the influence of the water-peddlers and anti-tax people. Perhaps if they knew someone who had a child like young Willie and then helplessly watched him sicken and die they would have more readily agreed to the project. Enough of them did agree to make it happen, and in the end, there were cannons fired, rockets sent aloft, happy bells chiming, speeches, cheers, music, and a sudden display of a great gushing fountain, celebrating Boston's end of water hunger, never to be repeated.

Charleston was still using cisterns and wells to catch water. The city had but one anemic artesian well which produced not enough at all. Little clean water and poor sanitation in a flat and swampy region is a bad combination, and there were regular consequences. One of them would strike my heart to its core.

The problems around Charleston were bad enough with regular fevers like yellow fever, congestive fever − which doctors call malaria now − and any number of sicknesses that killed scores of citizens every year.

I overheard many saying young Willie Lincoln's death was God's judgement on Lincoln for going to war against the Southern states, though there were also many who expressed sorrow for the death of an innocent child. A child so like all those young men marching and parading on Citadel Green, many who would not return. God's judgement?

A vengeful god.

In March we heard of the Battle of Hampton Roads in Virginia, foretelling a change in naval warfare the like of which the world had never seen.

Southern forces in Virginia had raised from the hastily abandoned Portsmouth boatyards the 250-foot-long remains of a steam frigate named *USS Merrimack*. The U.S. Navy had scuttled it at the war's opening.

The hull, engines, and boilers were repaired, and the mastless deck was fitted with a novel concept for warfare, a structure with slanting walls. Within this shelter were mounted fourteen guns. It was covered in plate iron, the first "ironclad" employed in battle. It was renamed the *CSS Virginia*.

While in France I had heard of a French steam-and-sail warship clad in iron, launched from a city on the Mediterranean. I was traveling home before it ever saw action.

Home.

In the sea battle at Hampton Roads, the "Rebel Monster," as some in the North called the *Virginia*, advanced and defeated the instantly obsolete wooden warships the Federals had stationed nearby. The very next day upon returning to the battleground to sink more helpless vessels, the *Virginia* was surprised to face another ironclad ship again unlike any on earth. This was the 180-foot *USS Monitor*. It had been quickly brought from New York and was armed with two smoothbore cannon in a rotating iron turret.

The battle was joined. The two unique craft whaled away, doing some damage each to each but neither gaining dominance. Anyone would agree that a rotating turret on a maneuverable shorter platform was a superior design over the larger, underpowered *Virginia*, which took an hour to come about, its tightest turn about a mile in diameter.

But designs of warships were forever changed. Ironclads were demanded by navies the world over from that point on.

The city of Charleston built two ironclads during the war to protect the harbor. There was an event to raise money for those ships that brought me to a new point in my life. That story will come in its time.

*   *   *

This seemed the right point for my great-great uncle to pause. A one-hundred-year-old man, even one this vital, must rest.

I shook his hand, still firm but also fragile, and slipped from the room as his attendant entered.

I would return the next day, but my time was drawing short for this work as I must soon return to Chapel Hill and my studies in business. But tomorrow's session was worth staying the extra day at the guest home, where that evening I enjoyed the best vinegar-styled barbecue I have ever tasted.

At 9:30 in the morning I arrived with my notepad. Uncle Jonathan had a cup of coffee near him and as he began, I had a thought that old people are more durable than the young.

They have seen more of life and aren't as surprised when things happen.

*   *   *

19

MY CITY

One day in the spring the newspapers reported the story that was not at first believed, of a battle in Tennessee. Many assumed there must be an error. The numbers were too high. It was eventually verified beyond doubt.

April brought the tale of sorrow, terror, of the profound realization that this was not to be a short, victorious war and independence with little cost. This war was to be a real horror.

In a battle at an unknown landing on the Tennessee River two large forces met in a day of cataclysm.

Union forces had taken strong points on the river and threatened the Memphis and Charleston rail line

Confederate General Albert Sidney Johnston, veteran of many battles and three different armies (including the Texian), led a surprise massive assault one morning that overwhelmed the Union camp. The retreating Federals were pursued. Johnston, while personally commanding his men from his horse Fire Eater in a peach orchard, took a bullet in his leg, which severed a major artery. He quickly bled to death and Charleston's Pierre Beauregard took command, that same soldier who had commanded the assault on Sumter almost exactly a year earlier.

The Federal troops were led by a new Northern general named Ulysses Grant.

The Confederate charge drove the Federals back to the river and Beauregard commanded a rest. He would complete the victory the following morning.

Beauregard's command was reinforced, but so was Grant's.

The next day battle recommenced.

Neither side wished to be seen as the loser, so both pursued the fight with gusto. Union forces were able to reoccupy their lost campsite and Beauregard withdrew to Corinth, Mississippi. Naturally both commands claimed victory. They shared nearly twenty-five thousand casualties, an impossibly high number.

This number was so huge that many believed the reports from Shiloh must be mistaken. Indeed, the number killed was about seventeen hundred on each side, but factoring in the wounded, missing, and captured it was a great blow to the Southern Army, and equally to the Northern.

Well, not quite equally, as the North had a larger reserve to draw upon for replacements; that is, if the replacements could be convinced they should join the army and march into an enemy's hostile homeland. Luckily for the Federal government there were many new immigrants, German and Irish, willing to sign on for the bonus money.

Charleston did not get many of the wounded, as the Confederate Army of Mississippi was mostly made up of Mississippians, Louisianans, Tennesseans, Kentuckians, Floridians, and Alabamians. They mostly went to their home states to recover or die.

Charleston then learned of the fall of Fort Pulaski, sealing the Harbor of Savannah, our neighbor just a hundred miles to the south.

Then we heard the most shocking news, that New Orleans was taken.

New Orleans, that polyglot cosmopolitan city, dominated commerce in the Gulf of Mexico. It was the largest city in the Confederacy and had been the third busiest port in the United States. It supplied all the interior of America with import and export services. Now it was in the hands of the powerful Northern enemy – not my enemy, but the enemy of all my friends.

This foreshadowed the capture of the Mississippi River which would divide the eastern states from Texas and Arkansas, also Confederate, also in the rebellion against the United States of America. These stark events drove the Confederate government to a heightened state of agitation. It passed the Conscription Act, which provided that all able-bodied men between the ages of eighteen and thirty-five must join up for a three-year tour.

I JONATHAN

My choice of not joining the army was now a crime.

Supplies and imported goods were still available, and ships running to and from Nassau, Havana, and Bermuda could still mostly evade blockaders.

I continued my work with Tyrone, delivering goods from the depot to homes and plantations, or from the docks to the commercial district. I always carried my rucksack of possessions with me, and now stayed in the shadows when possible, out of the gaze of those who might see me as a likely candidate for arms, or worse – from Boston!

At first when working so obviously for the good of the city or delivering the goods of commerce, I was unquestioned.

Often to avoid easy detection I would stay with Jacob and his family in his home instead of the warehouse. There I ate and slept out of sight of those who would wonder why I was not drilling with the other young men my age. I had no desire to tell of my origin, and I was in the unusual situation of being nearly alone, at least among white men my age, in not training to kill anyone. I did not see this element of my nature as a philosophy or a religious statement. It seemed, and still seems, the normal and natural state of a healthy human: to not kill other people.

War is made glamorous and attractive by men who seek greater power, without the basic concern that actual death and suffering of their brothers is the result. Without enough concern, anyway. And grief of loss can actually be converted into revenge, and used to generate more soldiers, more armies. And armies require the tools of war, which means great profits for some.

And like a spent horse at the end of a hard-run race, after the profits have been made, too many men are dead and wounded. The profiteers must wait another twenty years or so for a new generation to be born, to grow, and to be fooled into deadly folly.

I've seen this cycle three times in my life so far.

The dynamic of family life at Jacob's was a study in philosophy.

Jacob was a successful tradesman and businessman. Some of his own family were owned by others, and yet he maintained a good home where his kin could find the solace available in a land of slaves and slaveowners.

His wife Chloe, whose freedom he had purchased years ago, supplied good meals and a comfortable dwelling when his sons resided there. Jacob had come to terms with his life and was making the best of it, each month putting aside some money for the eventual purchase of all his blood family.

One of the benefits of Jacob's business was that he earned some of his pay in goods such as the brace of chickens he had gotten as part of that day's trade.

Chloe was a former house servant and knew cooking. That night she baked the birds and served them with greens and tomatoes. I would often sit and eat with the family, bringing them what I could.

The older of the two boys, twenty-year-old Esau was not pleased with his lot, even though Jacob had finally managed to buy and grant his freedom. They would discuss things such as his future.

"Daddy, why do you go along with these men? They are fighting to keep slaves!"

"Son," said the patriarch, his face a mask of solemnity, "This is the world we have. We will do fine."

"That's not the point, Daddy. They want to keep slaves, and even if it isn't me, it's my friends. Your friends."

"I didn't make this world. But listen to me." His tone was steady and quiet. "I know this world. I found a way to live a good life. You will too."

"No, I won't," stated Esau. "I will not stay in a place that owns human people."

"Where will you go? Do you think there's a heaven on earth you can get to?"

"I want a chance to get ahead, to make a life away from injustice." The young man looked toward the door.

"Esau, are you talking about going to abolition land?"

"Daddy, the Yankee troops are freeing slaves all over, even in South Carolina."

"Yeah, those poor folks. I heard about those field hands, following the Yankee soldiers around camps. They don't have much of a life."

"They will! Some are joining the United States Army."

"So they can burn their owners' houses."

"Yes!"

Jacob was silent for a moment. "That's a sad state. Burning

the same houses they built." He chewed thoughtfully as we all awaited his next statement. "I don't know how this war will end, but I know I will not burn down the house I built. I am talking about my city."

"It's not your city, Daddy. It's the rich white man's city."

"It's my city, too."

"Well, it's not my city. I'm going to go North." Esau pulled away from the table and challenged his father with a steady gaze.

Chloe and the younger son Eli were silent.

Jacob met his challenge and replied, "Son, if you go, you won't find heaven up there. You won't know anyone, you won't own a home, you will be lost. And they may not treat you as good up there as you expect."

Esau stood and the shared gaze of father and son was like a tug of war.

"I will not be anyone's property. Not even yours."

Esau left the table and went out the door. I never saw him again.

20

VERY LIKE A WALTZ

For Charleston, there was now an obvious need for armed craft to guard its harbors. The individual state governments had to raise money to build their own defenses, supplemented by public fundraising events.

Auctions of paintings, fine imported jewelry, cloth, glassware, furniture and other objects d'art brought in money that would build the ships.

A grand party in Hibernian Hall was announced in early May of '62 to raise funds for an ironclad. It was hoped that a good ship with iron plating, cannons, and a ram in the prow would clear blockaders from the North and re-open South Carolina's trade.

Tyrone, always competing well with the German shops, supplied much of the dainties for that fundraising party. I drove the mule cart four times to the event, each time with a king's ransom of sweetmeats, dried fruits, flour and baking materials, cups, bowls, candles and bunting.

The afternoon of the grand party was an event for all the families in Charleston including the wealthy families still in the area, and the soiree glittered with women in fashions and men in gold braid or black silk.

The city band played stirring marches, instrumental state songs, and a peculiar soft number that spoke of thoughtful longing and love, expressed by brass and woodwinds. The piano was alternately played by Abe and by Mrs. Barringer, and kept a lively tune in the hearts of the audience. People gabbed and gossiped about who was going to be married to whom before the regiments went north, or what a shame about the young men who died or were made lame in the latest battle.

But mostly the party was up-beat and happy, with the previous year's glorious victory at Manassas behind them and expectations of the swift victorious conclusion to the war ahead.

A four-foot model and large detail drawings of the ungainly craft to be bought by the event were on display, and I'll tell you it was not a pretty ship. It had a "casement" on top of the hull, rather like an enormous inverted loaf pan, oblong with slanting sides and fearsome cannon tubes protruding from it, and with a long piercing ram at the bow. The slanting walls would deflect shot; the ram would puncture the hull of the Federal ships.

My friend Charles who had witnessed Sumter's bombardment with me would stand by the model and its drawings and describe some of the attributes and reasons for the design of various elements. He loved that stuff.

Because of steam propulsion there were no graceful masts on the model, no sweeping prow or high sides. The craft was for the business of sinking ships under steam power in calm seas. It was a blunt weapon made for the harbor, unfit for blue-water sailing.

At regular intervals calls were made to the crowd for donations for the ship to be built.

As entertainment, women created "tableaux" of a scenes from the plays of Shakespeare, including Romeo and Juliet's balcony scene, one from A Midsummer Night's Dream with fabulous costumes, and another from Antony and Cleopatra. Jenny's Aunt Peggy attended with her dog Pierre, and had helped set the scenes. I noticed that there was none from Macbeth, or Othello.

Cakes were raffled, cash bids were called for tunes for the band to play.

Isabella from the burned house had recovered enough to serve at the party, and though scars had forever marred her face, her health had returned. She was actively helping her wealthy mistress pour punch and collect donations.

I returned to the event near its conclusion to load my wagon with leftovers and recovered party supplies. I saw little Timmy of the Light Brigade poem, older and now in uniform, and struggling with emotion as he stood near the piano. Abe was playing a slow and sad tune, very simple, mournful even – a dirge.

I carried on my work and when done, I saw Abe writing on a paper and handing it to Timmy.

Both wore solemn, even tragic expressions.

Abe stood and put his hand on Timmy's shoulder, seventeen years old now, and taller. He shook with sobs, then turned away and walked out of the room. I never saw him again, though I later heard his wild story.

Abe noticed me and waved me over.

"Poor lad. He wanted me to give him something. He said, 'To remember you by.'"

I had seen Tim enough to know that he was at war within himself. He was from a prominent family, and was always compared to the standard of his big brother William Ledger, one of the three who had sworn oaths in blood beneath that live oak tree the night of my masquerade at the party.

William, with his great stature, manly beauty and adoring followers both female and male, was destined for greatness. Men like these have always fascinated me, as they do everyone, I suppose. They become leaders as a matter of course. They are often so full of love of themselves that they do not even notice it from others. It is the daily experience of their lives.

Timothy with his mild and gentle manners had long wrestled with his fate and even his desire for masculine company. He had admired Abe and his talents, as did we all for his artistic abilities, but even more so, perhaps more personally.

Abe's interest was in the fairer sex, so Timmy Ledger's hopes were not to be satisfied with him; nor probably anywhere in the manly society in which he was born. He joined the army. The fiery fields of Virginia were his destiny.

"So, I transcribed and gave him the tune I played for him." Abe played it for me, slow, simple, sad. You have probably heard it. In these latter days the army plays it on the trumpet at funerals, at the close of day. Sad, mournful even. I think Abe, the Jewish composer from Charleston, based it on a French tune, but I'm not sure.

Abe watched the doomed young soldier leave the room and turned to me. "I cannot believe there is no justice in the world." He turned and drifted into the next room where Mrs. Barringer was playing a marvelous interpretation of what I took to be a polka, but was playing it slowly with much embellishment, very like a waltz.

In days and months to come I would reflect on the music of those two musicians, one so bright with creation and the other so innovative in her interpretation. Two would-be lovers joined by their music, but forever separated by two score of years.

Should they have been?

Timmy left on the train the next morning, to camp, and was later involved in the Battle of the Seven Days.

Despite his apparent gentle nature, he put his heart into the service of his country. His ultimate commander after the general in charge was wounded, was the same Robert E. Lee who had the year before commanded in Charleston, and saved the hotel during the fire.

General Lee was an officer of less than heroic proportions, yet carried himself with grace of command that demanded obedience and service, even reverence. Many thousands of men held under his spell danced into fields of blood and fire at a word from him. Such is the willingness of men to be led.

Timothy Ledger marched into those fields.

The battle where he fought was ranging back and forth in a wooded area, and from what I was later told, little Timmy got the bit between his teeth. The anxiety that battled within his heart and brain was brought forth, and perhaps he was inspired, lifted and driven as he was that night he recited The Charge of the Light Brigade.

During one of the Federal charges with his comrades falling about him, he lifted a revolver in his left hand, raised a saber in his right and leapt to the top of the earthwork with a great roar.

Little Timmy became a berserking giant.

He charged into the ranks of the men from the North and

147

fired and slashed, a lion amid lesser lions. His own squad, seeing him so inflamed, rallied behind him and they swept the area. They followed the blazing warrior who Tim had become. Now with a saber in each hand, he sought to destroy all on this hateful earth. He drove all before him until he was fired on by a trio of New Yorker soldiers, and fell. He was destroyed, his breast opened by the Minié balls exposing the great broken heart that could find no satisfaction in this world.

Perhaps he will be satisfied in the next.

Later his body, pierced and shattered by many balls, was searched. The Federal soldiers found in his pocket the tune Abe had jotted down for him as a parting gift so many miles and hopes away. The New Yorkers originally from Ireland – as were many of young Timmy's comrades – thought it was some kind of code and took it to their commander. The general was named Butterfeld I think. He guessed it might be musical, and shared it with the company bugler, who interpreted it as a melody and played it. That gentle, sad tune worked its spell and was instantly reverenced.

Abe's composition was quickly adopted and replaced the military camp signal of taps on a drum head for "lights out." It has been played at military bases and funerals ever since.

Later, after the event as I was loading Tyrone's pans and wares to return to his warehouse, Isabella came up to me.

She looked at me with trepidation and spoke with hesitancy, no doubt self-aware of her brilliantly scarred forehead and cheek, yet by now resigned to her new appearance. Both eyes shone clear; her right had forever lost its eyebrow. She kept her left side to me as well as she could.

"Jonathan, they told me it was you who found me."

I listened but could not speak.

It is true I was tired, exhausted really, but I was fascinated by this mysterious woman, now marred forever, and when she spoke I felt her gentle inner light.

She did not look horrible. She was not a monster. But she could perhaps never be called beautiful.

"Uh, yes…." I expounded.

"I want to thank you."

Thank me?

I am a man without home, country, or family, hiding from those who want me to learn to kill, begging the charity of a former slave and an expatriate Irishman. I am the one who should thank my benefactors even to be permitted on a black firefighting team, not one who should receive thanks.

I gathered my wits about me. "It was my honor to be able to help you." To help anyone, really.

The world is a hard place. I had seen people die and would soon see the deaths of many more. Some I only saw suffer. A very few I recognized as happy.

This woman without blame was disfigured in a catastrophe not of her making. This woman had healed but was not made whole. This woman was now viewed by the world differently, diminished.

She nodded and turned to resume her work.

Did she still hope to find a mate, one to win her in her present state? Was she looking forward to a life of bitter spinsterhood, finally dying alone?

As I left the Hall late that night at the end of my day's labor, I sought out Isabella finishing up her day, and with a great emotional effort, I took her hand in mine.

This woman and I shared each other's comfort for the rest of that night. And later, many nights after.

21

WOUNDED AND RELIEVED

The first night with Isabella was one of little conversation. We huddled in my little space in a corner of the warehouse, screened by a wall of empty crates where I would sleep in private squalor. Neither of us spoke more than a word. We shared a chaste enough embrace, a touch. We were both hesitant to engage in a conversation which would break the spell.

She needed me, or at least someone she believed she could hold, could trust, if only for a while. I would learn more of her story in the days to come. I needed...well, the needs of a man, but also a friend.

We simply held each other that night, fully clothed beneath the blankets with little more than a simple brush of lips against each other's cheeks, sharing breath. We were wounded strangers, thankful that we could share our warmth and hope that the time of simply grasping each other in companionship would last the night, not interrupted by sleep.

The silent whisper of her soft breath on my face and the scent of her hair was something I had not experienced before. My heartbeat quickened and elements of my body responded to the nearness of a woman, her soft shape. My prior hesitancy of intimacy left me unprepared for my reaction, as I had been years and miles ago with Laura in the darkened empty room. This night I simply enjoyed and endured the exciting sensations which kept me awake, and exulted when this woman grasped my hand.

I had succumbed to sleep despite my rapid pulse and electric senses, and I found myself opening my eyes and awakening in the

150

violet light of morning, as Isabella slowly disentangled herself from my embrace and stood over me.

She straightened her dress, smiled a lovely smile below that crimson scar, and then she was gone.

Despite my best efforts, I was accosted by the Home Guard.

The police force was disbanded when martial law was established in 1862, and many on the force joined either the 1st or 2nd Infantry Regiment. The 2nd went to Virginia and glory, the 1st stayed in Charleston to defend the city and keep order as Home Guard.

While walking to the docks to see if Tyrone could use a hand, two enlisted men stopped me and demanded my papers.

I had none, and offered a note showing I had overseen transport of slaves. This did not have the desired effect on these men, and they ordered me to follow them to the lockup now administered by the 1st Regiment.

While walked up Mazyck Street to Magazine, my friend Kerry the policeman hailed us.

Kerry being older had joined the 1st Regiment, and stayed in Charleston as a Home Guardsman with the rank of Lieutenant.

"Men, I will take charge of this man."

That is all it took.

Kerry had weight of rank, and most of the youngsters in the regiment were in awe of him.

The boys looked at each other, then saluted the officer and turned back to their duties.

"Jon, me son, I want you to always carry a formal note from Tyrone that you are his overseer and his drayman, and that your duties are necessary for the government."

If I was vital for the government, would that be the same as helping an enemy of my country? Yet the friends I now had were here, not up north, save maybe my childhood chum Edward.

Kerry walked me to Tyrone's office but did not enter. Kerry was Irish after all, not Scots-Irish.

I thanked him and received the document from Tyrone, which mostly kept me from trouble, save for my troubled soul.

In mid-May we learned that Jacob's son Esau had joined a few people and stole a 150-foot transport steamer, *The Planter*, which had operated in the area for years. They fled the city, if not the war.

Now this was a celebrated theft by the ship's pilot, a slave named Robert Smalls who after the war became a member of the South Carolina state legislature. He had planned this theft for some time.

He waited until the captain had docked the ship and left it on business. Then he took aboard some of his crew's family and friends and left Charleston.

He sailed past Fort Sumter with the flags of the Confederacy and South Carolina flying, wearing the dress clothing and straw hat of his captain. At a distance he saluted as the captain had always done when doing regular business. Then he drew down the flags, replaced them with a white sheet and headed straight into the arms of a Union blockading ship just out of cannon range of the Confederate batteries.

The *Planter* was such a regular fixture in the area that this was a shock to the town. The white officers were blamed for leaving the ship in the hands of slaves. In fairness, there may have been no hint that those men weren't complacent in their status as property, if you can consider that fairness. It was an obvious fact that owners trusted slaves with their property and lives every day.

Jacob had not tried to stop his son when he left. He was not completely against his son's attitude. He was satisfied that he had lifted himself and his family from a lower state to a higher one, and would face the future as part of the community that he was helping shape into a better one.

But he had given his son freedom to work out his own life as he determined best.

News from the war continued to find its way to Charleston, as did ships running the blockade, and continuing streams of young men to be trained in the arts of war.

We heard of the theft of a locomotive by spies from Ohio, and of the train's successful pursuit through the mountains of North Georgia and Eastern Tennessee, and its capture. Its dispossessed conductor had chased it on foot, then demanded use of another engine and finally regained possession of the company's stolen train. The spies were tried in Knoxville and jailed. A few escaped before the end of the war.

The news of the Battle of Seven Pines at Fair Oaks Station read like a novel when it was reported.

Apparently, Union forces under McClellan came very close to capturing the Confederate capital of Richmond. They had extended their forces, and Confederate troops under Johnston took the chance of cutting them off from their supplies. Many Northern troops were captured.

The Federals were able to reinforce, as was the Southern Army. Thousands of men were killed, captured, or wounded. As often happened, neither side won but both claimed victory, and both armies retreated.

General Johnston was wounded and relieved by General Robert Lee, who led his men, including young Tim, to victories and death.

22

THE EMERALD LAND

One day I was sent on another delivery to a plantation north of the city. It was named Dodona after the sacred Greek grove I suppose, up near the hamlet of Hanahan about twelve miles north of Charleston. There I again found Isabella.

The managers of the estate had offered hospitality to a cousin dispossessed by the Federal occupation near Edisto. The owners and their close servants had retired to Columbia, leaving some of his family household living in various outbuildings.

Refugees from the Port Royal area had established a community there among the earlier residents and their slaves. Isabella had found her own living space on the estate with help from her employers whose house had been destroyed in fire. The wealthy had mostly removed to their mountain properties, and Isabella lived in the cook's quarters, in a small apartment of the big house next to the kitchen. She supervised cooking and housekeeping staff. The owners took their primary cook and servants with them to Columbia, farther from the dangers of war.

I arrived late in the afternoon with a load of woolen cloth and thread, and was to stay overnight in the big house while the wagon was loaded the next morning. I would be returning with uniform pants and shirts, which were made on this plantation by women from the city. I parked the wagon by the service door and as I turned, I saw Isabella in the doorway. She leaned against the frame and she saw me. She looked thoughtful at first, then quickly sent me a smile of welcome.

She was at work again in the kitchen overseeing preparations of dinner for other women who were doing the sewing.

The seamstresses were mostly of the planter class, women and girls doing their part to support their brothers, husbands, fathers who were serving in uniform. Indeed, I realized I may have been the only young and able white man on the estate. Among the women sewing was Jenny Haywood's mother, who entered the kitchen to speak with Isabella, and recognized me from the night of the fire.

"You're the man who quieted our horse that night in Charleston."

"Jonathan Vander, Ma'am. I was glad to be of help."

"Well, we are in your debt, young man."

She turned to Isabella and discussed serving tea, smiled at me and left.

Isabella was now hesitant with me after seeing me addressed so courteously by a planter's wife.

As she began the arrangements for the tea cart, Jenny Haywood came into the kitchen and smiled at me. Though she was dressed in working clothes, a house-dress with apron suitable for sewing, she stood with the air of privileged command, typical of her class.

"Jonathan."

She walked to me and observed that I also was in working clothes, though ruder than hers. I stood, of course.

"It is good to see you," she said.

"Glad to see you and your mother. How is Martin?" I asked, though I was a little hesitant to inquire how a soldier was in war time.

I knew something of his story. Martin's plantation adjoined Dodona. He was of a large planter family with lands to the south as well, owned by first and second cousins. He was the scion of his branch of the family. His father died when he was thirteen, and Martin had worked since then in keeping up the plantation, taking up more and more of the duties as he grew. His mother told him in no uncertain terms that he must stay in school. So Martin, with the help of his two older sisters and his mother, managed the farm while he was attending his studies.

When the time came for advancement he enrolled at The Citadel as had his friends and schoolmates, and so was included for military service when the troubles began. He immediately took up the duty of training the raw farmers from the area to be soldiers, and was commissioned as lieutenant when the cannonballs began to fly.

His mother was left to manage the plantation. They had a good overseer, not too harsh, and his older sister had married a landless man who agreed to help look after the place as well. The farm was as secure as such a place could be, with an enemy army nearby determined on burning it down.

Martin studied bookkeeping and accounting at The Citadel as well as classic literature and arms. He had hoped to continue building his plantation into a more profitable enterprise before the call of battle took all of his attention, all except for what he must dedicate to his woman – to Jenny.

Jenny gave a brief thoughtful look, I expect recalling me at the plantation party where I'd met Martin, rather than the night of the fire. "Oh, still fine, though I wish he would come home. I get a letter from him every week or so. His regiment was just in that fight at Williamsburg."

That was one of the early battles in northeast Virginia, "The Peninsular Campaign" as it became known in the North.

There was a scent of lavender around her, even while at work sewing.

"Well, give him my regards when you next see him." I was aware of the change of my status since the social event of a year earlier, when I at least pretended to be at the same social level as she was. I was ready to end this uncomfortable conversation.

"Are you still with Mr. Tyrone?" she asked.

"Yes, mostly."

"Very well. I'll tell Father. He will want to know after you helped him that night of the fire."

So she smiled and took her leave.

As the house servants unloaded my wagon, Isabella, having sent out the tea caddy, returned and told me to sit. She brought me tea, again flavored with strawberry, and fresh cream.

"Jenny has been good to work with. She hinted that her father might want to hire me."

She paused, then spoke slowly and carefully, "Jonathan, I'm sorry I had to leave you so soon that morning," she said, "I was hoping to talk to you before I left town to come here."

In my usual shy way I was unable to form a good conversation with this woman who had decided to become my friend.

156

The scar on her brow was visible beneath the hair worn low over her eyes. It appeared to cause her no pain. I smiled and tried to make conversation, but I was tongue-tied and could not form words that would make any sense. I had personal feelings for her and wanted to share them, but could not.

The world is full of pain and sadness. The world is full of wonder and love.

We sipped in silence. It was not unpleasant to share a moment of quiet with a young woman and a cup of tea, trading glances and smiles. Sometimes the best communication is not verbal.

When I'd finished my tea I told her I would see to my mules, and she suggested I return to the kitchen for supper.

I drove the wagon to the stable and left the mules with the grooms. The animals seemed glad to be at a place of rest, though mules have their own thoughts unknowable to men.

Isabella set me a plate at the kitchen table, and I ate alone while the sewing women had supper in the dining room. Isabella was in and out of the kitchen and was really too busy to pay me much attention. When finished I walked out to the porch then past the slave shacks, many with swept dirt yards in front. I passed under the live oak trees to the edge of the rice fields.

The fields were clear of workers that time of day. The rice rose before me like a plain of emerald. Channels of water had been cut and dug in the low ground, hard work that, and the field spread out in acres lush and moist. The rice grown here was a staple of the diet of these workers, the city, and the army.

Night was slowly coming on and the boundless sky was brilliant with sunlit clouds. A pair of blue herons, necks tucked back for long-distance flight, sailed high above the scene.

I considered the remarkable land, and enjoyed a moment of peace.

I had brought other goods to the plantation with the cloth, including some wines, and that night I feared I was being presumptuous as I carried a bottle in my satchel into the service doorway.

I entered the now empty kitchen where Isabella met me to show me my room, and when inside the doorway she took my hand.

"The last time we were with each other was so good. I had forgotten...it was so good to be with you, Jonathan."

A day's work will make a man smell like an animal, or worse. But the aroma on a woman, the hint of perspiration can be like a vapor of morning fog, but warm, like steam from a mug of tea. Deep, unseen, mysterious, and arousing to the senses of a man.

I felt a rush of blood in my veins at her touch and again the breathless and heady feeling rose in me.

She stepped closer to me and embraced me. "Jonathan." She kept her head bowed, so I could only see the top of her head.

"Isabella," I said. "Isabella."

"If you can stand the way I look..."

There was no denying her disfigurement, yet it meant nothing to me.

"Oh, Isabella."

She turned up her face. Her eyes were closed as she drew me to her and kissed me.

There are stormy times in one's life when there is no joy, no hope. There are times of war, where news of death of a friend might come any day, of invading armies, the constant dread of smallpox, fever, life's end. These are times when any simple pleasure is welcome.

Isabella became my joy, and later my hope.

23

INVALUABLE COMFORT

My living quarters in the warehouse had become uncomfortable in my furtive attempts to remain incognito and invisible to inquisitive recruiting officers. I became a vagabond about where I slept. I would take my rest with Jacob's family at times, and at others simply sleep where my feet would take me after a day's work, and perhaps a pint at Murphy's. All of my property lived in my rucksack, including the coins and key Ricardo had left me in his jacket.

Once I slept in the observation post in the steeple of St. Michael's Church where a friend was on station. I would occasionally rest in the slave and freeman tenements between King and Queen Streets.

But when I could, I would travel the roads to Goose Creek, to the plantation house where Isabella slept.

The plantation was still being maintained by the overseer and the hands. The rice and other food crops continued to flow into the city, some carried by me in Tyrone's wagon. It was a half-day's walk, and it was often an easy matter to duck out of town and stay if need be for a couple of days.

I had never before lived with a woman, and it was a revelation on several levels. The rhythm of sleep was different, the warm sensation of being in bed with her, the smell of her hair, the caress of a soft touch, a lilting voice before or during sleep, were all a new world. Sharing closeness with her, sharing quiet breath. I felt the gentle tones of life with my mother from long ago. Contentment.

And there was another element of sleeping with a woman. We

shared physical love.

I cannot doubt that some were critical of us. I am sure there was some talk among the sewing matrons about our habits, yet even the most proper and mannerly of them were human too. They had lived human lives and knew that especially in these times a few moments of comfort were invaluable, though I'm sure they thought a marriage certificate would have been in order.

Neither of us was then ready for that.

I usually arrived late at the plantation and discreetly departed before dawn. I saw no need to openly flaunt socially unacceptable behavior, even among forgiving souls.

Though we slept with each other whenever we were together, we could not share our bodies often, and not nearly enough to completely satisfy me. Some times, when Isabella let me know the time was right, I learned to enjoy how God had made the two genders different from each other and to become wholly aware of joy. I learned then that there is nothing in this life more pleasurable than plunging yourself fully into a warm, moist and welcoming woman.

And I was aware of the purpose of this God-given joy, not for sensation alone. We did not produce children, and I must admit that Isabella had complete control over this, often by satisfying me with something other than the complete act.

As she demonstrated and later explained to me, Isabella was worldly in ways I was not.

In the quiet of night as we lay together, we would share the stories of our lives. I would tell her of the dancers of Paris, and the new architectural forms coming out of the Beaux-Arts school, of the flying man, the prancing cavaliers on parade, of the ice desserts and crepes and other foods not available in Charleston.

She told me of her husband.

She was born and raised in Chicago, Illinois, and from a respectable family. They were not gentry but kept a decent hotel near the train depot. The eldest of three girls, Isabella was married at seventeen to a twenty-five-year-old man named Ben from St. Louis. He worked at the rail yard.

Ben's mother had died when he was a toddler and his father was out of his depth raising the child alone. The man gave the boy up to an orphanage, remarried and moved to Ohio. Ben grew up at the orphanage until he was fourteen and able to get a job. He travelled a

160

bit until he came to Chicago where he began working.

He was a good worker if a bit of a dreamer. He read Melville, Cooper and Poe. After marriage to Isabella in the family hotel they moved in with her parents, and a year later she became pregnant.

A baby boy was born, but the child was very sickly and died within two days: her first catastrophe.

Isabella was heartsick and Ben became despondent. He blamed Isabella and began drinking to excess, and cursed her for ruining his life. He missed work and spent days away from home.

This was an emergency in the family and her father and mother intervened, found him in a tavern, and brought him home.

He went back to work, but was not in good shape. He was distracted and began to talk to himself.

After a month her parents thought it best that she and Ben take some time away and visit a family friend in Charleston where her mother had been raised and perhaps make a new start.

Ben continued drinking. He haunted the low grog shops and began telling anyone who would listen that Isabella was a witch, a demon, a poisoner, a baby-killer. Isabella worried her husband was going mad.

She wrote her parents but got no response, and finally she read in the paper about the fire in Chicago. The news story said several blocks of buildings were destroyed and an unknown number of people died. She heard from a childhood friend that her parents were among the dead and missing. That was in 1857, three years before I ever met her.

And then Ben was gone.

He took all the money the couple had and disappeared from Charleston. Isabella thought he either took passage on a train, maybe to California, or more likely followed the example of one of his favorite authors and signed on a ship to the South Sea.

So Isabella, in her shame, began working.

The family of her mother's friend helped her find the sort of humble work she had grown up with at her father's hotel. She had done such household work ever since – accepting her lot as a failed mother and wife. She held people – men especially – at a distance. This changed the morning she was rescued from a burnt house, as her parents in Chicago were not.

She wanted no more children, and she wanted no more

husband.

I listened and hugged her, and wondered what she did want.
For now at least, it appeared she wanted me.

The results of the party to raise funds for construction of the
gunboat were successful, and then we learned that the state
government had previously allocated $300,000 to build such a ship.
The money raised by the ladies and other public organizations was
applied to a second boat and both were constructed.

The first was launched in August and named *Chicora*, after an
ancient mythical paradisiacal kingdom in what is now South
Carolina. Oh, that we all could live there, in the magic land of
Chicora!

The second, christened *Palmetto State*, launched in October.

For the rest of 1862 and into the following year the Federal
cordon of blockaders grew in strength and effectiveness while the two
ships of war stayed at their dock.

Oh, but there was another event I should mention first.

24

THE DARK WAVE

The war was to our north, our south, and to our west. Charleston itself had seen no great activity since the conquest and occupation of Sumter, but with Federal forces having taken Port Royal the previous November, the Northern Army was threatening, continually probing and sending out raiding parties to plantations, burning crops, freeing slaves.

As often as we could after our day's labor Isabella and I took company with each other. We shared the simple satisfaction of our bodies beneath a sheet and she took whatever precautions she decided best to prevent an unwanted child. I could not see myself as a father then. I hoped I would become a good one if the time were to come.

And then in June of '62 battle came to Charleston.

The city was not only a vital port for the Confederacy and valued for the amount of war materiel imported there, it was also where the war had started, and so held a special place in the hearts of those who desired to defeat the rebels. It was an emotional and a strategic target.

We had heard the cannon fire in the distance days before then, and one day the field artillery were too close. Newspapers told us of the fight, and we heard lots from the soldiers who fought it, too.

The islands west and south of Charleston are low, swampy masses of muck, marsh, impassible fields of pluff mud, crabs, channels of shallow water, oysters, gnats and bugs – just miserable land for an army. More than a century earlier all the land of commercial value had been put under cultivation. Areas a few feet above high tide, where sandy spits and low dunes allowed it, had largely been planted in cotton. The South Carolinians built forts on these.

Actually, these were fortified batteries rather than forts, meant to bombard and repel invading troops and keep Charleston safe from overland invasion. It was from this direction that the British had successfully taken the city just eighty years earlier during another war of independence.

Rapid movement of troops and equipment were impossible. Roads, if you can call them that, were often a single plank over foot-sucking mud. They allowed soldiers in single files to travel to earthworks dug by hundreds of slave workers and fatigue parties of soldiers. Redoubts and gun emplacements were erected designed to halt a force trying to advance over the jelly-like field of stinging mosquitos. Not that any force was expected to attempt such a move at that time.

The commander of the Union forces on James Island left to confer with other commanders at Hilton Head a few miles south of Port Royal about their upcoming coordinated assault on Charleston. He left a brigadier general named Benham in command with orders to hold his positions. It seems orders like this are sometimes heard by the short-term commanding officer as permission to achieve a great victory while his superior is away.

About six thousand troops were ordered by this temporary Napoleon to march over the mud slurry and take a lightly manned gun emplacement on the narrow neck of dry sand near the area ironically known for years as "Secessionville."

This did not work out well for them.

The battery to be attacked was built around a 200-foot lookout tower, and so it was called the Tower Battery, later renamed Fort Lamar. Before dawn in mid-June after a day or two of sporadic artillery dueling, a large body of Federal troops advanced from the south.

The Union force was so large that the commander apparently felt it would easily overwhelm the battery. His staff did not challenge that view.

A Michigan brigade groped through the dark toward an embankment where about three hundred Confederate artillerymen and a few sentries maintained a watch, such as they could after three days of extreme labor. They had worked non-stop for a week and more in getting their cannon properly emplaced and defensive works dug and structured.

The defenders were exhausted and enjoying their first few hours of sleep in days, even in the light drizzle. Many were nearer their spades than their arms.

There were a few pickets and guarding troops in cotton fields in the damp dawning of what proved to be a bloody day.

A company of Michigan infantry leapt out of the darkness and surprised some of the watchers. A few got off some shots before they ran toward the defensive positions at the battery, and some were captured.

The advance force of Federals then sat down and rested while more of their troops came up to join them. On this remote swampy island on the coast these sons of wheat fields and iron mines prepared to march and battle.

In their hundreds the Michiganders advanced through the cotton fields of James Island, up the narrowing neck of dry land toward the defended fort. As they came, the sound of the drum roll from the emplacement revealed the element of surprise was lost. The advance became a charge. The men ran stumbling over the field rows.

The defenders woke and scrambled to prepare their defense from the dark wave rushing toward them. As the attackers drew near the line, a series of blasts and flame exploded from the mound of sand and broke the charge. Cannons fired canister and staggered the Michigan drive.

Confederate soldiers in the distance heard the growing battle and rose quickly to aid the exhausted defenders. The soldiers ran in the dark misting rain. Many hurriedly dressed as they scurried forward on the slippery boards of the footpaths, buttoning and tying and buckling, juggling their weapons in the dim light.

A few rifles played over the top of the fort and succeeded in pinning attackers to the ground. The charging Federals were devastated by the cannon blasts. Their line split right and left away from the center of defense as more troops advanced from the rear.

There were enough of the first line left to re-form and they charged, joining the fresh troops in attack. Some on each flank actually scaled the parapet and entered the fort itself, and charged the active gunners with bayonets. Others crested the mound and fired into the artillery crews as they frantically reloaded and fired their pieces.

The defenders were in a desperate state, and the chances of the Union forces taking this fort and opening the way to Charleston grew probable.

The Federal hope was to take the road to Charleston, which had no other good defense against them. Charleston was a center of the railway to Florence, Wilmington, Savannah, and to Columbia and the heart of the South. With control of this strategic city the war could be over in months, or even weeks.

As the Michigan men made inroads into the fort, the desperate artillerymen stood by their guns, loading and firing; members of the Confederate fatigue parties continued to defend.

Yells of the Federals as they charged and of the Rebels as they struck back blended with small arms fire, moans of the wounded and the clank and thud of blades, and of muskets used as spears and clubs.

In the rear of the fort a corps of Louisiana infantry had suddenly arrived. They rapidly formed a firing line and began methodically sweeping the Federals from atop and inside the walls. More soldiers came to the aid of the remaining artillerymen, loading and running their positions.

The Michigan infantry scrambled back over the parapet outside the earthworks.

A Connecticut regiment moved up to support the attackers and were preparing to charge, but their formation was disrupted and halted by retreating men.

Rifles of the Southern relief forces competed from the mounds with more numerous rifles of Michigan and Connecticut from the field.

Members of defending artillery crews slumped, exhausted, wounded, dead and dying about their cannon, as new soldiers took up their rammers and learned their craft from survivors.

Each blast of canister from the fort swept small crowds of men from the attacking line. They often fell in groups of families and neighbors, who together had grown up in the bucolic fields of New England or the lake country of the Midwest.

A determined volley from a group of survivors from the first

Michigan wave destroyed a company on the Confederate right, and as the Union men moved to take the cleared position within the fort another reinforcing battalion from Charleston arrived at exactly the right moment to prevent the fall of the Rebel defense. They cheered as they advanced to secure the vacant section of the line led by their commander who was struck in the chest and fell, still waving his men on. They lined the top of the mound and began a systematic fire into the dawning field of blue.

The weight of troops still moving toward the fort was slowed as Southern reinforcements checked their advance. Now it was a matter of rifles against rifles, thousands of them in the hands of the attackers in a field, hundreds of defenders in a protected fort, with four cannon and a mortar.

Wave after wave rallied to take the battery, some shielding in cotton rows, some attempting to march through the impassible pluff mud on the right and left of the fort. The resolve of the attackers was matched by that of the defenders, all amid drifting rain, flying metal, the rush of rockets, shouted orders, cries of men, hurt and dying.

A Union lieutenant was knocked down by a cannon blast that entered his thigh. On the ground, he demanded his men to hand him a rifle, fired into the Confederate line, and demanded another loaded rifle. Shot after shot from their leader heartened the men to continue their fight.

Then a Massachusetts regiment marched onto the field.

Row by field row the riflemen advanced, finally drawing up to the stalled troops of Connecticut. The fire into their front began to tell on them as well.

Morning came very slowly that day.

At about five o'clock, a murky and rainy dawn, the New York Highlander regiment moved into the battle amid the cheers of the remaining Michiganders. They boldly approached the Confederate fort left and here they too were met with canister and grapeshot. New Yorkers fell amid the Michigan troops who first came so close to winning the fort. There was no victory for them on that field, and many drifted to the marsh edge where there was some scrub protection but little hope for advance.

Some of the Highlanders rallied and charged through the ditch and up the fort wall, climbing over the bodies of the fallen. They were joined by remnant survivors of the Michigan troops who had nearly achieved victory earlier.

As they neared the crest, Confederate fire again stopped them and drove them back to the base of the wall, into the ditch, and to the side of the field.

Then a regiment from Pennsylvania, the "Roundheads," moved up to support the New Yorkers. They marched quick-step to organize in the center of the field and charged.

The New Yorkers rallied and were again atop the parapet, firing down into the fort.

As the Roundheads rapidly approached the ditch below the wall, they passed though the now immobilized Massachusetts regiment, the wilting New Yorkers now rebuffed from the parapet, and the totally spent and stunned Michigan troops.

They charged in high spirits across the same field as the other troops watched in horror.

Confederate cannon again opened fire and swept waves of Roundheads to the ground, mixing their blood with that from the earlier attackers. They too found what shelter they could in the cotton rows.

Another fresh New York regiment was ordered to the field. As they neared the action, elements of several regiments fleeing the battle disrupted their formation. Some of them broke and retreated along with the bloodied soldiers from the first efforts. Some stood in their line and received in their bodies shot and grape from the fort.

The battle at that time was a stalemate. The attacking troops were exposed and at greater risk. The Federal commander at last ordered a general withdrawal and most troops began an orderly, slow and deliberate march back four hundred yards to the hedge, out of range of canister and accurate rifle fire. The organized march of retreat was so brave and disciplined – as if on parade – that many Southern defenders found themselves appreciating the self-control and discipline of the defeated troops and some cheered them.

The hope of taking the Tower Battery failed. There were still actions as additional regiments from Rhode Island and New Hampshire tried to make a difference on the right flank of the fort, but no advance was possible because of the formidable defensive position on the narrow neck amid an impassible swamp of muck and the continuing rapid reinforcement of defensive positions.

All the blood, cheers, fire, pain, the deaths of young men who might have returned to family and sweethearts were for naught. If successful, the attack would have been revered in American history as the battle that squelched the Rebellion. Instead, the "Forlorn Hope," as it was briefly known, is largely forgotten, a minor defeat for U.S. troops in a war where greater battles of tens of thousands were engaged. It was a minor victory for the Southern forces, though unfortunate, really, as it enabled the South to fight another three wasteful years.

The Federals lost about seven hundred men; the Confederates about two hundred. Nothing was decided that rainy morning, except for the men who died.

Men from Michigan, Pennsylvania, South Carolina, New York, New England, Louisiana. A few years earlier these men would have together cheered the birth of General Washington, the founding of the Republic, and toasted the bounties of American freedom.

25

COLORS OF THE SKY

Later after the battle Tyrone had me take some sweet pastries out to the men remaining in the field, sent from Jenny's Aunt Peggy. After a morning of blood and murder a flaky sweet tidbit would be a welcome refreshment, or perhaps some kind of macabre humor.

As I pushed the handcart up the road I passed the discards of the troops who had traversed the roadway that morning. Coats, blankets, a few rags, some bloodied.

Negroes and a few poor whites from the city had begun to collect the discards. The most serviceable items had been gathered. A few citizens were walking or riding the sandy roadway toward the day's "victory." Many were searching for missing sons and brothers. Some were taking food to those still on station, as was I. It occurred to me that the vaunted victory spoken of rather hysterically in the city was another army's inglorious defeat. Must all contests be thus?

I reflected again on my purpose. Was I aiding an enemy? The people of this new nation, as they saw themselves, were engaged in war with my country. Was I helping them?

Earlier I had resolved never to act in a way which would harm my countrymen. Bringing some comfort of food to these boys who so recently had endured such distress was not acting against my country. Was it? Should I not act to prevent all men on earth from harming my homeland?

Homeland. Home?

I drew near the field of suffering and raised my eyes to the horizon. A small flock of white herons lifted away from the marsh. Someone was playing a flute, a somber contemplative tune, a lilting melody.

The tower rose high above the earthen walls of the battery. A squad was drilling, though not with the spirit of victory felt by the citizens of the city. Orders were called and the grim, tired boys tramped, stopped, and slapped their muskets.

Workers were repairing the earthworks. Two weary officers discussed the renewed fortification. A team of slaves was shoveling sand and muck from a trench, their sing-song leader calling them to move in a rhythm that created shelter from firm ground and changed the very earth into a weapon.

A young fresh-faced lieutenant approached me and directed my cart to a refreshment area near others holding flagons of water, breads, tea, and other foods donated by the town. The lieutenant smiled amid the destruction. I suspect he had not been present to witness the action of that morning.

I put down the barrow and as I left, a detail of soldiers from Louisiana complained that the breads of Charleston were just not up to the quality of the New Orleans baguettes they longed for. Having lived in Paris I understood.

I turned toward the Field of Men and walked to the side of the battery. There I saw the trampled and ruined field where my countrymen had died spread before me.

Smoke still drifted from the field, though it was too hot for heating fires. The grounds had not yet begun to stink much, as it would when I returned the following day.

The landscape was not so destroyed as I imagined it would be from battle. Groups of people were settled onto the ground as if at a picnic, though they did not stir. There were clumps of men lifting figures onto carts, and there were figures in repose, not moving, yet without attendants.

I stepped onto the ground rather in a state of amaze. I heard some moans, complaints of the soldiers on grim detail, and the chirping of birds. A breeze from the sea drifted through.

I walked across the land and imagined that but a few hours before it would have been impossible to traverse. Minié balls had been flying, most missing their marks – not all. Bushels of canister shot were broadcast across this muddy wetland.

The harvest was laid in the sun, awaiting collection.

These men from New England were my neighbors. What of

their comrades from Michigan? They came from far to the west, and with little to share with Boston Yankees like me other than similar language. And the Union troops from Pennsylvania, were they my countrymen? Yes! All were brought to this place for the purpose of fighting the soldiers of South Carolina and their allies from Florida, Georgia and the other rebellious states. Also my countrymen.

A body in a group of blue-clad figures was in a graceful pose as if in a vignette on stage, except he was on the ground, never to hear the applause of an audience. His demeanor was that of a hero achieving victory, though his position belied that idea.

One of his mates covered by his torso gave a movement of his hand free now of weapon, and free forever of purpose. I walked to him.

His face, lightly bearded and with eyes of bright sky-blue, gasped and murmured. "The colors," he whispered. I had no water, no balm, no easing of his pain nor his fate, a passing soul in a land far from home.

"The colors in the sky..." he said, and I turned and looked up. There was cloudy overcast. The sky was grey. I turned back to the lad with the auburn locks. He was not angry. He was not anxious. He blinked. "The colors..." and he grinned as he passed this world.

I looked closely into the blue eyes, now without life, and saw the reflection of heaven. The clouds shown in them as they lost their luster. They were gray, yet had a tinge of amber.

I turned again to the heavens, and never since that day have I observed the sky in innocence.

I fell in with Dr. Jinkins's detail. I helped load some injured and brought them to the hospital.

The doctor was kind, no-nonsense, purposeful and direct. The perfect military surgeon. I worked with him again later in the war.

We carried men until the wee hours, then slept in a bed recently vacated, whether by living or dead I did not know.

The next morning I returned to the field.

The Federals were fighting to preserve the Union. Because they believed all the states, North and South, were one country. All on both sides were my countrymen.

As I pondered such philosophy I wandered through the stamped-down grasses which had so recently heard cries, groans, calls, and blast of absurd battle. Some spots remained pristine, without a footprint. More was truly tortured earth, where hasty trenches were thrown to hide from rifle fire.

Some spots were black-stained with the life leeched from men.

As I wandered further afield in rather a trance, I came to a shoe protruding from a thicket. It became apparent that the shoe held a foot, with a leg attached to a body whose soul had fled, one of the hundreds who had met Eternity the morning before.

He was a large man, perhaps from Michigan, and he lay as if in comfortable repose. I pulled away the brush under which he had crawled and was astonished by his face. During the night, apparently the creatures of the swamp had taken their liberties with this flesh, which had fallen into their domain. It was difficult to look upon.

The crabs, birds, the rodents cared not that their meal was my countryman, a being created in sacred form. They sensed food and began their methodical natural work.

The animals of the swampland live dangerous and competitive lives. The tides of the sea rise and fall like the chest of a sleeping giant, bringing in and washing out the waters like the breath of life. This is all a creation of God.

Perhaps this is the true image of our Creator – not a man, not me, but the entire world system in which man lives. And in which he dies. Even the crabs in the swamp are His creation, even the birds pecking the flesh of a man killed by his fellow man, my countrymen.

"They missed him."

The apparent contradiction of this statement startled me as much as the voice itself. If he was missed, it was not by the ball which killed him, nor by the scavenging creatures which had begun to devour him.

The voice continued, "It'd be pretty rough for his wife to see him like that."

The man who spoke wore gray uniform pants and a loose white shirt, a kepi on his head. He appeared to be in his mid-thirties, still youthful enough for camp life, and with a weathered veneer. Despite his military hat and rifle he appeared as more farmer than soldier, which I suppose most of the army was less than a year before.

"What do you mean, they missed him?"

"The recovery parties. They were all over the field yesterday picking up their dead. This is one they missed." He took a carved cane whistle from his pocket and blew three short blasts, which was apparently an expected signal. Two stretcher bearers from the battery began walking toward us.

"I picked up a couple of our dead yesterday, too. Bad business."

"Yeah," I replied. I didn't have much more to say about it.

"They came up on us in the dark, but didn't expect the pluff." That phrase could apply to many of surprises in our lives. We meet an impossible difficulty we couldn't foresee. "I didn't expect the pluff."

I was somewhat familiar with this frothy mud by now. It was more like thick soup than land. A man could stand in it and sink to his waist. If he tried to walk, well, he couldn't.

"They charged pretty strong at the fort, and there was a lot of them, but the land is so narrow here..." He squinted in the sunlight and I swept my eyes over the grassy waste. "Well, they couldn't spread out. When they tried, they got stuck in the pluff and couldn't move. Clustered together like that it was bad work for the cannon."

The stretchers came closer and the soldier waved them over.

"I'm Billy Smith, from just north of Columbia." He held his hand out to me and I grasped it firmly, more to take my awareness away from the wretched sight of the dead soldier than in friendship.

"I'm Jonathan Vander from..." I hesitated, "from Charleston." I hoped my accent was close enough not to be questioned.

The soldier continued, "I joined up three months ago. If the Yankees take Charleston, they could ride the railroad clear into Columbia. I never thought I'd see our own country invaded."

His own country.

"Yankee." It was always a source of pride when I was young. Yankee ingenuity. Yankee trader. Yankee determination. Billy Smith used it in derision, as if it were a horrible insult to a horrible people.

"How come you're not in uniform?"

I said, "I'm with the Cooper Fire Brigade. We're keeping pretty busy these days."

"Yeah." He eyed me coolly. "We marched through the burnt part of the city." What could I say?

The bearers arrived and with kerchiefs over their faces rolled the corpse onto their stretcher. It was stiff and bloated, and it rolled uneasily. Billy and I stepped back. The hot sun was wearing me out.

"Good to meet you. And good luck." I turned to walk back to the battery.

"Good to meet you. And Jonathan," I turned back to him. "Good luck to you. When the time comes, I know you will do your duty."

Duty?

Those words would weigh on me. I did eventually find escape, through the door Ricardo's key would unlock.

In July the papers told of the Battle of the Seven Days, somewhere up to the north. Southerners were dying, including Timmy. Northerners were dying, all Americans; all men of our blessed earth, leaving this world.

26

THE FLYING MAN

Days after the Battle of Secessionville I was preparing for a short trip Tyrone had planned for me. I stopped by Murphy's to settle up, and perhaps have a glass. There were the usual characters including a group of soldiers in high spirits preparing for deployment. They sang lively songs of Ireland between bantering and joking among themselves.

They had names like O'Brien, Owens, O'Reilly, O'Keiff, and were, because of their heritage, known around town as "Company O." One was a German American named Adolph Wetherhahn, but in community with his mates he went by "O'Wetherhahn." The adapted name actually sounded pretty Irish.

While in the tavern I met an interesting character who spent part of his life suspended in air.

The new fashion in the army was to send silk cloth bladders filled with gas into the sky with a spectator hanging below it in a wicker basket. There had been an effort in Savannah to produce such a vehicle for Southern forces and it was being shipped to Richmond, where troops would benefit from knowledge of enemy movements as seen from a temporary high position.

The call had gone out that the government needed silk, so silk was given, donated, and impounded. It came from dressmakers, storehouses, deliveries from blockade runners and their agents. Enough material was gathered to produce an envelope bubble that could hold enough coal gas or whatever they used for aerial buoyancy.

Well, the silk gathered was to a large degree meant for fashion and dresses of society women. The final product, folded and sealed in moth-proof oil cloth on its locomotive transport was a pink, lavender, marigold, and crimson patchwork suitable for a celestial two-step waltz among the clouds. It was known as the "Silk Dress Balloon," and must have been a gay sight over a deadly field.

It required men of perhaps limited judgement to pilot such an experiment. And so, it happened that the aeronaut named Alexander paused on his transfer from the Georgian coast to the Virginia battlefields in the harbor town of Charleston. He had stopped to imbibe, perhaps not a bad idea in his line of work. I sat near him at the bar and he told me of his employment.

He didn't look particularly different from anyone else.

When he told me that he flew and before mentioning the balloon, I did not dismiss the thought out of hand. I had seen a man actually fly before in my days in Paris. That unusual acrobat wore a peculiar suit as he performed in the Cirque Napoleon. It was finely knitted hose which extended from his feet all the way up his legs, his torso, up to his neck, and down his arms. It was like tight winter drawers but with no visible flap in the back, and it caused a wild reaction of scandal in some, to display the male figure as if nude. The fellow I was sharing a dram with that night was not dressed in this manner, and I believe that probably avoided some comments from Company O and other clientele of that particular establishment.

In Paris one night three years earlier I sat in an audience to view that other flying man. His name was Leotard, and as he brazenly stepped out into the great room a murmur rose from the bleachers and seats. He moved with head upright demonstrating a confidence I certainly would not have felt in that suit, especially considering what was about to happen. He knew he could amaze the crowd, make them gasp and cry. It is why such a man would risk death. And for the adoration of women, of course.

The Frenchman rose from the carpeted floor up a ladder, rung by rung by rung to his flying apparatus, composed of cords and poles, not a silk bladder.

This American flying man in Murphy's would rise from the ground enclosed in his apparatus below the balloon.

A curious group of boys and some men of Company O had gathered about him as he spoke.

"The earth looks different when viewed from the sky," he said. "And so does the sky. When you rise through the clouds, they are thick and sticky. You can grasp a handful and squeeze it into a ball of hail! Above the clouds you can see the stars and planets, and sometimes strange birds you can't see from the ground."

I think he probably saw quite a bit of moonshine up there, myself.

He continued, "When you look to the west, you can see all the way to California. You can see the Indians riding across the plain, chasing the buffalo. When the sun shines at the right angle you can even see the slopes of the Rocky Mountains and the flash of gold in them."

This tale was pure nonsense, and some of the men rolled their eyes, but the youngsters were enthralled.

"To the north you can see the Great Lakes, and the snows of Canada, with wolves and white bears roving the drifts. The Philadelphia shipyards and New York docks are busy as can be."

It was a pleasant enough entertainment, to take the mind off the oppressive thoughts of the armed Federal squadrons patrolling outside our harbor, the gathering ranks of troops to the south, the brothers and sons marching away north.

The men continued to buy him rounds of ale and he continued to speak.

A great silk balloon would carry him aloft, above trees and buildings, nearly to heaven itself. From this perch, tethered at the end of an anchor rope a man, that very man, could view the array of troops gathering for an assault on the city, or other units or works. And of course, they could view him.

That man had drifted in the sky up with the birds and clouds, close to the angels. I expect the air was cooler up there. Silent? Amid the honkings of geese, could he hear the engines of the boats: the drums of the mustering troops? Gunshots? Did Northern sharpshooters try to dislodge him?

One long hemp line was his only link to the world of mortals. If that tether were to part or unbend, whither would he sail? Up to the sun, like Icarus, to melt and fall into the sea? Surely his flight would not take him to Europe. Perhaps to the Bahamas, or Madeira. No, slowly, slowly he must fall, and he would finally meet Atlantic waves and a remote, lonely, watery death.

That flying Frenchman also depended on ropes, but two of them kept him from falling. Only one kept that man from rising to the

178

stars and moon, even heaven itself. Or a very high Hell.

But tonight he dwelt among us on earth.

I left him to amaze his audience and to prepare myself for my next day's journey.

27

ETERNAL FLAMES

The action at Secessionville so close to the city convinced Jenny Haywood's family and many others to leave the area – at least until the South's victory was more certain and things calmed down.

Like many in the Low Country, Jenny's family would travel to the mountains of North Carolina for their summers. Loyalty to the city in its plight had delayed their trip in '62. The events of Secessionville spurred whoever was left to leave right then. There was too much action in close proximity.

The typical route to the mountains was a train ride to Columbia where the family would spend the night as baggage was transferred, then board the train to Greenville, where another hotel stay was arranged. The following day a cart of baggage and a carriage for the family would depart up the road to North Carolina and on up the Buncombe Turnpike. Much of it was steep, and much of it was planked. If all went well and there was no lay-over for visiting or shopping, the entire journey to Flat Rock took four days.

As for me, it was becoming impossible to avoid being seen about the town, so I asked Tyrone if I could leave for a spell. He was very understanding as his own business was flagging somewhat, due to lack of a steady source of merchandise and the loss of his customers as they left the city. Those who did remain would pay top dollar for what they wanted if it could be had.

I offered to help move Jenny's family. Mrs. Haywood had hired Isabella, since her previous employers had lost one home and moved inland. She and the Haywood's black house servants would accompany the family. Tyrone arranged a delivery to a customer in the area where we were traveling.

This worked out well for me.

Salt was in great demand for preserving meat, especially where hogs were slaughtered.

Tyrone dispatched me with Rhythm Tommy and a pair of wagons up the coast to Georgetown where saltworks were processing seawater. We couldn't ride together, but I heard him singing and talking in rhyming sentences on the road behind me as he drove the second team of mules.

I think the mules liked him.

Saltworks along the South Carolina and North Carolina, Georgia, and Florida coasts had been in service for many years. Hundreds of families made their livings on the works boiling seawater in large pans until all that was left was the granular residue needed for food preservation.

The Northern navy had raided saltworks in Virginia and on the coast of North Carolina as part of its effort to cripple industry. The shortage was telling, and people would carefully brush and collect the salt from preserved meat when it was to be cooked. For inland families the mineral was precious.

The saltworkers kept fires going constantly, fed with cartloads of wood from the forests near the coast.

After arrival, Tommy and I had a fine dinner of fish the locals caught. Despite the war, life was not much different for the Negroes here, living their seaside lives of fishing, boiling water, and cutting wood. If not molested, life would go on for the workers. Their white owners were making good money from the sea's mineral, and it was producible as long as there were no raiding Federals. Their sons were away in the army or perhaps avoiding service among the islands and forests along the coast. Many in rural areas near the ocean were not as strong in the Southern cause as those on plantations or near a city.

I spent the night in a shack near the works and before retiring, I walked along the beach by the constant fires of the salt pans. Out to sea were lights of a blockading boat on its patrol. Its crew could see our fires as well.

The saltworks were there well before the war began, and would be there long after it ended.

We arrived in Charleston with many bushels of salt and delivered them to the train station where Tyrone had arranged transport. I took one cask to the house of Jacob for his family.

28

TRAVELERS' REST

Tommy from Jacob's crew was to accompany us to the mountains, so I was assured of his sort of musical entertainment.

I climbed into the baggage car for the ride with the slaves, but was directed to the last passenger car, which had some servants in it, both black and white. The Haywoods took three servants, Festus, Horace and Isabella, so I had companions for the ride, along with Tommy. They had other servants at their North Carolina home, which Mr. Haywood's father had named Green Mountain Meadows.

I dozed and read amid the stoppings and startings along the route: Summerville, Ridgeville, Branchville, Gadsden, all the turn-outs and stops along the way until finally reaching Columbia, the state capital.

The city was bustling. Troops trained at Columbia's military school called The Arsenal just as they did at Charleston's Citadel. Later I heard that this city accidentally burned to the ground at the end of the war, and the Arsenal never reopened. The Citadel closed when the city was evacuated but reopened a decade later and still exists today.

We spent the night at Nickerson's Southern Hotel, a well-run establishment with rooms for servants as well as the guests. I had a comfortable pallet in a room I shared with five other white men.

Breakfast was ham and grits, of which I was becoming fond, and biscuits. Wheat flour was still available.

We boarded the Greenville Railroad early the next morning, and finally arrived in its namesake town after 8 p.m. I traveled with the baggage on that leg of the route.

Jenny and Mr. and Mrs. Haywood traveled by hack to the Mansion House Hotel. I remained behind and oversaw lading of the baggage onto a cart, then Tommy and I drove to our hotel. I slept with the family baggage and the servants in the house near the stable.

Early next morning the family and servants rode stage coaches up toward the Buncombe Turnpike to stay at a stage-house built long before by a man named Cook, now owned by a man named Goodwin.

Many who made the trip from Greenville to Asheville, North Carolina, used that house. It could sleep thirty people in somewhat crowded quarters, another indeterminate number in the outbuildings where I was lucky enough to sleep, and even more in tents on the grounds where most of the servants slept.

The house was well-run, with stable hands dealing with the stage and draft horses and mules.

We were nearing the high country, and I could see the ledges and hills to our north. The air was notably cooler than in Charleston, and with the steep countryside the creeks flowed more rapidly than those about the Low Country.

It is tiring to travel even for the wealthy, which I wasn't.

I found a chair on a small porch in the building I was to sleep in, and I sat and watched the expert groom handle the horses as he removed the harnesses, watered, fed, and put them in their stalls. Other horses and mules stood in the pasture. We would have fresh animals for the journey the next day.

War had not come to the mountains yet and there was lots of traffic up and down the pike. Farmers drove their produce carts and herded animals to slaughter. Soldiers on leave camped along the roadside and travelled past us on their ways to visit home. Some of them stayed home past their furloughs and refused to go back to the war.

I turned my eyes farther away and saw the fields bright in the sunlight, corn, tobacco, a garden with beans and tomatoes, potatoes, watermelons, all the regular eatables. I thought to myself, "I could live here."

I pondered life of workers there. They saw hundreds of people pass through, while each of them remained in place. The baggage, goods, private riding horses and people flowed like a river through the site, the workers taking their payment and tending strangers. Yet I suppose some became friends with the travelers over the years and decades as they passed through year after year.

The next morning Tommy and I were up and moving in the cool pre-dawn gloaming, our fresh mules eagerly stepping on the upward incline, a long pull for them but this job they daily did, the purpose for their lives.

Tommy hummed and chanted with words and wordless voice to the rhythms of the mules as they walked.

As we rose in altitude the shrubby cedar trees made way for the deeper woods of oak, pine, chestnut and poplar. Step by step, up the long windy turnpike, and closer to heaven, I guess, where Mother must be. I am not certain that Father would be with her, if he was up there at all.

Several coaches passed us that day. There were regular pull-offs, wide spots that allowed passing. The coach bearing our masters passed us a little before noon, the family waving as they rolled uphill, followed by one bearing the servants. Isabella called a greeting as they passed. The horses moved at a faster pace than our borrowed mules and were less encumbered by baggage, supplies, wine, brandy, and Tyrone's salt.

There were several important Charleston families in Flat Rock where we were bound, including those on the estate of a Secretary of the Treasury for the Confederate government.

The estate we were to stay at was about six miles from town, west and a bit south. We rolled past several grand entrances. At one point the road was exposed on an outcropping which allowed us to pause a moment and view the expanse of the Carolinas from a high point. I pulled the mules to a stop, though they wanted to proceed. Mules have a different appreciation of nature than do men.

I guess men vary in that also.

There was a cool breeze in our faces when we stood out from the trees.

The world looks different from such a high point. You could make out some tilled and fenced fields among the vast forest, and little homes and barns. One wondered what lives those miniature people shared that day. There were likely miniature cows to milk, tiny trees to cut, and probably small dining tables where tiny families gazed tearfully at small empty chairs.

We came to the private roadway shrouded by evergreen trees of a spruce variety. The darkening skies gave little light under the trees as we opened and passed the gate into the evening dusk. I latched the gate after the cart passed and viewed the sweep of the property. I could see where sheep had clipped the lawn, and a milk cow returned my gaze as she chewed her evening cud.

The coaches with Jenny, her parents, servants and Isabella had arrived hours earlier and I guessed they were unpacking and getting themselves ready for dinner.

The large house was white and well-appointed with windows and shutters. It had a spacious wrap-around porch and stood on a rise at the end of the long straight drive. A welcome column of smoke issued from one of four chimneys. Dogs began to bark, and a sleek hound came out to challenge me, though we quickly made friends.

I stepped up on the board and moved toward the house. The mules seemed to know that was their destination and made their steady progress without encouragement. The army had taken most of the decent horses for its cavalry and those mules would be in demand by the military before long.

Two bright setters black and white spotted with deep booming voices bounded toward us as we came close to the house. They frolicked about us, apparently recognizing that whoever the mules had brought were friends of the estate.

The mules drew us to the doorway and halted. Two servants lived there permanently, and they had spent the previous days airing out closed-up rooms and chasing spiders from corners, opening closed chimneys and making beds. They unloaded our baggage and supplies and gladly welcomed us to "their" home where we would spend the next few weeks.

The house would have been nicely set in Charleston itself. It wasn't as large as the Haywood house in the Low Country, but was well furnished and appointed, with six bedrooms, a large dining room that could seat at least two dozen guests, proper chandeliers, and two formal staircases. The house also had a formal parlor and an informal parlor dedicated to a large desk, a sewing room and other sundry rooms. It was a modern home for the wealthy.

There was also a brick privy house, a two-seater.

Beyond the house to the north was a falling hillside with apple trees bearing a heavy young crop, the rows dropping from sight with the curve of the hill. A little further beyond was a steep forest reaching a blue crest. I walked to the side of the house where I could see the mountains rising in the distance and I breathed deeply, tasting the "champagne air," as Low Country folks termed it.

The summer sky grew a darker blue with high clouds of fast-fading brilliance, their orange matching the color of the lamp glow in the porch's shadows. I drew in a large breath – clean, so different from the heavy atmosphere of Charleston. We had left it only four days before, though it seemed an age.

Travel weary, I entered the house and its gay comforts.

29

LIMITATIONS

Our first two days at Green Mountain Meadows were recovery from the journey. We enjoyed the succor of the good food available from the orchard and farm. Milk flowed, bread baked, cabbage fried, and tomatoes were mashed into sauces. We ate food the like of which we had not enjoyed for months.

Jenny spent her time writing to Martin, and hoping her letter would find its way to him.

The two African servants who lived at Green Mountain Meadows had two children, a boy of seven and a girl a year younger. They and the three newly arrived black servants cared for us in a manner that showed none of the anxiety of some of my Negro friends in Charleston. I think the mountains were another world for them. Here in the mountains they may not have had close friends and relatives who were directly endangered, such as being pressed in service to dig earthworks near combat, or carry supplies to battle areas, or to watch their children sold away. They were far out in the country, far from all but the echoes of hardships and barbarism created by nearby warfare – as were we, a welcome respite.

Or perhaps they were biding their time in that safe cove, awaiting their freedom and a new future, as were we.

Isabella's room on the first floor was being used for storage and wasn't ready for her as yet. I was to sleep in a cove in the basement, but until her room was cleared and set, she had my space so Tommy and I slept in the stable. Mrs. Haywood would never consider that I would stay in the slave quarters, and though she must have known of our relationship, she would never consider the thought that Isabella and I should sleep together unwed under her roof.

We had arrived in the first days of August with our separate cares among us, to this land of plenty. Indian corn was being harvested and dried as was the first of the tobacco. Some earlier varieties of apples had already been harvested and cooked into sauce and butter. The pears were growing larger, still hard as rocks, but promised sweetness in November. The walnuts and chestnuts had long dropped their blooms, and the fruit was swelling and ripening in the high branches.

The farm estate seemed so removed from the war and its concerns.

Our third evening there, after the sun set and the evening began to shed its daylight, I sat on a chair overlooking the meadow and watched the children running after fireflies, or lightning bugs as they call them here. They fly slowly and light up to entice each other for breeding, so they're not at all difficult to catch. They gave a magical sparkle to the fields, in synchronized flashing as horses munched and wandered on the green among them.

I drew on my pipe and watched the two carefree black children, kings of their world when their parents weren't in sight, playing with the dogs, chasing each other and the fireflies. I had run and caught our New England variety of firefly as a child, and I felt the world was mine to take as my birthright. Did those young Negroes think the same?

Yet I imagined it was only a matter of time before someone would say a word, or ignore their presence, or slightly or even directly insult them because of their blackness. This was before emancipation, so they could even be sold away from their families. They were doomed in this world. Indeed, though born here, they would not even be given the basic rights of other Americans who came to this country from a different one. At some point there would be a pall upon their view of life's future.

Yet each of us has our limits, our limitations.

I would never be a professional boxer, or an emperor, or owner of large mines or factories.

Some people were too short or too tall, some had bad eyesight or were deaf, or easy to catch ill. I was none of these, and had good health generally. I was well coordinated, and if not quick of speech, at least not dumb.

Each within our limits, to make the world as we can.

But to begin as less simply because of the circumstance of birth for an entire race. This cannot be argued as fair.

30

XANADU

My third day in the mountains I harnessed the mules to the cart still holding the casks of salt and set off to deliver it to what the servants said was an amazing house nearby. Its owners had decided to spend the rest of the war in Europe. They had fled to Nassau, and from there to England. They had taken with them four trunks of fine clothing and a bank draft of unknown value, though I expect it was worth quite a lot. They left everything else behind.

Their material possessions near Flat Rock included their mountain home – which was mostly shuttered – with an elderly Negro caretaker to watch and manage the place, and who had the owner's permission to access the accounts. Eight field hands worked the farm.

The rest of their property including their Savannah plantation estate they left in charge of another overseer, who was probably stealing them blind and planning his own escape.

Isabella told me the servants spoke of my destination in awe, that it was a wonder set in the wilderness.

The drive to the structure was about four miles up a formerly good road, then in need of some repairs. The repairmen were all away.

The early morning mountain air was still thick with cool mist, the shade dense with scents of trees, grass, ferns, herbs springing from the forest floor. Birds called to each other in avian lust, a gentle breeze moved the treetop canopy above, and there was no war. There were no worries, no pain, no memory of the rotting death of

191

Secessionville. All was clean, an unexpected Eden where souls heal. It was a fairyland without sorrow and with its own natural music – a lifting joy, so very unfounded in the shocking truth I had witnessed only a scant three weeks earlier.

The turn-off to the property led in a zig-zag manner through the woods to the gate, which was quite invisible from the main trail.

As my mules ambled up to the gate, I could see down the lane a worker with a pruning saw trimming trees and bushes along the drive. He saw me, waved, and walked toward me.

"Hello, good morning, Suh," he cried, and showed an impressive broad smile. I suppose he was about seventy years of age, with slender strength and hair mostly white against his very dark skin. His clothes were the closest thing to livery I have seen on a gardener, of heavy canvas cloth, neat and well-kept.

"Good morning," he repeated.

"Good morning, Uncle," I said, unsure how to greet such a welcoming stranger. "I am staying with the Haywoods at Green Mountain Meadows."

"Oh, yes, Mister Haywood's house. Please come this way." He shouldered his blade. "Will you share some tea with me?"

I assented, and he climbed up on the cart with me and we eased around the driveway curving around the gentle crest of a hill to the front of the house. Deep green hemlock trees and arborvitae and other shrubs created a park-like setting for the lonely home.

I was not expecting such a gracious welcoming, especially from a working groundsman, and was somewhat at a loss. "Is the master at home?" I was unsure how best to phrase this question, for even though I expected that he was a slave, he may not have a master – perhaps the state of many men both white and black.

"No, Gentleman has gone to sea. He sent me a letter telling me to continue to keep the place up and welcome all Southerners." I wondered, and not for the last time, if that might include me. I had grown to wish it would. I was not going to disabuse the man of my origins.

I learned his name was Xenophon, if you can believe that.

This was a smaller house than the one at Green Mountain Meadows. It was built on one level, and at first appearance was rustic.

As we unloaded the sea salt into the kitchen, the thin and

apparently elderly man demonstrated great strength.

When we finished, he led me through a tended hedge, which opened onto the back porch of the house. There were shady trees about, but the roof stood in the sunlight. He walked me around the wooden porch to the front of the house which faced away from the drive. The porch was furnished with items made of twigs the diameter of my thumb, craftily woven, wired and stapled and tied into the shape of tables and chairs, cushioned with horsehair-stuffed cushions. But what defined the shady porch most was the view.

An orchard of fruit trees descended from the porch on the northwestern slope, planted so to delay spring bloom until danger of frost was past, as northern slopes warmed last. Some trees were burgeoning with pears and apples. Cherries, peaches and plums had already been harvested and preserved.

I have seen many striking sights in my life, but I will never forget that mountain view. Because of the slope, mountains above the tree tops climbed to the northeast and row upon row of horizon lifted clear into the blue and cloudless sky that golden morning.

Birds soared in the distances, sailing black against the gentle sky and soft hills. I reflected on the grace of such a sight, and I must have lost some time in the practice.

Sunlight glanced from the leaves, flashing as the breeze fluttered and swept the branches. The wind whispered a cloying welcome as it caressed my cheek.

"Who lives here now?" I asked in a hushed voice, not wanting to disturb the scene.

"Nobody in the house, until Gentleman comes back. Just me and Cassie."

Cassie appeared behind him, a strong-looking woman of indeterminate age, a dark clear complexion showing no emotion or expression, as if judging me to be friend or not. She was holding a tray of tea, cornbread, jam, and cheese. As she set the tray down, she hesitated, then briefly smiled and did not speak.

"Set down and have some tea," spoke my host. "I don't get many visitors up here." The woman silently withdrew to the deeper shade of the house. It wasn't real tea but it wasn't the yaupon variety like we had on the coast. It was a spicy and fragrant drink made from the roots or leaves of the sassafras tree that grows in the mountains, and the sweetener was honey.

Xenophon explained to me that he and Cassie lived in the house which the owner named Xanadu after the subject of the poem by Coleridge. He oversaw the field hands, the house and grounds, and kept the accounts. He and Cassie kept the kitchen garden, a milking cow, chickens, and two plow horses. A row of neatly kept slave quarters over a low hill housed workers who kept the place flush with produce. I later learned that there was another more remote cove that held more workers, more fields, more livestock.

Other than the workers, they had rarely seen people in the past two years, and were glad of the visit. We ate our bread and sipped our tea, and watched the sun play on the mountains.

"How many are up at Mr. Haywood's house this week?" He asked this very conversationally. Most Africans in my experience in the South would not have presumed to share tea and bread at the same table as a white visitor, but Xenophon's state of social hunger made him perhaps less circumscribed in his manners. Or maybe he didn't care.

I explained that there were three residents and seven servants. A third of the house was not covered well because a fallen tree had crushed part of the roof, and some were bunking in the barn pending repairs that might not be completed before the war was won.

"Well," said my host, "Why don't you ask Mrs. Haywood if I can host you here?" He leaned back in his chair with a smug expression of playing the host, yet I think he was anxious for outside companionship. "We would be happy for the company."

I have never lived where I had actual servants and never in so large a maintained house. My mind drifted to imagining myself as lord of such a home.

"Mr. Xenophon, that is a very kind offer."

"Better call me Zeke. That seems to work better. So, let me give you a note to carry to Mrs. Haywood and we'll see if we can get you moved in for a week or so."

The old man called, "Cassie! Bring me a pen and a note card."

I wondered that this man, himself a slave, would order another slave as if he were her owner. Or perhaps this is the way of men, to assume that women are their inferiors, and perhaps even their property if they are wed. For those who wish their own freedom, can they deny it for others, due not to race but to gender? But it seems the way of the world and will not change. Of course, that is what they said of black slavery as well, and that certainly appeared to be changing.

He lit his pipe and offered me one, which I accepted. Hygiene among strangers seemed more relaxed in the remote setting. I sat and mused in the hearty smoke. After a bit more conversation I drove the cart back to Green Mountain Meadows as evening fell.

I carried his card to Mrs. Haywood, who was pleased to have me vacate, as she knew that the barn was crowded, and that I would be more comfortable there. "Zeke says he has a room for Isabella as well." Mrs. Haywood and Jenny understood what I was suggesting. They were aware of our relationship, and despite the propriety demanded under their own roof, they realized that we would be most happy sharing a room at the other house, out of sight and mind. Mrs. Haywood for all her Southern fervor and mannerly strictures was a kind soul.

Isabella packed a bundle and brought it to the cart.

She wore a simple calico shift with a distinctive blue and black pattern of flowers on a white background. I would always remember her in that dress, bright white with a blue and black print in that bright mountain sunshine.

She sparkled like a dew-fresh plum.

31

PRISTINE FORM

The week Isabella and I spent together at Xanadu was the most enjoyable, least worrisome time of those years for me, perhaps of my whole adult life, and I think for her, too.

On our arrival Isabella and I followed our host, exploring the house, and it was a wonder.

The main parlor was furnished in dark mahogany, carved and upholstered velvet settees, chairs and wide sideboards displaying china and silver coffee and tea pots, cups and flagons, all the accoutrements of a wealthy household.

The main room had a large window with eighty glass lights looking across the porch to the mountain view, line upon line of aqua horizon. We appeared to be floating above the verdant trees. There were rich Persian carpets and broidered curtains, sconce oil lights and a magnificent chandelier in the dining room. These were not used by Cassie and Zeke by themselves, but in honor of our visit the host and Cassie lighted the candles and lamps. The room shone with the brilliance of a king's hall.

"The lamps burn whale oil," said Zeke. "We still have some in tins in the basement." This was now unheard of in the South, with its surplus of turpentine oil and very limited access to the valuable fuel harvested by Yankee whalers. There was much in the house retained from the days of a wealthy, worldly owner who shared but a bit of his lavish possessions with that mountain home, his fourth house.

The wine cellar was still fairly well stocked. Not just with the

Charleston favorite Madeira, but wines from Burgundy, Rheims, and Bordeaux. Zeke and Cassie did not partake, though they did open a bottle for us on the occasions of dinner in the big room.

It was most gracious of our host to play the attendant, a role he had practiced his whole life. Now he was giving us a great gift, perhaps the greatest in his power to bestow, and I was nearly in tears at his generosity.

We had changed and brushed, and though not in formal dining clothes, we each felt as good as we had in months or years.

Isabella sat on my right, showing me her unscarred profile.

We were served a joint of roast pork with turnips, carrots, onions, all in a sauce where some of that wine might have been used. Side dishes included mashed potatoes and a green bean of local culture, a "greasy bean," it was called, flavored with bacon.

The fare was not fancy in the French style, yet when served on silver and porcelain trays and chargers by an attentive servant in clean livery, in the magic glow of oil flame, and against the embroidered tablecloth covering the intricately carved table, the sunset view of mountains through the window, my woman beside me, I was king.

But the most satisfying of times I had that glorious week was at night, with Isabella.

After dinner and a pipe and tot in company with Zeke and Cassie, Isabella and I began our evenings together in the most modern individual bathing facilities I had 'till then experienced. Apparently the owner, "Gentleman" to Zeke, had designed that spacious and well-lit room for his own satisfaction.

The privy house was outside like everyone's in those days, though also lit with sperm oil, but the availability of fresh water for cooking and cleaning inside the attached kitchen was a true luxury in that mountain palace. Water was channeled from a mountain brook near a spring, to the kitchen by a system of hollowed tree limbs, and out again through a similar system. A constant flow of water was available in the kitchen as it fell into a basin and then was channeled through the floor to a tile drain. In the winter it could be shut off by deflecting the log channel at its source and sealing the port in the wall.

From the kitchen basin a valve in a pipe carried water to the bathing room where it was available to another very large basin with the turn of a cock. It was really quite innovative. I think even Charles might have approved of the engineering.

From the large basin, a drain in the bottom and two outlets with channeling pipes led out, one to the heating pot and the other to the "washtub," if that is what this wonder can be called, but it was not for clothing. That water-fast tub, formed of hardwood of some kind and covered with hammered copper, was more than three feet deep and four feet broad, more than six feet long.

The thought of immersing myself in the bathing basin brought back early memories of my mother sitting me in her clothes washtub for my weekly scrubbing, which I generally found pleasant. She would pour water from the teapot into the wooden vessel to create a warm medium for me, but it was a small container compared to that basin which proved a new, wonderful experience.

The bathing room was large, about ten feet by twelve, with counters and mirrors and lamps. Brushes were laid out, and soaps, and a razor, scissors, and a vase of cut flowers – a touch of beauty from Cassie I suppose.

Zeke, ever the most thoughtful host, had started the heating of water in the forty-gallon heating tank adjoining the tub before our meal. The water had been caught in a copper tank above the tub and an oil flame was burning beneath it.

Today, bathtubs and indoor plumbing in most houses are very common I suppose. Even indoor privies! But this bathing tub was a nearly unheard-of luxury in those days.

That night was a night of wonder.

After we had shared a delicious meal with the good company of Zeke and Cassie, we were to share a time together the like of which neither of us had experienced.

I can't really tell you everything I experienced that evening, other than it changed me.

Isabella and I in that room rediscovered each other. Though her face was scarred forever, and I was not lately groomed, in the reflected light of the whale-oil lamps, the steamy water filling the copper tub in the warm room as we undressed, she and I both came to realize her great beauty. The form of her body was not diminished by the December inferno. And as I knew her then, it would not have mattered.

She shyly yet also proudly raised her eyes to mine slowly, and began to smile.

Tonight, she knew she was Venus.

A scent of lavender rose from the warm basin and gave an unworldly element to the room, of comfort and joy.

I slipped my feet, then my whole body into the heated water, and dipped my head beneath the surface. I stayed suspended for a moment in the liquid warmth, and I let it permeate me entirely. In that moment I felt complete and well, as if I were newly upon the earth, unblemished by memories of loss, pain or anguish, or any bad thoughts. I brought my head up and looked at the silhouette of Isabella viewing herself in the mirror awash in steamy and golden glow.

"Come to the water. There's room for both."

That was a time of soap, of warm fog, of rippling friendship and a sense of glory.

We used the brushes; I shaved my face. Then in our newly shorn and pristine forms we shared together the bed of the owner.

The heated water of bathing made our skins more sensitive to each other's touch, and the lamps' glow revealed us as two new creatures of purest understanding of the joy of life.

We each hugged the other, covered ourselves with quilts, comforters and blankets in the cool mountain evening, the first of a week of them that August. We fashioned ourselves king and queen beneath the rich brocade, and told stories of our childhoods.

Each night after our meal and goodnights to our hosts I carried a lamp to our room, sealed the heavy door, and we held each other's hands.

To hear love poetry when not living the reality of it is not to believe it. There is an ethereal spirit that covers and envelops you and makes each breath feel like a rush of a flowing river. There was nothing in the world of war, of hate or death. There was no pain, no scar, no fear, no loss. But to say our joy was the absence of bad would not be the whole tale.

Each extended look into the other's eyes, even the moment of dropping our clothes to the floor and joining together was just the prelude to completely having the other, holding and becoming one with the other, so that there was no other. Only the one we had become.

As I said, to hear this without living the reality of it is not to believe. But perhaps you have lived it and will remember.

If not, you may think me mad.

32

CASSANDRA AND ULYSSES

Isabella and I would take walks in the very early morning through the dewy woods. We passed through fields of shady ferns dripping with dew, and over chuckling streams, drinking in the clean air rich with scents of hemlock trees and green growth. We walked past and through wonders of massive boulders the earth had thrust out, bedecked with wild geranium, trillium and other wildflowers. We would hold each other with our eyes closed and listen to the awakening sounds of life about us.

This world I loved. The quiet sounds so far from those of war or preparation for it, away from the city, in a land of plenty with a loving woman.

This is how I thought of the mountains. I still do.

Cassie and Zeke shared breakfast with us in the kitchen where there was an abundance of fresh eggs and milk each day, and the Southern delicacy of ham and grits which I now loved, dotted with butter and sprinkled with salt, or even cupping a pool of gravy.

I learned to milk the cow, an experience I never mastered when visiting my mother's father in New Hampshire so long ago. There is an art and craft to the practice, and an appreciation of the sensibilities of the female bovine. I tried to be gentle and not disturb her natural pleasant disposition. After the first time she seemed if not completely satisfied, at least complacent at my touch.

Isabella helped Cassie make cheese, and they butchered some stew chickens for dinner. Those plus the tomatoes and greens from the garden and a corn pie with apples were a treat.

The farm's cellar was soon to be stocked with onions, turnips, potatoes and winter squash and pumpkins. Summer squash, beans, tomatoes and greens filled our table each night.

One day while the women were gathering fruit and flowers Zeke showed me the library, a room whose dominant feature was four shelved walls laden with books.

The volumes ranged from animal husbandry and plant cultivation to philosophy, history, literature.

"This is one of my favorites," Zeke explained. He held forth a translation of The Odyssey. He looked at me wryly. "That man Odysseus was a smart one."

I mused on my own journey, its turns and trials, and me without the wit of Ulysses.

He turned and ran his hand along the thirty or so books on ancient Greek history and literature. One was by an ancient Greek also named Xenophon. He turned back to me.

"Cassie is not her real name," Zeke said.

"She ran away up here two years ago. She told her owner that the South would lose if they went to war, and he didn't believe her. He was angry and was going to sell her, so she ran away. I found her when I took Gentleman to the train station down the mountain, and I saw her hiding in an alley. I put her in the carriage and brought her up here." He smiled at me. "She's happy with me, I think. I call her Cassie after Cassandra, from Troy," the woman who warned the Trojans of disaster and was not believed.

It was not common in those days for slaves to read. I considered it a shame, and understood if they could read, they might get ideas about freedom, the way other Americans did. This slave was quite literate. And he seemed happy in his world of mountain beauty, a woman's company, and freedom.

At least I guessed he would be until the South won the war and his master returned. But then given his personality and intellect, he may well have been happy in any circumstance.

* * *

As Great-great Uncle Jon finished speaking, Mrs. McKay came to us and announced lunch. I was invited to stay and dine with the pensioners. Biscuits and chicken stew were on the menu.

We went to the dining area where a sign said, "We Share These Sacraments Together," and Uncle Jonathan introduced me to several of his friends. One elderly man named Adams had served as a drummer boy with a Tennessee regiment. I thought it indiscreet to ask if he was in the Confederate or Federal Army, as thousands of Tennesseans served in both. Though a decade or so younger, he appeared older than my great uncle.

There is no accounting for parentage, and each of us is blessed or doomed. My mother had died at forty-three from cancer of the chest.

Still, at ninety years old, Mr. Adams had lived a long life.

When we had finished our tapioca, Uncle Jon and I returned to the parlor and to his tale.

*　　*　　*

33

BLACK HUMOR

I returned to Charleston after that wondrous week with Isabella at Xanadu and resumed my labors for Tyrone. Jenny and her parents came back a couple of weeks later with Isabella and their other servants.

Despite darkening visions of future events for Charleston, there were still parties, feasts and balls whenever there was the slightest excuse for one. The few soldiers returning home were welcomed regularly, albeit with diminishing variety of refreshment. I was sent with a cartload of whatever delicacies Tyrone had available to one such event at the home of local gentric royalty. I helped unload the cart and stood by the kitchen door as the evening's entertainments began.

The usual matrons and their staff were present, dressed in their finest livery. The older non-combatant men attended, as did soldiers recovering from war. Many were happy to retire from conflict due to their wounds; some were eager to regain the field despite infirmity.

Mrs. Barringer was the pianist at this event. I had heard her before at the ironclad fundraising party and other events but she was always playing second to Abe. Here she was the main entertainment. She was a gem.

She opened with light music, much from Foster of course, and "I've Left the Snow-Clad Hills," (which I recalled as popular before my Paris excursion), and several pieces from Hayden. It was a pleasant background to the lively conversation among the matrons and the rather few young women. The only one I recognized was the black-haired and fair-skinned Carla.

To my joy, Isabella was attending as serving hostess and stood behind the punchbowl in her own style of elegance. Damn the scar.

The men, mostly in uniform, many battle-wounded, entered the home, some with a servant assist, some in bandaged arm or visage. Their uniforms told of their regiments, and I realized that before me was arrayed a history in tableau of conflict and battle.

Some had stood with Stonewall Jackson at Manassas. Some had ridden with Stuart in the "Critter Corps," as the cavalry was sometimes known, and some were now serving in the Home Guard.

On they came, halt of walk, wrapped and bound in their best uniforms, brushed and splendid – some mended. And as they entered, the five or so young "ladies" in their anteroom made callow and hapless jests.

Whispered one of a soldier with an eyepatch, "Oh, look, he has his eye out for you!"

Her friend said, "They look like they are all under the command of General Disrepair!"

Carla, on seeing a soldier who had an arm amputated: "He will ask for your hand."

A third, not to be outdone when a lame officer arrived, "Here is Major Disaster! He will put his best foot forward!"

Though callous that evening, these girls were not mean of spirit. They in their way were witness to the diminishment of the strong manhood of their homeland, the company of whom they had hoped to enjoy, savor and reward for a lifetime. Theirs was a youthful lament of their state; their men fighting and falling, or returning unwhole.

Said the last, "Oh, I think I must engage the man who has completely lost his head over me!" Their giggles belied their own sorrow.

I looked to Isabella, and we locked eyes. We did not smile, but we each warmed to the knowledge that this painful and pitiful scene was spared us, was not of us. Whatever the world may bring, it hadn't brought us to this, not yet.

Mrs. Barringer played "In the Hazel Dell." Without lyrics sung it was a kind and warm tune, a gentle set for conversation.

In the background some women spoke of frightful rumors they had heard, of fears of being murdered by their servants while they slept and their men were away, of helpless white babies being strangled while at the breast of their black wet-nurses, of elderly women stabbed in their beds, of slaves setting fire to barn and house and owner families as they fled to follow the Federal Army.

The host called for a reading, and one of the younger men rose to recite the poem, "The Bingen on the Rhine," a gruesome choice.

A soldier of the legion lay dying in Algiers,
There was lack of woman's nursing, there was dearth of woman's tears;
But a comrade stood beside him, while his life-blood ebbed away,
And bent, with pitying glances, to hear what he might say.

That clean youth, still whole, stood bareheaded in the turpentine light and spoke the lay. At his tones, men grew more somber; women hushed. One woman sniffed as the lines brought us to that bloody African field.

Tell my brothers and companions, when they meet and crowd around,
To hear my mournful story, in the pleasant vineyard ground
That we fought the battle bravely, and when the day was done,
Full many a corpse lay ghastly pale beneath the setting sun:

What kind of person could make such an error, to recite this macabre rhyme amid a gathering of mutilated soldiers and widowed soldiers' wives?

His trembling voice grew faint and hoarse, - his grasp was childish weak,
His eyes put on a dying look, --- and he sighed and ceased to speak;
His comrade bent to lift him, but the spark of life had fled, --
The soldier of the Legion in a foreign land is dead!

I compared this recital to the earlier one of the "Light Brigade." Both made me shudder, but I understood that this one told more of war's toll than its glory.

The sniffing woman burst into tears at the poem's end, and a pall was laid over the entire event, quite the opposite of the entertainment's intended purpose.

Mrs. Barringer sought to salvage gaiety and played some pieces eminently danceable. Yet no one danced. Those able may have thought it poor taste to dance when some honored men present could not.

She strove to uplift the assembly. She forced a sweet smile as she played "There's Music in the Air," and then "Listen to the Mockingbird." All enjoyed this tune, though those who knew the lyrics shared more somber looks. She began "The Sword of Bunker Hill," but it was not appropriate and she closed after the first stanza.

"Root Hog, or Die" was more approved. Some of the men, outnumbering the women at the party by three to one, actually sang along with newer lyrics about their victory at First Manassas.

Then she played "Twinkling Stars Are Laughing, Love," and took that tune from love ballad into a new land.

You may know the tune, or you might not have heard it in this Twentieth Century. That sixty-three-year-old entertainer at the keyboard led the crowd into a journey of her own heart where they were more than willing to travel, away from their earlier gloomy thoughts.

I have always admired those people (not politicians) who put themselves out on stage, on a theatrical set or at a musical venue. They stand (or sit) in front of an audience and open the chambers of their hearts, let the audience into their inner spaces to share their most private feelings and cares. And what if they are rejected by the crowd?

I hope she would have decided that rejection mattered less than her own expression to the world.

Her rendition of new variations of "Twinkling Stars" brought all there together. Some knew the words and reveled in them; some made their own words. At last they were brought out beyond their cares and were swept into the music of that wondrous expressionist who had carried them out of earlier gloom.

I stole a glance at Isabella and her flashing eyes caught mine, and were themselves twinkling like stars, perhaps sharing my thoughts of our next time in each other's arms.

Finally, the pianist ended, though her exploration of the possibilities of that simple popular tune might make all of us wonder at what our simple lives could be with a bit of free improvisation.

I hoped any more poetry would be only lays of love and beauty.

34

CALL AND RESPONSE

As summer faded in 1862, Charleston daily became more deserted of civilians.

Empty houses were sometimes inhabited by "squatters," but many yet had a caretaker or were checked regularly by the owner's relatives or representatives. Their owners vacated for safer lodgings in Columbia, Nassau, Bermuda, or even farther away.

Some of the homes held soldiers and artillerymen manning the batteries at White Point Gardens and other area emplacements.

The Haywoods packed up their most important goods from their home and moved to the mountains, "until the war was won," Mr. Haywood told his reluctant wife. The Charleston house of the Haywoods was occupied by one servant as were homes of two neighbors in Charleston. Isabella remained to manage these homes and servants and to look in on Aunt Peggy when she could. The Dutchess, as I always thought of her, refused to "abandon my city," and retained her city house with two servants and her poodle Pierre.

There were more drunks on the streets now, and the Home Guard was beyond its capacity to keep them clear. Lucky for me.

Scavengers, and some of them were soldiers, would steal metal fittings, guttering, hinges and the iron decorative work of houses. They would sell these to buyers and metal shops. Lead and all metals were at a premium. All that could be found was used to manufacture bullets, buckles, equipment and weapons to pursue the war.

The musician Abe had taken up residence in one of the houses on Legare, just north of the devastated area of the fire of two years earlier. He also was looking after the property and house servant for one of the wealthy refugee planter families. Everyone loved Abe.

Once I walked by the house where he lived, and he was playing a tune on the piano. I did not recognize the melody, but it was joyous. As I listened, another piano from across the street joined in the music. Theirs was not exactly a duet as there was enough physical distance between the two that their notes weren't completely synchronous and weren't harmonizing, but rather calling and replying.

The music slowed, and each player improvised so that one would phrase a stanza and the other would answer, each time one then the other playing off the previous notes but changing it. A musical conversation without words.

I paused that evening as the shadows grew and recognized it as a wordless song of love. Abe, the twenty-six-year-old musical genius and Mrs. Barringer, the sixty-three-year-old creative master.

Pondering how these two could call, respond, call, respond was like watching a pair of dancers on a stage, or birds courting.

The music became more somber and sad; this love call became sorrowful and told a tale of two born out of time from each other, as the two pianos were too far distant to play a traditional duet. In their music there was no age difference. They were both of the age of now.

The performance of these two was so intimate that I felt I was intruding. I turned my steps to the house where Isabella dwelt.

The changing melody haunted my mind and heart.

Isabella was the caretaker of the house where she stayed, and when I could I would share her bed. We each recognized our need for this companionship, and both of us believed our time together to be temporary and tenuous. Yet I cherished these hours. She was after all someone's legal wife, though she neither expected nor desired his return. One time she disparaged herself to me because of her situation and her damaged appearance. I shushed her and told her

210

she was as beautiful as any woman on earth, though she chose not to believe me.

Remembering that time in the North Carolina mountains I had no doubt of the truth of it.

Myself, I was still in a pit of self-pity for my orphaned and dispossessed condition and would not submit anyone to permanently share or endure my state.

When I arrived to her after a furtive day of rough deliveries and avoidance of authorities, we would not speak much beyond dinner preparations, then we would fall together in bed, engage each other's attentions and sleep without other commitment or any promise. The next day I would leave, usually before sunrise.

We shared the warmth of our bodies in the careless world.

I continued delivering for Tyrone, though there were more times now when I had to avoid the recruiting men who were curious as to my being healthy yet not in uniform.

This was no small effort. Sometimes I affected a limp. Later, when I misplaced my foot where a mule's foot was about to step it was no pretense, at least for a few days.

I joined Jacob in the fire brigade when he needed me. Often when we were at work near the fires in the dark, face and hands sometimes became smeared with charcoal, and I may have been seen as just another black fireman. Most people didn't care as long as I was working to save their homes, and mostly I stayed out of sight.

The night can be anonymous of color, of care, of anything.

News of yet another battle, a Southern victory of course (if you believed the papers), preceded by a day the flood of men into the hospitals, new victims of failed politics, and for some the delivery to their final rest.

These latest sons of glory had met their challenge at Second Manassas, that same battlefield they had taken by storm only a year earlier.

Again "Stonewall" Jackson's forces amazed their enemies as attack after attack shattered against the brigade's resolution. The day after these repeated attacks, the Union's General Pope sent his strengthened forces to finally defeat the entrenched stubborn brigade. He had not realized Jackson had also been reinforced by Longstreet on his left flank. That general fired his artillery and ruined Pope's advance, then sent an astounding twenty-five thousand Confederate soldiers in an overwhelming charge. Pope withdrew in haste and got away with his army mostly intact.

Glorious for the South, and all in vain.

Thank goodness.

I was growing more to love and identify with the people of Charleston. I wished the war would end, that the troops and their families would return to the city to a new life of peace. And that I could be accepted as one of these gracious and kind people, proud in their innocence, adapting to life in a changed and freer society.

But the war continued.

After a few weeks the dying had died, the healing had healed, the lingering continued to linger. Then another battle, even more violent, more glorious, more vain happened in Maryland. Its jetsam flowed down the railroad tracks to the houses of pain, of healing, and of failure, even to Charleston.

35

LAURELS OF GLORY

The newspapers heralded the Battle of Sharpsburg near Antietam in Maryland as another great victory of the warrior heroes from the South. But then the lists of dead and missing came by telegraph just two days before the first trains arrived bringing wounded to Charleston. Most stayed in Virginia of course, closer to the battlefields. But many found their ways down to Raleigh, Charlotte, Columbia, Charleston, and Savannah.

The battle in Maryland was close-run and hard fought on both sides, with maneuver and counter-maneuver. I had a flashing thought of the chess genius I had met in Paris. He was a miracle.

I had seen him set up six chess boards at a sidewalk cafe', each with a fine, intelligent opponent, and he would carelessly stroll up and down making moves in each contest and effortlessly defeat all half-dozen competitors without even a pause.

He was from Louisiana, son of a wealthy man, but he did not return to serve his country in its rebellion.

If he had been in command of the armies could he have as easily defeated the Northern generals as he had the six chess players? Or perhaps he saw there was no winning play.

In September President Lincoln used the claim of U.S. victory in Maryland to proclaim that slaves were now free, at least those in states that were in rebellion. This held some import on several levels, not least to the darker skinned Americans who could then claim ownership of themselves.

It also meant that the Republican President of the United States of America, who held no direct power in South Carolina except around Port Royal, proposed to deprive the ruling class of the Southern states of many thousands, indeed millions of dollars of their property. And that property was guaranteed by the very United States Constitution which gave Mr. Lincoln the authority of rule!

That is one way of looking at it.

But anyway, when the war was finally over and the slaves were freed and the planter class was again in power, it was as obvious as can be that the South would forever after remain solidly in the Democratic Party. Can you ever imagine it being otherwise?

The first morning rumbles and whistles from the north heralded the arrival of trains bearing the wounded to Charleston Depot. Fearful families had ridden or walked through the sandy streets to the station in silence. The trains slowed to a stop and seemed to rest before anxious crowds made their ways to the doors. The walking wounded stepped off. They then helped their fellows limp toward the breasts of the families they had marched away to defend.

The national symbol of the Confederacy now appeared to be a red spot on a white field as every butternut or gray-clad patient bore that emblem, oftentimes on multiple locations on his head, body or limbs, or perhaps where the limb should have been.

The long dragons of transport breathed their hot steam as they disgorged men. Then each was laden with the goods of death and fresh souls and turned its oil-lit eye again toward northern fires.

The trains kept arriving and followed no discernible schedule by then, bringing home troops on leave – or perhaps reprieve is the term. What reprieve can there be for a man who faces the fire of hell, witnesses his friends fall, and is convinced that he should and must return yet again to kill his national kinsmen? Then to journey home where his family is suffering its own privations, always knowing he must return to the flames. What of the teachings of the faith he was born in, which must condemn him to eternal damnation? What reprieve is this?

214

I JONATHAN

What reprieve for the woman who desperately holds the son, husband, father, brother to her breast, shedding tears of joy, thankful for the warmth of his body, kissing the hands that have killed to protect her? What balm is there to gaze into eyes that have seen Death Himself in the dreams before the battle, on the very faces of his beloved comrades, and most horrible, on the brows of the ravening enemy whose only purpose is to drive a shiny point of metal into the very body holding her now? What joy is there in kissing lips still warm, arms still firm, holding the flesh of her flesh, knowing that a year, or a month, or even a week hence that flesh may be sharing a dark, damp pit of corruption with a hundred others, or scattered to fragments across a blasted field?

What sons of New York accountants or of Pennsylvania mechanics and farmers will have lost their futures to the battles where their lords directed them? Of my Massachusetts schoolmates who served, their travels to the foreign lands to the South would not be a happy tour of sightseeing and holiday, but a mission of murder and woe.

And yet the families of these men hugged, cried, and held their dear ones to them as if in this one moment the turning world could stop and the fresh-faced boy who left them the year before would be with them as they were at that moment, forever.

But the world does not stop turning. Seasons change, and the blooded veteran who joyed in seeing his father's house, who once more stroked the head of his beloved sister, who shared a last breakfast with his mother – again shouldered his rifle. One more time he climbed into the rail car for the advance to the front, to tempt ravenous Death as he does murder to men.

So, the trains brought home the survivors of battle to take what succor they could from the drying country, to accept the hospitality of a grateful but increasingly paupered city.

Music was arranged with what was left of local bands, often elements of the remaining fire crew musicians, or ever younger cadets from the Citadel. Sometimes the only music available was from plantation servants who played banjos and fiddles with perhaps a flute and tambourine.

Those men who could walk on their own stepped from the trains, lifted their baggage and scanned the city for their families, for their previous lives, or just to view a city mostly intact.

The three who swore the oath beneath the great oak tree were reduced to two. Tall Louis had met his end at a place in battle with the ominous name of the Sunken Road. Kit toted Louis' bag along with his own. His eyes showed careworn shadows from days of mourning for his friend, and for other comrades unknown to Charleston.

Proud William shouldered his bag and carried something else with an air of reverence, a small wooden box.

There arrived at the station a ghost: a fine carriage trimmed in the livery of the lost Ledger Plantation from John's Island, with a Ledger servant driving. The plantation itself had been harried, occupied, then burned by Federal forces months ago.

I arrived at the station just as William and Kit ascended into the carriage seats and rolled away to the hotel their family had arranged for them.

My duty that day was to carry two passengers in my wagon to their homes. They did not ride up with me, but rode in the back, within coffins. As with many of these burial caskets, the top of the boxes was lifting from the writhing of tortured dead bones, unhappy in their enforced repose. As the body cooled, the joints drew into resisting forms which pried the nails from the coffin tops. Coffin screws were no longer available; they had all been used, and the routes of import from the north were closed. The coffins I carried that day were tightly bound with hemp rope to keep the lids from lifting completely.

I turned the horses to the road leading to the old racecourse and the home where my cargo was to be delivered. As I was leaving the station, I heard a call and halted my cart.

"Jonathan!" I turned and saw a travel worn Martin, Jenny's fiancé, limping toward me. "Jonathan."

Well, he had made it through alive. "Hello, Martin." I stepped down and shook his hand. "Put your bag on the cart and jump up." I thought better of saying that immediately and helped him step up. His wound was not as disabling as many others I had seen lately.

Martin's mother had died, and he was to spend a week at his plantation of Castle Oaks to get things in better order before returning to Virginia. He had lost some of his childhood friends in battle, and now his mother was dead. The structure of his personal world was crumbling.

"It's good to see you, Jonathan. Do you know where Jenny is?"

Jenny had felt it her duty to return to the city to help as she could in the war effort, by volunteering with Doctor Baily at Roper Hospital. And she also hoped to see Martin again if he were to return on leave.

"Jenny is likely at the Hospital on Queen Street for a few more hours. Maybe you could clean up a bit." Martin looked down at his clothes and up at me in agreement. I was in the unusual circumstance of being cleaner than a man sitting near me.

He said no more but turned his eyes around the city as I quirted the mule. He didn't need to say anything to me of where he had been. I had heard tales of the horrors of the battlefields and the diseases of the camps. Since learning the news of the Ledger boy Timmy who had presented poetry at the Queen Street mansion nearly two years ago, I didn't want to hear any more of this disgusting news. I had hoped there would be no revelations of tragedy for me here. I was to be disappointed.

Martin scanned the town as we made our way through it. The streets showed little activity other than soldiers making their ways home or to hospital. Most families had moved away. Martin's mother had stayed at his plantation up near Goose Creek where she had died of fever.

Scores of laborers were in the outskirts of town digging defensive works, especially on the north west, the avenue the British had used in their grandfathers' time. Those enemies had tried to force the harbor but were repulsed by citizen militia behind their forts of palmetto trunks. Eventually their forces landed on James Island and marched overland to take the city. The Battle of Secessionville in June had reminded the citizens of that defeat, and Charleston was not ready to allow that again.

In the town itself there were, other than soldiers, mostly men staying behind to guard their homes, their businesses, their city. A few women remained. They gathered to sew clothing and goods for their men in the army, and to care for the wounded.

As disabled soldiers came into town by the trainload, they overwhelmed the hospitals. Makeshift infirmaries were established. Soldiers were detailed to run the sick houses, and the local women supplemented the labor. They brought bandages made from old bed sheets and petticoats. They brought cakes made from flour and corn meal. Some even donated precious coffee brought in by the blockade-running ships, which still plied the guarded waters between the coast and Nassau.

These low fast boats brought in delicacies and luxuries no longer available in the South, but prices were high, and cotton was no longer to be exported by order of President Davis. The idea was to drive up demand and force England and others who were hungry for the stuff to support the Southern effort. Orders didn't stop people with means from carrying it out for sale.

Cargo from the blockade runners was transported on guarded carts. The cargo I carried that day needed no guards.

Most of Charleston's soldiers were buried where they fell. Very few made the journey back to their homes where their families could place them with their ancestors.

I drove by the Mills House hotel where William and Kit were resting on the balcony surrounded by other soldiers and civilians. With drinks in hand they were calling, "Lieutenant Martin Tenate! Report for duty!" The mayor was with them on the very balcony where General Lee had directed such fire control as was possible during the Conflagration. I remembered his reserved face lit by the flames' glow during the excitement and devastation as he calmly gave orders.

I lifted Martin's bag from the cart and carried it for him up the steps, where a worker at the hotel greeted. "Mister Martin! Welcome back. I am glad to see you well, suh." He gave me a cautionary look as I hefted the bag up the stairs behind Martin, as if to ask what business someone of my class had in the building. But I waited for the soldier as he carefully preceded me up the staircase to his floor.

Two Zouaves and a trio of Florida Grays cheered Martin as we entered the room. I set the bag down and turned to leave. "Thank you, Jonathan. If you see Jenny, tell her I will be with her soon." I walked across the room to the stairs and saw his friends William Ledger and Kit sitting somberly at a table with some of the family and friends of Louis. My curiosity made me pause to listen.

William opened the small casket he had carried earlier and drew forth a Testament. Tattered and worn from long study, the cover was creased and wrinkled. Louis's father and uncle were there, each of them tall and dark like the late hero. "This was Louis's comfort for many a long hour in camp," said the soldier, and handed it over. The father reverently placed it on the table before him.

"He was killed repelling the enemy on the Sunken Road," told William in his deep voice. A company of Georgians was ordered to hold it at all costs, but when their number began to fall, Louis, Kit and I ran to join in their support."

Kit gazed into the far distance as he recalled the day as William spoke. "Row after row they came, and they fell like wheat. We stayed at that road for hours. Our rifles grew hot." William looked away into that same distance. "Finally their massed guns were too much for us, and we began to fall back. Before Louis could turn to withdraw, he took a bullet in his neck. He looked at me as if to ask if this had really happened. He sank to his knee, then sat down."

William sat a moment in memory. "He was holding his bleeding neck and told us to bring his bible home to you and his mother. He said to protect Charleston and the South. We renewed our oath taken under the live oak last year. And he breathed his last.

"Our forces retook the road.

"We carried our fallen comrade to a large tree on the field and placed him below it. There is no shame in sharing a resting place with many others who were laid in that ground made holy by the blood of brothers. Louis will rest in the shade of a mighty tree, and we two survivors will hold true to our oaken oath. We swore we would not rest until our land was free and sovereign. We will remain true, and honor Louis with our arms."

"Aye," said Kit.

Their hair was now quite long, and reached their shoulders. Their beards were three inches and more, though recently washed and combed. William, the larger and more vigorous of the two, had a fast-growing face and was beginning to look like a Viking hero. Kit had always been the quieter and was more fair. His beard grew less fully, rendering him more like pictures of Jefferson Davis than of Jeb Stuart.

They all took a few moments of silence to remember their friend, nephew, and son. Though the table was silent, on the patio the soldiers began a ribald song directed to a passing pedestrian, obviously one of the rare women still in the city, and not gentry from the tone of their attentions.

Next drawn from the soldier's cask was a glass, used on the rare occasions when a drop was found from a friend's brandy horn.

Next was a gold ring. This was to be for Carla the black-haired woman, to whom Louis was prepared to propose marriage at the moment of their army's victory. I wondered if I was the only one present who knew that she had left Westward with another man two weeks earlier.

From the room below came the tones of a piano playing a lovely melody from Italy, so at odds with the sorrow at this table. As that melody ended, a more lively tune began, and the moment was over.

So quickly do memorial moments pass in this hurtling world.

I had heard enough and left.

While I was in the hotel for those brief moments, someone had visited the back of my cart and placed wreaths of magnolia leaves upon each casket.

36

WONDERFUL THINGS

My first delivery after leaving Martin at Mills House was to an undertaker on the town's northeast side. The dead fool was slid into the room behind the chapel to be prepared for the next in a long line of funerals the following day.

Then I drove to an absolute horror at the next home.

Just south of Line Street, on Nassau, I pulled up to the nice but modest white house. A matron and some of her friends were celebrating on the small piazza with tea of some sort and some delicate cakes. They were congratulating the mother who was giddy with relief. She had just received word that the soldier son she had been mourning since reading of his death the night before was not killed. He would be coming home on a train that day.

I did not wonder who was in the tormented casket in my wagon.

As I pulled up in front of the house, they all became silent, but not the mother.

She dropped the teacup from her hand and it shattered. With her mouth grotesquely open and her eyes unnaturally wide she began a low groan that grew into a howl, higher, through the octaves into a screech which did not end.

The women around her tried to comfort her, but she went mad. Her friends forced her into the house, and as I shifted the sad load down my ramp plank to the carriageway of the house I continued to hear the wild echoes of her distress.

I prayed the woman would find peace somewhere, somehow.

I replaced the magnolia wreath upon the box and left as quickly as I could.

I went to Roper Hospital. The area all around was still a ruin from the Great Fire. A few soldier-nurses were on the porch sharing some medicinal whiskey, quite unashamed as I walked up. The men's eyes were hollow, their faces vapid. They had worked long hours washing linen, carrying food, emptying bedpans, cleaning the dying, transporting dead bodies, perhaps their own brothers.

It didn't take much imagination to understand their condition, grievously wounded without wound.

There was a popular poem going around later in the war that said it best, told from a woman's vantage, and it moves me yet.

Here is a part:

> *Somebody's darling! So young and so brave,*
> *Wearing still on his pale sweet face—*
> *Soon to be hid by the dust of the grave—*
> *The lingering light of his boyhood's grace.*
>
> *Matted and damp are the curls of gold*
> *Kissing the snow of that fair young brow,*
> *Pale are the lips of delicate mould—*
> *Somebody's darling is dying now.*
>
> *Kiss him once for Somebody's sake;*
> *Murmur a prayer, soft and low;*
> *One bright curl from the cluster take—*
> *They were Somebody's pride, you know.*
>
> *Somebody wept when he marched away,*
> *Looking so handsome, brave, and grand;*
> *Somebody's kiss on his forehead lay;*
> *Somebody clung to his parting hand;—*
>
> *Tenderly bury the fair young dead,*
> *Pausing to drop on his grave a tear;*
> *Carve on the wooden slab at his head,*
> *"Somebody's darling slumbers here!"*

Each year another generation of life is born, innocent babies pure of spirit, like a constantly flowing spring whose waters run down into a river, there to be polluted and spoiled. Yet the fountain continually springs anew.

I shared a quiet moment of sorrowful camaraderie with them, then stepped into the halls of pain.

Everyone wasn't moaning and the smell wasn't as bad as my last visit, if you can say that – more of ammonia than rot this time. Some beds were empty now. I saw no doctors. I asked one of the attendants I knew where Jenny might be, that a soldier she knew was looking for her.

"Jenny's gone. She and Doctor Lebie went to Wilmington."

All of us had heard the kind of town Wilmington had become, and I couldn't believe she had run up there with the doctor. He was twenty years her senior, and was married himself! But I had seen things in these past years I thought would never be possible.

"Dr. Lebie and Jenny went to Wilmington? Why?"

The attendant was not shy about sharing information. "Oh, he went with three of the girls."

I had no answer to that.

"They're having a problem up there and asked for help."

"Oh. What kind of problem?"

He looked out toward the harbor. "A boat brought the fever." Yellow fever.

I had heard it was a raging epidemic in the Bahama Islands and all feared it would cross on a day's voyage to our shores. It had come into Wilmington with a vengeance.

Jenny and the others weren't safe from this creeping and invisible evil. This is not like cannon or rifle, or even an attacking dog. This was like devious poison, more like what had killed young Willie Lincoln. Yellow fever is not always deadly, but often it is, and there was little to be done.

I shuddered.

I bade the attendants goodbye and took the cart back to the stable. I quickly unhitched the mules and went back to find Martin.

He and I had never been close. I felt admiration for him and the great good fortune of his birth, his prospects as a planter, and his great luck in courting Jenny – both of them the class of Carolina princes, and she a rare beauty. I had envied this perfect couple since the day of my arrival in Charleston when he spoke with her at the teetotal soda shop and again when I had "chaperoned" the couple the night of the plantation party. I respected that he had clear vision and knew what he should do with his life, though his plans had been interrupted.

I walked to the Mills House and inquired for him.

"He's resting after his wash," said a servant.

I sat in the parlor and waited his awakening.

As I sat there my engineering friend Charles Gallard passed through, speaking with an academic-looking man in a pristine gray uniform.

"...So, you see we can do wonderful things!" exulted Charles, with that light in his eyes I had seen before. He turned toward me and smiled with a wink. Later he would tell me the astounding plan he was discussing though I didn't really comprehend what he meant at the time.

The gray professor walking with my friend nodded and did not smile. He put on his braid-bedecked hat and they walked out into the sunlight.

Martin came into the lobby I told him where his fiancée' was. He had to go to his mother's graveside, then report back to his regiment before he could have a chance to see her, and charged me with carrying to her a letter. I expected that it was love poetry.

He was stoic as he left me, but his cheek was wet with tears.

37

HEAVENWARD

Christmastime in 1862 was celebrated with less cheer. The limited use of the coal gas street lamps in the dark months made the town more dismal.

Yet another great battle was fought in December. Fredericksburg.

The familiar process repeated itself: the wounded rode to hospitals and the dead to their places in the ground.

A few businesses sported wreaths and greenery, but there were no street decorations. The isolated holiday displays only heightened awareness that most were not celebrating. The children were mostly gone. The women were mostly gone. The native sons mostly gone. Many stores were closed.

I had delivered rice and salt pork to a home with some of the city's few remaining children on a day visit. The family was preparing to go to Columbia, seen as less vulnerable.

The kids were playing dress-up, and as I took tea with the mother, we watched the children pretending to drum or to hold sticks like guns. One child had his left arm inside his shirt and displayed the empty sleeve, a mother's growing little boy playing a veteran whose arm had been blown off. The woman's eyes filled. She sniffed and told the boys to stop playing and take a nap.

Most of my errands were horizontal, across rubbled and deserted streets or sandy lanes, but this one was vertical in nature, not by balloon, but via old fashioned steps. I was on an errand for Tyrone, delivering a note to the heart's desire of a woman named

Louise.

The sunlit roadways and sidewalks of Charleston were eerily quiet. A cart filled with furniture and parcels rattled along a cobbled alley. The black driver gently guided the old mule with his load of some master's possessions, taking them where they would be safe from whatever may come. A few dogs should be searching about, but they had all been captured and put to the butcher's knife by meat-starved soldiers as the hunger blockade worked its way.

Killing one's pet, the friend one knows, seems impossible to me. But men who have had no meat for weeks might come across a scavenging cur and put it to the knife, if desperate enough.

I suppose I could do that.

Isabella in her house-tending had contacts who knew people still catching fish, and her household could usually produce some marine meat or at least edible crabs.

As I passed Archdale Street and onto Meeting a company of soldiers carrying spades noted my passing. Their sergeant glared at me and the small envelope I carried.

I began to limp a little.

He marshaled his tired-looking charges to their next assignment, whatever that might be. Their duty as ditch-diggers was made necessary by the shortages of slave workers, most of whom were moved to reinforce the works at Morris Island and Battery Wagner, until those emplacements fell. Then to Sullivan's Island and the outskirts of the city. Some fled to Union camps.

Those troops looked weary and less hopeful. They shouldered implements and pushed their barrows to prepare the next planned site of a line of desperate defense. Should another attack at Secessionville succeed or should Sumter fall, the enemy must be fought in the streets of the city itself.

I skirted the new breastworks these soldiers had dug and continued to St. Michael's Church.

St. Michael's was a white deserted shell. God's house and perhaps God was still inside, but I did not think so. The bells had been removed from the steeple and were secreted inland farther from the danger of Union attack. Some churches had donated their metal bells to cast into cannon.

Christian sacrifice?

All the portable tools and items of worship had been sent to the temporary home of the remaining congregation in the north of the peninsula, out of reach of Northern shells.

But the church was not quite deserted.

The bell tower sans bells was the highest point in Charleston. It is from that spire that lanterns were hung to signal fire companies where they should drive their engines. A lamp on a pole on the east or west side directed the men that the fire was in that direction, like that awful fire just a December earlier.

The tower's height also had at least two military uses. The forces from Charleston placed in it a man who could observe enemy movements beyond the battery, beyond Pinckney, beyond Sumter, all the way past the harbor entrance.

The other military use was employed by those attacking the city: it was the point used to orient their long-range cannon fire. That artillery target was my destination.

I opened the door from the hallway off the vacant and cavernous sanctuary to begin my trek up the steep stairway, toward heaven. Indeed, as I climbed the steps I felt more light-headed and considered that I was approaching a level nearing the angels, and I wondered. If the Confederate dead from Charleston are buried in some unnamed field on some unknown farm or nameless forest, might their spirits return, using the bell tower of St. Michael's to locate their native city and seek the places of their childhood? If man has a soul, perhaps I was entering the company of angels. Or perhaps all soldiers are damned by their actions to eternal hellfire.

Much of Boston and all of Charleston is very flat. I had never had occasion or practice of stepping up in such a long stair and felt the burning in my calves which must be wholly unknown to Zeke and other men of the mountains. Each stair squawked and squeaked and announced my approach to the sentinel in the silent bell tower.

When I reached the top landing where the observer stayed, I found that it was Theodore Watkins of the Signal Corps, who I had met during the days of the signing of the articles of separation. He recognized me.

"Hello, Jon. Have you not yet been conscripted? Or, rather, which uniform would you wear?" I saw that his uniform was buttoned up against the cold, and his coat and a muffler were also employed.

"Ted, you are looking well. I heard you were at Manassas. I

am glad you are unhurt."

He turned his eyes away, then looked to me again. I handed him the note.

"Oh, from my Louise! Jon, sit by the fire while I read the note!"

There was a small stove in the tight area, and the wintry wind blew through the open viewing space. Christmas is icy cold in Boston, but I can tell you from a definite experience that Charleston is not Nassau and is not tropical, at least not in December. I gladly crowded the firebox as Theodore read his love letter. As I watched his lips silently whispering, his face would change and react with each word.

Most men are made to be loved by women, and without this there is a great hole which can never be filled. I feared my choices had made me more of a hole than a man.

But I had found Isabella, for as long as that could last.

Theodore read his letter with all his attention. When finished he began again, savoring each syllable and comma.

A tip-tip-tapping noise alerted me, and Ted leapt from his stool, still cradling the paper, and bent his attention to the telegraph key mounted on a small shelf. He made notes on a pad with his stub of a pencil.

I stood and peered out of that aerie onto the scene of Charleston Harbor. A brass telescope was mounted on a solid wooden tripod, daubed with lampblack to prevent sunlight reflection and aimed at James Island. I thought it best for me not to attempt use of the instrument while an officer of the army was otherwise occupied.

The sun had passed the meridian and the water shone a dark gray-blue. A few boats punted about, hunting fish and carrying people to or from Forts Moultrie or Johnson. Several boats were plying between the city and what must have been Battery Wagner. The day was dark due to light overcast. I could make out some shapes in the distance against the dun water: the blockading fleet stood a threatening patrol.

The clacking ended, and Ted took a moment to translate the dots and strokes to letters, then words. He smiled and shared the message.

"This is from General Manigault, the artilleryman. Actually, it's a lieutenant on his staff. He says his brother is at Battery Johnson, and precisely at 2 p.m. will begin a message that I should acquire and

228

transmit back to him. He says he will pass it to his brother's fiancée."
Ted's eyes narrowed and he smiled his crooked smile. "I shall be
eavesdropping on a stranger's love letter."

I believe he thought it was irregular to use army
communication channels for the transmission of love-making. Yet I
wonder what legionnaire of Caesar's army would have hesitated to
send his Penelope a letter up the Appian Way if a Republican courier
was headed toward a marketplace near his household.

Ted checked his watch, then aimed the magnifying device
toward the battery, and saw the man. "Oh, yes, he is using the French
flag system. I hope he transmits in English; my French is deplorable."
I knew his French to be excellent, but Theodore was always a humble
sort.

The older wig-wag signals used by both armies to coordinate
troops and firepower had great limitations. The French semaphore
style of flag waving is much quicker and more precise, capable of
creating letters and actually spelling words. Both armies began to
adopt it, and the surviving army employed it after the fall of the
South.

The message flew across miles of sight lines and electrical
wiring: "My heart beats only for you....oh! that we should be together
again in the moonlight, beneath the flowering peaches...my thoughts
are of you and no other...your happiness is all I can hope
for........." Nothing new, nothing original. Yet nothing is so craved
by one's love other than such words, and the expressed hope that they
should join their lives together.

Theodore was enthralled by his intrigue, his misuse of
government property. He was too captivated by far. His routine was
so dull, viewing nothing and reporting nothing, only occasionally
enlivened by transmission of the essence of human existence, one
lover to another. And, occasionally, by a flying explosive ball of metal
aimed at his perch.

The sentinel made his report to the brother of the signaler,
tapping on his telegraph key the personal notes of another lovestruck
couple.

Shadows were growing longer.

I made moves to exit, but Ted persuaded me to share the
contents of a basket with him ere my descent to mortal ground. The
ginger molasses cake made of corn flour rather than wheat was crude

and simple, and so delicious a morsel of delight! Yaupon tea was stewing on the stove, and we ate silently, smacking lips in communion, a cup with sticky rough delicacy.

Community.

38

SANCTUARY IN A STRICKEN CITY

Leaving Ted's perch in the tower, I made my solemn journey down to what now seemed the underworld – the streets of the city as the sunlight faded. The walks were deserted except for an occasional furtive scavenger or looter in alleys between the big houses.

All was silent save the sound of the breeze through the empty alleys and streets.

As twilight deepened, I wondered at the danger now lurking here, not from the Federals, but from common criminals who hide in every city. No gas lamps were lit any more. I felt the comforting heft of my Bowie knife and was not afraid. If I encountered one man, my blade would either defend me, or, well, the grave waits for all of us.

In the distance around a corner I saw a shrouded woman accompanied by her African maid, carrying a small lamp and rushing somewhere without male escort.

The two were bundled against the chill and moved swiftly. It was not proper to be unaccompanied like that, very unsafe on these ungoverned streets. I thought I recognized Jenny's maid Festus. I ran quickly to overtake them.

"Run, Missy, someone's comin'" cried Festus, as she turned to confront me with a drawn knife, or perhaps a bayonet. The other figure turned a fearful eye on me above her face scarf.

"Festus, Jenny, it's Jonathan Vander."

Unsure at first, then each of them stood in relief, but then renewed pace toward their goal.

"What are you doing out here this time of day, without an escort?"

Festus did not answer. "Good to see you, Jonathan. You gave us quite a fright. Please, if you have the time to accompany us I would be most grateful."

I suggested we slow our pace to display a confident stride. "Where are you going?"

"I have an engagement. Father would not have approved, and our man Coffee was not at home when I received the summons."

Summons!

"Yes, Ma'am, I will be happy to escort you," though my sorry workman's clothes did not appear well compared to her fine cloak, still smart after two years of privation and blockade.

I walked in front of the small party. Festus brought up the rear.

We did not go to the Huguenot Church, though I do not recall which church we went to. Each of them was emptied, dark, locked. Some had become homes of derelict men, both slaves and hiding soldiers. We turned off Meeting Street. I recall feeling myself the protector of the women, and not the guide.

"In here," whispered Jenny, and we turned our steps into a narrow path between buildings. It was paved with stones but overgrown and rank with vines. The lamp's glow threw crazy shadows of fern and leaf.

We stepped through a gate to the back door of a chapel. Jenny tried the latch, but it was sealed. As she raised her hand to knock, the rough door swung inward: deep shadow. I waved the lantern in and saw feet, and a tunic of gray. Bright buttons, and the thin face of a friend.

"Oh, hello, Jon. Have you brought me a Christmas present?" It was Martin, glowing darkly in his mended yet spotless uniform. He was clean-shaven and smelled of the barber.

Jenny replied. "Martin!" That was all she said, all which needed saying.

232

Festus and I followed the loving couple. A dark figure shuttered and bolted the door behind us and padded behind. Martin shared with Jenny that he was the only one of his friends who could steal away from the army for a very few days, and he risked punishment.

We walked through the empty hall into the larger chapel, echoing dark and vacant, like most buildings in that part of town. Pews were empty. They waited in vain for their congregation to participate in communions, christenings, weddings, and funerals.

I had seen enough funerals.

We entered an antechamber off the main room. As I entered the small sanctuary, if sanctuary existed in this stricken city under siege – or anywhere on this earth – I saw the white cloths on the altar, brass candlesticks (all the silver had long been hidden or sold for the Cause), and the plate of bread and the cup. I was now at a wedding – secret and unauthorized.

Who should authorize a wedding? The city? The state? God Himself? Those two young people whose lives were interrupted by a war planned and directed by another generation were about to take authorization upon themselves.

The minister was Reverend Poste, the same Tennessee preacher who prayed to sanction the plantation party that night on James Island. He lit two more candles, ensconced them in their places on either side of the altar, and carried a vase of rare winter flowers to the table draped in white. A church servant, the tall and thin black man who had locked the door behind us, laid a pad in front of the altar and stood behind the podium near the choiry. Festus stood beside her mistress.

"Jon," said Martin, I would be honored if you would stand beside me."

I felt I was being "Shanghaied," a term I had picked up in Boston before my European adventure. Apparently some ships lacking a full complement of sailors would hit unsuspecting men on the head and lock them up on a ship headed to far ports, maybe Shanghai, China. When they awoke, they had no choice but to serve on the ship.

In other times, if anyone had asked me to be the groom's man in my sorry state of disrepair I would have refused. The soil of two days' work was on my body and my clothes would have only been appropriate to a New England scarecrow. And I knew Martin slightly, really. He was an enemy of my country, and perhaps of his own if the South was to lose. Revulsion filled me at my own sins and unworthiness.

I walked the steps to stand by him.

Reverend Poste adjusted up the altar, looked right and left, then walked to the side of the far pew. From there he lifted his stole, the only vestments in this secret ceremony. He had removed his overcoat so that the black stole would show against his white blouse. This removal of a formal cloak perversely lent a greater air of formality to the event.

The wedding ceremony I had earlier begun planning for myself and Laura was to be in a large church with our families and friends in the pews. My childhood chum Edward was to have stood by me, not some shabby workman acquaintance I barely knew who smelled of sweat. I imagined Laura in fine satin and laces, flanked by her sister Fanny, and schoolmates. Hundreds of candles would have lit the sanctuary. A refined minister in austere cleric garb would lead the ceremony, not a country-bred preacher in a lonely hidden ceremony like this one, in a dark church in a doomed, decaying city under siege.

Reverend Poste stood a bit straighter. As he walked to the front of the sanctuary this plain preacher, a common man of the back woods, he became a man of God. He radiated a Presence and turned our impromptu, ragged gathering into a holy ceremony, joining two young souls into one.

"Dearly beloved, we are gathered here together in the sight of God to witness and bless the joining together of Martin Tenate and Virginia Haywood…"

His flat Tennessee accent rolled through his mouth and out into the deserted holy space. Its echo deepened his voice, and his simple words became rounded and as powerful as pronouncements of a prophet.

The long day I had finished began to tell on my consciousness and attention. I was drawn into a trance.

Those two fragile lovers gingerly treading the fine line of the law of Man and God gripped each other's hands, desperately hoping they could somehow achieve a happy life together. Their innocence would have been a high jest to a cynic like me, except that there – and I suppose everywhere – when a couple honestly joins together in lifelong promise, they share an act to bring about the greatest life hope of man and woman.

As I recall, the church we were in was not one of those that uses perfume incense smoke. But I could swear my own days-old odor was driven away, and the musty smell of the closed-up sanctuary was lifted and replaced with sweet airs of flowering spring. Maybe it was a scent in the candles.

My drifting attention returned to the altar. The minister was silhouetted against a candle's illumination, and his dimly lit form added to the unreality of the scene.

"I ask you now, in the presence of God and these people…" I noticed the eyes of Festus and the African servant widening briefly and met. By using the term "these people" the minister would have caused at least comment had there been any of the regular congregation in attendance. Of course, the congregation would have assumed it was meant to include only themselves, so it wouldn't have mattered. A smile was shared by the blacks as they realized that here, at least in this community, and in the eyes of God, they were indeed "people," not property.

"Martin and Virginia come to give themselves to one another in this holy covenant."

Our greatest hope.

"Enable them to grow in love, and peace…"

A vain dream of peace, at last pronounced aloud. The vows were exchanged, solemnly.

"I, Martin, take you, Virginia, to be my wife, to have and to hold." The man's eyes were glistening.

"From this day forward, for better, for worse…" Worse was to come.

"In sickness and in health," in a world of so much sickness, such fragile health.

"To love and to cherish, until we are parted by death…"
What could be more likely than parting by death? How many of his
classmates are even now moldering beneath foreign soil?

And I was struck by the thought of this boy's selfishness, that
he would marry this young promising girl, herself bursting with youth
and health, to enjoy her love for a night, and then go off to war and
die. What hopeless hope that he would come back to her, alive and
healthy? He had already been wounded in the field once, and would
return to battle soon, where the gods of war were screaming glory
and eating blood.

I felt revulsion then at my participation in this unholy
sacrament. I felt I should flee.

So you see my rainbow of emotions during this ceremony.

"This is my solemn vow." The full eye of Martin overflowed
down his cheek. I saw that Jenny was also weeping. The hopeless
darkness of the future lay before them on their wedding day.

As the bride began to speak with tremulous voice, I looked at
her maid. She was openly crying for her lifelong best friend. What
could these tears have meant? Another range of thoughts cascaded
through my mind.

"I, Virginia, take you, Martin, to be my husband, to have and
hold, from this day forward, for better, for worse, for richer, for
poorer, in sickness and health, to love and to cherish, until we are
parted by death. This is my solemn vow."

She spoke the promising words quickly and strongly. She
meant them completely.

The minister spoke: "This ring is the outward and visible
sign…."

Martin started. "Wait." He had no ring.

And in this travesty of a wedding ceremony, where I stood as
nothing more than a shameful stand-in for a real friend of the groom,
likely William Ledger, my spirit again failed. A moment before I was
ashamed to even consider this charade as anything more than a
means of a lusty boy to deflower a pure young woman. Hasn't that
been my own reasons for the sham of decent treatment of a woman?

236

And what was I doing to Isabella? The thought of her forlorn and vain hope of being a good wife and mother, only to have her child die and her husband abuse and abandon her. And now my great sin in living that selfish and fruitless way with her.

I stepped back from the altar and looked at the kneeling couple. They didn't care about a ring at this point. The ring was nothing but a symbol, as the minister had said. Their faces were glimmering in the light of the candle flames.

But there was not lust here. There was something else, something pure that I had seen before in Mother's face. And in Isabella's.

They gazed into each other's eyes and whispered. Reverend Poste said, "We can proceed; the ring is just a symbol, and can be given later."

Once again, my emotions reversed course. "Wait." I drew forth from my rucksack a U.S. silver dollar which was of the secret pocket hoard of coins and key the Mexican left me in his jacket. It was an 1859 coin, still shiny and with the head of Liberty on it. "It is no ring, but has some value. Repay me when you can." I whispered as I handed it to Martin.

His eyes looked steady into mine as he slowly took it. "Thank you, Jon." He turned to Jenny.

"Virginia, this is your ring. I give it as a sign of my vow, and with all that I am, and all that I have, to honor you and to give you the best of life in my power. It represents my love and my promise to return. I will have it fashioned into shape and bring it to you when I come back." She grasped the coin and held it to her breast.

If this seems very gallant, gracious and generous of me, well, I suppose it was. On the other hand, I knew that Tyrone was going to pay me my wages when next I saw him. And I had food, more than most. And I still had two silver coins and a gold doubloon left from Ricardo's gift. In fact, by Confederate standards of that time I was well off for a laboring man.

The minister took a brief, reflective pause, then passed the wine cup around. Madeira. Then he broke bread and afterwards each of us shared a brief taste of each, including the slaves. As Poste put the crust into Festus's hand, she whispered to him. He looked in her eyes and nodded, and returned to the married couple, still kneeling. At this point, the service was nearly over. He leaned in and spoke a few quiet words to the couple. They exchanged glances and nodded.

The reverend returned to the couple, turned and nodded to Festus, and she began to sing. You may know the old song:

> *There is a balm in Gilead to make the wounded whole;*
> *There is a balm in Gilead to heal the sin-sick soul.*

Her soprano was clear and strong. The slave custodian moved to stand behind her and hummed in a deep bass harmony, a singular and haunting sound in that empty and echoing chapel, but with words which moved me greatly, and spoke to my delicate and fragile state of mind.

> *Sometimes I feel discouraged, and think my work's in vain.*
> *But then the Holy Spirit revives my soul again.*

"You have declared your consent and vows," intoned the minister, "before God and this congregation, or rather this gathering. I announce to you that Virginia and Martin are man and wife." The minister then looked directly at me. "Those whom God has joined together, let no one put asunder."

I do not believe that he meant that I might put the union asunder. I believe he was commanding me to safeguard this union and not let anyone else put it asunder.

Funny how things work out though.

39

ANGEL OF ST. MICHAEL

One day in early 1863 after months of chiding by the Courier and the Mercury newspapers, the two warships *Chicora* and *Palmetto State* got up steam and charged out into the sea.

The early morning was heavy with fog as some smaller gunboats and the two ironclads quietly ventured out of the harbor, past Sumter to spring an attack on the Union ships closest to them.

They worked independently and rapidly overpowered several boats, ramming one, much to the surprise of the fleet. Two were damaged to the point of sinking; several others barely limped back to Port Royal.

This big morale builder for the citizens was announced in several papers – that the blockade was broken and Charleston was again open for world commerce!

That was a bit optimistic as the blockade was, after two days, completely restored, except for the continuing ingenuity of the blockade runners.

My habits had changed since the Conscription Act forbade me from flaunting my civilian status and appearing regularly in Downtown.

Once while returning from a visit to Isabella I was stopped by a patrol of two of the Home Guard, with Kerry nowhere in sight. These men were in no mood for debate.

"Show us your papers," demanded the younger of the two.

He was missing his right hand. The elder, a large Georgian, seemed more forgiving, and stood silently looking about us.

I gave him my document of my value from Tyrone and my latest bill of lading. He was not impressed.

Since martial law was declared in May of the previous year, there had been varying degrees of compliance and order. Though on that day there was order in the order.

The sergeant asked, "What is your name?"

"William Gallard," I lied.

"Why are you not in uniform?"

This episode of my avoiding taking an armed side in national tragedy ended with my dead good friend Ricardo again buying something for me: my freedom. In exchange for a chance to remove myself from the city, I gave up the doubloon coin of the treasures he had secreted in his jacket two years ago. I kept the two remaining silver dollars, and the key.

It was perhaps a chance to buy escape for the soldier and sergeant as well. That gold could have bought fare to far places. I never saw either of them again.

That evening I met with Tyrone and he sent me to his farm.

I hurriedly left for Wadmalaw Island, a fertile region to the south and west of the metropolis where Tyrone had an interest in a plantation. It had been highly profitable. "Sea Island Cotton" was grown there, and though Tyrone had but a twelfth share, it paid well for him. I didn't learn until later where he put all of his profits.

All the families of the plantation owners had left the surrounding area because being closer to Port Royal meant exposure to raids from "Yankees."

Several plantation homes were burned to the ground on Edisto Island, and on one occasion a roving band of soldiers scared me and the remaining hands into the jungle. The house was left undamaged except for anything that marching soldiers could carry off including most of the chickens.

Though these invaders were from my homeland I did not feel I could approach them under those circumstances. And why should I?

240

The slaves of Tyrone's plantation mostly remained in place. There at least they had a bed and could find food – though some young men evaporated into the woods. Trails led away from the cotton fields and toward the camps of the invading troops where, I suppose, they became workers and even soldiers.

If slaves join the winning side in a war, are they then masters?

The situation on the plantation was too tenuous for me to remain at the location, so one day I packed some cornbread and walked back to Charleston. I arrived after dark and slid into my old warehouse pallet again. The next day Tyrone, ever my benefactor, planned to send me on a delivery of lime to a plantation on Long Island, though I guess now everybody calls it "Isle of Palms."

Anyway, before I made that trip, I witnessed the biggest battle yet to try forcing the harbor.

Union naval forces had been building up at the entrance for months, and finally the dam broke.

Nine ironclads, monitors and the powerful *New Ironsides*, a sail and steam-driven casement ship, attacked with all their fury.

It took more hours than expected for the morning haze to clear and to prepare the Union fleet for the effort. It was late afternoon before the ships' guns fired on Sumter. The attacking fleet was answered from batteries Moultrie, Wagner, and Gregg. Fort Moultrie was commanded by a Jewish officer, cousin of Abe the musician. These defensive forts together with the guns on Castle Pinkney, the James Island batteries and those on the city peninsula itself totaled more than three hundred eighty land-based guns for harbor defense.

If the ships meant to gain the harbor and fire directly into the city, they must pass through or over the floating booms of logs chained together, and then dodge floating torpedoes. And there were the two slow but heavily armed ironclads.

My engineering friend Charles was involved in the design and manufacture of some of the torpedoes and later asked me to help in making them. We shared a secret about that, which I will tell you later.

The town was aware of impending battle, and when the show

began, those who were not preparing the town's defenses went to the rooftops of buildings near the harbor to view the scene. I was among them, and could see out to Sumter from the waterfront behind the battery near White Point Gardens. I stood with civilians in the cool air. Some had telescopes or opera glasses.

We could barely see the ships trying to form a line of battle, but the flagship ironclad with masts had some difficulty, which delayed deployment of the fleet and caused confusion before the first shots were finally fired.

We saw puffs of smoke before we heard the reports. When the cannon began in earnest, the boom-boom-boom began to fall over itself – a sustained rolling bass like distant tympani drums struck by drunken demons.

Later the newspapers told us more than two thousand shots were fired at the attacking squadron, with more than five hundred striking their targets. Pity the men in these ringing tins of iron!

The sea tide as well as the tide of battle began to turn against the Federals and finally the attack was cancelled. Several Union ships were badly damaged; indeed, one sank and later its fine guns were recovered by an expedition from Charleston.

My Rebel friends cheered as the fleet withdrew, and I must admit to my embarrassment that I did, too.

But did they think the Federals would not try again?

Murphy's was lightly crowded that evening as most of the younger men were far away. There was much discussion among the men there of the day's events. Desperate bravado seemed the tone that night; statements made of how defenses of the city would always prevent invasion as had been proven twice by then, and would forever guarantee the town's safety. This was forlorn hope even among those victory-talkers, as more and more of the city's people were moving away, some to other countries.

In the tavern I met Policeman Kerry, whose mother I rescued from the fire more than a year earlier. He and another associate were "out of uniform," as it were, having placed on the bench beside them their hats and their coats with military insignia. Otherwise it was

242

considered bad form for the city's guards to sit in a dark saloon and drink.

"Jon, me son," said Kerry in his booming lilt, slightly in his cups, "Where are you off to now?" He knew I was always on the move.

"Another delivery for your friend Tyrone," I replied. "Long Island."

I asked about his mother, and he told me with welling eyes that she had passed the week before. His tone was reverent as he spoke of her.

She had lived in some rural part of Ireland I had never heard of, Kil-something, and spoke the Irish language her whole life. She and her husband farmer had had four children, three of them sons, working their little acre and digging peat from the bog.

Until the potato famine – the Great Hunger – they lived a happy enough life, if one of no luxury. One son went into the army, one studied for the church away in Dublin. The officer I knew was the youngest of the three boys and was sent away at eighteen when the family was near starvation. A cousin had called him to come to the New World.

When he told me this, he looked away, cleared his throat and quietly sang the slow and sad tune:

> *So pack up your sea-stores, consider no longer,*
> *Ten dollars a week is not very bad pay,*
> *With no taxes or tithes to devour up your wages,*
> *When you're on the green fields of Americay.*

Like many thousands of Irish he passed across the ocean to America. Most sailed to Philadelphia, New York, Boston, Baltimore, some to New Orleans and Charleston, and spread all over America. I had seen some of the Irish immigrants near the docks when I was a child, and my mother kept me from getting close to them. They were considered criminals and loafers, thieves. And worse in Boston: they were Catholic.

Kerry had come to Charleston, lived and stayed with his

uncle, working as a drayman just as I now was until a friend who joined the Charleston Guard told him he might work there too, being a big strong fellow. And so he became well established in America.

When he heard his father had passed away, he saved and borrowed money to pay his mother's way over. She had been living here for nearly three years.

He drew from his cup and turned his glowing sad eyes to me.

"She never wanted to learn the English. She said it was the language of the oppressors." He took another deep draught.

"Jonathan, in her final hours she spoke of the angel sent by St. Michael to save her that night."

Now that was a singular feeling, to have a man tell you that his mother's last thoughts were of yourself, as an angel.

"She thought of you 'till the end."

He pulled up a nearby chair and I slumped into it by his side. The big man put a heavy arm on my shoulder and gently wept.

After a moment, "Best keep moving. The home guard has been told to keep an eye out for you in particular."

I completely understood, though it was a violation of Kerry's duty to tell me this. Perhaps they thought there was more Spanish gold from me. Women and children had been advised to leave the city earlier. At first it was largely ignored, now Charleston was getting more dangerous. The city's population had thinned out and was overwhelmed by soldiers being trained, deployed, healed, or buried.

I knew Tyrone would continue to employ me, would not reveal me to the authorities. He paid me little, but could have paid much less with my situation as an anonymous fugitive to hold over me.

I thanked the officer, finished my tankard, and returned to my corner in the warehouse, back into the shadows.

Next morning I went to Tyrone's house to plan the next day's early delivery, timed best to evade observation.

I walked with circumspection through the edges of the town avoiding anyone and made my way down Elliott Street. The live oak leaves were glowing green and threw dappled shade beneath the bright branches. I hoped to take a short lunch with Isabella. I had not seen her for more than two weeks, and I admit to longing for her.

Usually her days were taken by going about her duties of managing the servants and shopping whatever was available for her households, checking the three houses under her charge, ensuring servants still living there were keeping to their duties, minimal as they were, and that the houses were kept clear of squatters.

During this period some plantation families who had moved away left field hands and house servants behind. Many were being sold to plantations inland and upcountry while they could still bring a good price, and many slave families were leaving their parents, cousins and grandparents.

Some servants tending houses for absentee masters had invited one or two of their "cousins" to live with them, at least for a while.

Isabella did not turn them out unless she thought them untrustworthy. Their presence inhibited scavengers from stripping the house of any remaining metal or furniture as had happened to so many of the fine old homes of Charleston. Besides, they were simply seeking temporary shelter from whatever storms they feared in their own world.

As do we all.

Isabella was in the kitchen in the early afternoon and answered that door with a knife held behind her back. When she saw it was me, she put down the knife and welcomed me into her arms. We held each other for several minutes saying nothing, sharing familiar warmth.

I told her of my planned delivery to the north of the city, which would take me away for some time. We embraced again, and she felt my need.

She was ever kind and thoughtful to me, to everyone really, and she went out to speak with the kitchen servant as I waited in the pantry.

She smiled as she returned to me, beautiful. Her scar, blazing red, didn't bother me. It was just a part of her I was growing to love.

The sun was bright that April day.

This woman had found me. She had borne burdens beyond the ken of most men, and had been battered by oppression of the heart, through chance and circumstance, and then by her own husband. She was abandoned in a strange land. What little harbor could I give her?

Yet her kindness persisted. Her good humor was quiet and distant, yet the urges of goodness were strong within her heart.

She took my hand and led me upstairs to her bedroom, and in that glowing spring afternoon awash in greening sunlight rippling into her chamber, she untied her apron, stepped out of her shift, took me in her arms, and Isabella loved me.

Late that evening I oversaw the loading of the mule cart for the next day's delivery. Well before dawn Jacob's young son Eli and I hitched the pair and began the journey to Long Island.

Eli was about twelve years old and tall for his age. His figure was nearly that of a mature man, and his manner was steady, less unruly than his departed older brother Esau.

The roads were fairly busy until we crossed the Cooper River, and then the Wando where I presented my papers from Tyrone, just like a slave would have to present his badge and orders. The guards at the ferry and bridges eyed me in my civilian clothes with disgust, or perhaps envy.

We arrived before sundown, and the delivery was to Jacob who had work up there. He agreed to employ me as an overseer, mostly for appearances as I was handling brick more than men. He gave orders to his crew of six and returned to Charleston in Tyrone's wagon with his son. The city had much masonry work to repair and build even beyond the nightly repairs on Sumter, and the area of the great fire never did get rebuilt in those days.

The plantation overseer where we worked was a short, stout German. He spoke good English, though he used a syntax that I thought was often humorous. I chose not to describe it as such to him or anyone else. We were building a new outbuilding. The owners were still confident of Southern victory despite the apparent determined opposition from the giant nation to the north with its limitless resources of men, equipment, and a growing resolve.

I was there for two weeks when Tyrone sent a message that he had another more exotic assignment for me.

*   *   *

Another night fell on my Uncle Jonathan. Nine o'clock was late for a centenarian, and I told him I would return the next day. Indeed, his story would not be available for anyone to hear in a very few years; he a young man during the War Between the States, and now so very old.

As I walked back to my bed I looked up at the unchanging stars between the trees and tried to imagine what my choices would have been in the days of Jonathan's youth. I was born in a Southern state and knew nothing of the world north of Virginia.

I suppose I would have joined the fight, and not for the freedom of men, but in defense of my country.

Uncle Jonathan was a man out of his world. He adopted the one where he lived and yet could see it from an outside perspective.

And now he saw that world of war from a great distance of eighty years.

The next morning we walked around the home for a few minutes for his daily exercise before taking our seats in the parlor.

His eyes were glistening bright as he spoke, clear and crisp; a direct channel of memory to me.

*   *   *

SECTION THREE

STEALTH AND DASH

40

SEARCH BY SMOKE

Given all the other conditions, it is amazing how accurate the shot was.

I was deep in an early morning reverie, preparing my pipe on the pitching deck amidst the spray, clouds pressing down on the ocean and seas rolling at about four feet. A five-pound ball of iron flying two feet by your head can quickly draw your attention on the present. My reflection on my past few days vanished in an instant.

But I got ahead of myself.

Tyrone had called me back from the masonry job on Long Island and sent me to sea on a shopping expedition.

He competed for the best merchandise from the blockade runners but had difficulty getting it. Tyrone paid agents to bring in tinned hams but would instead get back spoiling salted bacon. He requested bolts of fine silk cloth and was brought hogsheads of black cloak buttons. Once he paid for any fashionable items women could wear and was brought bundles of white kitchen aprons. And he would have to bid for other imported smuggled goods with other shop owners, especially the ones owned by the Jewish families along King Street.

He decided to send his own agent and he knew I was eager to get out from under the eyes of recruiters.

I slipped in to see Isabella before I left. I kept to the evening shadows. She expected me and wore that dress from the magic nights in North Carolina, the cotton floral print in blue and black. She let me in and we went to her room. We quietly shed our clothes and went to bed and loved, she quieter than usual and holding me gently as if I was fragile. When I awoke that night and again early the next morning she was not asleep, just quietly cradling me against her breasts.

I rose and dressed. I kissed her goodbye before dawn.

I knew I would miss her sweet caresses. I still do.

There was lots of activity at the port in Charleston the morning before we left for the British colonial town of Nassau, far to the south. That city was making lots of money as a transshipping center between Europe and the Confederacy.

Our ship was loading on the Cooper docks. Hundreds of bales of pressed cotton and great skeins of hemp swung onboard by cranes and tackle, and the muscles of the Negroes. Workers moved methodically from long practice, slaves and freemen overseen by white foremen.

It was from this dock that the steamer *The Planter* had been stolen by Robert Smalls and Esau Johnson the previous year.

Our boat was named *Gawain*. Long and low to the water with sidewheels about midships. Its graceful structure reminded me of a racehorse, or perhaps a greyhound. In fact, I think there was a blockade runner named *Greyhound* at one time. But really with all the cotton piling up it was more like a pack mule, filled and stacked with bales and casks of turpentine. It was also loaded with coal from two different warehouses, and the water tank was topped off.

The ship was painted a dull gray to blend in with sea mists, and its retractable smoke stack could reduce its height profile.

The last time I rode a seagoing vessel I was nearly killed under a mountain of water, and on landing found myself marooned, bereft of family and sweetheart in a land preparing for war. I boarded that gray craft with trepidation.

I suppose the cruise was daring, though it was seen by millions of my countrymen as simply illegal.

250

Heavy, dense cotton bales from the steam press were hoisted atop one another onto the deck of the ship until the boat resembled something like an Alp.

As the light grew dim that cloudy afternoon I saw the workers perform a task I had never witnessed. The bales were being fumigated. But it wasn't to kill weevils or chase roaches out from the dense fiber bundles; this was to strangle human stowaways with rank smoke and force them out and on deck. The fumigation crew carried long poles to prod victims among the cotton bales. Metal boxes with smoldering fabric and leaves inside were carried around the ship, and while one man used a bellows to force air through the box another directed the smoke through a sort of stovepipe. It shot the choking fumes into the spaces where it turned out men could and did hide.

One man squirmed out, dusty, coughing and spitting, and was taken by a Citadel cadet detail with a rough sergeant. I wondered whether he went back to his barracks and whatever punishment was given deserters trying to get out of the country.

I wonder what punishment they would have given me.

But my papers from Tyrone were in order today. There was little interference with those on task of running the blockade.

And then voices gasped from between some more of the bales, and two haggard looking men in soldier's uniforms staggered forward. How they were able to secrete themselves between the huge blocks of cotton without being crushed to paste I cannot say, but there they were, hacking and struggling to breathe. They were held by the crew and taken ashore, joining the other. Were they all tried and imprisoned? I doubt it. Men were in short supply. I expect they were given muskets and sent north to fight alongside comrades who must have kept a wary eye upon them. Or maybe their comrades themselves later joined in an attempt to leave the hopeless war for home, or just away, maybe westward.

The search by smoke continued, and another figure roused from the cargo. He scrambled to the top of a bale and gasped. He was dressed better than the recruit, and it turned out it was Charles Gallard!

"Ahoy, Charles," I cried. He coughed, and waved. "What are

you doing?"

My friend lowered himself to the deck and walked toward me. "I was just checking to see if I could evade the procedure."

Two cadets from the Citadel walked over to take him in tow. He protested, "No, I have a ticket. I'm legitimate on this ship."

Charles retrieved a ticket from his coat, and one of the cadets examined it. The captain of the ship walked over, looked at it, and confirmed, "Yes, he's a passenger." With a cautionary glance at the legal stowaway the captain returned to his duties. The cadets seemed nonplussed and decided to return to the dock.

"Charles, you continue to surprise. Why are you going to Nassau?"

"I've got to choose some ordinance." He had been experimenting with new designs of torpedoes as well as performing his regular duties with artillery shells and charges. "I'm working on a special project. Perhaps we can talk on board, later." I remembered seeing him that day at the Mills House, discussing a mystery with the professor officer last autumn.

He hustled off to shore to change from his odiferous and smoke-stained clothes.

By sunset I had eaten a good meal and used the privy in anticipation of an overnight voyage. All passengers went aboard. They were mostly business men, though there were two mothers with children and a rather striking woman, a Mrs. Trent, traveling alone, supposedly to meet her husband who was already in the Bahama Islands. I would not call her buxom exactly, yet she had a remarkable profile from any angle. She carried herself in a way that would lead one to wonder about the details of her feminine physique, and many eyes followed her as she went below.

Everyone had been directed to wear only black at night – not even a handkerchief of white; no lights and no smoking were permitted on threat of immediate death. This sounded drastic and may never have been implemented, but truth is that any sign could have betrayed the presence of the *Gawain* to the blockading ships of war. It seemed incongruous with the rules of stealth that there was a lot of white cotton aboard.

Adventure it was, but in deadly earnest.

The captain gave the word, and the engine's fires were lit. The clean hard coal began to warm the boiler creating steam, which was directed to the piston and then to driving the wheels as the ship cast off its moorings. The sun had set hours before. It was totally dark except for the glow of lamps on the wharf and a few on nearby boats.

As we moved downstream on the river into the harbor bay I glanced back at the dock and saw Isabella standing near the warehouse near a lantern, watching our boat slowly drive to Sumter. Her face shone white in the lamplight beneath a slacked hood covering her scar.

I had told Isabella I'd be back, God willing, in less than a month. Some ships made the passage and back in less than a week. Some never returned. She had packed some food for me which I had taken aboard earlier. I watched her as she turned to stare at me with a stark capturing gaze, firm of chin, sorrow in her eyes.

I thought of her life, a pretty young woman marred with her trial by marriage, then while recovering something of a reputable station, marred again by fire and "defaced," as it were, and slipping to a state of desperate survival that led her to take even me as a companion. Me in my own low state.

Now she survived as a white serving girl with a bond of casual convenience to me, impossible to be called anything like marriage, and with no hope of anything better in life, no future beyond this. What a prospect!

And now even I was leaving her, if only perhaps for a few weeks.

I waved. She stood still and stared at us. This public yet deeply private scene struck me to the heart. I waved again and watched her standing as a statue as she shrank in my sight and finally was lost in the darking mist.

What was she seeing? What was she hoping?

How would she greet me when I returned?

From the stack came a very fine exhaust, not black and heavy as from the smaller boats running about the harbor. *Gawain* burned high quality coal imported from Wales or Canada. Some said it came from Pennsylvania. It provided little visible smoke, which helped blockade runners evade the telescopes of searching Federal ships.

Coal from the mines in Virginia, Tennessee and North Carolina is softer and smoky when burnt. Hard coal was valuable, like the guano from the Pacific islands was for the farms of South Carolina, far from such a source of concentrated fertilizer. I wonder if they use Pacific guano in Wales.

The view of a darkened city from the deck of a boat passing into danger is thrilling. Not good really, but thrilling.

We passed by Sumter, the fortified outpost in the harbor whose walls and battlements had by then been pounded to rubble by the bombardment of Federal warships. Cannons still protruded from the dark mass, perhaps more imagined than visible as we cruised past the ruining citadel. Every few weeks the Federals (my brothers!) would pour shot and shells onto that manmade shoal, reducing its brick walls ever more. Yet there was a garrison of men on Sumter, and their flag flew. Each night workers came to the island for repair. Soldiers rotated in and out to keep watch. They lived a ragged life in tunnels dug in the foundation of that artificial island made of broken bricks atop New England granite.

Perhaps each of us digs our own tunnels to hide in.

A hooded lantern blinked a signal; our ship replied, then came darkness and silence, save for splashes of water on the hull, the rhythmic throb of the engines, and the electric whispering of passengers. Our darkened *Gawain* swept into a sea of hidden warships.

No smoking was allowed. The glowing tip of a lit cigar could be the beacon that revealed us to blockading Federal vessels. It could raise a cry, "Look! A runner heading out!" to sell cotton, and to bring needed food, materiel, and weapons to continue the war. To kill loyal Americans.

All non-crew were ordered below and to remain silent until the ship had passed the cordon of blockading ships. This was a part of General Winfield Scott's "Great Snake" or "Anaconda." The plan was devised by the venerable old commander of the U. S. Army who convinced President Lincoln at the start of the war that the South's seaports could be blockaded and strangled, as if by a great constrictor snake. Squadrons of ships, he said, would end the sea trade of the rebellious states and prevent their supply from friendly interests in Europe.

It wasn't completely effective as three out of four times the blockade runners made it out and safely returned. But it certainly added a level of danger. After all, those Federal ships were armed and the blockade runners were not.

The crews manning the runners were mostly English or Scottish or other foreigners, though I think I identified more than one adventurous New England Yankee posing as Irish or Welsh. I wonder what they might have thought of me.

Our crew was all dressed in black or dark gray. The captain had run ships to and from Nassau four times since the war had begun. And because of earlier service for the government in Washington, he had long been very familiar with shifting sandbars, tidal patterns of the inlets, tactics of the blockaders, and the quantity of money he made every voyage. All was paid in Yankee gold or British sovereigns and deposited in a British Colony bank.

The captain had been a coastal surveyor in the U. S. Navy for a decade before the war began and had offered his services to command a warship for the Federal government. He was deemed by a clerk in Washington too old at sixty-two years to command, and was rejected. Perhaps his sensibilities were hurt. His vigorous nature would not let him rest, so he was hired by a firm that would pay him handsomely to employ those skills he had so completely developed.

All lights on Fort Sumter were quenched, or at least shuttered so that the silhouette of our ship would not eclipse a lantern's glow when viewed from the deck of a blockader out to sea.

We passed out of the harbor, and the ship's master directed the steersman as we wove over the changing channels through the sand bars.

We turned up Maffitt's Channel to the north, easing along Sullivan's Island past Fort Moultrie and up the coast. Our boat was not racing but making quiet swift headway in gloomy mist. After cruising carefully northward we turned to the open sea about three in the morning with no sign of a horizon, nor of a pursuer.

Federal ships were out there, but were invisible that black night.

The *Gawain* could sail in as little as eight feet of water depth. The Federal boats had much deeper drafts and coming within a quarter mile of shore was a risk. Several in past months had been grounded, leaving them open to the guns of Forts Moultrie, Johnson, or Sumter.

I wrapped myself in a dark oilskin cloak and rose to the deck.

The oilskin was warming and the sea not too rough. I felt rocked in a cradle of gray on an ocean of black, with the heartbeat of engine throbbing beneath me. I drifted to sleep on deck with sky above me and plumbless deep below. I awoke in the early fading gloom wishing the sun would hurry into the May sky so I could safely light my pipe.

The journey from port to port can take as little as thirty-two hours, but using our circuitous route of evasion we didn't expect to see Nassau for three days.

I have seen the sun rise from the ocean many times in my life. That time, as black faded to gray, I knew light would make our craft visible, this mountainous pile of cotton driving even more eastward now.

And that is when the early morning cannon ball thumped into cotton beside my head. I mentioned this earlier.

A Federal ship had fired a shot ahead of our craft earlier to order us to halt, but I never heard nor saw that one.

The marksman on the blockading ship put his missile on board the rocking, cruising platform well over a mile distant, to near where I had been resting. That seemed to me really quite a feat.

My primary reaction was to duck.

The distant crack of the cannon arrived shortly, and I looked around at my fellow passengers in the early dim light to see their reactions.

"It must be the 'crack of dawn,'" quipped Charles, who had

stepped nearby.

I saw crewman and passengers in various positions of collapse, alarm, and crouch, except for the ship's master employing a telescope, the first mate steady at the wheel, and the young matron Mrs. Trent on deck in a dark blue frock. She stood quite erect and boldly followed the gaze of the captain toward the other ship. The bleary dark shape of a pursuing Federal blockader was becoming more defined.

We were all aware of the danger of the passage, though when a piece of hurtling metal came among us our emotions became something more than a simple thrill.

Some men in a chase like this would become anxious, furtive. Some would act angrily. The captain acted as if this was normal procedure and spread his cool confidence among his crew and passengers. Perhaps in his world of chase and evasion this is regular rote of action.

The sun broke from the clouds and bathed the Federal ship in a celestial glow. It seemed to glint from it. I watched its light sweep in progress across the shaded waves between the Yankee boat and our own like a drape being pulled from a window.

The ship was definitely closer.

"She'll be within easy range soon, Captain."

As the sailor spoke, I saw a flash of fire from the other ship. As I watched, a puff of smoke in the distance dashed away from its side. Then we heard the crying shriek as a ball sped past close to our bow.

"Fine shooting," stated the captain.

A passenger named Jones was having none of this praise. "Captain, we cannot countenance cannon fire! We must surrender! There are women aboard!"

Mrs. Jones was made of sterner stuff. "Hush, Willie. Let the captain do his work."

Then Mrs. Jones stood on tip-toe to view the pursuing ship. She was dressed in white that morning, and Willie stood beside her, crouching and shielding their daughter. The ten-year-old struggled to get a glimpse of the attacker.

The captain moved serenely to the very bow of the ship and

trained his glass upon the sea before him. Charles and I watched the approaching craft as the sun slowly climbed toward its zenith.

More shots followed. Charles spoke, and I listened to his soliloquy of muzzle velocity, ballistic arcs, how cannon barrels are rifled to improve aim, and even of methods of gunpowder storage. How does one learn all these things? When broken into the abstract, the flying iron around our boat was not so frightening, except when another thudded into one of the large bales of pressed cotton on deck.

"More coal," commanded the captain, "more pressure."

The sun hung like a beckoning lantern higher above the eastern horizon.

The Federal bow-chaser barked again, and the ball splashed a few yards to the side.

Everyone was ordered below deck, and I complied. The well-proportioned Mrs. Trent remained above to converse with the captain and he allowed her company.

"Two points starboard," called the captain, and the wheel turned.

The *Gawain* responded and became more lively.

We had almost no exhaust coming from the boiler burning the heavy and expensive Welsh or Pennsylvania coal. Its cost depended on prices from coal smugglers plying between Northern ports and Bermuda or Halifax, then to Nassau. Lower grades of coal released plumes visible for miles, easy to spot by the blockaders who constantly searched for tell-tale smoke.

Our ship the *Gawain* was designed in Liverpool for invisibility as much as was possible. It was low to the sea and painted like fog, though its cargo of cotton bales bulked its profile. It was powered by a large steam plant that drove sidewheels, which allowed fine maneuverability in port and pretty good speed on a calm sea, about twelve knots. But it was not really a match for some of the Federal blockading fleet, loaded as it was.

The captain had no choice but to run further east for the open sea. We were given chase and the pursuing ship was gaining.

I heard the captain call for "cotton," which when soaked in

turpentine can replace coal as the fuel for the boiler, and can quickly increase the temperature of the boiler. We carried an unlimited supply of cotton and about four hundred barrels of turpentine.

There is always a danger of disaster on a ship driven by fire, especially if it carries a cargo of turpentine. Breaching the first keg of the liquid added a dimension of risk, and running the steam drive at a temperature and rate of motion beyond its design heightened the thrill. I think there weren't any folks aboard who enjoyed this level of excitement. I went below, more to avoid the immediate challenge of the contest than for any other reason.

As the rhythm of the motor increased, I heard a "thump," which I guessed was another shot from the other boat, once more hitting its mark, though I hoped only absorbed again in one of the bales above. It is amazing to me that the gunner could estimate the range, elevation, and motion of his and our ships to the degree that he could place the ball aboard us.

I heard deep splashes as the engine shafts whined at a higher pitch, and sidewheels thrashed the waves.

The steely Mrs. Trent came below with a wild grin, her eyes glowing with the rush of her blood. "The captain is lightening the ship by casting adrift some of the cotton! What a chase!"

Yes, what a chase.

She was more elated than concerned. To lighten the load the captain ordered bale after bale cast overboard; thousands of dollars bobbing in the open sea. I wonder sometimes what became of those cotton rafts, the result of hundreds of hours of planting, tilling, harvesting, ginning. I expect some that may have drifted close to shore were salvaged and sold, slightly the worse for wear. The others, thousands over the period of the war, perhaps became homes for seabirds and comfortable fiber for nests.

Our ship was less lofty now, like a snowdrift melting in spring sunlight.

As each ton of fine cotton was set adrift the speed of the straining *Gawain* increased, though the pursuers were still gaining.

I returned to the deck and witnessed the quiet efficiency of the crew as they dumped the cotton overboard A trail of white treasure bobbed in our wake. The smoke stack was hot and poured a radiant heat to the sky as wheels churned the water. A band of cloud appeared on our port beam, and the sky seemed to have grown darker. By then the day was progressing toward noon.

Another shot flew overhead missing *Gawain* by more than a hundred feet.

The Federal warship was growing larger, and I could see the bow wave, white against the dark sea.

The captain changed course again, and drove us more northerly, still eastward. The engine drove yet faster.

Another bale splashed sternward.

Like all blockade runners, *Gawain* had no arms other than the captain's revolver which could easily be dropped overboard. Any blockade runner captured with arms aboard could be charged with piracy, and the attendant penalties involving twisted hemp were not worth the slim chance of winning a battle of arms against a U.S. warship.

"Six more bales, from the bow," ordered the captain.

The heavy bales were dragged and levered into the waves, and bobbed in our wake as *Gawain* shuddered to a faster pace.

With increased speed of the engine, danger of boiler explosion also increased. A boiler explosion in the open sea could mean only doom for most all on board. But that was the challenge.

This was the cost of profit.

The lightening of the load had a dramatic effect. The disk of the sun crested to zenith. In a few more moments we finally could see the result of the captain's orders.

Our pursuer was falling behind.

"It's the Drift," said Charles. I glanced at him and saw him smiling, raising that eyebrow to a high altitude.

The captain of the Federal vessel also recognized he was failing and turned the broad side of his ship to ours. Flashes and smoke rippled along its side. Seconds later larger shot landed in the water to our rear, not well aimed. We had drawn out of range, and our lead was growing.

"He crossed the stream of the North Atlantic Drift," said

Charles. He told me that a stream of warm water flowing from the Gulf of Mexico up to England travels about three knots faster than the water closer to the coast. Our captain had played the following ship and had timed our path to use this speed advantage to boost us away and out of range.

I have never been good at reading the sea.

As a youth I passed the wharfs of Boston with their tall masted ships loading at the docks, stevedores wresting the world's goods into my hometown. Loitering boys along the wharf known as harbor "chucks" would offer to work, maybe getting jobs as stevedores themselves, or maybe as seamen. Some became cutpurses. And I'm sure by now some had joined the army, at least for the enlistment bonus.

The seamen I have known and shipped with could read the sea. They would watch the birds, clouds, fish and dolphins, the angle of the waves, slight changes in the roll of the sea. They could tell how far off we were from shore, or that a blow was coming.

The men on the deck of the *Gawain* went about their duties, no longer unlashing and rolling bales overside, but trimming the tiller, looking to our pursuers, and to the sky, to the sea.

I could not see invisible signs these sailors can read.

A falling mist joined the spray from below. The sea, the sky, the air all were becoming water. I briefly wondered if since there was water in the air, was there air in the water? Not much, I think. I suppose in seltzer.

The scene was eerie. The gently falling rain dampened the deck and spitted off the stack of the engine. Fire in the boiler roared distantly, the wheels beating water. The crew stood attentive like statues, watching their work as the wind pulled at their coats. Any danger of being seen by a pursuer quickly faded in gray rain.

As the rain fell harder the captain directed the ship to turn three points to the south, more toward the Bahama chain of islands. As I made to go below deck the indomitable Mrs. Trent was alighting holding her umbrella aloft, so I stood aside. She went directly to the captain. I moved toward them as he shared that he had positioned us

261

for running to the drifting stream that pours from the Gulf of Mexico up the coast and eventually to Europe and the land of Vikings, as Charles had deduced. This is apparently common knowledge among blockade runners. It is effective but takes the boat off course and can delay the voyage for days.

The rain was a blessed extra from heaven obscuring our flight.

On deck we were of gay spirits, and some spirits flowed freely. The sailing crew was not as free as we passengers.

Finally a blurry sun touched the sea and began to squash as it sank. Darkness came upon the deep, *Gawain* changed course to the south and reduced speed to conserve fuel.

The captain switched to the cheaper coal and insisted on all lights out and dark clothes only. And silence.

We went to our berths early, glad for the day's salvation, yet anxious to see what the new day would bring. I was sick on that voyage, queasy anyway, but from mortal danger, not from wave motion this time.

I would return to my reverie that evening and pondered my life, the choice before me. Yet another choice that would mean the world to me, to Isabella, to others. My world, and their worlds.

The night was clearing now, another black watch on the barren sea, dark but for the lively starlight, an occasional falling star, and the imagined distant, dim sense of breaking shoals.

God looked out for us that day as He had done the previous night and would the following week. But I hope I never grow to count solely on Him.

*　　*　　*

Uncle Jonathon was tired, and I let him pass into sleep. I gathered my notes and as I left his room, I noticed a small wooden box on the shelf by his bed. I could have looked inside it, but I thought his privacy should be granted. I couldn't give him much at his age, but I could give him that.

*　　*　　*

41

NAUTICAL LIMITS

The next morning was windy, a beautiful clear day made more beautiful by the lack of an enemy ship looking for our blood. In fact, the blockading fleet and the U.S. ships in international waters did not want to sink the blockade runners but wanted capture. Each member of the capturing crew would get a portion of the value of the cargo and a portion of the price of the ship when sold.

The earlier diversion into the northerly drifting stream had pushed us a hundred or more miles off course. As we fought our way against the current southward we had burned much of the softer, smokier coal while working our way toward the islands. Now we were down to the last of the expensive smokeless coal, as we plied into the sailing routes between Europe and Nassau.

The traffic on that route flew many flags, though no ships were in sight this morning. On deck, Charles was lounging with a bale of rope for a pillow and writing something in a tiny journal or booklet he carried aboard with him.

"Charles."

"Hello, Jon. Uneventful escape yesterday."

He had a childish light of mischief in his eyes, though you would think a man of thirty-three years would have had the child burnt out of him by that age.

"Are you escaping the South?" I asked. He carried nothing with him, it seemed, except for a stout, short coat and the small booklet and pencil.

He folded the book away. "No, Jon, sometimes a man needs a little adventure. I am afraid South Carolina will always be my home, for good or ill."

His face was still a bit smudged from the smoke the dock guards forced into the spaces between the cargo. As the light grew the smoke stains shaded his face, and it looked like shadows in a Dutch portrait from a Paris museum.

I said, "There are battles a bit to the north giving more adventure than many men want." I did not wish to tempt him to those, though.

"Oh, cat and mouse," he told me. "Hide and seek. Diversion, decoy, deception. That's the kind of adventure I'm after. I want nothing to do with murder." Philosopher, him.

As morning passed into dull afternoon, Charles napped under a piece of sail cloth on deck. I took what rest I could in my cabin. Passengers ate a bite, cold ham and cornbread. The sailors had their own mess. I don't know what.

Passengers and crew came on deck to take the sun and for relief from the cramped quarters and the smells below. Sunlight glanced off the waves, and it seemed a happier world. During the past night the seas had been a bit rougher, and some passengers were ill. Now there was less of a chop and the sailing seemed nearly pleasant.

One of the crew cried, "Sail ho!" as he spied a form on the northwestern horizon, black against the blue.

The captain walked the deck and looked at the shape with his spyglass. "Federal."

Two leagues off our starboard quarter an American frigate showed its colors. She began to advance. The southwest wind was in her favor on this course, and our engines were burning coal judiciously. Our supply was growing low.

The captain swore an oath plainly, without care whether the gentler sex heard him. A mother shook her head reproachfully and her little girl's eyes widened as she smiled.

"Full ahead," ordered the captain. "Bear southwest."

We felt the wheel shift us to a new course as the rhythm of the engine increased and the boat surged ahead.

The ship was a regular racehorse, even with a heavy load of cotton.

Though I represented an owner I did not venture to voice an opinion. My estimation of the crew had risen through the decisive action of the day before and I was inclined to respect their judgement.

The weather was brisk and clear. The tops of the waves blew mist in our faces if we peered over the gunwales.

The ten-year-old girl was a joy of inquisition as she crawled and leapt over the steamer, now bereft of high piles of cotton bales towering above though still well loaded. Her mother occasionally called her to heel, but often let her run amok as perhaps she had done herself when a youth.

"Helm aweather!" called the captain, and the ship was redirected into the wind from the west-southwest, continuing into the regular shipping routes followed by lawful transports from that other British colony of Bermuda. We did, in fact, espy another ship flying the King's ensign and laid a course following her. She was a small sloop, perhaps a messenger, but with her British Union colors aloft we strove to keep pace with her, she flying across the wind and making good time. Perhaps we should be adjudged a convoy.

The masted Federal frigate could not sail well into the wind. The small dispatch vessel did not care so much. She pressed on in the gleaming sun, dashing sparks off the curlers and strode out of sight, as the other sinister ship (my brothers!) endeavored to close with our boat.

U.S. ships patrolled waters far beyond the nautical boundaries of the continent. They could legally stop and board any ship they thought was from the Confederacy, as it would be an American ship to their thinking.

The captain swept the glass across the horizon completely around the circle and held it at due east. I looked that way as did all on board, fearing yet another pursuer.

We saw the tall forms on the horizon, but the captain saw them better. When he had determined the nature of the ships he collapsed his prospect glass and turned to his mate. The sailor turned, spoke briefly to the man at the wheel and went below, returning with a folded cloth. He bent the material to the flagstaff, and a large red flag sailed on the wind. It was the Red Ensign of a British merchantman.

Well, we all knew we weren't British or even under their protection, and that this deception was illegal by any laws of the seas we had ever heard of, but I learned it was not an uncommon ruse.

The British government did not like this, but the idea that a ship flying this flag would likely not be molested by ships of the U.S. Navy was a tempting ploy for blockade runners in dicey waters.

Gawain turned its prow to match the bearings of the distant specks of ships on the horizon.

The Federal ship strove to come closer. I have no doubt that the captain of the U. S. frigate was completely aware of our situation and the trick our captain was playing. Ever since the international embarrassment over the Mason and Slidell incident, when two Confederate diplomats were forcibly removed from a British mail packet early in the war, U.S. captains were very careful approaching a sovereign nation's ship, especially if it flew a British flag. That incident nearly a caused war between the United States and the United Kingdom, which might have guaranteed the South's independence.

Once burnt, twice shy.

The Federal ship struggled to keep its distance against the wind, until *Gawain* was within half a league of the British convoy, but then turned and withdrew, no doubt in disgust.

Late that afternoon, long after the Yankee (I still shudder to use that term in such a way!) left us, we left the British convoy without officially signaling to them.

Night was falling again. The captain slowed the ship until the quarter moon rose warm from the sea. White islands of sand and palms drifted by as the last of the anthracite coal was burnt.

We returned to gently applied cotton fuel until finally a day later we limped slowly and smokily into Nassau harbor.

42

JEWELS AND OBSCURE EQUIPMENT

Have you ever been to Nassau? Well, I'm sure it's different now.

We were a steamboat among a few others, but also among many small local sailing craft. Some of these were rigged with the roughest of spars and booms, seemingly hacked alive from local forest trees, bark attached.

Native Negro freemen fished in boats driven by wind and sail, maintaining them as they could in a functioning and unrefined manner. They cut the branch, they rigged the ship, they sailed the bay.

Yes, they were crude and homely. They caught the fish, they fed their families.

The number of boats and ships filling the harbors was astounding. There may have been war and boys dying in America but in the Bahamas, folks were living high.

Our craft was modern, sleek, swift. Our captain was intelligent and clever. Our cause was mercenary, maybe even immoral, and we had arrived.

We waited our turn to get a slot on one of the docks. Charles and I jumped to the dock and walked up the street as the cotton winches began their toil, loading onto waiting float trucks and their teams of mules or horses. We went to our hotel and I slept. Charles was gone when I awoke.

My goal was the banking house Tyrone used.

It was an amazing walk past the line of ships loading and unloading, and through streets filled with vendors and warehouses. Every imaginable item was available, and lots I had never imagined.

Boston had merchandise from all over the world, but I think Nassau had goods from the moon and Mars.

One shop had every type of liquor on earth, including what they called "Oozoo" from Greece, and they offered the finest whiskey made in a cave in remote Hebrides. There were even some of the exotic liquors I had sampled in cafes and saloons of Paris.

A dealer of firearms was apparently doing a brisk trade in exotic and elaborate fowling pieces including some from Japan or China. In a glass case he had an assortment of silver- and gold-chased dueling pistols.

Imagine fine weapons created to be used in civilized dueling, when the great duel of nations was happening less than two days' sail to the north. They were elaborate and pretty, these jewels of death.

Shops dealt in drugs from Holland and India, cloth from Luxembourg, spices from Anatolia, wine from Burgundy, Italy, Spain, and of course Madeira.

One shop had all manner of leather goods piled in neat disarray in a fragrant deep and dark warehouse, the rendered flesh of bovines, pigs, sheep, and other animals I could not recognize. Belts, shoes, fine English saddles, riding crops, even coats. What beautiful carnage!

I purchased a woolen coat for myself similar to those worn by the crew of our ship, and I found a shop with toothbrushes. I had lost mine long ago and my oral health had suffered. I bought two dozen and would give some to the family of Jacob Johnson.

The sign on one business proudly stated that it had Yankee hams, salted and smoked in New York City. Casks were being loaded into a cart attended by four Confederate soldiers. They weren't in uniform, but their military bearing, jargon, and accents proclaimed their origin.

A book vendor had several editions of northern newspapers and periodicals less than a week old, and I purchased some.

Several U.S. sailors were in the streets unaware of or oblivious to citizens of their enemy country. British were everywhere, and the streets were filled with the accents of London, Liverpool, Glasgow, and the native sounds of Bahamian Negroes, lilting and musical.

I heard some boisterous music and wandered to the site of it. The band was playing the most joyous and lively music with a trumpet, a sort of bass bugle, drums, and cymbals. It's the music of a festival in the Bahamas called "Johnny Canoe," their New Years' celebration, and it was apparently something to see. I regretted that I would miss it as we were to make sail at first opportunity.

The Bahamas is made up of mostly free blacks and "coloreds," as they called mixed-race people, with some white Europeans and Americans scattered in the commercial district.

The blacks and coloreds fished and worked the fields, though some had commercial businesses. I was told that during the "Johnny Canoe" celebration, the world was turned upside down, as they say, and common blacks were feted like kings!

England had abolished slavery in Britain and in all its colonies before 1820, so all the blacks at this port were free. Indeed, any slave from America or elsewhere who could make it to the Bahamas was instantly recognized by the British government as free.

Why was the United States so late? Not a real question: money. It was just too profitable to maintain this barbaric and obsolete institution, despite the higher goals of the American Constitution and Christian philosophy. So we had a war.

Hot food was available on the streets: fish and rice, fried pork, hashed meats and corn mush.

Oh, and spies were everywhere.

As I looked down alleyways leading off the main street, I could dimly see in the distance magic potions and dancing bears, maybe a fairy or ogre in the shadows. Observation down another alley surprised me with the sight of a very tall white woman with a towering head of crimson hair, standing in plain view of the city with the most brightly rouged lips, cheeks, and with bare breasts. I don't recall if she had a pretty face.

Yes, Nassau was a wonder in those days.

I was in that city for three weeks, mostly because the captain had to supply the ship, load more hard British coal, and wait for the dark of the moon. The cotton was sold and I was able to find some of what Tyrone wanted in silks, brandies, and carpets of all kinds and sizes from Turkey, Persia, and the looms of Belgium. The actual bank transaction was completed rapidly. The town made its money while it could.

While in town I visited a bit with expatriates of North and South, toured the shops, and learned the political news from home.

Many in the North were not pleased with the President's actions and blamed him for the death of tens of thousands. Some said, "Why can't we just let the South alone? We don't need them, and we can still buy their cotton." I didn't know the answer, but I know that many in Boston were solemnly committed to destroying the practice of slavery. Did they believe that enough to send tens of thousands of their sons and neighbors to their deaths?

Apparently so.

More than two weeks away from Isabella and I was growing restive. Living with a woman and sharing intimacies creates demand in a man's body. This is my own experience. I'm not speaking as a medical man.

I reminded myself that we weren't married and I had made her no promise. I owed her nothing, and she owed me nothing; we each just needed and used the company of the other.

I located the alley where the bare-breasted woman had been and found an establishment part-way down. I was told of it by a Pennsylvanian civilian at a tavern near the hotel.

My habits had long been solitary, and I admit to a callow nature regarding other people, especially the opposite sex. This may be the result of my dependence on my mother throughout the decade and more of my youth.

Though I do not see shyness as a vice, I find it can be inconvenient at times.

I walked into the house and was approached by an older white woman who spoke a British accent from what I guessed was a poorer district of London.

"Hello, sir. Can we offer you a cup of tea?" Her eyes were appraising my purse by regarding my clothes. I stammered a bit.

She yelled, "Jasmine!" I thought she was calling for the tea of which I had heard, not the flower, yet three girls came from a back room. One was a striking beauty of butterscotch complexion, chestnut hair, and bright green eyes. She wore a sheer bodice with nothing beneath other than that with which God had blessed her, a stunning sight.

I must admit I fled, embarrassed and ashamed. Yet still needy.

I returned to my hotel room alone.

My mind conjured images of the form of a lively and

beckoning Isabella in a soft haze of glowing oil lamps, in a warm mountain room far away.

After a few quick moments I was able to relax, and then I napped. I gave a silent thanks to the memory of the girl, and the hope of a more corporeal experience with her on my return. In her grace she had never refused me.

Later, as I wandered the streets, I saw the construction of a large and glorious cathedral underway, though it was called a Methodist church. The war profiteers were apparently soothing their souls by buying glory to God. Not a bad idea, I suppose, if you can't or don't want to stop the killing.

Charles had gone to some instrument shops and had some mysterious bundles of gadgets and obscure equipment. He had also arranged for some explosive powders and fluids, though he swore me to secrecy at that time. I think it's all right if I speak of it now. After all, that was more than seventy-five years ago. And besides, the other side won.

I asked him, "Well, Charles, will this help you win the war for the South?"

"Win?" he said. "Neither side will win."

Well, that wasn't an answer, but then it wasn't the right question. He was right, of course. The North lost hundreds of thousands, even more men killed and wounded than the grievous numbers lost by the South. But the Confederate government was eradicated. Charles was a philosopher.

On the way to the ship I picked up a few things for myself, and some gifts for friends.

I went into a jeweler's shop and debated buying something for Isabella. It could not be earrings or a necklace. She would look at herself in the mirror to see them and would be reminded of her disfigurement, the ruin of a once-pretty face. She had never accepted that she could be pretty again.

She was, though. I felt it every time I saw her.

As the craftsman tap-tapped at some jewelry item at his bench I looked at his offerings.

I wanted something she could see without using a mirror.

A ring?

I decided on a bracelet.

43

INTO THE NIGHT FOREST

We waited in Nassau for a cloudy night, but the weather held clear. Finally the moon was only a sliver, and we prepared for sea, as did several other runners. Most were bound for Wilmington as the cordon around Charleston had grown tighter.

Gawain was heavily loaded with munitions, barrels of beef, hundreds of bottles of wine, coffee and tea, bolts of wool and silk cloth, shoes, salt pork, soap, wheels of cheese, bundles of telegraph wire, medicines, shovels, olive oil, stationery, belt buckles, four barrels of sperm oil for shore signal lights. And one more unusual item: a handsome riding horse.

This horse was a fine chestnut gelding a bit over sixteen hands high and about three years old. I was told it was a gift, a "Dutch Warmblood." I had heard of warmbloods though I was unfamiliar with the breed. He looked like a strong and lithe horse. He was nervous on deck and would not like the sea swells, though he got his sea legs eventually. An attendant groom was with him at all times for the expected two-day voyage and did his best to keep him calm. That was very difficult later in the voyage. I wondered how he would react to cannon fire and I was to find out.

His final destination was secret, though I could only assume it was meant for an important government official, or perhaps a military officer.

I had the same small berth as that on the run out. I was able to acquire a case of coffin screws, which I knew were in great demand, and a small box of a dozen bottles of women's perfume from France. Each vial would be worth hundreds of Confederate dollars, or perhaps thirty in U.S. currency. I also bought an assortment of finely worked Belgian handkerchiefs, a small bundle of luxury compact enough to easily transport, and a quantity of tins of bicarbonate of soda needed by every cook in Charleston.

I put these items in my berth as I had no space dedicated to my private cargo except for my small bundle of clothing in my rucksack. The screws were not labeled as I believed superstitious crewmen might have thought something so ominous might not be a lucky cargo. The coffins I transported the previous fall showed the need for the screws, to keep the dead from rising in protest at their needless sacrifice. Best to seal the unholy mistakes of men in tight boxes. Bury them in the ground with honors, and leave them to the hungry earth.

The captain's cabin was, I was told, crammed with luxury goods of all kinds. There are advantages of being captain, though there was always the danger of capture and imprisonment, or even hanging if the captain was a former U. S. Navy officer.

We had re-coaled with enough smokeless hard coal from Wales or England for a round trip, and braced ourselves for the expected cat-and-mouse chase with blockading ships. I expect there were large fortunes made by English shipping companies bringing coal from Wales, England, and Canada to the storage dumps, then selling to the ravenous boilers running the secret journeys to America. I suspect there were some millions made from the hard Pennsylvania coal available at some depots.

About nine o'clock the big sidewheels eased us out into the channel. We crept north along the south coast of Hog Island to Rose Island, then northeast, finally slipping to the south around New Providence Island, north to the passage between Great Abaco and Grand Bahama. The boat turned to the shadowy open sea like a swift stag entering a night forest where wolves prowled.

Stars peeped out of the darkness as we left the lights of the city behind. A few lanterns were visible along the horizon. Mostly they were coastal boats of the islands, though we knew Federal pursuit waited for runners like ours to creep into the night for swift flight to resupply their enemies. Our pilot peered out toward the British lighthouses to find his course in the trackless waters.

Gawain's passengers were not the same as the voyage out, of course. They included a very relaxed veteran arms merchant or perhaps salesman who may have himself taken a shot or two, or perhaps a measure of grape. He was dressed in a hunter's coat, was full of bravado and went by the unlikely name of Kilcannon.

He spoke with a nervous lawyerly looking man obviously on his first run through the blockade. He glanced wide-eyed about him constantly. Two younger men stood in heroic poses. They appeared to be volunteers coming back from England or somewhere to join their brothers' war: more fuel for the fire.

The redoubtable Mrs. Trent was also aboard in a new traveling dress. She had perhaps eaten well and gained some girth about her waist over the past three weeks. There was lots of good food in Nassau, especially at the homes of the various European business interests and Confederate supporters, perhaps with discreet messages from foreign powers, or from industries, lovers, agents, and generals. The added thickness of her waist could, I suppose, have been bundles of messages, or documents. Or maybe she had found she could transport six or eight corsets for later sale.

Charles was early adeck, scribbling in a notebook figures, calculations, shapes and notes, figuring his measures for torpedoes and other devices.

We slowly passed distant watching patrol ships, if indeed they were on post there. The horse stood uneasily on his wooden turf, hooves clad in felt to silence his nervous stamping. After a few hours we slipped below decks as the engine's vibration lulled us to sleepiness, a nervous sleep for some. My feet rested on a case of coffin screws.

The morning dawned broad and calm. A pale vapor from our steam plant rapidly dissipated, as slight smoke from the hard coal rose nearly vertically. Our motion kept pace with the breeze as the exhaust lifted to scramble with other airs of the ocean.

Charles met me on deck after rolls and coffee. This reminded me of fare I enjoyed in early morning Paris. I mused that there were many thousands of Parisians there eating rolls, drinking coffee that morning, and even today that we will never hear of, nor they of us.

We spent a pleasant day discussing memories we carried back from the British colony: of the gay music and dancing of bands that would later play at their winter festivals, and the joy of the happy Bahamian families greeting their men as they brought their catches to port at dawn – simple joys desired by all people.

We lunched on smoked ham and fresh bread and I learned of Charles's dealings with some of the munitions traders. He had purchased new explosive materials and equipment for his torpedo experiments, wires and batteries and such, and some fabulous long-range exploding shells that had a timer. The shell could be set to explode after a specified period after leaving the muzzle of the cannon, thereby spreading a rain of metal fragments over enemy forces. It sounds gruesome, and its result was even worse than you might think. I'll tell you some of what I saw of it later if you have time.

To me, the most fascinating part of his expedition to the town was the contract for rockets. Rockets had long been used for illumination for night warfare. They were used during the original bombardment of Fort Sumter against Colonel Anderson's forces, and of course in the attack on Fort McHenry described by Francis Scott Key in his poem "The Star-Spangled Banner." They were also employed as signals by Federal ships in pursuit of blockade runners. Some ancient Chinese generals, as I recall, had used exploding rockets in warfare against their enemies, and more modern killing rockets were used in the late Mexican war. Some had been used at the Battle of Secessionville the previous year.

Charles had a similar idea that they could be used to carry a weapon into the ranks of Federal soldiers far from the Southern forces. He had discussed with me the theory of the rocket and had bought the ingredients and materials to produce an object that could carry an explosive charge many miles.

His idea was to build a rocket with a second level of ignition that would fire after the end of the primary flight that would push the exploding shell another distance. A rocket fired from, say, Richmond, could conceivably travel all the way to Washington and land a charge on top of the White House itself! Despite all his circles of heavy gun emplacements, troops, and flying cavalry, Mr. Lincoln may not have been safe from a rocket-borne shell from above!

By this time I felt I knew Charles well. He was not a harsh man. He would not have wished to inflict harm on anyone or even on any animal of any kind. He preferred fish to warm-blooded meat. His was a gentle soul, enthralled by the possibilities of technology and science. He was not a dangerous man of himself, though his ideas could be used by those willing to do harm. There are always warlike men eager to use science to defeat other men like themselves, even if in the process they destroy gentle people around them.

I occasionally saw Mrs. Trent with the other passengers and with the captain, charming them all. She was no doubt delightful company at a dinner party and quite a conversationalist. Despite the scents of the sea and the ship, there was a distinct aroma of spice about the woman, and she wore it like a summer pinafore; a cloud of careless joy surrounded her.

She stepped over to Charles and myself and began a light discussion on the social scene in Nassau. Charles was somewhat known in the upper circles of Charleston and Columbia as a free-thinking inventor and philosopher, and more importantly was from a respectable family, and usually dressed well. Her lively demeanor and range of voice was musical and rather hypnotic, and her eyes were a deep black. They flickered toward me every so often, to keep me in her trance as she poured her direct charm onto Charles.

I don't really recall the words she spoke, though I noticed that Charles told her of the munitions he was transporting, and that he worked on torpedoes and other explosives in Charleston Harbor – items that should not have been spoken of beyond official offices. She hinted she was interested in my presence on the runner, and I told her of my work as an agent of Tyrone. This seemed to satisfy her, though she made a comment, which could have been a reference to my old neighborhood of the South End in Boston. It was as if she read my hidden accent and knew my origins.

I realized her talents and finally recognized her as one of the valuable and able spies of the Confederacy. I doubt her name was Trent at all, perhaps having drawn that label from the Trent Affair, regarding the capture, imprisonment, and negotiated release by the British of Mason and Slidell.

She drifted away over to the two young recruits and shone her charms on them. "She is quite good at her profession," stated Charles. I nodded. "Had she stayed with us any longer, I would have revealed how many grains of powder I calculated for sharpshooter cartridges, and described the placement of the cannon on Morris Island."

We marveled at her effect on the helpless young soldiers-to-be as we shared a draft from Charles' demijohn flask, sweet French brandy such as a Mexican had once bought for me. Mrs. Trent then returned to discussions with the munitions dealer and then the small man in a short top hat who seemed quite flattered by her attention. I wondered what secrets he was sharing with that fair agent of the government of the Rebellion.

At least that's who I think she was working for.

The two of them strolled over to the horse and shared intimacies, her gentling voice calming both beasts.

44

MYSTERIOUS CRAFT

On the afternoon of our second day the *Gawain* kept to open sea and would approach Charleston from the north, the route we used when we were outward bound. Our lookouts reported a U.S. ship to the west, between us and our destination. We were fighting a headwind from the southwest. The sun was not yet low and our fuel was diminishing.

The Federal ship was running before the wind, its smoke flying ahead of it.

Charles came over to me and said, "At this rate of speed, if we turned southeast, the ship will catch us in about five hours."

So, by the next morning I would be charged with treason and packed away to a Yankee prison. I would spend Christmas in a New York lockup.

But Charles had a sparkle in his eye again.

I noticed that the smoke from our stack had become black and thick, not like the wisps which had come from the hard coal we stocked for that run. The ship was directed more southerly, and the engine quickened. The bow wake grew white and foamy, and the narrow boat leaped into the rolling waves. Its wake sent ripples to overlay and blend with the natural rhythms of the water's surface.

The chase was on. The sun was falling toward the horizon, and the space between our crafts narrowed. Blockade runners had no weaponry. U.S. Naval ships had no such limitations and the captain of the pursuing ship demonstrated this.

As I watched the approaching vessel I saw a flash and shortly heard a whistling whine.

I don't recommend this experience if it can be avoided.

The churn of the sidewheels, the rumble of the engine, the splash of the waves, these sounds are all right. But when a whistling piece of cast metal flies by your head you realize there are some sounds you never want to hear. The next sound was a distant pop, the report of the cannon following the shot at its own leisurely pace.

This was a repeat of the attack on our voyage out.

That first shot was not very close, and was sent afore the ship as a warning to halt. The captain conferred with his mate as dark, soft coal smoke flew from the stack. It was now retracted to reduce the ship's profile. We turned southeast and the engine increased the speed of its piston.

The sky darkened over hard blue waves.

The sea is freedom in its most raw, most unforgiving form. The clear and open horizon can lead you to white shores of frozen ice, or soft hills of green, or welcoming bays and lagoons of warm sand and flower-draped women who know nothing of shame, nor of deceit.

Our freedom, vast in one direction, was rapidly becoming constricted in another. Again I heard the whistle, and the shot barely crested our smokestack.

"This is exciting! This is living!" Charles had a rather unorthodox sense of pleasure. The report of the cannon reached my ears. "Don't worry, Jonathan. Our chances of reaching a friendly port are still more than sixty-five percent! Remember the moon won't rise until after two tomorrow morning!"

I don't know how he came up with these things.

The disk of the sun was now nearly touching the horizon's rim.

The ship chasing us was a sight to behold. I could see sailors and gunners on its deck, golden gray in the light. Activity on the warship paused, and again the flash.

This time the whistle was interrupted, and a great dull thud shook the ship. The horse neighed in fright.

"They have our range!" Charles was so enthusiastic it was

unnerving. The shot had burrowed into a bale of blankets. Charles stated, "The ironclads have proven themselves in battle, but for unarmed flight, I prefer a cottonclad!" Our ship was now bereft of cotton, though not of casks of gunpowder.

The figures on the boat trying to kill us moved in rapid precision to reload the weapon. Our boat turned two points more to the east, and our smoke streamed black in a dense ebony cloud, a dark contrast against the dimming sky. The captain had allowed a binnacle light to be lit, which must have been occasionally visible to the pursuers. He began smoking a large segar.

Sunsets can happen quite quickly at sea. Less than twenty minutes after the sun sank below the horizon the sky and sea were nearly dark. The pursuer was less than a mile off and had a rate of fire from its bow chaser of about six minutes, though the last shots were rather wild and didn't threaten. Our captain had planned this out well, given limitations of a heavily laden boat with a known destination and no defense.

At last the sea and sky were so gloomy that it was night.

A smoky lantern was tied high atop a crate on the thwart seat of the ship's dingy, and a bundle of several segars was lashed to the mast. One was lit, the boat was hoisted over the side, a small sail was set, the tiller tied, and the dingy was cast off, bearing easterly.

Immediately the smoke tumbling from our stack became nearly invisible hard coal smoke, and the wheel was brought three points to port, to a bearing of south southeast. The binnacle light was shaded and the captain tossed his segar overboard.

This looked like a simple and easily exposed trick. But it worked!

Everyone on board had been sent below decks except the mate and the captain, both dressed in black. We could hear the engines of the warship to our south and we listened in the dark. The U.S. vessel was pursuing a phantom ship running to Bermuda.

As the sky of stars spun and changed, the captain ordered a change back to the softer, cheaper coal, and our burner sent a column black and thick, invisible in the gloom to any peering spyglasses. The horse was restless and grunted a bit, despite the groom's efforts of calming.

A brisk wind was rising and blew all clouds to the east. The stars on a clear night at sea can be a startling soup of glowing light, creamy against the blackness of infinity.

Charles pointed out ascending Jupiter and Mars. The final stage of the waning moon would not rise until much later.

Mars was the planet nearest to us, and Charles described how its journey about the sun was related to the way a mortar shell describes a parabolic course, using the gravity of the larger body to describe its trajectory. Though in the case of the mortar shell it falls again to earth, and neither Mars nor Earth ever falls into the sun.

Jupiter has four large moons, each of which moves in its own parabola about its massive planet, perhaps complicated by its neighbors. Each Jovian moon could be large enough to support seas, and maybe boats like ours. So, I wondered whether some creature like myself, on some sea of Io or Ganymede, bracing for a dash through danger, might be looking up at the sky and seeing our dot of a planet, and pondering the existence of creatures on that disk of light. I raised my arm in a slow wave of greeting, or recognition, or perhaps of despairing wonder at it all. Then I turned to the dark sea and wondered at the strange world below our keel.

Morning rose – still air with gray clouds. Far to our northeast a lone steamer, likely a ship of commerce, was a smoking dot on the horizon. The captain put his burners on a diet of hard coal, and we slowed our pace, not wanting to reveal ourselves to any outer band of patrolling craft. *Gawain* swam slowly, awaiting the setting of the sun. The horse seemed more content as he munched the grain brought for his comfort. He had somehow grown used to the ocean's movement, and the seas were calm.

Horses grow so rapidly that a period which to a man would seem brief may be a large part of his life. So perhaps younger animals may grow used to strange conditions faster than humans. So I speculated.

That day dragged on with periods of tension and languor as

we awaited its end. A sheen of cloud scudded from the west, and in the last glow of the sun the colors of the sky showed dull red; then a brighter color, then a few flashing minutes of a hot orange before darkness – a red sky at night.

The engine stepped up its pace and the rhythm of the sidewheels grew more rapid. The ship was making good speed now, perhaps ten knots, racing to its home port, or perhaps another fate.

It was now quite dark. The crew kept a lookout on the port and starboard beams for lanterns of ships guarding the approaches to Charleston.

The captain was taking us to the coast somewhat north of the city near Dewees Island. Patrol lights were visible in the distance, but too far to worry us yet. Lights on shore were lit for bearings for runners like ours. One was put about two hundred yards inland, the other just atop the dune nearest the shore. The inbound ship could line them up and be guided to a channel clear of sandbars and safely approach land.

As the *Gawain* neared the shore, I could see breaking waves close to the beach as our prow turned south for the run along Long Island. Misting rain had begun to fall. Rain may be a bother to most sailing men, but to blockade runners it was a godsend, masking us from watchers.

We were not delaying our journey then, as this was the most dangerous time for us. Patrolling ships were thick about the entrance to the harbor, and as we ran up along the shore of Sullivan's Island our chances of being detected grew greater.

We were less than a mile from the entrance to Charleston Harbor, and keeping a close watch on the bobbing patrol lights on the near horizon when we very nearly rammed another ship. It appeared out of the gloom, running without lights like us. The steersman turned hard to starboard, and the boat slipped past our port beam.

No paddle wheels, this craft was apparently screw-driven. It was sailing northwest, probing just outside the harbor, more slowly than we were, as we turned hard to starboard, to the west. We passed about twenty yards from each other, and the blockader didn't notice us until we were nearly past it. The horse slipped and staggered to regain its footing as it neighed loudly. The groom had earlier put a cloak over its head to blind it to the lights, and he drew near to comfort the beast.

We heard the whistle from the Federal and saw the pursuer come about to intercept us. As it turned, our captain gave the order to change course and put on more speed. The vibration of wheel paddles hitting the ocean quickened and the prow of the *Gawain* swung eastward to open sea.

Our pursuer in his excitement misjudged the sea bottom and ran its keel aground on a bar before it could complete its turn. Its whistle blared again, and two rockets glaring red shot into the cloudy skies above us, a bright signal to its squadron.

So again the Federals were in pursuit.

The shallow draft design of the *Gawain* had already shown its advantage for coastal sailing. Now the power of its engine was its strength, and it flexed its muscles.

There were no other ships near us other than the grounded Northern craft, which having alerted its comrades was reversing its screw to back off the sandy bank. A Drummond limelight from that ship illuminated us in our flight. We saw movement now from the distant lights of the blockading fleet as they all moved closer to shore, trending north.

The grounded ship fired two more red rockets into the sky as we escaped their light. Two of the ships drew closer to us, perhaps fourteen hundred yards, following us out to sea. The captain then ordered us more northerly and showed us another of his tricks for evading capture.

He barked an order to one of his crew, who went below and returned with a bundle of gear. He worked in a dark mass of shadow and then to my shock, a fiery flame leaped into the night sky. Then another, two bright red rockets directing the pursuing fleet to chase the blockade runner to the east, further in the direction we were not heading.

The Federals were fooled and leapt after the phantom at least a mile south of our position. The *Gawain* ran quietly and dark to the northeast, past the moving cordon of patrollers now heading out to sea.

We cruised slowly north unmolested and unseen, about twelve miles out, past the fires of the saltworks lining the coast around Georgetown.

Morning broke with a stiff breeze from the southwest. The captain had determined Charleston was too closely watched. He would take us north to North Carolina's Cape Fear River, to Wilmington, which should be more easily attained.

We stood further out to sea for the next day slowly cruising northward, far to the east of Murrells Inlet. We bided our time scanning the horizon for ships, though the few we saw were either neutral to our existence, did not see us, or didn't recognize us as a Confederate blockade runner. At sunset the *Gawain* drew nearer the coast. There were no cities there of any size, and we followed the contour of the land. The line of white breakers to our left undulated in the forever rhythm of our earth, where we all are only temporary passengers.

In the dark we ran along the shore and used the salt fires to gauge our distance. From Georgetown north, Carolinians were boiling seawater to harvest the mineral. We carried no salt in our cargoes that I knew of, but it was in demand high enough that people would burn fires day and night. I recalled the hot work I saw when Tyrone sent me there last summer, before my trip to the mountains.

Our coal reserves were running short again as sunrise neared. The ocean was black but the eastern sky showed a hint of a horizon line as we came up on Oak Island near the entrance to Wilmington. Northern navy patrols would be tired from their night's surveillance of the coast. A fresh shift would soon take station with renewed vigilance.

A multitude of soft sand islands sit at the mouth of the Cape Fear River and its two major inlets. There is no way to guard all passages. Also, there were several strong Southern gun emplacements at the river's mouth, with rifled cannon whose accurate range with a thirty-two-pound shell was a mile or more.

Rather than wait for another night with diminishing fuel and a small but waxing moon to deal with, the captain judged to run to

284

the river in the dim morn, before the forenoon watch took station on Federal boats. Coal was loaded in the burner. The horse was hooded. *Gawain* made way swiftly.

The captain's years as a coastal surveyor served him well, and though he knew the sandbars shifted in every storm and from year to year, he gauged the sea bottom and judged where the bars were for this entry. This is sea craft mysterious to me.

The beat of the wheels again quickened.

Gulls and terns, ospreys and pipers flew out to observe us in the freshening wind. The glow on the sea horizon shone a definite light blue to the sky. Waves blew spindrift from their peaks.

The hooded horse was not comfortable, and neither was the groom.

Horses do not really belong on board a ship, and the young gelding was restless from lack of exercise. He stamped and pawed the deck in agreement with my own thoughts. I sidled closer and softly sang my proven horse-lullaby, "Doo-dah, doo-dah, doo-dah."

Mrs. Trent came on deck and gazed fore and aft with a stern face; no party here.

There were no Federals to see as we raced along Oak Island to reach the safety of the guns of Fort Caswell, Fort Campbell, and Fort Holmes at Old Inlet.

A horse patrol on the beach saw our ship and raced up the beach to alert the cannons for our need for protection.

A gust pushed our boat toward the coast, and the captain directed his men to keep the boat from the shore. That is when we realized a Federal patrol vessel was bearing toward us from the south. We were nearly within range of his bow-chaser.

Gawain clawed its way from the shore, losing speed as it did, and the blockader came closer.

The wind gusted again and shook the boat. The horse whinnied and stamped.

In the lightening gloom we saw the flash of the blockader's gun. I could not see where the ball landed.

We ducked close to the deck to avoid the wind and peeped over the gunwales to view the chase and the forts we were approaching. The guns were about a half-league distant.

Again, the flash from the other ship. I heard a zoom as the projectile flew overhead.

I looked aft and saw the captain coolly smoking a pipe. His eye was not on the belligerent ship but on the coast, the sea, his craft.

Again the shot from the Federal, the ripping sound of a shell. As we watched the other boat there was an enormous splash just to the side of the pursuing ship, then a loud "BOOM!" I looked to the shore and saw smoke in the lightening air drifting from the battery on the point ahead of us. I turned back to the blockader and saw it pivoting quickly to the west, exposing its heavier cannon. It let loose a double flash, its small broadside from two guns in parting. Both shells sailed wide of *Gawain*.

Another shell from a shore battery sailed over the retreating gunboat, over its top but directly in line with it. The Federal quickly ran out of its range.

Gawain now drove toward the mouth of Old Inlet and all aboard felt relieved, including the warmblood horse, which smelled land for the first time in days.

The wind continued blowing, and then as the engine slowed we could worry more about running aground and foundering instead of flying projectiles and the explosives on board.

When we got close to Fort Fisher and were very near a safe home, the sun had not broken from cloud but there was a growing grayness. A mist rose slightly from the river on its way to the sea.

The land was still. We could see the far silhouettes of the searching Federal gunboats behind us, far enough to be out of range of Fort Fisher and the other dune emplacements.

We saw figures on the beach watching our progress. These men had been manning guns there for more than two years. No doubt they were bored and tired with only an occasional bit of excitement like this morning's.

As we passed the forts that had fired in our defense we waved and the captain directed the engineer to blow the whistle in thanks. The sun crested the horizon and though we were tired from lost sleep and anxious hours of the passage, we were elated.

45

QUICK AND DONE

We continued up the Cape Fear River toward the docks at Wilmington, past Smithville, past Battery Buchanan, through sandbars and islets on to the city itself. We passed the tree where legend tells of a bottle of brandy hung to greet boats coming to town. Captains would order a pause to share from the bottle that had formerly hung there, and several blockade runners were anchored no doubt sharing a dram among themselves as had been done for the past century. Thus the "dram tree."

A pilot boat came out and told us we would have to wait twenty days before progressing up river to the city because of a quarantine from yellow fever that had gripped the town earlier. Twenty days! Some boats were doing this. Our captain would not.

We did not pause but maintained our course toward the docks in Wilmington where a small boat with an armed guard positioned itself before us and demanded we halt. We did so, and the captain and the commander of the guard boat spoke briefly. I did not overhear the discussion, though I later heard the captain had convinced the lieutenant that the horse we carried was an urgent gift from the King of Prussia or someone, and was to be delivered immediately to some high Confederate official or general.

The captain's power of persuasion, whether vocal or metallic was such that he was permitted to pass. As the boiler smoked, we coasted to the docks newly built to service the trade worked by the blockade runners. The older docks were in some disrepair and not much used as they were splintered, sunbaked, unsteady looking, only fit for small fishing boats.

We docked shortly after noon and immediately all passengers disembarked before the local authorities could detain them and keep them aboard what should have been a vessel in quarantine.

I stayed near the ship until Tyrone's portion of our cargo was registered with an agent at one of the Crenshaw warehouses. I oversaw its unlading, arranged transport of Tyrone's goods to Charleston, and paid off the captain the balance of our fares and portage fees.

Charles arranged with the local garrison to safeguard his munitions, equipment, gear, and exotic explosives. We met at the end of our business and proceeded to seek the hotel we had been directed to. It was a house whose owners had died or deserted the city and was then administered by an agent of the family as a boarding house for blockade runners, merchants and other transients.

Wilmington had never been a very large port city due to its distance from open sea. During the war its remoteness became a strength.

The small city was genteel before the war. With the needs of the blockade-running services it instantly became cosmopolitan in a ribald sea-faring way. This was not a welcome change to many of the older families.

When the yellow fever epidemic struck in late 1862, hundreds of citizens died and most of the surviving residents who could afford to flee did so, allowing the city's gentle urbanity to become a raucous and free pleasure center offering a wide and unprecedented variety of entertainment and distraction.

A military camp had been established to the north of town with an impromptu parade ground, a hospital, a goods depot, and a campground for followers of the military. The men's wives and some parents would be there, and the ever-present undertaking and body preserving services. This science was rather new to America. A steady stream of wounded and dying soldiers came to this place from the terrible battles in Northern Virginia and beyond. That was where I would find my buyer of coffin screws.

I had a couple of Yankee dollars in my pocket, so after putting my rucksack and parcels in our hotel we went into town for a meal.

As Charles and I walked into the city I was struck by the extremes of music and unusual dress among the habitants. Most of these people were not natives of Wilmington but were sailors and blockade runners, largely British, and of course there were the people who made money servicing them.

We entered an eating establishment and found tables of young English gentlemen dressed in colorful uniforms like horse-racing jockeys and marching band members toasting each other with brandies, gins, and barley beer in bottles. Bottled beer was a most expensive and luxurious habit then, and these men decided their money, won by adventures not unlike our own earlier that day, was best spent on that and later on the exotic ladies who were plying their trade in theaters-turned-dance houses, and in most elaborately decorated private rooms. The women were from North and South, and from England and from the corners of the globe.

But perhaps I should not speak more of this. Let's just say any imaginable pleasure was available for those visitors. Maybe more than you can imagine, at least that was the case for me. I call them visitors because I believe none of them made Wilmington or America their homes.

Wilmington was not quiet even in the early morning breeze. Two blockade runners that came in earlier were preparing for another dash to the islands, a new chance for fortune. They were loading the pressed and baled cotton aboard, men barking orders or following them. Mules and men drew loads to the dock; cranes swept them aboard.

Carts of crates – arms *Gawain* had brought – rolled down the street toward the encampment of soldiers. They were assigned months ago from Charleston to protect Wilmington's northern approaches. There was general consensus now that the Port of Charleston was effectively closed to Southern shipping, which left Wilmington as the best place on the eastern seaboard open for trade, and that was chancy as we had recently experienced.

A breeze was rising, and with the freshening wind and approaching storm there would be good cover for ships seeking to sail out. Bad weather was good weather.

The arms were carried to the military encampment north of town near Island Creek, and I caught a ride with one of the drivers. The elderly black man spoke sadly of his horses and named them, and how the army had requisitioned them, and how he missed them. The mules he then drove were small but willing animals.

Riders carrying dispatches passed us twice on the road, not hurrying so apparently there was no imminent emergency.

We arrived near the camp about noon. There was some excitement as the arms dealer who had made the passage with me was going to demonstrate some of his wares. Tables, tents and targets had been erected on an open field and a meal was being prepared for the guests. The overcast skies and the gusting breeze did little to dampen the curiosity and excitement of the presentation of new rifles and ordinance.

The assembly of guests included officers from the nearby camp, but also representatives from cavalry regiments and from the government in Richmond. Other characters were about, perhaps town leaders and an honor guard with a few soldiers, though there were no Federal troops within a hundred miles or more.

The regiment at the camp was the South Carolina 24th Volunteers who I met at Secessionville the previous year. What I saw and heard on that marshy field haunts me yet. I remembered that I had spoken to Corporal William Smith and thought I would inquire if he were available to renew my acquaintance.

I approached the encampment and was challenged by the sentries. Since I was not in uniform and not attached to any unit, I was told to wait where I was. Eventually one of the men returned with Corporal Smith, who greeted me with a smile. "Hello, Jon! Good to see you!"

"And you, Billy."

He saw the pea jacket I had bought for the voyage home. "Jon, are you a sailor now?"

He invited me to take a cup of tea.

We walked to a nearby cook fire with sitting logs about it, and he poured me a cup of the Yaupon tea, which was the common drink since Chinese tea was exorbitant yet available to those who could pay. Some was carried to America aboard *Gawain*. We sweetened the Yaupon with molasses, a Southern product still in ample supply. It completely overpowered the flavor of Yaupon.

It may seem a brutal and crude drink, yet it was satisfying in its way, and under different conditions might be considered a delicacy.

Billy was not the youthful thirty-five-year-old I recalled from Charleston. He had seen more of the world since then. We spoke, and he shared a tintype photo of his wife and child. I told him of some of my adventures on the run to Nassau. He became silent for a moment, then spoke.

"I wonder where this war will lead. The first year we all thought it would be quick and done. We would just all go home and be about our business, just with a different government. Why would the North care if we went our own way? We were all supposed to be independent states.

"But they did care, and they invaded. How could they expect we would not resist? We beat them back again and again, and killed so many of them that they filled their army with foreigners, like the British did with the Hessians during the revolution. Our ranks were just men defending their homes and their way of life."

I pondered for a bit on this. To defend a way of life based on something fundamentally wrong, how can that be worth defending?

This was the world he was given, and we are each born into our different worlds. Defend your home? Yes, of course. Defend the land you grow your food on? Yes. Defend a way of life based on the ownership of others?

I wonder if I had been born into his world and knew no other, would I question it?

Billy started again, "Now they expect the Union Army is moving into East Tennessee from Nashville. I heard a rumor that we will be heading that way soon, through Georgia, I guess. I'm not sure I see a good way out of this." He took another sip of tea.

"I'm sorry about all this, Billy." That's all I could say.

I'm sorry. Not worth much.

Later I learned that he had stood with his countrymen at the battle of Chicamauga in northern Georgia, a Confederate victory. Billy took a bullet in the guts, languished on the train south to the hospital in Macon, where he died three weeks later. It was not a victory for William G. Smith.

Corporal Smith is buried in the Confederate Cemetery in Macon, at Rose Hill, where neat rows of tombstones stand as on parade in nice military order. Wives and veterans held a service for the soldiers interred at that cemetery, "Decoration Day." I think some now call it "Memorial Day."

He seemed like a good solid man doing what he thought was right.

I wonder what happened to his wife and child.

I'm sorry, Billy.

Lunch was being served to the important visitors, and my shipmate Mr. Kilcannon, the arms merchant, briefly took a moment to wave me over and offer a meal before going back to his important customers. Charles was also there, dressed in his important person clothes. After the army officers and government purchasing agents had served themselves, we each took a plate and went down the line. There was plenty left over in the way of ham, beans, bread of corn and wheat, roasted chicken and turkey, potatoes, yams, and a sweet pudding. We sat and servants came around and poured us coffee, likely newly brought from the British colonies. We ate that meal nearly as fine as was available in Nassau, and it was one of the last good meals I recall eating that year.

While dining I heard a gunshot, which did not upset anyone at our outdoor lunch. We saw a demonstration of firearms about a hundred yards away, and after finishing my meal I went to see the new machines at work.

Most quantities of Confederate arms were purchased on contract through a Department of War agent named Huse. The independent dealers who could bring in a quantity could often sell them at a good price to regimental representatives who were unable to procure them through regular channels.

I drew near the field and heard Mr. Kilcannon extolling the qualities and capabilities of his weapons. There was a Shakespearean quality to his speech. He spoke of the weapons' grand power, stellar craftsmanship, of lofty purpose – oh, the feats of heroic wonder a man could achieve with these marvels! Upon these arms sit laurels and victory! Let smooth success be strewn before your feet!

One firearm I found rather remarkable was a handgun that fired seven rounds and could also fire a blast of shot, like a scattergun. The cavalry officers tilted their heads together and whispered at what a battalion of horsemen armed with sabres and these weapons might accomplish. The handgun was apparently developed in Louisiana and produced overseas. It became a favorite of the Stuart cavalry.

Another arm was the Whitworth Rifle. These long arms fired a machined slug, long and hexagonal, through a hexagonal barrel bore. It looked heavy, and some had bright brass telescopes mounted upon them.

"This is the finest sharpshooter's rifle on earth," declaimed Mr. Kilcannon. "With this rifle, more modern than any available to the troops of the North, an accurate shot may be placed on an enemy at a distance of two thousand yards! Imagine, removing from the field an advancing opponent at a distance of more than a mile!" I noted that the telescope was not a frivolity, but seemed necessary at that range. Perhaps he was exaggerating a bit. Still, that was quite a boast. A few months later I was unfortunate to see the verification of Mr. Kilcannon's promise of those rifles in the hands of defenders at a battery on Morris Island, and on Fort Sumter.

The marvelous Mrs. Trent had made an appearance and seemed to have lost enough weight overnight to restore that wondrous figure. She was making her goodbyes to some local dignitaries before leaving in an expensive carriage with a lucky general. Many envious eyes watched as she rode into the distance with the officer, to what end I can only guess.

I scanned the attendees and found a small gaggle of undertakers, or so I assumed from their dour dress and their solemn, unsmiling yet glad demeanor. I approached them and told them of my case of coffin screws, and showed them a sample I had brought with me. An immediate and understated bidding began, and I was quickly guaranteed a price that would give me a profit of twelve-hundred percent. I accepted a small deposit, signed a promissory note and walked over to a table displaying unusual firearms. These included Enfield breechloading rifles and a fine row of bright swords, both for infantry and cavalry.

Among the unusual arms were elaborate dueling pieces, fowling rifles, fine shotguns, a repeating rifle which foretold the future of at least one battle scene at Chicamauga, and a series of handguns. The one that caught my eye was a repeating revolver of French manufacture that could hold twenty cartridges. Imagine having the power of life and death of twenty men in the palm of your hand. This is a power no one person should have.

I bought it, lest it fall into the hand of a madman. And I also bought the cartridges.

Charles was still in deep conversation with a government-looking man and his advisors, perhaps from the War Department. They were apparently concluding some business, as they shook hands all around, and shared segars. Then they bid farewell, and Charles walked toward me again, his fuming Havana leaving a fragrant trail of blue.

"Ho, Jon! A beautiful day, a fine day. Let's get back to town. I heard of a venue we should see."

This day was not beautiful, and the gusty wind had settled more into a dark steady blow from the north. We returned in a carriage with a townsman who had turned a profit selling Madeira and Cognac Brandy to some officers on post. We shared a pleasant conversation on the road discussing the mercantile nature of the war.

Charles spoke about new inventions and possibilities of transportation and explorations. I was mostly silent, thinking of what I must say to Isabella and must do when I returned to Charleston, which I was now beginning to admit was my home.

I touched the bracelet in my pocket.

46

PERHAPS SOME GOOD

As we rolled into Wilmington, the nightlife was beginning to get underway. The two blockade runners had eased down Cape Fear River and awaited dark to make their dash. Charles and I went to our room, and I arranged for my parcel of screws to be delivered to the embalmer. We tidied up before seeing what the evening beheld, despite the rainy weather.

We visited a tavern for a drop of ale before venturing to the address Charles had for his evening party. We weren't very hungry after the heavy meal we had for lunch, so we ate lightly – some peanuts, a salad, oysters.

After our second pint we ventured out onto the street. The rain was steady, and we put on our oilcloth capes and pulled our hats low.

A hack pulled by a mule and a nearly lame horse carried us to the address, a large house on the southern outskirts of the town lit with a thousand candles, and with magical music emanating. We were "greeted" at the door by a large white servant, perhaps a sailor, who in a rough English accent asked politely who we were and who we wished to see. Charles charmed the man, and gave his card. Soon the host, a young third son of an earl or something, ushered us into the parlor.

The youthful lord was dressed in evening wear, a trim coat over a waistcoat, very formal, yet was careless in his speech and manner. A good match in kind with Charles.

His was a large house. The parlor was decorated in fine furniture, and there were unusual teak tables, settees and such about.

The current tenants had draped the rooms in the most fabulous manner with long sheets of colorful silks and cushions that minded me of a Turkish sultan's palace. There were tea sets of elaborate gold and silver, carvings of jade, ebony, ivory, and bone.

Music emerged from an alcove. A man who looked like an Eastern Indian was seated on a cushioned settee, and he played a stringed instrument called a see-tar or something to that effect. Its music was unlike anything I had heard, a cloud of ethereal joy that wafted through the air and itself smelled of perfume. Well, actually when I think about it, there was perfume in the air from pots of burning incense. That smoke could have been intoxicating itself, but the music led my mind down a tiled hall of mystic ruby to the chambers of Aladdin.

There were perhaps fifty men in the house. They seem to have been mostly British as well, with a smattering of Americans and at least one odd Dutchman. These were mostly blockade running gentlemen and their officers dressed in the most outlandish colors and styles, or in formal after-dinner garb. Some looked like actors in a comic musical production, dressed in gay silks and colors, with buttons and epaulettes, tassels and braided cord. The men were being waited on by women in the most revealing and lascivious dress, either formal bodices with outrageously short skirts, or transparent blouses and Arabic pantaloons. There was one woman dressed and groomed exactly like a young gentleman, except she had no clothing at all on her upper torso save a conservative collar and bow tie, and cuffs on her wrists. Some women were quadroons, some of European extraction, with accents of France, Ireland, perhaps Russia, and some of an exotic look and sound of the East, perhaps Calcutta or Bombay. After listening to the French accents of two of them I suspected they were from that province of Gaul known as Tennessee.

The colorful gentlemen were of high spirits, joyously toasting each other, singing snatches of song. They were drinking bottled beer and ale, sherry and champagne.

The night was young, spirits were high, the women were alarming, the wine was flowing. These young men had lives of adventure, a thrilling ride on the high seas in wartime. If captured, they were breaking no laws and would be released to their parents, to continue their lives of adventure. Eventually they would, I suppose, enter the family banking or trading firm, become conservative businessmen and produce their own sons of empire.

That night in that pleasure palace in Wilmington I could only imagine the life of leisure these adventurers lived, and like a too-sweet dessert, I believed I could only have stood for a taste of it. But it appeared an intriguing dish.

In one corner of the home was a darkened room lit with a few candles, and a small group of philosopher kings. They were enjoying a taste of the little Green Faerie. I had not shared a drink of Wormwood since Paris. Was it "l'Heure Verte?" Yes, apparently so, or at least it was somewhere on this spinning globe.

I entered and pulled up a chair.

They poured the absinthe, the color of the gem peridot, and I placed the spoon with a sugar cube. It clouded into louche, we drank. Shall we grow mad, and commit crimes? The soothing Hindu music seemed to deny that, so we sat and spoke, a free discussion on all subjects.

I thought they were talking in tongues. At first, I could catch a word now and then. Eventually I understood it was a dialect of Northumberland, or Carlisle, or some obscure variety of English, though one apparently was speaking something related to Flemish. I don't know if he understood any of the others, or they him, but they shared a camaraderie in which I joined. Each of us broke forth of the most urgent and weighty matters of the day. I don't recall any of it. Except one part about the nature of spiritual belief.

A man stated that the greatest achievement of the Roman Empire was the dissemination of Christianity.

Another said the Church had caused more death and pain that all the Roman and Greek gods put together.

The Dutchman called out the Reform movement as the salvation of the Church and, therefore, of mankind. Or that's what I think he said.

A Welshman said there was no God, nor any gods. There was only Mankind, and we should gather our forces together to save ourselves because we are all alone. And we should sing!

Yes, we men, we pots of churning chemicals and gasses and philosophizing speeches, should pause occasionally and sing.

I noticed out of the corner of my eye that there were two women, both with long dark hair and the whitest flesh, sitting next to each other on a crimson-cushioned sofa in the gloom, each stark naked, sharing a small, thin segar. They were speaking quietly, no doubt about their own view of Mankind's folly and their inability to escape it.

The wormwood was working my head at this point. I said rather hotly that without the Church, without the Bible, there was no objective morality. There was no real reason to live. There could be no right and no wrong.

I hadn't meant my brief wormy tirade to have a strong effect, but all became silent and reflective. One unintelligible man from the hinter regions of empire began to quietly cry.

And I didn't even believe what I had just said.

My true belief is that mankind has an inherent goodness which Jesus only captured in words that have thankfully come down to us, a guide to our better natures.

As we sat in the candle-lit room with the wind outside nearing a howl, the rain fell heavily. A man ran to the house and screamed, "For God's sake help them!" then ran to the main threshold and beat upon the door. He was met by the rough sailor in the hall and was let in, dripping gallons, and ran to our room disturbing our uncomfortable meditations.

"They need help!" he shouted into the room. "Captain Spivey's boat has run aground in the storm and is being swamped!" One man from Northumberland or somewhere jumped to his feet immediately.

"Captain Spivey, that's Ralphie McEwan!" That statement got a reaction from several of the imbibers and philosophers. "C'mon, lads!" As a man we all stood and left the room to the candle, to the Green Faerie, and to the two forlorn nudes in their own introspective reverie.

I had no reason to join the British adventurers other than that people needed help, and I might perhaps be able to do some good. The party house was on the southern side of the city, near the shore. The men at the house seemed mostly to know the captain of the boat and formed an able crew to help. We went to the boathouse where a small steam launch was tied.

The men got the engine up and burning with turpentine and kindling, then cured wood. As the boiler became pressurized, much of the rest of the household arrived, sans the women and musician.

It was obvious there were too many of us to fit in the launch.

I JONATHAN

Six of us dragged a rowboat into the water and piled in. Others stood and watched us away as we cast a line to the steam launch. It was secured, and we were towed downriver under the dull black sky in the rain within about twenty minutes.

The stormy waters of the river became rougher as we neared New Inlet where the boat was grounded. It showed a grim rocking silhouette against the gray spray. Another boat from Wilmington was already there trying to help.

Three or four lanterns shone swinging above the ship's tilting deck, and as we drew near we could see a huddled mass of passengers bunched on the leeward side of the ship.

The rain slackened, but the wind was still high.

The launch cast us off, and we employed our oars to steady and drive our skiff. We rolled with the bubbling swells listing us to left and right, and neared the stranded craft. It shifted with each large wave that hit it broadside, spewing a cold spritz across its deck and onto the doomed passengers. The crew had already abandoned the ship in the longboats and made to the shore, the dastards.

There is something in the face of a doomed man or woman who seems no longer to care of the world's riches and wealth, clothes and trifles, but only of their lives, and perhaps those of their offspring. Indeed, one woman in sodden fine dress held an infant in her arms, and her face displayed an acceptance of the end of her world. This pressed a sense of dismay upon me and perhaps others in my boat, who so recently debated the value of a book of religion, and how the world would not survive without those thin pages of ancient discourse.

That woman in that instant saw the world very clearly.

We drew near in our unsteady craft to about ten feet, which varied with the rolling waves.

A man, not large, not powerful, perhaps a school teacher or an accountant, put his arm about the woman and took her baby from her arms. She gave a regretful stare into his infant eyes – a tearful face of sorrow I will never forget.

The man challenged the very universe, gave a great bellow and tossed the baby wrapped in a child's blanket across a dozen and more feet of lively swelling sea, the child breaching a flying curtain of spray, to our rocking boat. In an act of reckless salvation, I caught that missile of life. I held the child in my own arms.

Eyes wide and shivering, both mine and the child's, we shared a gaze into each other of a fate neither of us could have imagined.

What could have befallen that young life had he slipped into the water and sunk beneath the surface? What would happen to me, if I had fallen? Or what would have become of my mind if I had dropped that tiny promise of a man into the deep?

Four of the huddlers jumped into the brine and were brought aboard, and that was really all we in our rowboat could do. They were comforted as well as could be by a squad of us brandy-bearing revelers who had jumped aboard a small boat in the late night not really thinking, half in our cups.

And I who held that small life.

It took us nearly an hour to row and then be towed back to the dock; the larger steam launch arrived at nearly the same time we did with most of the remaining passengers, and no good words for Captain Spivey's crew, I'll tell you.

I heard later that one woman, apparently a spy, had leapt overboard and tried to wade to shore but was weighted down by forty pounds of gold sewn into her petticoats. Her body was found the next morning.

Four of the women from the house, now well-robed, met us and the larger craft at the dock. They had transformed into matronly angels of comfort for the storm-tossed people we brought ashore. One cloaked figure, formerly the woman in the mannish dress I think, became so solicitous of the infant I carried that I gave the tired and sleeping bundle to her to guard until he could be reunited with his mother, if she was saved.

In future years there might remain a legend of the flight of that child across stormy waters, a flash of nascent humanity in the night winds, but the infant's youth would never allow his own recall of that journey.

47

TO LIVE WITH CANNIBALS

My circuitous journey from Charleston was nearly over.

I reflected on the harrowing events of my recent travels: dodging cannon fire by my own countrymen, snatching a baby from a storm, my other adventures and experiences. I reviewed my place in this world.

Employed, after a fashion.

An orphan, yet a man.

An expatriate myself, though living in a country still calling itself "America."

Of the North, yet now of the South.

Mated, yet unmarried.

The day following the rescue of the people from the foundering ship I boarded a late train back to Charleston. Charles remained in Wilmington for a few more days to acquire some additional materials and to engage in discussions. There were few riders other than some of the traders, and freight, including the rugs and other goods for Tyrone. I had my pistol, a box of cans of baking soda, the small bundle of handkerchiefs, a box of French perfumes, and cash from the sale of coffin screws. And in my rucksack Ricardo's key.

And a bracelet.

I had chosen the bracelet without having to think. The jeweler in the tiny shop by the square in Nassau had a range of fine wares. He worked into each a combination of silver, gold and bronze. The Damascene swirls and folds of the metals told a story of how our lives are and twisted and blended, filed and polished, no two alike, yet all sharing common elements. The item was a beauty, a clasp to fit Isabella's fine wrist.

I eased into the wooden seat worn smooth from years of riders' backsides. Hundreds and thousands of passengers had occupied the same space I sat in. Each sat in the same place, each rode the train to a stop. When one passenger leaves and another sits in the seat, and the train moves, is it the same space? But then the rotation of the earth moves the train and the seat as well, and the earth's circling the sun even more. None of us can ever stay in the exact same place.

My exhaustion from the past three days drove me into a torpor, and between fitful naps between stops, my thoughts turned to Isabella and our upcoming reunion.

My unrelenting expectation was that I would again share her bed, and my body began warming in anticipation. And I began to see that this should not be the highest act in our lives, not the final goal for us. Whence from there?

The train finally pulled into Florence where, fatigued as I was, I saw the freight transferred to the train to Charleston and boarded it myself. Schedules were fluid now, and the train began moving in its own time. I took another space on a bench and returned to my reflection of the future for Isabella and me.

Would her husband return from his travels and take up with his wife once more? That did not seem likely. If he were indeed mad, he may have been dispatched by his rough crew-mates if at sea. He may even have been marooned on an island to live with cannibals, if he could get along with even them.

Would Isabella and I never be more than furtive lovers, hiding in shadows when the proper people weren't watching? That is no way to live. It was not fair to Isabella, and I realized I should break it off.

I would choose the despair of Ricardo over the hope represented by the bracelet.

Then what?

I touched the bracelet in my coat's inside breast pocket. It warmed me. I recalled the nights she comforted me, and I comforted her, and our glorious magical time in the hidden mountain palace. Even that memory of her gave me some comfort in Nassau.

What could I offer her? My nature being so depressed I feared

I would not make a worthy companion. And what of her? So calm of nature, yet sweet, competent yet vulnerable, alone in her life except for me.

I knew what was right. There was really no thought needed for this. I felt I was her husband in all but name, and she was my wife. She should be given the choice. I owed her anything I could give her, and I resolved to become a better man. She was more than worthy of anything I could give.

Having chosen this, I saw an open channel for the rest of my life, our lives.

I made up my mind to propose marriage to her, all I can give her, and hope that she would accept me. I doubted her husband would return to her, if indeed he was still alive. If he did, well, we would take up that challenge when it appeared, and perhaps have him jailed for cruelty and abandonment.

My path was now clear. I regretted that the bracelet was not a ring.

We finally arrived at the train station in Charleston at four in the morning. I spoke with a porter who offloaded the goods from Nassau and watched over them while I walked to Tyrone's office.

That's where I learned that Isabella had died.

48

COFFIN ISLAND

Tyrone's share of the blockade enterprise was successful to the extent of his hopes, if not a bit above.

Munitions and military supplies had taken most of the cargo space onboard, but he had generated much from his share and had arranged to leave some of his funds in the form of promissory notes in Nassau with a British bank. Just in case.

He was satisfied, even happy, despite the news of Isabella he conveyed.

Tyrone was sitting at his desk amid papers on spindles and notes, and invoices stuffed between pages of ledgers. The small window at the back of the room shone a dim light somewhat obscured by the dove that perched on the outside sill.

"Jon, Isabella died four days ago." I had just been landing in Wilmington then. He was somber as he spoke. "She took sick with congestive fever a week after you left and finally failed. These damned swamps and their foul airs. Poor lass."

I stood in my shock without words. The dove on the window sill gave its sad call, startling in its volume. I fingered the bracelet in my pocket. It should have been a ring!

I knew that scores of people died each year in Charleston from that and other sicknesses, though many recovered and lived for decades. Usually it was the older who died, the infirm. Not people like the woman to whom I was about to offer my life. Perhaps I had broken her heart when I left, another man sailing away, probably abandoning her. Perhaps her spirit failed at last.

"She passed at the house of the Morays, where the servants took her when she got sick. She was nursed by the servants, and they finally brought the doctor, too late."

I stood mute, thinking of what I had been planning to say to her, to encourage her, to bring her into the light of a better world. We would run to the mountains and marry, where her past life could not find her.

He told me she was buried two days before at the potter's field south of Goose Creek.

"Jon, my lad..." began Mr. Tyrone, but he did not finish.

I did not wish to hear or think of her weakening, her face growing cool and ashen, her coughing and labored breathing. I had lived before with that image with another I loved and was glad to not witness Isabella fade in distress, finally into shadow. So in my selfish way it was a blessing that I had not seen her at her terminal end, but could only remember her as vital, loving, smiling sweetly beneath that friendly scar. I wished our last parting had been more joyful; I wished I could have shared that I had been ready to give her my name, everything. I wished that I had died with her, holding her hand as we crossed over.

I left the building, out into the stygian gloom of midsummer glare.

After learning of the death of Isabella I was despondent and again fell into habits I practiced before the fundraising party for the ironclads. I spent my evenings at Murphy's, or among the German drunkards, or just alone with my bottle under the scrub oak by the bank of the Cooper north of the city, where I first treated my sorrows with the Irishmen, and kind Denis's bottle.

When in the city after dark I would wander the lanes of the lower battery area, past the house where Isabella had held me the night before my voyage. I noticed there was still candlelight from some houses, including the one where Jenny's Aunt Peggy and her poodle lived.

I would pass the docks silently like a spectre, would even go on long walks at midnight to James Island and Hanahan. Isabella's death was my lost chance at a normal life. I kept the bracelet with Ricardo's key, as perverse talismans against hope, and felt sorry for myself again.

News from Virginia and Tennessee continued good and bad, though many citizens were finally realizing the war might not end in a resounding Southern victory. It was even becoming evident in Charleston that the Americans would not quit.

Well, both sides were Americans, so I guess that was at least part of the problem.

The Federals had been beaten badly in the Charleston area nearly every time there was anything close to a parity in battlefield numbers, and at Secessionville even when they outnumbered defenders more than ten to one.

Defenders always have an advantage, and on Morris Island the waves of attacks broke like water upon the castle of sand and cannon known as Battery Wagner, which guarded the harbor near the isle's northern end.

Capture of the Rebel anchor island of Morris was long seen as vital to opening Charleston Harbor to Federal warships. It protected approaches to Fort Sumter and dominated the harbor inlet on the south, as did batteries on Sullivan's Island to the north.

Cannon fire from this emplacement kept the attacking ships literally "at bay," by keeping them out of the bay.

Since the blockading fleet arrived two years earlier, their guns had bombarded Fort Sumter into rubble. Yet by the middle of 1863 a few guns remained on the island and could still direct accurate fire on the ironclads and other ships. Each night more than a hundred workmen and a thousand sandbags were ferried there to make what repairs they could.

The fleet decided to direct attacks on the Morris Island batteries that protected Sumter and guarded the southern harbor entrance.

The Federals established themselves on Folly Island just south of Morris Island weeks earlier. The Southern commanders debated whether their opponents would try again to move on Charleston through James Island or whether they would attempt to move north onto Morris Island to threaten Sumter. To do that they would have to go through the "neck battery," so called because it sat astride the narrowest part of the island between areas on each side, which flooded during high tide. It was later named Battery Wagner.

When it became clear that Union troops would try to march up Morris Island, the battery was hurriedly reinforced. Slaves and soldiers performed enormous work lifting defensive dunes to protect the batteries, and turned the site into a fortress.

After harsh bombardment the Federals boated over from Folly Island, some falling into the water before gaining the shore. The commander led the charge – wet, hatless, and bootless, riding a captured donkey. He progressed up the island on his steed in his stocking feet.

They met little resistance until they drew near Battery Wagner, which had been heavily bombarded by Union monitors. The Southern battery had returned fire with accurate aim, hitting the ironclad flagship sixty times and finally causing the flotilla to withdraw.

The infantry advance on the fort was forced to fall back to rapidly dug defenses. The Federals settled in to begin a slow movement up the island.

The defenders dug more elaborate redoubts and bomb-proof holes and brought the most accomplished sharpshooters on earth to keep the attackers back, armed with the exquisite long-range rifles I had seen demonstrated by Mr. Kilcannon in Wilmington.

When the Northern observers peeped through spy-holes in their trench mounds eight hundred yards from Wagner, the sharpshooters were often able to place a hexagonal bullet through the very eye of that soldier.

Progress northward on the island was very slow. A new form of warfare was developed. Trenches were dug for protection, and attackers gradually crept toward the enemy. Wire was strung as obstructions in and around the trenches to hold the enemy back should they attack. In that war against the Kaiser a few decades later, use of wire was a standard tactic. I think the whole trench-and-wire warfare concept was invented on Morris Island.

In years past Morris Island was known as "Coffin Island" and had been a plague colony. Many unmarked graves were discovered as the trenches were dug. Holes for fresh water collection were often contaminated by the decades-old corpses of anonymous burials. As you can imagine, morale for the Federal troops there was not high.

Attacks were planned, put in motion with support from the fleet with heavier and heavier cannon, and each was repulsed – like waves rising and falling against a shore.

The lighter guns of Wagner were buried in the sand, as were many defenders who concealed themselves in rice barrels set into the earth as bombproofs called "ratholes." One observer at Fort Sumter reported that on one day more than twenty-five shells per minute flew into Wagner during a ten-hour bombardment.

After one all-day shelling, the eighteen-hundred defending troops arose to meet an advance by the Federals. Many at the battery had little sleep for nearly a week and were stunned by the day's constant bombardment. Yet they arose to repel a charge by five thousand soldiers. The 54th Massachusetts Colored U.S. Regiment led the attack.

The charge was expected to be an easy walk up the beach. No one believed any living thing could survive within the earthworks of Battery Wagner after the day's furious bombardment.

The attack was not planned in earnest, not coordinated to guarantee a victory, and so faced a surprise.

Artillery from Sumter, Wagner, and James Island fired on the beach where the 54th charged. The tide had come in and some soldiers waded through breaking ocean waves as they advanced, or through knee-deep swamp. Others crossed the searing sand of a late July afternoon.

As the sun set the attackers charged the fort, and the bearer of the colors was felled. The flag was immediately seized by another of the 54th, who charged up the walls of the fort with the other infantrymen. He was shot numerous times, yet refused to hand the flag to comrades who offered to take it.

A few Federals succeeded in entering the fort. Some demoralized Confederates cowered in their ratholes, yet mostly the Southerners stood by their posts and guns and stopped the charge. The supporting troops from Pennsylvania, Connecticut and New York recoiled at the unexpected fury from the earthworks and hesitated. They did not advance to help their black Massachusetts comrades.

Nearly all officers of the attacking troops were killed. Undone and shaken, the remaining Federals beat a clumsy withdrawal. The wounded bearer of his nation's flag, William Carney, later received the United States Medal of Honor. When he returned to the rear, he stated that in his possession the flag never touched the sandy beach, and he became the first black U.S. soldier awarded the congressional medal.

A company of light infantry had been posted in the rear to maintain order during the charge and were prescribed whiskey to stimulate their energies in the South Carolina heat. As retreating soldiers of the 54th fled from the leaderless field, drunken rear-guardsmen tried to prevent their return. Armed with sabers, the inebriated soldiers of the U.S. Army slashed the retreating Colored troops naming them cowards, those men who had actually charged into the fusillades. At last these rear-guardsmen were overwhelmed by retreating soldiers.

The ocean tide continued to rise. Wounded men near the water's edge slowly drowned. The wails of the injured and dying could be heard by the defenders above the surf throughout the night.

So, the attack known as the Second Assault on Fort Wagner failed, with fifteen-hundred Federal casualties versus about two hundred down on the defending side. Accepting it to be a longer-term objective, the Federal infantry began a two-month siege on the sandy shore against the resolute defenders.

That heroic charge, that valiant defense, was little heralded in the press as there were forces at work elsewhere that July of 1863. Vicksburg had fallen, which opened the Mississippi to Union boats and forces, and cut off the Trans-Mississippi forces of the Confederacy from their armies in the East. Great draft riots in New York threatened to divide the Union even further.

And there was Gettysburg.

49

THE FLASHING SEA

The morning after that battle on Morris Island a general truce was called. Each side recovered its dead and wounded. Jenny had returned to the city from her Green Mountain Meadows and once again volunteered at the hospital, thinking of her secret husband Martin and praying someone like herself might help him in whatever distress he might find himself on some far-off field.

Doctor Lebie asked me to help him after the battle, and I agreed to accompany him in a small steam launch. The Doctor had with him two assistants, including Jenny, with a man's cloak over her dark dress hiding her gender from Charleston onlookers. It would have been unthinkable to many that a woman of her station would brave the scene of a battle's carnage. Men at the battery were in exhausted states of depression, shock, and general apocalyptic desperation.

She noted my appearance, and somberly nodded, perhaps remembering the evening in a dark chapel when I stood witness to her marriage to Martin. And she had heard about Isabella.

We arrived on Morris Island about 9 a.m., and it was a mess. The battle was another attempt of a vastly superior force to overwhelm a well-armed and absolutely determined defense. The beach before the earthworks was a still field of woolen blue. Still except for scavenging gulls.

After a glance I set to work to sort and bury the dead and load the wounded aboard boats for the hospital in Charleston. Battery

311

Wagner had been under siege for weeks, months. The hospital was in a tin-topped dugout dune and hot as blazes.

The doctor was cutting or otherwise preparing the men for transport, and Jenny was supervising loading of the launch. I helped move the stretchers from the shelter to the boat.

Some men survived their surgeries and went their ways to live their lives in distant lands, to eventually be buried without their complete bodies.

I wondered if those who expect the Rapture believe the body will re-join itself in mid-air, or if the body will grow a replacement arm. This thought was fleeting, and too abstract to consider on this beach of corrupted flesh, where reality abutted your senses and demanded a callous view of life and death.

Seabirds were everywhere.

I could walk along the waterline as I helped gather bodies without much emotion now – constant shock had become my world. I could calmly look in the dead face of a young Negro soldier who lay half buried in the shoreline sand, his sunken eyes and head facing the sun and his gaping mouth and throat full of washing sand.

The sun glanced its rays off the rippling sea, sparkles and flashes on blue-gray water. Hours earlier that gentle sea had hosted boats bearing flashing cannon whose fire had set the stage for this devastation.

Jenny signaled to me that another was ready. Her blue smock was stained now, streaked with the crimson blood of some seventeen-year-old child caught up in the battles of a world he never created, and from which he would soon depart.

She did not show the emotion of the fair sex that I expected. Her slender jaw was set in a clench, her lips moved in a whispered prayer. There was no doubt that she was laying her greatest blessing and hope on Martin, away in a field or forest in Virginia or Maryland. Her brow was clean and tense. She commanded in a workman-like way, and I considered that had the world been different and accepted doctors of her gender, she may have become a doctor herself.

As I lifted and carried the young men to the boat, humanity by the pound, I watched their faces, now slack, no longer masters of their fates, some grimacing in pain, some not conscious, but more often with a look of resignation and pride and general despair. They had done their work and were willing to take the consequences. I wondered if I had done the work I had been given, and what that might be. I did not realize that I was doing it even then.

During the truce many soldiers in blue uniforms were mixed with those in grey, and all within our purview were taken back to Charleston. Later the newspapers would chide and criticize those who showed mercy to my countrymen fighting for the Union, even calling the nurses, doctors and orderlies traitors. What would the Federal papers call them?

Before turning to resume our duties, we each viewed the strewn sandy plain before us. Smoke from campfires in the distance swept to the west before the sea breeze as the truce allowed each side to gather its fallen.

Gulls soared and wheeled overhead.

The Federals recovering bodies were black soldiers uniformed with red trousers, unlike those they were lifting. There wasn't much detail to make out, but the red pants or leggings were visible at a distance. Wind whipped low with stinging clouds of sand as they loaded remains into wagons.

When I returned to transport another casualty, I saw Jenny shading her eyes and looking across the field of despair where so many young men lay fallen.

Closer to the dunes was a wagon with a shade canopy and other figures around it. At the limit of my vision I could make out some taking more time over the prone figures on the sand. One was a woman, and as she turned toward us, she shielded her face from the wind and sun. Her skirts billowed from the breeze like Jenny's.

I saw she wore a dark blue dress, and at first glance I saw on her chest a white apron or towel also stained with blood. She rose from her charge and glanced toward the works of the Southern battery, and as she turned, I saw the stain on her chest was in the shape of a cross. What Christian, smeared with blood, would ever hope to wear such a device! Or, perhaps, that would be the best sign to wear in such service.

Eventually years later battlefield medical personnel did wear an actual "red cross," the inverse of the flag of Switzerland, where an international organization to aid wartime sick and injured had been founded.

As the distant nurse pulled the bloodied towel from her

shoulder, she saw Jenny. Each saluted the other with a slow wave of the arm. They shared a wordless communion of sadness perhaps only possible between women, the potential mothers of sons. Children who could end up blown to crippled pieces – or perhaps worse, who could work weapons to destroy other men. This is why women are not allowed on a battlefield. It would become obvious that the whole horrid exercise was contrary to nature.

This was a remote, sorrowful empathy of the angels of this field, and I felt unworthy to share this event.

"Miss Barton!" called the distant voice of an officer, and the Federal nurse looked to a new charge brought by stretcher bearers. She waved again to Jenny, and each turned back to the work at hand.

Sometimes I wondered that if the South had prevailed in the tragic war, Jenny might have been the world-famous nurse of the battlefield, instead of Clara.

*   *   *

I had listened to Uncle Jonathan's story, taking notes all the while throughout the morning, past the noon hour.

Mrs. McKay came in and told us we must suspend to eat, but my uncle resolutely dismissed her. He was in full recital mode and would not be interrupted.

The kind lady told us she would hold some sandwiches for us. He continued.

*   *   *

50

DOING THE OPPOSITE

When the boat held its fill, we made our way to the city.

The wounded were mostly sleeping, drugged and groggy from opium or whatever balm the doctor had administered. Some moaned lowly. One got up on his elbow and looked over the gunwale at the bay. He was black, wearing a blue jacket and no doubt wondering at his future as a prisoner of a slaveholding government.

We passed by Sumter and saw the sentinels on the walls staring at us in silence, perhaps contemplating their own fates.

More launches were plying the bumpy water. Some were accompanied by dolphins playing in the wake and bow waves. Wake may have more than one meaning, especially on an evening following a battle.

As we neared the wharf a crowd of citizens, slaves and soldiers met us and helped bring the warriors to wagons and to the infirmaries. The few women who still remained in the city peered into the faces of the wounded, searching for a son, hoping not to find him there.

I felt a definite twinge in my jaw as I trucked the wounded and dying from one room to another, some finally to the back where wagons took them to the charnel site. Their beds were now open for more of somebody's darlings, old enough to catch a bullet.

I call them children, but they weren't all young. Some were grown men who came to believe it was not right to ask the boys in the family to defend their homeland while they stayed in relative safety, protected by a wall of their own descendants.

But most were mere boys.

I don't mean small boys, but they were at the age where their adult strength was growing to its greatest. Their minds were quick and sharp. They could march, sing, aim, and fire a deadly weapon. In all this they were men.

Lately they learned from their elders that it was manly to join the army, to join these great machines of death. It was an adult thing to line up in great numbers, and on the order of another young man, to shoot hot lead into boys just like themselves. The opposite of Jesus's message.

They were children.

Anyone who had lived long enough to see the world, the dangers and evil of wars, would not have been fooled. Anyone but an imbecile.

At what point is it better to live under hated laws than to turn into a killer?

The women's charity brought foods and coffee to the hospitals. Coffee was very difficult to find, smuggled in from Bermuda or Nassau, and so was very expensive. This gracious gift from these wealthy women was brewed and brought to the bedsides of the wounded, sick, and dying.

One older soldier who could perhaps have avoided service due to his age had been stricken in the chest and lay on his deathbed. He was lucid and spoke clearly, and as he gazed intently at a blank wall, he named his father, his grandfather, his great-grand father, and his great-great-grandfather. Then his father's mother, her father, his father, and on.

He spoke crisply, precisely, and was still reciting when I left the room. When I returned in less than a half-hour his body was being lifted from his bed, which was being prepared for the next dying soul.

* * *

My uncle took a moment of rest, and leaned his head back upon the high chair back. He closed his eyes and breathed deep; then, eyes still closed, he lifted his head and began to recite again the old poem we all know:

Into a ward of the whitewashed walls,
Where the dead and the dying lay—
Wounded by bayonets, shells, and balls—
Somebody's darling was borne one day.

Somebody's darling! so young and so brave,
Wearing still on his pale, sweet face—
Soon to be hid by the dust of the grave—
The lingering light of his boyhood's grace.

*   *   *

Jenny stayed with the men in the hospital. I returned to help clear the beach while the truce still held. I wondered if God chose who was to die. But it seemed to me that often the wrong men die, and the wrong men keep living.

Soldiers who were helping me gather the dead would sometimes ask who I served with. I spoke of my work with Dr. Bailie and Dr. Lebie, and that seemed to satisfy them. Some had been tended by one doctor or the other. I think they believed me to be a corporal or sergeant assigned to him from a regular division, though I never represented that I was.

I helped load and supervise the soldiers moving the bodies of their comrades and friends onto the barrows, and carried them to the area of graves. We picked up parts of men as well.

One piece of a man I picked up was a ruddy forearm, blown off by a load of grapeshot, severed at the elbow, and retained no shred of uniform. There was no way to identify, much less reunite that arm with the body of its former owner, living or dead, Federal or Confederate. The fingers of that soul's limb curled as I grasped the arm. I noticed a ring on the small finger, a simple wedding ring, unusual for a man, but why should a wife bear the symbol of constancy and remembrance if not the husband? Perhaps he held it as a promise to give his beloved when next they met.

These two or three pounds of flesh and bit of metal told a tragic story.

I pondered the loss of the man now most probably dead, of his widow, of orphaned children at home. Their father was lost on a

317

distant field serving for a cause of one side or the other. At that point, what did that matter? The man dead, the widow and children alone?

Yet the gold band showed that he had loved. He had been willing to commit himself to another, and perhaps for a time to find solace and joy in a world so void of goodness, of justice, of comfort.

I had been willing to commit myself to Isabella. She was gone. I had nothing of her but a bracelet she had never even seen.

I carried the arm to the pit which held other arms, legs, feet. I reflected what these hands may have done in their lives: driving plows, shoeing horses, making clocks, penning contracts, caressing lovers, wives, a grandchild. The legs and feet would have walked many miles, run races, danced.

All were now buried together in a forgotten pit on a desert shore.

I clasped the disembodied hand in fellowship, and squeezed the arm that the fingers would return the embrace.

I shared the world's doom with this remnant of my brother.

51

FORM OF THE BEAST

Charleston streets were ghostly at night.

The city had been under intermittent bombardment from Federal cannon on James Island since the summer of 1863. The occasional blast of a falling shell chased nearly every person still in residence out of the city's southern peninsula. Most civilians had already moved out of town, and by now there were almost no white women, and no children – except those wearing uniforms and given commands.

I made my way to the depot where Tyrone had directed me to take the load of medical supplies he had bought from another blockade runner. The turpentine-fueled lantern on our cart cast crazy, dancing shadows on the crushed shell and sand road. The medicines we were carrying were so valuable that the cart was under guard. Tyrone had succeeded in hiring two Irish workers, each of whom carried a club. Both had knives in their belts. I had a knife, too. And my French pistol hidden in my coat. Nobody knew what our cargo was except me.

Morphine and opium were at a premium in those days. Many women across the state, wives – often widows now – were encouraged by the authorities to grow their own poppies and harvest the gum from the buds. A nick by a knife on the bulbous stem would cause poison sap to drip down the plant, to be scraped off, collected, then bottled for further refinement by the medical corps. That drug from the lovely blooming plant allowed doctors to shear off the limbs of the women's husbands and sons without the violent animal struggles hopeless men will sometimes perform when they realize they are being mutilated.

The opium we carried was very high grade, much more potent than the homegrown product. It was imported from Asia through the British colony of Jamaica, then secreted in fast blockade runners among the bags of sugar and coffee, gunpowder, books, boots, silk cloth, firearms, and other necessities, contraband, and frivolity.

The Irishmen were quiet for a change, not joking or speaking. One, a veteran, had been wounded at Secessionville, and though mostly healed was missing most of his right hand. He was still able to wield a club. The other one was older, both quiet. I was not comfortable around them tonight. Both reeked of perspiration and whisky as they plodded beside the cart, their foot treads silent compared to the shuff-shuff of the mules' hooves on packed oyster-shell and sand. The cart creaked as it rolled over the road, but mostly all I heard was damning silence.

The city had become grim and resolute in its need for survival through the war. The dark roadways and walkways matched the mood of the somber shadow figures marching toward the train. Gas lights still illuminated the streets in some parts of town when needed, but most lights were a few lanterns held by soldiers and train station personnel. Burning piles of debris lit faces and silhouettes of guards, workers, featureless men who waited.

We were all waiting.

Jenny had departed Charleston once again to be with her father in Flat Rock.

Despite the rallying statements in the newspapers telling everyone about the glorious victories the South was winning, we knew what the waiting would bring. The growing toll from the limited resource of young men told the true story.

The hour was midnight as we approached the depot. Church bells, those that remained in their towers, were silent that late at night. I looked for the representative from the army medical corps who had already paid for the drugs and medical implements. We came up to the depot and waited, not quite in the light of the lantern by the track, but close. As we waited, a rumbly feeling gripped my guts, and I feared another bout of the looseness which had afflicted me earlier. The rumble became more pronounced, and I realized that it was not inside me. I could hear it. A dark train entered the station.

As it neared, several noncommissioned officers led a squad of armed regulars to the tracks and ordered everyone to back away, to leave the area if not working in their special detail. We wheeled our loaded cart out of their area, back near a row of warehouses.

"Are you Jonathan, from Tyrone's Mercantile?" whispered a man standing in the blackness near the building. I held the lantern up and looked him over. The doctor was dressed in a dark suit, white shirt, and worn bowler hat, elegant once. Now he was gaunt, with the pasty complexion of the exhausted. He was tall and stern, careworn and older than his years. I guessed him to be about forty years old, but his eyes showed he had seen much more; no doubt many lifetimes had passed under this gaze.

"Doctor Moor, please show me your receipt."

He showed me a paper signed by Mr. Tyrone and that was good enough for me. I had him sign for his delivery. He was accompanied by four privates, a sergeant, and two slaves, one black the other high yellow who could perhaps pass for white. But if he were to do so, he would be given a gun and sent to his death.

The Irishmen with me opened the tail gate of the wagon and stood aside as the African sons of America wordlessly transferred our load to their handcarts, later to be shifted to a waiting train car bound for Hades.

As I stepped out of the way onto a landing platform, I felt a twinge again in my right jaw. How can lifting a leg cause a pain in your jaw? I have heard the Chinese have a medicine based on one part of your body effecting another, but I don't know.

"I must be off later tonight," the doctor said. "There is movement of the troops to the west, and this shipment may be exhausted in a very short time. It hurts to think that this will be enough only for some of them." He paused, losing composure as he turned toward me pleading. "They cry when I cut them."

Who wouldn't? I'd heard this before, and had seen it at Battery Wagner, and didn't want to dwell on it. Bloody stupidity.

"Safe journey." I turned away and that is when I saw the Beast.

I have witnessed bears fighting dogs and was impressed by their strength as they slapped away their ravening tormentors. Mountains of flesh and tusk called elephants are used to move logs and the heavy gear of circuses, and are awesome to behold. I have traveled across the ocean sea twice and seen whales hung from ships' cranes for butchering, the sad, harmless giants. All of these were naught when I consider what man had wrought.

Balloons, cannon, sharpshooter rifles, monitors. Rifled long-ranged cannon were bombarding the city now.

Rockets, torpedoes, mortars, Greek fire. What other demonic inventions were possible?

My gaze that dark hour was of a sight I had never considered before. The mass of gray clad troops which had moved us from the trackside was now looking as a man toward a shrouded form, lying prone on the flat bed of a railcar behind the dark train. As the shroud was lifted, I saw the form, large as a whale, and became aware of its purpose.

Inventions are created to ease man's efforts in his various endeavors. What I saw was an invention to improve his ability to destroy, to kill.

The madness of man is boundless.

The metal shape appearing from the tarpaulin was that of an iron segar long enough to be smoked by Zeus himself. Or rather Poseidon. The bolted and welded tank looked like a long and round boiler from a stretched locomotive, only much longer than reasonable, and with a streamlined front and rear. Rather, call them bow and stern because this was a sea vessel. And what sort of sea craft would be brought into Charleston in the dead of night, this beleaguered and besieged sea port? No fishing boat, no pleasure craft.

The top of the ship had a hatch, but not of wood. This hatch was of metal and appeared tight against any intrusion of an undesired element, such as seawater.

I JONATHAN

This was an underwater craft of war.

The faces of the troops turned toward the warship as a last bold hope for the salvation of the city. Chains were attached to the submarine boat. Cranes and tackle and skids began to ease it onto another car bed, which would take it to a launch site.

Before I could watch further, my company and I were ordered to move on, and we did. I released the workers and they went their ways. I was tired, weary of dark intrigue of contraband late at night in the company of stinking sullen Irishmen. I was a witness to a new device of murder, while being the deliverer of a balm for easing dismemberment of children.

God must look down on this world and weep. Is this the natural state of his progeny, after being driven from Eden? Will the sons of Abraham and the pupils of Christ be ever such?

And of my own state then. Isabella! My forlorn hope of finally finding a life! Is this fair to me? To you, my lost darling?

No.

No one noticed, and therefore no one cared that I had kept one of the bottles holding the black syrup of opium. I turned the wagon toward the warehouse, to my eventual rest, and another day of wasted labor, a little closer to death however it will come to me.

*　*　*

True to her word, Mrs. McKay brought us food, and we ate lunch late that day.

I left my uncle to his nap and walked around the block, then down Main Street. I passed the Carolina Theater building where some construction was going on, and walked on down to the creek. It was good to stretch.

I was slowly coming to the understanding that I may be the only person who can write down this story of a man's life who had lived through so much.

My field was to be business, not literature or art or whatever this is to be called. I doubted I could do a good job, but there was no time, no time.

I walked back up Church Street to Uncle Jon's place where I waited in the parlor until his nap was over and he came back to me.

He seemed to want to get right to it. He also knew there was not much time.

* * *

52

FINGER OF GOD

It had become obvious to General Beauregard and his officers that Morris Island was losing its value as a viable and defensible base. Week after week of threat, bombardment and outright assault had not taken Battery Wagner, which in August of 1863 could still defend the entrance to the harbor. Yet it was wearing.

Several times a day a courier would mount his horse and dash from Wagner to Battery Gregg at the extreme northern tip of Morris Island with his report, braving shot and shell from Federal sharpshooters and monitor cannon. The horse would be watered, the reply would be penned, and the courier would again mount and fly amid missiles to the shelter of the dune walls of Wagner.

The trenches slowly drew ever nearer the battery; the movement of supply boats became more hazardous.

Finally the order was given, and the troops began to withdraw at night, boating to Charleston under cover of dark.

There was debate on shooting the small gray horse the couriers had used so well. One of the soldiers stood fast and would not permit it, so as the men left, he blessed the beast and gave it water and what shelter he could when he left.

The flags remained flying above Wagner and Gregg when the last soldiers left the forts abandoned.

For three days the Federal forces believed them to still be defended despite reports by Confederate deserters that they were empty. They did not approach, remembering the futile attacks of July.

At last they realized there were no defenders.

When the Federals occupied Wagner and Gregg, they found a redoubt vacant except for the messenger horse that had so intrepidly done its duty along that dangerous and barren coast.

Years later I returned to the beach of Morris Island, and in the gusting airs I saw streams of windblown sand lifted from the surface of the beach. They flitted across the ground like the souls of men buried beneath the shore, seeking escape from that tormented land to a safer and more restful place.

I wonder if their search was in vain.

In mid-August guns of the U.S. Navy turned on Fort Sumter again. They were joined by shore batteries, and a huge bombardment began that threw more than one thousand shells in the first twenty-four hours. After five days the fort's guns were not firing. The Federal assumption was that it was no longer effective as a battery, and they were right.

The heavy guns had all been dismounted by the blasts. Most were removed and mounted at Fort Moultrie on Sullivan's Island north across the main channel.

Charleston sent a few sharpshooters to Sumter so that at least a minimal means of attack was available against opposing batteries.

Sharpshooters are not the same as regular troops. On Sumter were four of the most fearful and unusual man-creatures I have ever seen.

They dressed more like wild game hunters than soldiers. There were no bright buttons nor buckles that could reflect sunlight and present targets to opposing sharpshooters. Their eerie eyes were covered in smoked glass with rough-ground lenses appearing gray except for the very center of the lens, where a large, dark pupil-like center made them focus on their targets without distraction.

These men were not excitable youths who could be goaded into charging a gun emplacement or running up a hill at defending troops. Generally silent, these were methodical craftsmen.

They would usually deploy themselves hundreds of yards in the rear of attacking or defending troops, on a hill or berm where there was a clear view of the field. In this case hundreds of yards of seawater separated them from their game.

The Whitworth Sharpshooter Rifle was long, with a

hexagonal twisted bore instead of regular grooved rifling. A machined slug fit the channel of the barrel and was driven by a powerful charge of powder. It was often fired while the shooter was in a recumbent pose, or prone. The rate of fire was not rapid like that required from a soldier on the line. The sharpshooter took his time.

The shooters would survey the target areas with powerful binoculars, an invention of the French, to determine their mark. Artillerymen were often targets, up to forty-five hundred feet away. The gun was charged with powder, then the hexagonal bullet was slipped down the muzzle and rammed home. The marksman would lie back against a support of stone or post, or on his belly with the rifle barrel supported by a forked rest, and view his aim down the long barrel.

He was in no hurry.

Because the slug was so heavy relative to common Minié balls, wind was not quite the factor as with lighter rounds. The one-in-twenty-inch twist of the rifling made the shot, if well aimed, highly accurate. It was said that Queen Victoria took a try with the weapon at a demonstration and shot the bulls-eye from a target at four hundred yards. But I think most monarchs don't go into battle these days.

When the sharpshooter was ready, steadying his rifle, adjusting very slightly for the sea breeze, he took a deep breath and slowly exhaled. When he felt the aim was true, he gently squeezed the trigger.

Because of the distance to the target, the victim would often not hear the report from the long rifle. The puff of smoke was not seen. To he who was targeted, the day was still bright and fine; the gulls spiraling overhead were a gay sight. Waves sparkled out to sea.

Perhaps he had been hoping that the cook would prepare some of the fish his messmates had caught that morning. They had brought out some line and hooks and had earlier cut poles from a stand of cane on the other side of the island.

He may have thought that he must remember to write his mother later that day, after his shift at the Columbiad, after firing four or five balls at that mound of broken brick called Sumter off across the water, which now resembled a volcanic crater.

He probably wondered whether men could still be alive there after the walls had collapsed, after their cannon had been silenced.

There were no weapons there to fear now.

Perhaps his last thoughts were of his mother, of a delicious meal, of the beauty of God's creation.

When he fell, it was as if the invisible finger of God had gently touched him and bade him rest.

Across the water the sharpshooter stood to survey his handiwork with the binoculars.

And slowly reloaded his rifle.

53

INVULNERABLE TO BULLET
OR BLADE

The monitors attacked Fort Sumter again.

It was a pile of smoking brick rubble, it appeared sterile of life. So the American Navy decided to claim it.

In the middle of the black night of September 8 a force of about five hundred soldiers, marines and sailors was towed in open boats near Sumter. The boats were rowed to occupy the crumbled fort. They expected at most only a skeleton staff of watchers and signalmen amid the ruins.

More than three hundred armed soldiers awaited them, and they were as ready as they could be. They had received a signal from the gunboat *Chicora* warning of the expedition and when the marines and sailors drew near, a withering rifle fire from the fort met them. As they drew closer to the ruin, guns of the batteries Moultrie and Johnson previously sighted for this expected move opened up on the fort's beach. Cannon from *Chicora* fired on the Federal boats.

As they landed, the surprised force immediately sought shelter in piles of blasted brick while being shot at and hit by hand grenades, firebombs of turpentine and pitch, and hundreds of brickbats.

The supporting boats thought better, withdrew, and the men ashore surrendered with a loss of more than a hundred twenty-five killed, wounded, and captured.

Jacob Johnson was still my friend and benefactor. Some nights I joined in the fellowship of the fire companies, now largely manned by Negroes. His company was battling fires during a busy week.

329

Incendiary shells caused much of it. A call was sent to us to fight a fire on the island of Fort Sumter itself. There had been an explosion.

By that time in December the fortress was reduced to broken bricks with few wall fragments still standing. The men inside the fort had dug tunnels and caverns in the rubble where they would maintain their weapons, sleep, eat, and prepare to defend their harbor while living in subterranean misery. Despite regular shelling by Federal monitors outside the harbor, the defenders could still sometimes remount a few rifled cannon of good accuracy and direct fire onto the floating menace.

Some of these metal boats, called "cheese-box on a shingle" because of their design, would receive as many as a hundred strikes in a few hours from big guns on supporting batteries at Johnson and Moultrie and Sumter. One can only imagine the life experienced by the crews encased in the floating metal batteries. Inside they were washed by rolling seas, cooked by the bright sun, and pounded into ringing senselessness by the hammering of twenty- and thirty-pound iron balls on the steel plate only two feet from their heads!

Thousands of shots fired from the fleet onto and into the fort had completely blasted Jacob's carefully laid masonry fortifications into shattered fragments. I recalled the walls I witnessed being laid by Jacob high on his scaffold and his crews when I first arrived only three years previously.

The men lived below ground with their stores, their munitions, their whiskey, ready to rise and defend the lump of rocky ruin.

No one knows what caused the Fort Sumter explosion that December morning in 1863, just a few days after the night attack by the Federals. Some say it was a lantern knocked from its perch, igniting spilled whiskey and then gunpowder.

When the powder lit and exploded, men were blasted to bloody pieces, and others were concussed into senselessness, some never to recover.

Stunned and deafened men staggered from the holes and dragged their comrades with them when possible. Then the rest of the stores caught fire, as did the caves' supporting timbers.

The fire raged for days. Our fire crew and several others were called to the ruined fort. We spent two hours on a large launch steaming our equipment to that tragic isle.

Jacob, now the leader of our fire company and a past foreman of the masons who built this place, surveyed the ruin of his handiwork in a cool, emotionless gaze.

We left our small steamer by the lights of the fort's lanterns. We carefully walked to the smoking and glowing holes leading to what most certainly was hell.

I briefly imagined those fiery holes as openings to a giant kiln, where the bodies of men were fired and glazed into stoneware soldiers, a regiment invulnerable to bullet or blade.

We were there for three days and really couldn't do much good to save anything. The fires were too deep. The smoke prevented access to the burning rooms, so we flooded them with water, then pumped them out.

While we cleared the holes of the burnt flotsam and items stored in the caves, I came across the charred fragment of a club. On it was scratched the markings, "A. Dblday," and I recognized it as a baseball bat, the property of the foul-tempered lieutenant Abner Doubleday. I recalled he did not like my appearance that morning I was found floating in the dingy after poor Ricardo's party. I reflected that it was good for me that he did not have that club at hand that morning.

I suppose it had been quite some time since baseball was played on the island.

The injured were transported to the city. Bodies were recovered. Fresh troops arrived on the third day as we were gathering our gear, exhausted from our labors. The fort's commander ordered his band to play as we left, and the strains of "Dixie" could be heard as far as the occupied shores of Morris Island. Some of the Federals cheered when they heard the music, honoring the face of resolution presented by the hopeless garrison as the sun was setting.

As we pulled up the river to the city docks with troops who had been relieved, a small civilian band played. The music was not a lively tune but not yet a dirge. I clenched my teeth in the chilling wind to forestall chattering and again felt a sharp twinge in my right jaw.

Each of us was greeted by members of the town. Some of the ladies' auxiliary who remained presented us with small bundles of tea of some sort, cookies, and dried ham. On each of us, the white men anyway, the ladies tied a blue silk ribbon around our right arms. They asked our names, and noted them down. I had been given a greatcoat from some missing soldier as protection against the bluff breezes coming off the bay, so I apparently was seen as a soldier.

That event with the ribbon is what I later found such an ironic element of my life, though my realization came well after the war.

54

SANCTIONED BY SATAN

Morris Island was captured. Sumter was a wreck. Charleston itself was thus far inviolate.

Federal gun emplacements around the city had sent a cannon ball or two into town every few days for months, but the bombardment began in earnest January of 1864.

We received a shot every few minutes for the first week or two, and though the damage was not overly destructive, the effect on the minds of the people was profound. A man might be going about his business such as preparing his morning toilet, and from the sky a shell would crash though a house into his parlor and explode, making a mess of a room meant for gentle talk and quiet relaxation. Suddenly it was a blackened chamber of shredded carpet and blasted furniture.

Or a ball would flash onto a street and leave a hole to remind all passersby of the blind wrath of men who knew you not. One couple was awakened an early morning by a ball flying through their roof, into their bedroom and through their bed itself, between the husband and wife lying there. It was rather a miracle neither was hurt, though it could easily have been taken as a disapproving sign from On High of their nuptial contract, or at least its continuing consummation. Or perhaps a sanction of the union by Satan.

I sometimes wonder if that union produced a child.

One eighty-three-year-old gentleman was out for his evening constitutional walk when a shot from a four-mile-distant cannon visited him in a flash and left with his leg. All that remained was lameness for the rest of his life.

One may wonder what those men cleaning, loading, aiming,

and pulling the trigger on the weapon were thinking as they took target reading on the spires of the town's churches. Perhaps mere target practice, not really aware of the distress of the citizens, of the elderly cripple, of the permanent fright of the population. Perhaps revenge for a fallen comrade.

I would arise from my warehouse pallet or some doorway or vacant house and survey my world. Striding forth with my pack, I remembered the curse on my head, and felt that I destroyed the world again that morning.

If I were to tell that to the people I see every day it would only have confirmed in their minds the current popular opinion of me. Well, they can all go to Hades. And I would see them there.

The previous night in my drunken agony I had realized that this was my great destiny, most probably: to wander the slums of this city receiving fire from the sky as it degrades and burns, finding satisfaction in decay, and hating every fine thing I saw. My universe had devolved into simple carnage. My chance for redemption died with Isabella.

At night when a shell containing "Greek fire" found a flammable target and the fire leapt into the night, amid the screams (or worse – silence) of the family whose home was burning, fire crews including ours raced to the scene and began pumping and clearing out what could catch fire around the blaze. As water pumped and our axes flew, it seemed that the aim of the distant enemy was directed at the glow they could see in the sky. So we dodged (or at least feared) flying metal from above among the lapping flames and collapsing walls. Those nights of smoky labor wore us out, as often the blazes spread to neighboring homes or business buildings.

During one of those conflagrations a fire crew working beside us was struck directly by a falling ball that smashed their pump engine to fragments. Two of their members were killed in that instant, and two more failed later. As I sought to steady one of the surviving horses from their pump carriage, my horse-lullaby failed to calm him enough to prevent his thumping me soundly on my right calf, and I limped for days after.

The survivors in the shattered fire crew righted themselves and continued their work. They eventually joined other crews or a rifle company, where they might achieve whatever vengeance they felt they could on powers commanding the faceless enemy in the distant swamp.

The increased bombardment also had another effect.

The iron sub-water craft known as *CSS H.L. Hunley* had had several mishaps in its history, including at least three times sinking with entire crews of eight men aboard. All the crews died on the first two sinkings. On the third event, which happened in Charleston harbor during training, three men escaped and the toll was only five dead sailors. They had been attached to the *Chicora* and had volunteered to work the submersible.

Lowering gray clouds of dread gathered ever deeper about the town as resolve to survive lingered.

A new crew for the submersible was formed. The defenders were desperate to strike blows against forces that were now putting hundreds of shells and balls onto my city.

The *Hunley* was without doubt a flawed weapon, yet its potential was evident to everyone. Hopes were that it could be an element of offense and perhaps break the cordon of restraint of the port.

But it was obviously a most desperate act.

Torpedoes or marine mines were used to protect many harbors in the areas of the Rebellion, and the Confederacy had some success in the use of them. I have heard it said that more Union ships were sunk by Confederate torpedoes than the number of ships in the Confederate Navy – not many I suppose.

Other stealthy craft had been deployed with various degrees of success. They were known as "Davids" and had rammed explosive torpedoes into the sides of blockading ships.

The original *CSS David* was the prototype for those boats. They were about fifty feet long and shaped much like the *Hunley*. These boats drew five feet of water and worked very low on the surface, driven by a small coal-fired steam plant. Water was drawn into ballast tanks to partially sink them for concealment. This worked well, and on dark nights some could approach ships of the blockade to ram their hundred-plus-pound charges into their hulls. At least one successfully damaged a blockading ironclad enough to send it back for repair.

That was something, I suppose.

Charles was drawn into design and manufacture of these and other torpedoes. Mostly they were anchored to float about the entrances to the harbor between and among the large tree trunk booms chained together to prevent forced entry.

Charles was respected and known for his inventive abilities, and was set to work in one of the warehouses by the Cooper River docks.

We spoke of this work, and he told me to report to him. Together we worked on some of the torpedoes with powder brought from Wilmington and from other manufacturing sites away from the coast.

He and I sometimes worked alone without others about.

"Jon, the war is lost. Whatever we do now will only delay the end and cause more to die." He was not sad about the war's end. "Or, we could save men's lives," he said. "You know, President Davis hates these mines." He said that if Federal ships got close enough to trigger a torpedo, then the city was already doomed.

Charles wheeled a barrow of sawdust to our workbench. Between the two of us we filled several of the explosive barrel devices with it and sealed them with wax and pitch. We made a score or more of these "dud" mines.

We weren't the only makers of these devices, and some were effective like the one arming the *Hunley*.

The *Hunley* differed from the davids in that it was totally submersible, a true underwater craft, forty feet in length, an iron coffin less than four feet in width and about five in height. Power was supplied by the muscles of a crew of eight sailors crouched over a long hand-driven crank.

Originally it was designed to tow a charge on a rope behind the boat, submerge under the target ship, and draw the bomb underneath to the keel where it would detonate. Various experiments and attempts had proven this method was problematical and tangly. The night of the attack on the *USS Housatonic* the torpedo was mounted on a twenty-two-foot spar, affixed to the front of the segar, like a knight's lance from the books of Sir Walter Scott.

Charles and I had not prepared that device.

It was February, and cold. The sun had set early, and by 7 the night was black but for a waxing moon just in its second quarter.

The metal boat launched from Sullivan's Island. The water was still, and the men moved the *Hunley* by cranking its screw propeller into the sea. They drove it at about one mile per hour, attack speed for this vessel.

336

I JONATHAN

I did not hear the blast, but read of it in the paper.

Out of the dark an unseen enemy approached a quiet ship filled with men far from their northern homes. The cold night, a ripple on the water, and then a sudden blast killed several men and threw the rest into frigid waters.

The ship rapidly sank, and cries of the survivors carried across to the boats searching for them. I was later told an eerie blue light shone on the water, signaling the success of the attack by the *CSS H.L. Hunley*, which was not seen again.

Apparently the iron craft, with a speed of less than two knots and perhaps damaged by the proximity of the blast, was unable to fight the current and its own weight. It slipped beneath the surface paying no heed to desperate men within their coffin of a weapon.

A chilling story, in all ways.

Later in the month we heard of another great Confederate victory, this time in Florida. The story I heard was that at the battle of Olustee three hundred local militia defeated six thousand Federal troops.

I learned long ago that not everything heard, especially involving warfare, should be believed.

SECTION FOUR

LOST
AND SAVED

55

FIRE IN HIS BLOOD

Desperate city.

By summer of 1864 only the obtuse or fanatical believed the South was winning, or even had a chance of winning. But appearances were important. Not to me anymore, but to the city, bombarded day and night.

The shells continued to do little physical damage except when they started fires. But a mental pall shaded the actions and thoughts of everyone.

When not working for Tyrone I found myself walking aimlessly around the empty doomed city, like the wandering memory of my dedicated devotion to Isabella rattling within my breast. Her bracelet in my pocket mocked me.

By the time I realized I loved her, I realized she might have known me only as a cad, even a rogue.

Martin came home on a troop train, mostly empty. It may have been an unauthorized journey.

Jenny and her family were living in their house in the mountains now. As I passed the rail station, I greeted the lieutenant as he stepped to the terminal platform. He looked more worn, though still upright and handsome.

"Jonathan!"

He told me his friend William Ledger had been wounded and sent home. He knew no more, and wanted to visit him before looking in on his family's property. His sister had moved to Columbia to avoid the distress of Charleston. Columbia had its own worries, but was not under steady bombardment and threat of imminent sea attack.

Martin and I went to North Charleston where the Ledger family had moved, out of range of the "Swamp Angel" cannon. William had arrived that early morning.

The Ledger's house servant greeted us and led us to the parlor where the family of William was sitting. They were all in tears, grieving in silence as was their way.

"Martin, I'm so glad you could come," said William's father. "He was struck down while leading his men into battle."

It was late in the war. Too late.

The battle had been fought in a place with the happy name of Cold Harbor.

A man who had been in the fight stepped into the room, a sergeant who had taken up the task of attending William in his distress.

Here is the story he told us:

> It was a cloudy day, and the Yankees had pressed forward until the brigade was forced to retreat. Minié balls and canister were flying all about. Our colonel was killed and the men of his command were failing.
>
> A friend of Major Ledger's had an arm taken off by a cannon ball.

I learned later that it was Kit who lost his arm, one of the three I had overheard that night of the plantation party beneath the huge live oak. Louis had been killed earlier. The sergeant continued:

> Captain Ledger was just promoted to major, and was obeying orders to fall back. The retreat was beginning to get disorganized.
>
> During our withdrawal the fire in his blood got the better of him and he stopped and turned to face the Federals.
>
> Believe it or not, clouds parted for an instant,

340

and a beam of sunlight illuminated the ground
around him. It was like magic.

"Charlestonians!" the major cried in his
baritone.

The retreating men slowed and turned to see
him atop a small sunlit rise.

Major Ledger drew his sword, now sun-sparkled,
and stood like Telamonian Ajax facing his foe, his
gold braid gleaming, his cockade rippling in the
breeze, the shine of his blade, and his deep rolling
voice calling to his men.

"Charlestonians!" The call charged the men
with a thrill of marshal fervor.

All of us stopped our retreat, and as the flag
bearer brought the colors near this new Southern
Ares, we rallied to his call.

"Charlestonians!"

I'm from Savannah, but at that moment I
wished to God that I was from Charleston.

We were swept into battle fury as he stood on
the reeking field.

These words from a lowly sergeant. Even common men of the
South ache to be poets.

I looked at Martin who had, I suppose, seen such things on
battlefields he had crossed. He was gazing out of the window at a
flower garden filled with blooms and butterflies, but I believe he was
seeing a different scene.

The sergeant spoke again:

The whistling air was filled now not with metal
and death, but with victory and glory, a promise of
triumph!

"Charlestonians! Forward!" the major called.
And as a man we came.

Bullets picked at our uniforms and drew blood

on some. Occasionally a comrade would fall, but our tide had turned. With a strong resolve all of us halted at his command, dressed the line, reloaded our weapons, and began an irresistible advance.

At a wave of Major Ledger's saber, the line of soldiers stopped and knelt. We fired as one, and sent a blast of fire and smoke and a thousand missiles against the yet advancing enemy line. They slowed and staggered. Holes opened in their array.

"Reload!" cried my commander in a voice like a thunderclap.

A volley from the enemy flung a score of our men to the ground.

"Advance!" and we all began a new march.

We were about one hundred yards from the Federal troops now, and as they stopped to reload, the major called us to "Fire!" A blast of brimstone. "Charge!" With a great cheer and yell we all ran, and the Federals broke and fled.

Our voices rose into a trumpeting chorus as if we were all Hannibals astride raging elephants. Our warrior champion and his banners kept the pace, and we pursued our foes until the field was taken. A halt was called.

He ordered us to re-form and establish a defensive line. We were setting our positions and beginning to dig defensive trenches with many a congratulatory word to Major Ledger. He would no doubt be granted a field promotion to colonel after that day's action.

He had just sent a messenger back with a report and a request for reinforcements and rations when he quickly turned to me. He had a beatific look of victory on his face. There was a small hole in his tunic.

He staggered and fell to a knee, then sat down.

I leapt to him and he said, "Hold the colors aloft," and he coughed.

That is how the sharpshooter's bullet found him.

I helped carry him to the rear, to the hospital, where surgeons were up to their elbows in blood said there was nothing to do. "Put him on the train for home."

No one expected him to live for more than a few hours, but we sent him back to Charleston, and I stayed by his side, giving him water and food and even a glass of claret when offered by a lady in Richmond who visited the wounded on the train.

The sergeant wiped his brow. It was a warm morning, and he was in dress uniform, honoring his dying commander. "We wondered if he would survive and heal, but it became obvious that his labored breathing and coughing were not improving. We arrived here this morning about four o'clock.

"He asked for his friend, you, Lieutenant Martin Tenate."

I accompanied Martin down the dark hallway to a door opened by another servant in bright livery.

That room was filled with light.

William was lying on a bed under a golden comforter and on bright sheets. His face was pale beneath the sunburnt cheek, his flowing bronze hair and beard bathed in rays of sunlight streaming from an open window. The wails of doves chimed their sorrow. In the corner a minister whispered from the book of Psalms. About the bed sat and knelt young maidens and matrons, and his mother who toweled his calm face with a damp cloth wetted with rosewater.

"...The Lord Almighty is with us; the God of Jacob is our fortress..." quietly spoke the minister.

William's eyes fluttered open and he recognized his friend. "Martin."

Martin strode forward.

"He has been given morphine," said an attending nurse, carelessly demonstrating the family's wealth. "He feels no pain."

The minister continued, "O clap your hands, all ye people; shout unto God with the voice of triumph."

I recalled how I had viewed William and his two friends that evening at the plantation party, when they three had sworn by their sacred honor to never rest, nor cut their hair until victory was won.

"...He shall subdue the people under us, and the nations under our feet..."

At that time and since, I have thought how silly, how unrealistically glorified those three had been, imagining themselves as knights or crusaders gone to achieve greatness for their homeland in its irrational quest.

After achieving a great victory among his friends on the battlefield and now dying among his relations in his old family home, he was going to his glory a celebrated hero. I realized that through their eyes and his own, he had lived a perfect life.

The sergeant stepped to the head of the bed and faced the gathering.

The minister halted as his comrade quoted a poem:

> *Twas in that hour his stern command*
> *Called to a martyr's grave*
> *The flower of his beloved land,*
> *The nation's flag to save.*

> *Your own proud land's heroic soil*
> *Shall be your fitter grave;*
> *She claims from war his richest spoil --*
> *The ashes of her brave.*

A pause in the room held as a sunbeam fell on young William's face.

> *Nor shall your glory be forgot*
> *While fame her records keeps,*
> *Or Honor points the hallowed spot*
> *Where Valor proudly sleeps.*

His mother and sister sobbed and the room was still.

The priest began again:

"...Though while he lived he blessed his soul: and men will praise thee, when thou doest well to thyself."

The day was cool and sunny that June morning when he was buried. The funeral procession was like a celebratory parade with carriages, great bouquets of flowers, a color guard, a band, speeches of his bravery and honor, and his blessed life.

Later I discovered that his image was used as a model for some of those Confederate statues that were put up in county courtyards all around the South a few years ago.

His whole life he had always been the hero, and he never knew any other experience. In his reality he had lived and died the perfect triumphant commander.

It is interesting to try to view a man's life through his own eyes.

Wreaths and flowers were laid on the casket at the graveside beneath the giant oak where three years earlier three cavaliers had sworn their oath. As the first hands-full of earth were thrown, Martin turned to me and solemnly said, "Jonathan. Whatever may happen to me, I call upon your oath as my second at my wedding to look after my wife."

Well, this was not really what I expected when I found those women walking the dark streets of the city that evening. I had offered to lead them, only to escort them in some level of protection.

Martin was quite serious and held me with his gaze. "Swear. Again, on your honor."

I drew within myself and reflected. I could say yes, and if all went well (whatever that might mean) I would be free of my obligation. And if Martin were to fall, who would know what I had sworn? My honor?

"I swear upon my honor." I experienced a brief pang at uttering the words I knew I would never uphold.

Martin held me again in his aura, this child of privilege and obligation, this cadet officer warring against my country. What did I owe to him and his young wife?

"Jonathan, if the world fails, we can count only on one another. I do count on you."

The band played a dirge as we all went from shade of that grand live oak tree.

And as we left the grave, clouds covered the sky. Yet as the sun fell to the west it slid below the overcast, and an orange and golden glow lit the ground where the Conqueror Major William rested in eternal glory.

56

NOT LEGAL BUT COMMON

Beer is a wholesome food, as everyone knows. It is rich in starches and esters and goodness that keeps one healthy. It discourages parasites and purifies the kidneys and liver.

Murphy sold deep rich beer and ale. Some liked the very bitter ales, some the light lagers. My preference was always the ambers, the light browns.

In the days since learning of Isabella's death I frequented Murphy's more often and tried repeatedly to drink myself into perfect health, at least to the point where I could still find my way back to my pallet. The warehouses were less busy in those July days of '64, though more crowded with walking wounded and others trying to get back home, to catch a freight train, to escape the world around them.

One rainy evening at Murphy's while improving my health and dining on a savory bowl of roasted peanuts, I met Charles. He was just back from Richmond, that fragile capital of the Confederacy.

"Jonathan," he said in greeting.

He was dressed in a tidy brown suit and vest. He refrained from displaying his gold watch chain now. Such metals were in such extreme demand, and there were men about who were beyond desperate.

He called for a Madeira and paid for it with two U.S. dollar coins. The bartender did not question it, but gave him change in U.S. half-dimes and bronze pennies, not legal but common since the currency of the realm was so lowly valued.

"Jon, I've got funding for my project!" He was enlivened by the thought, a small victory from a government willing to try anything to stave off the inevitable. But it was just a passing thought to me, because as he spoke, I bit a peanut that drove the head flesh behind my right jaw into a spasm of grief.

An ocean of fiery pain lit up my scalp. My eyes must have shown the sensation.

"Jon, are you in pain?"

His startled and worried expression might have been comical, except that I was in another world right then, with knife-wielding demons slashing at each other above my jaw.

"Toothache," I stammered.

"Oh," he comforted. We both knew that the regular dentists were all in the army, as were doctors. We both also knew that the finest dental attention now available would likely be an elderly barber wielding a pair of pliers.

He ordered a brandy for me. "Here, for now this will help a bit, I think."

Memory struck me of the glass of brandy I had shared with poor Ricardo, bonhomme.

I quaffed the tumbler, less of a vintage than the dram from three years earlier, both in its quality and its lack of Richard's essence.

That tooth had bothered me for a while, more of a nagging tickle, but hadn't reared its power until that mighty misplaced peanut when it stood up on its hind legs and roared.

Charles kept talking, not really comprehending what I was enduring. "I heard about Isabella. I'm sorry, Jon."

Yeah. Sorry. The throbbing had subsided just a bit, and I tipped up the last of my pint. I called for another. Getting healthier.

"Tell me what you've got in mind," I said, not really thinking of anything but avoiding another brain blast, but willing to remain still and act like I was listening.

We went to a booth, sat, and maybe he didn't notice that I couldn't focus. Or maybe he did not care.

He spoke of things I did not grasp. Of parabolas, delayed fuses, grams and grains, compressions and resistances, and oh, my head!

My experience with teeth told me my tooth issue wasn't going to resolve itself. As I finished yet another volume of health-drink and ordered again, I recalled a bottle of opium I had secreted in my rucksack left in Tyrone's office. It held promise of at least a respite of relief sometime the next day.

The rest of the evening was nothing I remembered, though I did recall Charles helping me to my cot, thanking him.

57

ARGUMENTS AND INDIGO

Morning's grayness forced itself upon me, and in my dank awareness of the evening's liquid fortification I felt a pulsing throb. My tooth. This is something all men must face.

I had had luck in my life regarding tooth health. My mother imbedded a strong element of personal hygiene including brushing my teeth with soda. I had postponed the more severe tooth problems throughout my youth. But now at the ripe age of twenty-two years I faced that I must lose a tooth. So age we all, our mouths calendars.

I roused myself in the morning and leaned against the wall by my pallet. The pain in my jaw was a throbbing constant. I drew the bottle of opium tincture from my sack and drank a long sip in hopes of temporary relief.

I briefly considered taking the whole bottle, which I expected would ease my pains permanently. But first I would seek the counsel of my friend Jacob, who had been help in the past.

I made my way to Tyrone's office, and he was in. His business was slow, and he had nothing for me that day, so I took up my sack and left to seek out the house of Jacob.

It was something of an extravagance, but I took the omnibus, still running then and carrying a few servants and soldiers. I rode from the Exchange on Bay Street up King, to Line and beyond. I walked past the race course where hundreds of Northern prisoners waited their exchange, or movement to Andersonville, or just their next meal.

I JONATHAN

The race contests at the track those days was of a different sort.

Among the prisoners were some Negro soldiers captured from the 54th Massachusetts Volunteer Infantry. At first there was no debate about what to do with black prisoners. They were either escaped slaves or free men taking up arms against white slaveholders. In either case they did not deserve the same rights as white prisoners, and should either be returned to their "owners" or executed as slaves in insurrection.

That was the common argument at first.

In some cases, such as the Fort Pillow incident many surrendering black soldiers in uniform were simply shot. Though commanding officers ordered the men to stop before all were massacred, it had happened. That crime forever tarnishes honor of the Southern Army by any who hear of it.

Some Southern lawyers made an opposing argument to black prisoners' separate treatment: any man who wore the uniform of the U.S. Army should be treated as a prisoner of war, not as an escaped slave. Consider how the North's Confederate prisoners would be treated if the South chose to treat some soldiers of the United States without rights, without dignity.

The lawyer was persuasive, as were arguments and threats from the U. S. Government on its possible treatment of prisoners in their custody, and nothing was resolved before war's end. So captured black prisoners were often held with white prisoners, which was still a grim prospect.

I hurried past the track. Being white in a prison with scant food and blankets would be bad enough without worrying whether the race you were born into would make things worse.

I reached Jacob's house on Grove Street. My jaw throbbed with each step.

Jacob's wife Chloe greeted me. "It's been a long time, Jon. Glad to see you haven't been sent north yet." I was, too. She thanked me for the gift of baking soda I had brought from Nassau the previous year. She was making wheat bread this morning.

She fed me some cornbread and I gave her another present, a great gift, one of the last bottles of French perfume I had bought in Nassau. I had sold most of the rest at a good profit, and I had more money then than I had had since I was in Europe. Luckily it was mostly in silver.

And I still had a silver dollar from Ricardo's jacket. And his cursed key.

Chloe noticed my gingerly chewing.

"Bad tooth?" I grunted assent.

"What you going to do about it?"

Again a grunt.

I had nipped from the bottle of opium that morning. I was fully aware that it was a temporary remedy, and doom was falling.

"I think you need to see Brother Agur."

He bore a biblical name from Proverbs. I had heard of him, and of other "conjure-men," though I had not met any.

A conjure-man or root doctor was a folk medicine witch-doctor who carried on traditions of old Africa including healing, casting and undoing spells, messages from beyond, and more. Some called it "Voo-Doo."

Anyway, I had come to this house for some advice, and here it was. Chloe sent word via her littlest daughter Hanny to the house of Agur's mother.

While we waited, Chloe continued her work baking bread. She told me a tale of what Agur did once about three years before.

"There was a slave and master," she said, "who loved each other like father and son. The old master named Baker had a small farm, not a plantation really, where he still grew indigo dye plant along with his food crops. The old man was raised on an indigo plantation when he was a boy. There used to be indigo plantations all around."

She had mixed her batter, added the yeast starter and was letting it rise near the stove.

"Now this slave named Tobe was a boy of nine when he was given to the old man by a wealthy relative. Mr. Baker wasn't old then, just about twenty-five. He took good care of the boy who helped

352

around the house and farm, including growing and making indigo.

"To make indigo dye you have to farm the plants, then soak and beat the plants into a slush. Then you churn the slush like butter until the water gets thick, then strain it and let it settle to the bottom of the tank. Drain off the water, and that mud paste is dried and cut up. That's the dye you sell.

"Anyway, the man never found a woman he wanted to marry, but he had a happy life in the country, just him and Tobe, and God's nature all around them, growing older together.

"They would come to town together, sometimes both of them with blue-stained hands, and the man would sell his indigo to local dealers who sold it for dying small batches of cloth. It was good quality, but by then most people bought what they needed from new suppliers in South America.

"Eventually his regular buyers grew fewer and he had to travel to the upcountry to sell his dye. He left Tobe behind to keep the property up, pay his bills and milk the cow. He went to Greenville, Flat Rock, and eventually over to the Brown Mountains area of North Carolina where he was able to sell his dye. Tobe found that out later. The old man's bank reported a paid amount from the dealer he sold to up in Morgantown.

"Well, old Mr. Baker never did come back. Tobe grew more worried when he did not return. He was told to maintain the farm, and that's what he did for years until he too grew old and finally died. Some say of a broken heart."

I had finished the cornbread and was sipping the yaupon tea with honey. I did not see where this story was going. Sad, but pointless.

"Well, when they buried Tobe, they put his lantern on top of his grave. That's what lots of us folk do, lay some item owned by the deceased to ease their spirit, make it feel restful and at home. Some say, 'Live and learn, die and forget all.' Some say the dead don't forget.

"But Tobe was buried wrong. He was buried cross-wise to the world. His head was in the north and his feet were in the south!"

She expected me to draw something from this, but I did not.

"Well you see if a man dies a violent death then he should be buried north-to-south, but Tobe died a sad death, a quiet death, and should have been buried east-to-west like everyone else. Well, his soul could not get no rest!

"People would go by the old house and hear owls, or see lights above the grave, what we call jack-o-lantern. Every full moon the trees around his grave were full of strange noises and creatures. He was not resting in his ease."

Chloe's batter had rested and risen enough to knead.

"People knew Agur's family, knew some of them had 'the sight' and might well have an answer for poor Tobe's restlessness. So they were sent for, and Agur, his mother, grandmother, and uncle all came to the gravesite. They all looked worried and looked around them like they were beset with invisible dogs or demons or something. Only Agur stood firm. He was just a boy then.

"Agur was calm. He walked over to the grave and grabbed a handful of dirt from it, and he sniffed it. He held it to his ear and listened to it. He smelled it again, and then he tasted it.

"When he did that his family all stood away from him and backed up far away."

She paused in her labor and looked straight at me.

"He said he could fix this, and we wouldn't have to dig up that body that had been in the ground for six months."

Chloe began working the dough again.

"Later he told us part of what he did. He waited until midnight on the next new moon and went alone to the grave with a black cat and a white cat who were born in the same litter. The white cat was in a bag, and the black cat was in a cage he made of cane.

He took up old Tobe's lantern and cleaned and fueled it and made it light. Then, in that ghost light he held down that bag and hit the white cat on the head with a black stone and killed it, all in sight of the black cat. He took the dead cat out of the bag and held it close to the black cat, his brother, who smelled it and smelled death.

"Then he buried the white cat in the same grave as poor Tobe, set the cage on top of the grave, and opened it to let the black cat out. The cat stepped out onto the grave, looked around and up at the stars, and began walking to the west. That's the last anyone ever saw of that cat, at least around here."

She divided the dough into four large loaves and set them on a pan to rise some more.

"Agur removed Tobe's wooden grave marker and burned it in a bonfire, one hot enough to destroy that lamp, too, and threw the ashes in the Ashley River.

"And there have not been any more spooky sounds around Old Tobe's grave since then, and now I don't think anyone could even find it exactly."

As she finished, she looked up, as did I, to see Agur coming out of the woods trail and across the swept yard.

"Some people say that a few months after that, a black cat nobody knew ran through Morgantown. And sometimes there is a light up in the mountains just wandering about without any destination. But those of us who knew Tobe know what it is." She stopped talking and nodded.

Little Hanny came into the kitchen, wide-eyed, several steps away from Agur who was a curious looking fellow.

Agur, the mighty conjurer and necromancer was a slight boy, maybe eighteen, slender. He wore a sleeveless brown shirt over dark amber skin, shining and clear. His shirt was cut above the waist, and his light brown trousers were belted with a hemp rope. They were cut off at mid-calf, and his feet wore sandals.

His head was done up in a small turban much like Chloe's, but it was dark blue. His sharp cheekbones gave him a nearly oriental face, with thin eyebrows and lips, a broad nose and eyes of nearly clear water blue.

He had no facial hair, and if I didn't think it was impossible, I would say he had applied woman's makeup.

He did not smile.

"Brother Agur, this white man is our friend, and he has a bad tooth."

He looked at me in silence for a moment. When he spoke it was in a very deep throaty voice, quiet and slow.

"Do you hurt when you drink cold or hot?"

I told him cold, though nothing cooler than spring water without any ice now available.

He looked at me with those eyes for another full minute, never wavering. Mesmerizing me, I think. For a minute my tooth pain was completely gone. The blood rushed in my ears.

"Your woman died," he said, and was silent again.

After a moment he asked for a pen and paper, and wrote something on it, nearly filling it with his script. Then he got up with no more word and stood before us.

"Thank you, Brother Agur." Chloe then handed him the small bottle of French Perfume I had given her. I nearly tried to stop her, knowing its value, but said nothing.

Agur gazed at the little bottle in his hand, then looked again up at me and Chloe, turned without a word and slowly walked from the kitchen.

I watched him leave, and noted his gait was smooth and sweeping. He slowly walked down the trail and back into the shady wooded grove.

The notes on the paper he had written were in a fine hand, not feminine, bold and quite legible. When I read what the words said I could not believe it was a cure for anything.

The instructions were to hold a buckeye rolled in the right shirt sleeve, the side of my tooth pain, then to make a soup of boiled earthworms, turpentine, bacon fat, and some roots of plants that I did not recognize. I was to take this brew with me.

Part of the prescription was to go north to a part of the peninsula where there was a sort of swampy sand island meadow. In the center of the meadow at midnight, I was to sit on the ground and draw a circle around me with a live oak branch and drink a half-gill of opium, then the soup. And I must do this within three nights of today.

Now I don't know how that child knew I had a bottle of opium. I had told no one and had kept it hidden, but that was in his recipe. I still had about a half-cup in the bottle.

I had strong doubts about this and was ready to look for a

strong barber, but Chloe was adamant.

"That conjure-man tells you what will fix that tooth!"

But I was not convinced that I should drink worm soup and sit in the mud at midnight. I thanked Chloe and took my leave.

"Alright, Jon, but you come back when that tooth gets worse!" and she bade me give her regards to Tyrone. "I'll have that soup ready for you!"

58

BEARING THE WEIGHT

The tooth throbbed but not enough to distract me from getting back to town. I walked, then rode the public carriage to the Exchange, then walked to Legare to the house where Abe was house-sitting for one of his absent patrons.

There was no music coming from his house that day, but I wanted his advice. I had seen a witch doctor and hoped there was a Jewish remedy not as bizarre. I had heard of weird Hebrew rites that I did not want to believe. The strange rumors of Jews were completely at odds with the experience I had had with Abe, or with the other Jews I met in Charleston.

The Israelite community of Charleston is very old. They were among the first colonial families and were mostly of the Spanish traditions of Jews, which is apparently a bit different from the German and other Eastern European traditions.

Jews were usually not given the same respect as Christians in the North, while in the South they could become leading community citizens just like good Presbyterians and Anglicans. Before the war, Georgia had a Jewish governor, and there had been Jewish U. S. senators from Florida and Louisiana. The states of the North didn't elect a Jew until the next century.

How could a society of such liberal progress for non-Christian Jews be so backward in its attitude regarding slavery of Christian Negroes?

The Charleston Jewish tradition also was the first, I believe, of the Reformed worship service, now apparently the dominant style among Hebrews in America.

I JONATHAN

I arrived at Abe's about sundown and knocked on the door. The bell had been taken for its metal.

A servant answered and recognized me. Abe was not in at the moment but was expected back soon, and I was welcome to wait.

The furniture was mostly covered with tarps in the big rooms, but in a small parlor by the front of the house was a grand piano. It was decidedly not covered and was a monument to the craftsman's art, its lid open and displaying the science of its strings.

It said, "Chickering" on the keyboard cover, and beneath that, "Boston." Another echo of my youth came charging back to me.

One early morning when I was about ten years old, Mother called me to the door to look northward to the center of the city. We lived in Boston's South End, a neighborhood where the up-and-coming families were moving. We could see from the hill on our street a great plume of black smoke curling up to heaven. We later learned it was the great Chickering Piano Works Fire, and here before me was an instrument of graceful curve and exacting science from that workshop disaster from my memory.

I was admiring the piece when Abe walked through the doorway. He was in uniform.

"Abe. Are you in the army?"

"Yes, Jon. Or at least Chester is. It's good to see you."

His face was somber, not displaying the jovial musician. He was dressed in butternut trousers, blue shirt, and his kit was as good as could be had in Charleston at that point. A complete, second-hand uniform would make him one of the best dressed soldiers in the field.

"I'm going to join up with the 10th Volunteers in place of a man who can't go back."

He told me of the soldier named Chester who had been with the regiment since early in the war, since the Battle of Stones River near Murphreesboro, Tennessee. He had marched and fought in the Tullahoma Campaign, and at Chicamauga where Billy Smith was shot. He served at Missionary Ridge and all the other skirmishes and engagements of his regiment, until his latest one at New Hope Church.

His regiment was in the Army of Tennessee under General Johnston, one of the generals who won the First Battle of Manassas three years ago when Washington City was within the South's grasp.

Chester's regiment and division sometimes won and

sometimes was beaten. Recently the marching and fighting had taken them to northwestern Georgia. As the larger battles go, that one was not large.

Sherman commanded the U.S. Army's Military Division of the Mississippi and thought Johnston was in a strong defensive position. Sherman moved his command in a flanking maneuver, but Johnston had considered his action and ordered a mass of his troops into the path of the Northern movement.

Sherman determined that Johnston had only a token force in his way and sent an attack by three divisions. This plan seemed to be succeeding as the Confederate skirmishers allowed themselves to be driven back for three miles until Sherman's force encountered the emplaced main army of Johnston.

The cannon of the Confederates devastated Sherman's forces and stopped the advance. Sherman then ordered another advance on Johnston's right flank the next morning at Pickett's Mill. That attack was also anticipated and resulted in six thousand defenders stopping fourteen thousand attackers, with sixteen hundred Northern casualties generated in about half an hour.

Private Chester Jones had had enough. He looked within himself and saw someone who could not be criticized for cowardice or for not serving his country, and he could bear no more battle. He knew the war was lost and he would not be lost with it.

During a lull in orders he left and made his way to his hometown of Charleston where he sought out Abe. He knew Abe from his days playing organ at his church and hoped he would give him shelter until he could go to the family home near Summerville. He also needed some counsel.

Chester was shattered. He had lived through battle and blast, more than could be asked of anyone. Abe said that any little noise – a door slamming, a branch falling – would send him falling to the floor in a huddle, or scrambling under a table.

He needed to heal.

"But Abe," I said, "why are you going?"

"Jonathan, this is my city, my country. I feel that I need to go. Besides," he said, "Daphne is leaving."

Daphne Barringer, the pianist from across the street, the one who created such wonderful variations of polkas, the expressive artist. The sixty-four-year-old woman who young Abe loved.

"She's going to try to make her way back to Wisconsin." His voice was steady but his eyes were brimming.

"Isabella died," I said.

"Yes, I know."

A moment passed between us.

Many of life's miseries are driven by the women we love.

"George," he said to the servant, "Please bring us the cognac." Eau de vie.

As the servant went to the liquor storage, Abe walked over to the magnificent grand piano.

That mahogany beast of an instrument was a glory in solid wood artistry. The grand design of it is understated in its carving – more like the architecture of a large Presbyterian church than an Episcopal cathedral. Its pillared legs were massive and could bear the weight of the cast iron string frame and box. The cheek had a mighty scroll like a buttress to hold up the sides of the box, and the keyboard itself stood like a broad white beach beneath the music shelf and elaborate desk.

Abe walked slowly over to the bench and sat. He placed his kepi on the music desk and placed his hands on the bright ivory keys, which would be but a memory when he was by a campfire.

His fingers lay on the white keyboard as if it was an artist's canvas, and he began to play.

The music was the tune I had heard those months ago as I walked outside his house, with Mrs. Barringer playing, then answering, then playing as he alternated phrases in their love call.

George brought out the tray of brass, not silver, as those precious items of service had all been donated for the Cause. He set it on a table and stood silently smiling, eyes closed and listening. Perhaps he recalled guests being entertained in that house in days past.

The music began soft, a yearning call, then a gentle response. It swept into a swelling cascade of notes, like a joyous hymn, then faded to a whispering prayer, lingered, then slowly drew to.... silence.

He sat quietly, then turned to George, who handed him a snifter with the brandy gently curling up the side as he swirled it, and sipped.

I sipped mine as well.

The paintings on the wall of the absent family home owners

stood or sat in mute witness to the romantic ruin of two men. Or maybe three. I don't know what George had been through.

"Abe, I never told her I loved her. I was going to marry her."

He replied, "I told Daphne. And she told me." He turned his eyes to me, light brown and pained. "She said she received a letter from her sister and was summoned home. She said she always knew she would go, return to her family."

All who knew the two of them understood that the match was not viable, yet their love out of time was beautiful to see.

"We shared our love before she left." I was not exactly sure of what he meant. But it meant a lot to him.

"I'm going to take Chester's place in the army," he said. 'They will know I'm not him, but the way things are going, I don't think they will deny me his place. From now on I'll be Chester Jones."

My tooth began to throb again, and I swallowed another gulp of French pain relief.

"The army is nearer Atlanta now. I think I can get a train seat if I tell them I'm going to war."

Yeah, everyone wants to help a young soldier going to his doom.

"They buried Isabella in a potter's field. I never got to say goodbye."

"Go to her grave," said Abe. "Tell her goodbye."

I could not bring myself to tell him of my tooth distress. It would have spoiled the tone of the evening.

Then Abe turned to his instrument once again and began a familiar tune. The words resonated in me as I drained my glass, placed my hand on my friend's shoulder, and walked from the house.

These are the lyrics, as I can remember them:

> *When stars are in the quiet skies,*
> *Then most I pine for thee;*
> *Bend on me then thy tender eyes,*
> *As stars look on the sea!*
> *For thoughts, like waves that glide by night,*
> *Are stillest when they shine;*
> *Mine earthly love lies hushed in light*
> *Beneath the heaven of thine.*

362

I JONATHAN

His lingering tune followed me to the street, up Legare. I continued the song in my mind, my hymn to Isabella, as I turned onto Tradd, to Meeting Street.

> *There is an hour when angels keep*
> *Familiar watch on men,*
> *When coarser souls are wrapped in sleep—*
> *Sweet spirit, meet me then!*
> *There is an hour when holy dreams*
> *Through slumber fairest glide;*
> *And in that mystic hour it seems*
> *You should be by my side.*

I never saw Abe again. I suppose he was killed in the Atlanta campaign wearing Chester's name, buried with his countrymen. That wondrously talented Jew, in love with a much older gentile, who was now moving far to the north. He gave up his life for his country, and his love. Suicide by patriotic war.

I was still humming the tune, feeling sorry for myself as I continued to Calhoun Street and finally to Murphy's, which was slow that evening.

> *My thoughts of thee too sacred are*
> *For daylight's common beam:*
> *I can but know you as my star,*
> *My angel and my dream;*

Vagabond of life, with my rucksack holding besides my few clothes and money, my treasures: a silver dollar coin, opium, a bracelet. And a key.

> *When stars are in the quiet skies,*
> *Then most I pine for thee;*
> *Bend on me then thy tender eyes,*
> *As stars look on the sea!*

The brandy and the walk left me tired, and after three pints of

Murphy's amber, once again my friend Charles made an appearance.

He was in work clothes this time, his sleeves rolled up and hands stained with grease and smelling of machine oil and saltpeter.

"Jonathan, you have got to see this! You will call me Daedalus!"

I was in no pain now. He bought a pint and drained it, then led me to his workshop. He had gone from torpedoes to something else.

On the walls were maps and schematic diagrams, and a large slate chalkboard covered with gibberish that I believe were calculations related to flying objects, projectiles and rockets.

As nearly as I could grasp on that mournful, painful, ominous evening, his invention was a tube of gunpowder with another tube within. At the tip of the rocket was a charge that could blast a hole in the roof of the United States Capitol!

I admired Charles for all his imaginative creations, and I knew that with men like him mankind's progress was inevitable, especially if you think development of more efficient weapons is progress.

He waxed poetical as he described the potential of an array of these super-rockets. They could remove entire regiments from battle before they were even near the front. Yet I knew Charles did not want to harm men.

"I'm off to Richmond on tomorrow's noon train. Good luck to you, Jonathan." He warmly shook my hand. "We will meet again in happier times."

With that I was dismissed, and he turned to his work.

I was drawn to my old pallet and walked the street up to the warehouse. The next day I would find solutions.

I felt the bracelet in my hand and ran my thumb across the scrolling silver and bronze work, and passed into fitful dream.

59

SOMETHING OF VALUE

The next morning I awoke with urgency.

The city was failing.

Military rule controlled everything, at least everything that could be controlled. Orders were shouted and soldiers were marching.

The city was bereft of white civilians.

My tooth hurt. I took a swig from the opium bottle and determined to solve my dental problem that day, and then make plans to evacuate my adopted city.

I went to see Tyrone, and he too had decided it was time to leave. His various business interests had mostly worked out for him, and he was cashing out.

He was not a slave owner himself except in his share of the plantation, but he sometimes handled the sale of field hands. Many plantation owners were selling off their workers to people who had property farther inland as well as in the mountains. He didn't like this business and did as little as possible, but now things were moving swiftly.

Orders from his old customers now living out of town directed him to sell their hands, and he did his best to keep families together.

I went into his office, which was both in horrible disarray and orderly disorder. He was arranging transfer of stock, both inanimate and human.

He said, "Another delivery, Jonathan. If you can."

I could.

I was to take a very large and heavy wagonload of goods of all kinds, including some of the rugs I had brought from Nassau, to the

Goose Creek area. With that load I was to oversee twelve slaves there for their eventual transport to their new station.

This was a new kind of shipment for me. I assented, and while the wagon was loading, I borrowed Tyrone's horse. I went to speak with Jacob.

As I rode north in the city a far-reaching shot of a cannon shell fell through a house about fifty yards away. It was vacant, no one to be hurt. It reminded me of how random life can be. And life's end.

Jacob, like most black men, free or owned, was helping dig earthworks around the city. He was northeast of town that day on James Island, and overseeing a crew who were enlarging and enhancing the works between the Race Track prison and the Four Mile Tavern house.

I arrived and was challenged by sentries who appeared exhausted, alarmed, alert, and heartsick all at once.

"I have orders to speak with the chief of a work party, Jacob Johnson," I bluffed.

"Orders from who?" demanded the sentry.

My tooth was throbbing now, and I was irritated.

"Captain Tyrone," I created. He always considered himself a "captain of commerce," so I took that liberty.

The dispirited soldier didn't argue. He let me through and directed me to the near works where Jacob was overseeing six Negro workers and four white soldiers in enhancing the redoubt. That work looked about done.

"Hello, Mr. Jonathan. I didn't expect to see you around."

"Hello, Jacob. Mr. Tyrone has got me transporting field hands. Can I beg your son to come with me?" I explained the situation and that I was preparing to leave Charleston.

Jacob had been nothing but a friend during my time in the Holy City. He had helped me much more than I could ever hope to repay. He did so again.

"Eli! Come over." Eli was given orders to help me.

"Thank you, Jacob. I will never forget your kindness," I told him, and despite my poor condition of hygiene and his state of perspiration I shook his hand, then drew him to me in a hug, an overt expression of affection I do not share with men. He returned my embrace, and I again realized how strong the man was.

Eli and I shared the saddle and went to Jacob's house. The

366

horse's motion was smooth, yet my tooth became an exquisite monitor of minor bumps and vibrations.

As Eli dismounted, Chloe exited the house and greeted me. "How is that tooth, Mr. Jonathan?"

Her tone was such that she knew I needed the help of Agur's medicine.

I told her that Jacob had loaned me Eli for the day for the slave transport and told her that indeed I must get some relief from my pain.

"Well," said Chloe, "I'll get that soup ready for you. You come by tonight."

So my decision had been made. I looked forward to pain-free days ahead, and dreaded the night's trial.

"And I'll send Eli with something to eat."

I rode back, and spoke with Tyrone.

"Jonathan, I'm going away. When you get to Rosy Acres, leave that cart and livestock in the livery. I'll arrange for them later."

Tyrone had borrowed another cart, and it was loaded with the rest of his possessions, books, casks and sundries. He paid me the balance of my earnings and then handed me a twenty-dollar U.S. Liberty gold piece as well.

"I'd rather have paid you Confederate, but I thought I'd best give you something of value."

The coin was heavy, and shiny, and pretty. The woman's face on the piece was looking up, so different from the downcast faces of Charleston.

I thanked him and put it with my other coins, my last silver dollar from Ricardo, Isabella's bracelet, and poor Ricardo's key. He also gave me directions for one more task, which I'll tell you about later.

And that was that for Tyrone. He shook my hand, mounted his horse and was gone.

It was years before I learned that he eventually traveled back to Ireland. The money from his trading business, his blockade-running ventures and the sale of his plantation share bought him a modest estate in the county from which he borrowed his name.

I never did learn what his legal name was.

My cart was loaded. Eli arrived with a sack of lunch for both of us, as well as packed meals for the rest of our day. We expected to be back at Jacob's house by sundown, or soon after. Chloe had packed two baskets of food for the traveling slaves as well.

As he and I ate, me carefully chewing on the left side of my mouth, two white men arrived on horseback marching thirteen field hands. They had walked from up around the Ashley Ferry northeast of the city. The slaves were mostly women, some with children including one in arms. The oldest boy was about twelve, and the youngest man was about forty. I assumed the men between twelve and forty had gone into the woods and sought out the Union Army, along with their freedom.

I directed the hands to some water and shade where they could sit to await the next march, and to eat the corn bread and boiled eggs that Chloe had been kind enough to supply.

The overseers apparently thought their job was done when they made their delivery. The elder was a Kansan and appeared eager to drop off his charges and be on his way, probably to return to "Bleeding Kansas," perhaps now bled dry and safe from invasion. First he and the other man, his son I think, would return to the endangered plantation they had left that morning to remove whatever valuables they could sell or transport to their new destination. For them the post-war world offered great possibilities.

We spoke briefly and each signed papers. I was given the slave badges. The authorities were growing more and more concerned with the movement of blacks as the Federal cordon tightened. Many slaves were growing restive, with their promised liberty so close at hand.

Finally we were on our way up Meeting Street. We showed our papers and badges to the sentinels at important crossroads, who were used to seeing more slaves being sold inland. Late afternoon we arrived at Goose Creek and the "plantation." Rosy Acres was a new plantation, or at least had a new plantation name.

There was no plantation house, just some shacks and a sort of barn apparently used as a livery station where horses were watered, fed and switched out on wagons like the one I delivered.

The slaves were directed under a shade tree before beginning the next leg of their march to their own unknown futures.

As I turned toward the path back to the city, I saw a man walking to one of the slave shacks, seeming to talk to himself as he did. I recognized him as Tommy, the slave Jacob and Tyrone sometimes hired, the one who ate pâté with me on the abortive delivery to Edisto.

"Hello, Tommy," I called, and he turned to me and smiled.

"Hello, Mr. Jonathan, I never 'spect to see you again."

We stood in the shade of a live oak and Tommy told me, using a tempo of speech I would never hear from anyone else, that his owner had sold him to someone in North Georgia. He would stay here, attached to this plantation until he was sent for.

He seemed to take the situation with serenity, just another adventure in the life of a naturally talented rhymer, his whole body his instrument.

I shook his hand, which made him uncomfortable, wished him farewell, and turned to the road. He resumed his internal conversation and walked away.

After the war when he became free, I wonder what happened to him. Perhaps he became a dancing entertainer.

Eli and I started back on foot.

60

THE GLOOMY SUN

We retraced our steps now along the sandy road. Each step brought a stinging "thump" of my heartbeat in my jaw.

Just after we passed the old Six Mile Tavern I stopped and looked to the left to the place I knew Isabella was taken when she died.

Eli looked at me, and I told him that I had to say goodbye to someone buried there. He found some shade.

I walked to the field, lumpy and hilly where the numerous nameless people without property or family were laid, freemen and poor whites alike. Most graves weren't marked.

Many fresh mounds of sandy soil were scattered about. Some of the hills were in rows, some not. At the edge of the field was the swamp, which would someday I suppose rise to submerge the graves of these people. Even their graveyard would be forgotten.

I walked the field in its gloomy and sun-blasted heat searching for I know not what.

I stopped near a mound that could have been three weeks old. I sat down in the sun, nothing but my hat between me and the hot ball in the sky. I looked about and could not feel, see or hear anything that spoke her name to me.

I pulled the bracelet from my sack, looked it over in the bright sunlight and imagined it on her wrist. I quickly buried it in the sand and left the mournful place of people bereft of hope, of friends, of even names.

No one passed us from the north though there was some

traffic coming out of Charleston. Three times we met wagons loaded with family goods. Two had only two men, both armed. One had a man, his young son, and two servants. How long could such a household exist in the coming calamity?

After another mile or so in the shadeless heat Eli turned to me and asked, "Mister Jonathan, am I going to be free forever?"

Now I always considered myself wise in ways most men could not comprehend, and indeed I suspected most men did not comprehend that I was wise at all. But this heartfelt question from an alert lad, nearly a man, demanded a serious reply.

I tried to imagine a world in which I was afraid that I might become someone's property. In my family lineage I was probably fifteen or twenty generations distant from that. This boy was his family's first free generation since Africa.

But even now, at least on paper, free blacks could still be subject to enslavement in many places if they owed money or transgressed in other ways.

One foot before the other, and the boy waited for my answer. I gave it best I could.

"Eli, no one knows what will happen. Most governments of the world run by people who can read don't allow ownership of other men. And I can't help but think America is just about there." Too many words.

"Eli, I believe you will never be a slave."

His eyes did not change. No doubt he was weighing the value of my words, and that is the least one should do when hearing another's thoughts.

The walk from Rosy Acres took us the rest of daylight and an hour or two more. Eli, being black, was illegal if out after dark, and we had no lantern. The moon had risen about noon and was now falling to the west, lighting the white sand road. The only people we met were four uniformed soldiers coming out of town, and they did not challenge us in any way.

I suspect they were deserting before the cannon balls flew again.

We reached the house of Jacob, and as we entered Chloe beamed a large grin at me. She hugged Eli, told us to sit and eat, and served us a meal of fried chicken and cornbread that was most welcome.

Again, I ate around the pain. I knew I was nearly done with it, if the root doctor was capable.

I sat in the family home of Jacob, a humble businessman on the cusp of a great change in the world, our world, his world.

That man had succeeded in building a good life for himself, had freed many of his relatives. He treated others he hired better than most of their white overseers had. He had married well, and had earned and cultivated respect among the important men in town. He had become established as one who could be trusted to work when the town began to rebuild itself, if there was anything left to rebuild after the impending doom.

In his comfortable wooden chair, Jacob read Dickens to his family by the light of turpentine lamps. Chloe was at her sewing, and the children were in the wonder of their imaginations. I fell into the trance of the words as he read:

> ...*There is a drowsy state, between sleeping and waking, when you dream more in five minutes with your eyes half open, and yourself half conscious of everything that is passing around you, than you would in five nights with your eyes fast closed, and your senses wrapt in perfect unconsciousness. At such time, a mortal knows just enough of what his mind is doing, to form some glimmering conception of its mighty powers...*

Those freemen children were learning the thoughts of a great writer and might work with those thoughts as do professors and kings.

As Jacob read, the sturdy patriarch with his woman and his progeny about him, I realized he was the one I envied most.

Sad Abe, heart broken and breaker of hearts, went to war and died.

Charles, with his machines and inventions was satisfied enough in his creations, but I wished more than contraptions and calculations in my life.

Mr. Ledger had lost his sons William and Timmy.

Mrs. Trent spent her life in deception and evasion.

Tyrone had his money and not much else, poor man.

Officer Kerry had lost his mother.

372

I JONATHAN

I had lost my wife. But she never had been my wife, and oh, how I regretted that!

I could see myself happy in such a house as Jacob's, with such a family, with Isabella, she now buried in an unmarked grave at the edge of a rising swamp. I would have given her my name. Instead I had given her nothing, and knew that she was destined to be forgotten.

But I had yet something to give her, that she may be remembered a bit longer.

In my soulful anguish I clenched my teeth, and the lion roared – the rocket flared – the bell rang.

It was time to drink worms.

61

THE STARS EXPOSED

At about ten the children were abed and the father was preparing for the same. Chloe held me in a determined stare. She brought me the note Agur had written. And a flask of liquid.

I wanted to thank her and eventually I did, but at that time knowing I was expected to drink that concoction was something I could not face with composure.

The directions included a location for my cure. Young Eli led me there. He held a small hooded lantern at the end of a stick.

I followed the young man to the north and west of the house.

"Doctor don't like lights on a dark night," and indeed the night was very dark. The moon had set, the stars shone bright enough to cast a faint shadow.

He led me to a swampy place near the Ashley River, which eventually flows to meet the Cooper River at White Point Gardens where, as they say, the streams join to form the Atlantic Ocean.

We walked across a boardwalk floating on pluff. This was far from Secessionville and areas of possible military action – completely deserted of any men.

The boards ended, and more or less firm sand became the trail not much used by people, but maybe by other creatures.

We walked in the dim flicker of Eli's lantern, sometimes hearing movement in the grass of what must be called an isle of firm ground in the marsh. There were trees now, not large.

Despite my fatigue my senses sharpened as we neared the site, holy or cursed, depending on which church you attend.

The tooth pain was constant and heavy.

We came to a circular clearing and Eli halted. He removed the lantern from the stick and handed the oak wand to me. He handed me a buckeye, and I dubiously rolled it in my sleeve. I can't imagine how he acquired it.

He said he thought he should not enter the dark glade. He told me the rest of the instructions, turned, and left. With his lantern.

I stood alone in the dark at the edge of a secret ground in a Southern swamp with a bottle in each hand, a live oak rod at my feet and a buckeye rolled in my right sleeve. My tooth throbbed.

I wondered how I had gotten into this situation.

The alternatives before me were none good. I could weather the night, return to Jacob's house for my rucksack and use my gun to end my pain. That fancy revolver could shoot twenty times; should I use all the rounds? Seemed like a waste to use only one.

Or I could try to find a strong arm with pliers, except that my pain was at the point where I would not be able to concentrate on my location, or maybe even walk. No.

At the advice of some of my best friends I was ready. I moved to the center of the dale, scribed a circle all around me in the dirt with the lantern rod, turned my eyes to the stars, and drank the last of the opium. Then quickly and without thinking I quaffed the warm soup. I didn't consider its ingredients other than that my salvation was dissolved in there somewhere.

I wished I had brought a piece of mint candy.

It was midnight, or close enough for the instructions. A crow called.

I had never heard a crow call at night.

Now that the lantern was gone my eyes had become attuned to the darkness, and the illumination of the stars was bright enough to make out that there were scores of black tree roots all over the small field. I could not see the large tree, which must have been nearby.

I looked again at the sky and remembered some lines from the song Abe played for me as I left his house:

> *When stars are in the quiet skies,*
> *Then most I pine for thee;*
> *Bend on me then thy tender eyes...*

Oh, lost Isabella. My lost life.

My thoughts of her were not the simple childish attentions I had held for Laura so many, many years previously. Well, five years before.

My loss of Isabella was my loss of a good life with a good woman, hopes of a loving wife who could share with me this cruel world and gentle it a bit.

> *There is an hour when holy dreams*
> *Through slumber fairest glide;*
> *And in that mystic hour it seems*
> *You should be by my side.*

Self-pity has always been one of my strongest features, and I put my hands to my eyes and sobbed, alone in the dark, hoping some crazy wizardry would make my life a bit better.

I sat down heavily and landed on one of the tree roots, which leapt from my weight! The root turned and snapped its jaws, as would a young alligator.

The field was covered with juvenile alligators. I froze on the ground, without a clue of what to do.

The gator I had sat on squirmed away, disturbing some siblings as it did.

The night was cool and without wind. I began to sweat profusely. Some of that may have been the effect of the opium – or maybe the worm concoction.

Some of it may have to do with being surrounded by meat-eating reptiles, perhaps with a large mother nearby.

After a minute without seeing any coherent movement I looked about to see my best escape.

The starlight was bright, the lizards were still, the crow had not again called. A rustle in the bushes caused me to turn and see a dark shape.

I must admit that observing the quiet lamplit reading of a novel in a friendly family house now seemed the antithesis of this evening's entertainment.

The opium and root medicine were without doubt having some effect. My vision became more selective; the slightest lightness became brighter, and the dark areas of sight became stygian black –

no grays, just blackest black, silver and white, though mostly black.

I focused on the movement at the edge of the infested glade and recognized a thick man-shape, its silhouette dark against the low bush's shimmering leaves. It was hunched over, with starlight glinting from its coat. Then the figure stood erect, obviously a bear.

A bear!

There I was in the lonely swamp islet, in the dark, beset with alligators and a bear!

The beast stood tall and mostly still. It wavered a bit, but on his hind legs he looked almost graceful.

Black he was, yet the halo on his head and arms reflected a celestial sheen. On his breast was plainly visible a blaze of white in the shape of a ghostly heart. In my state of witchy drunkenness I could only imagine what that might have meant.

Fortified by the poison opium, I stood and faced the creature, still careful not to tread on reptiles.

We stood there and observed each other in misty light as some stars seemed to swirl from the sky and flow between us.

I do not think eating me was in the mind of the animal. I hoped he would prefer baby gators to humans.

It is fearful to face a bear. I tightly grasped the slender oak rod as if it were a weapon of some sort.

I looked in his eyes and at that mark of white on his chest.

I at last grew fatigued at our contest of wills, man and beast. My legs began to fail, perhaps due to opium, and I wavered on my left leg. I recovered, and saw the bear waver to his right.

Intrigued, I leant to my right, and he leaned to his left.

Perhaps I should have danced with this creature all night in the starlight, and a song may someday be written, but at that moment the crow cried again. The bear turned to the sound, then dropped to four legs and moved away, to mud or land I know not. I saw him or something like that bear once more at another later time, but for that night he left me.

My experience of that midnight and beyond was something I have never told anyone. So listen and believe or not as you wish.

All the young alligators left the field as if on command. They disappeared into the brush, perhaps to seek fish in the shallows, or some land creature smaller than myself.

I turned completely around in the circle surveying the field, seeking what wonders might next appear.

Silence and starlight within my magic circle.

Even in my state of excitement I was weary. I've not eaten worms before or since. I've developed a few theories, but I have no desire to conduct confirming experiments.

I turned about and sat again in the middle of the field as directed. I had had enough of this witchcraft, or mesmerism, or whatever it was.

No more bears, and the alligators had all gone. I lay on my back and gazed the heavens, wondering if Isabella was there among them. Had she had met my mother up there?

If you look at the stars long enough, they move, like the hands on a clock. Perhaps there is a mighty clockwork that God has set in motion. I wondered if he has to wind it.

I realized that my tooth no longer bothered me. Now there had been distractions, both reptile and mammal, and perhaps avian.

The crow called again, poor confused creature.

My eyes grew thick. I haven't used that expression before or since, but thick they were. I covered my face with my hat, and looked at the crown from the inside. It was very dark in there.

There was a silence on that mud island; a relaxation, and a submission to the forces of nature and the night.

As I lay there, most quietly, serenely, the thing occurred.

My hat levitated from my face and exposed the stars.

Before my face appeared a ghoulish sight – the stern face of a giant fiend black against the sparkled dome. Then bringing a candle or lamp of some sort, its face was illuminated. It moved, it stretched up and down – not in a coherent manner. I would have been stunned, but I was in another place now – quite relaxed, a spectator.

I noticed my toes and then my feet were tingling.

The Demon leaned over my face. I could see his eyes in his lamplight.

Crazy shadows swept across his appearance. His huge eyes were the most mysterious element. And I knew them.

This man, as I now believe he was, wore a pair of the shaded spectacles, the ones used by those sharpshooters on Fort Sumter the previous summer. Their sanded areola focused all attention on the clear center irises, magnified beyond nature.

This demon was Agur.

I JONATHAN

The slight and effeminate Negro boy, the deep-throated wearer of women's makeup who had sent me to that forsaken wilderness island, was now the demon conductor of my trip to Bear Island, as I named it in my mind. I felt lightning and thunder rattle me, though I saw it not.

He pushed me to sit up in the night, and stood before me enormous.

He wore what I'm sure were butternut Confederate trousers, and a Federal blue jacket. His head was uncovered, and in his hand was a small glowing jar of light – in the other a bundle of I don't know what.

The stars over his head were a wonder, and the Milky Way poured its cream on his shoulders, and it dripped down his elbows to the ground. He craned back his head and ate the heavens. He gave a great cry, and nature recoiled!

He stood tall, and the wind rose and rattled the bushes around his courtroom. His hair shifted in the wind.

Then he turned his other-worldly eyes on me, reflecting the spangled heavens.

His voice in the maelstrom was vigorous and entreating. He spoke in Tongues, in African dialect, with the harmonizing growls of five lions.

He bade me sit, and I did. He bade me stand, and I did. He bade me fly, and I did.

As I hovered amidst the stars above that swamp isle he reached up and stuffed into my mouth from his left hand more herbs, or roots or twigs, some diabolical elements, and I chewed.

He wore on his shoulder a wine bag holding water or some mild liquor, and I drank. I drank deep. I found myself sitting on the damp ground, I drank and drank and drank and drank from his wine bag.

That is the last I remember from that night.

62

BROKEN, BLASTED, PUNISHED

I lay alone and cool when I awoke the next morning. Dew hung heavily on my face and clothes. The sunlight was dim as yet, the mosquitos not yet in full feast. I looked around for alligators, bears, and God knows what, but saw nothing. Just weedy sand and wild shrubbery. I heard a crow call, and a flight of gulls sprayed across the sky in a dense crystal formation.

My head was in sensation similar to a watermelon. Yes, I think that is accurate. Overripe. I raised my hands to my head and found in my right hand a scrap of cloth. As I opened my palm, I saw a muddy piece of white, blue and black calico. As I unfolded it, I saw that it could be nothing but a piece of Isabella's dress, the one she wore our week together at Xanadu.

I sat for a while, and awhile more. I was a bit dizzy.

A Great Blue Heron alighted at the edge of the field, and I awaited the miraculous event I knew must follow. But he pecked about and decided I was not going to feed him. He flapped his enormous wings and climbed low over the trees.

All right.

I was not ready to admit that the previous night's experience was merely a dream, but I needed breakfast of some sort.

I slowly stood and surveyed the clearing where I had slept. Alligators? A bear? A night crow? The demon!

The scrap of cloth was in my hand.

As I lifted myself erect, I noticed the taste in my mouth, a bitter and caustic tangle of stringy material, juicy in its way, my own
380

saliva mixing with it.

I chewed it, and when it squeezed between my teeth it released more of a juice, I guess. Not unpleasant really.

I sat back down and kept chewing. I wondered if it were a fibrous oral poultice for me from Agur. From the Demon.

Then I recalled why I was at that location, my foul tooth.

Slowly I withdrew the balming chew and explored my mouth. The offending tooth was gone.

Gone.

I wondered if my missing tooth might ever reappear in another conjuring of the root doctor. I imagine some spells might require one.

So, the calendar of man may be judged by our passing teeth, and better perhaps to finally die with fewer teeth than to die sooner with a full set, as I had witnessed men do so often.

When I returned to Jacob's house about an hour before noon, Chloe greeted me and offered a pail of water for a wash and a meal of hot grits.

And that is how I experienced the Voo-Doo of Charleston.

Later that day after thanking Chloe for filling my stomach, I made my way to the telegraph office. I had to notify Tyrone of the completed delivery of the slaves to Rosy Acres, leaving me only one more task for him – to take another shipment of salt to Flat Rock.

Many soldiers were telegraphing to their mothers and sweethearts, and I had to wait an hour in line before my turn, and of course official military business took all precedence.

As I walked out after having sent my telegram, to my surprise I saw Jenny's father, Mr. Haywood. He drew me to a corner where we spoke.

"Hello, Jonathan, very glad we met," he began. "I am in town to tie up a few things and collect Aunt Peggy. She won't leave her neighborhood, and it's just not safe." No, I agreed it was not. I was surprised she had not left before the south peninsula had become so wild.

He asked me to bring Aunt Peggy Moray to him. He would

complete his business, which I later discovered included selling his house in Charleston and his endangered plantation. He had apparently found a buyer who was seeking a bargain.

Against all urgings and entreaties, Aunt Peggy had decided to stay in her near-ruined home on Tradd Street, sitting in her red rocker on the front porch, ignoring the occasional crunch and blast of a falling cannonball in her neighborhood. Despite desolation about her, she refused to believe her life could change – her world of large houses, kept gardens, teas and balls. The surreal life she was living was finally not acceptable to her relatives. And her neighborhood was wilding.

Grass grew waist-high. There were foxes. Ragged men hid in basements. The last of Aunt Peggy's servants had recently fled, and only her poodle Pierre remained with her.

As I passed the market and ventured across Cumberland I again saw the desolation of the burnt district. It cast a pall on the day. Like going from life to death. Bright sunshine glanced off the ashes and cracked stone. On one wall someone two years earlier had proudly painted the cross of the Confederate battle flag. It had faded and now resembled a ghostly "X," a symbol of failure and death.

I looked down the wide corridor that flames had cleared, and I recalled the night I sang to Mr. Haywood's horse. That next morning Jacob's crew and I found Isabella under the burned house on Queen, just a block from where I now stood.

I walked south to Broad and toward the deserted St. Philips Church I saw a figure in a pale walking dress with a large whitish dog. I recognized the Duchess, Aunt Peggy, picking through the rubble of a blasted wall.

"Helloooooooooo," I cried, and she lifted her tattered parasol and shaded her eyes with her hand. Pierre stood by his mistress in alert attention. The large dog had changed. He needed washing and brushing at the very least, and was missing an eye. His snout bore a mark made by a knife, or a bayonet.

"Who is it?" she asked.

I recalled then that the last time I had addressed her was at the plantation party so long ago, and that she would not recognize me in my present state.

As I walked forward I called, "Just a friend of the Haywoods, Miss Moray," which was more or less true. "Can I help you find something?"

Pierre crouched and growled, baring teeth.

"Well I come here every Sunday for church." Her dress was much the worse for wear and now quite ragged. "I was just checking to see if services were planned for tomorrow."

The building was obviously deserted, in ruin. In a way it represented many of South Carolina's institutions. This church had supported the war effort and donated its bells to be melted and recast for canon. It continued to give spiritual succor to the dwindling number of churchgoing families until an exploding shell from the Federal bombardment disrupted a service some time ago. From then on, the congregation met farther to the north of the city.

The shock of the city's change had affected her mind, and she had slipped into delusion.

Her hair was pinned up under a hat which must have been stylish in the '40s, and stray bits of her hair sought escape from so unfashionable a cover. She collapsed her parasol and used it as a cane as she toddled through the weed-grown sidewalks, the flower bushes unkept and unruly.

"Come, Miss Peggy, your nephew wants to see you." I reached to her to offer my hand, and Pierre leapt!

I backed off but he continued his attack, grasping my arm and tearing my sleeve.

"Pierre! Pierre!" the old woman cried, and he released his grip as I further retreated, stumbling. He stood growling, crouched and threatening as I tripped on a curb and fell backwards, tapping my head soundly on the pavement.

When I awoke Officer Kerry in Home Guard uniform was leaning over me, as was an alert Pierre. Aunt Peggy was disturbed.

"Jon," said Kerry. "Jon. Look at me."

He held his fingers up as my eyes regained focus. "How many," he demanded.

"Uh, two. Two."

Kerry sat next to me and laid his coat down and invited Aunt Peggy to do the same. He was a gallant Irish.

I lay for a minute and looked up at the sky, fluffy rolling clouds unchanged by the follies of men below.

"I do apologize about Pierre," said Aunt Peggy. "He is protective, now that everything has changed."

Yes, changed.

I noticed some of the serene clouds resembled a clipped poodle. Pierre's coat had gone to unkept wooliness, gray now, not as white as the clouds. More stormy, I thought. I sat up.

He was a proud dog that first night I had seen him, brilliant among the glamor of the plantation ball, the sweeping gowns, glittering uniforms. He was sharp and disciplined, groomed in a rakish style. Now he was reduced to savagery and would bite first without seeking permission of his mistress. He had lost all sense of cordiality, of propriety.

How often I would see this transition in men of the South! Not all, thankfully.

I gathered my senses as gentle Kerry surveyed the town. I reflected on how this guardian of his city had allowed me continued access to his province, this broken, arrogant, blasted and punished city. Once-bustling streets had become a wasteland.

Starving goats wandered in alleys and gardens that used to be so tended.

The fabulous homes were vacant, spoiling to ruin. Gutters and roofing metals had long since been scavenged. A few houses sheltered ownerless slaves or fugitives from the army, biding their time until the end – coming soon now.

"Miss Moray, it's time to go," said Kerry.

"Your nephew sent me here to fetch you," I said. I didn't relish travel with Pierre. I carefully struggled to my feet, as did Kerry. "Let me help you up and we'll get your things."

As she stood, she looked all around at the grim panorama and sighed. "We lived such a blessed life in our youth."

Yes, we did. All of us did.

And so did you, Nephew Ralph. Don't forget it.

63

MARK OF THE LOST

Aunt Peggy began to pack a large trunk of her items. Kerry and I convinced her to separate her belongings into two smaller baskets that could be carried, and we two men ported them up the road. Our little parade of Miss Margaret Moray, Pierre, Kerry and I walked to the north of the city where Mr. Haywood had made arrangements for the night.

Jenny's father had met his overseer and gathered the last of his documents. He was very business-like and had satchels and cartons of papers, much representing old business that had lost any meaning.

Jenny had pleaded and demanded to make the long journey in hopes of seeing her home city once more, and perhaps finding Martin miraculously home on leave, but that was not to be.

Despite his gender and age and though he kept up a brave front, I think Mr. Haywood was more sensitive than Jenny. She had worked in the blood of so many men, had carried disembodied limbs to the pit, and eased so many others' darlings to their rest.

I said farewell to Officer Kerry, who was staying with the city until the end. "I believe there will be a need for an experienced local policeman when the government changes," he said. This officer's service would be needed no matter who was in power.

I shook his hand, and again he drew me into a bear hug.

"Good luck on your road. Thank you for my last year with Mother. And may God hold you in the palm of His hand."

"And you too, Good Kerry," I said.

I ate with Mr. Haywood and Aunt Peggy on the humble piazza of a guest house as the sun set. We chatted about small things that matter in everyday life which would be totally overshadowed if we discussed what was happening to each of us at that time.

I returned to a last night in the warehouse, and next morning I saw them arrive at the train station in a carriage still bearing the crest of his lost plantation.

Before his removal Tyrone had bought another quantity of sea salt from near Georgetown and left directions for me to send it from his otherwise empty warehouse to the estate of "Gentleman," as Xenophon named his owner. There wasn't enough available from their local salt agent to meet the needs of the upcoming slaughter season.

A nation of automatons wandered the streets near the depot, onto the platforms and into the benches in the cars. Faith in their new nation may yet have hovered about some of them like a dissipating mist, but the incarnate facts were the returning cars with boxes holding the wounded, and bodies now home forever – and the movement of survivors out of Charleston. To retain the hope of their new nation they must abandon all they knew.

Except for soldiers, people at the station were moving with the pallor of dread on their faces as if marching in a funeral. With their servants they carried their bundles, casks and trunks onto the train. They appeared shattered.

Mr. Haywood said what seemed like final goodbyes to his friends.

I had nothing left in the city and asked to accompany Mr. Haywood and Aunt Peggy to Flat Rock. From there I knew not where.

A few soldiers about the station were alert and crisp, performing their desperate duties as they understood them, knowing it was nothing but a few weeks or months until Charleston itself must be evacuated.

Another train carried wounded soldiers slowly pulled to the depot, though more of us were leaving the city than there were wounded and dying coming in. As the battle-scarred staggered or were carried off, a familiar figure from the past walked by, paused, and turned to me.

"Jon!"

It was the third musketeer, friend of dead William. Kit.

"Jonathan." he leaned against a post and displayed the empty sleeve of his shirt.

I had nothing to say, though I was amazed at the change in the man.

He was about twenty-six years old but could have been fifty.

He had lost weight beyond the three or four pounds of his left forearm and looked gaunt. Strands of gray hair had woven themselves into his mane. He was a shadow of the proud figure from that night at the plantation when he swore never to rest until his energies and those of his trio of oak had wrested his home state from the talons of the United States, and created their own proud nation.

Where is his nation now? Where are his mates? What of his oath? Had he proven himself faithless?

His eyes were filled with anguish and flitted about as if he was hunted.

"Jon. I killed scores of them." His eyes darted. "I killed hundreds. Thousands. There was no end to them."

It must have seemed so.

His hand went to his sleeve where his left elbow would have been. I could see the scar on his right wrist from his blood oath.

I asked what he was going to do. "I'm going home," he said.

He was from a plantation near Mount Pleasant, as safe as any such place around Charleston. What would he would find there, and how long until it was invaded by Federals?

His eyes tilted downward, and he silently turned and walked from me. He found a ride up Meeting Street, to the ferry and to his family.

How this knight saw himself at the utter ruin of his quest I could only have guessed, and I was sad at the thought.

I saw to the secure loading of Tyrone's salt and boarded the train with Mr. Haywood and Aunt Peggy. She looked confused but resigned to her fate.

Passengers checked their train schedules, though I can't imagine why. All the numbers in rows corresponded with chalk figures on the wall, and none mattered now. Trains came, trains left like a flowing stream, each on its own schedule. The little schedule books were pretty, and I like a good fiction story as well as anyone.

I had expected to ride with the baggage this time, but rode up with the family. There were many passengers crowded in every car and Mr. Haywood wanted me to join their retinue to enhance their space and importance, and even their safety. I still carried my Bowie knife. My French revolver was in my sack.

I was cleaner than usual, though unshaven for more than a week. I was given a topcoat belonging to Mr. Haywood. After waiting many hours, the locomotive finally pulled out early in the predawn. The morning cool was quickly chased from the car by the heat of packed bodies, some snoozing, many in nervous conversation with their fellow travelers.

The trains all rolled slowly now due to the age and condition of the engines and the tracks. Maintenance was postponed during the war for lack of labor, materials and money.

The South had a system of trains and tracks that in some cases varied in gauge. Iron was in short supply and needed for arms, cladding for fighting ships – for everything. The South had only one major iron-producing area in Alabama, the remainder of demand fed by fewer and fewer blockade-running ships. And some black-market trading with elements in the North who cared more about commerce than holding the Union together. Or perhaps it was a cynical gamble that no matter how much iron was sold south, how much Southern gold came into the hands of the dealers, the Confederacy had no chance of success, of survival.

Summer's green pastures were a refreshing change from the stone, dust, and heat of the city center. The annual rhythms of farm life continued, despite the individual tragedies each family might face any day. Even after those fields were burned by invading Federals they would heal, sprout again in spring, become golden in autumn.

Workers still tended their crops and harvested the fields, which appeared as patterns of abstract lines from the windows of the moving cars. Some of the plowed fields, if timed with blinking of the eyes, evoked moving images as in magic lantern shows I had seen in Paris. I suppose that entertainment is now obsolete because of moving pictures.

Each town we stopped at took on civilians and soldiers. Many carried baskets of bread and cold fried chicken for the trip to the capital or beyond to the foothills and the mountains.

That train ride to Greenville took four days, twice as long as before the war. Everyone who could was escaping the bombarded city. The wealthiest rode to Asheville or Flat Rock, "Little Charleston in the Mountains," seeking cool and peaceful summer beneath hemlocks, far from malarial heat and flying shells.

Rail lines had been pulled up around the state and re-installed to stretch to centers of supply. It was a desperate attempt to produce a viable system of transport. Some rails on the less important lines were even made of half-inch iron plate fastened over wooden rails. Maintenance was constant and demanding, and never enough.

All trains moved slowly to minimize wear on the tracks, the engines, the cars. When a military shipment came through, all other traffic was sidelined as the goods, weapons, perishable produce and ever younger men were sent to fiery horizons. When we rolled through Columbia raw army recruits were turning out on a parade field. The men looked eager and determined, perhaps for not having been in battle yet. They received instruction on marching, forming, marching, marching. They had stern faces for young men, many of whom were destined never to become older.

Besides ourselves and other passengers, our train carried mail, food, and of course troops. This war used trains to get fresh soldiers to the killing fields much faster than possible in previous wars, and permitted death in unprecedented quantity.

As we rattled and clacked along, the conversation among the riders turned to the usual gossip, discussion of new clothing styles, and whether one would ever see a father, son, brother, or maybe Philadelphia or Chicago ever again.

Isabella had been from Chicago.

We had to spend most of a day and nearly all night in a rail yard. It was tempting to walk about the train, though we were warned by the conductor and crew to stay on board, as we would get little notice when the train would move. And, by the way, there were criminals who hung about the rail yards.

My French revolver precluded much worry on that point, but I stayed aboard.

The car's seats had at one time been comfortable, but in the period of those several days from Charleston to Columbia and beyond they became a device of torture.

From Columbia to Greenville, transferring twice, we continued to Flat Rock. Mr. Haywood and Aunt Peggy travelled by carriage. A hired cart and driver carried me and my cargo, along with trunks and cargo for other customers. Up and up winding, steep roads. After four days we had all adopted a vagabond style of life that was becoming normal.

Perhaps the natural state of mankind is nomadism.

We were accompanied by armed guards this time as there were deserters and renegades in the hills. I wondered if the guards were trustworthy.

We all slept in tents at the travelers' resting place by the Goodwin House, which overflowed with Low Country travelers like us. There was an obvious presence of armed men about, guards like the ones traveling with our caravan.

Travel-worn and exhausted we slept, and the next evening we arrived at Green Mountain Meadows.

Jenny was glad to see us all, but especially her father who assured her he had never been in danger.

She greeted me cordially and asked news of Martin, of which I had none.

She looked older, more careworn. She was strong, as she had proven many times in hospitals, the sewing factory, the fever clinic in Wilmington, and even on the battlefield on Morris Island. Since seeing her last in the days of the evacuation of Wagner she had grown a bit more plain, more resolute.

The house had more servants then, families and children. Much human property was being sent "up country" where it would be more secure from emancipation, at least for a while.

That evening after a meal of good pork, squash and biscuits, I sat on the porch and surveyed the scene.

I speculated how the world could change, though that would be a great change indeed, to transform the basic justification for a civilization: to recognize all humans as worthy of equal rights. It is a stated American ideal, but may be a pipe-dream never achieved. I drew the warm smoke from my pipe onto my tongue and puffed it into a small cloud as I listened to the happy young voices in the gloaming. I was growing used to the hole where the tooth had been.

As darkness grew and stars began to peep out, the children were called inside. In the cooling air the fireflies lifted from the ground and slowly sparked and danced into the maples, hickories and chestnuts.

390

The world can change, of course.

Witness that there are nearly none of the large wild cats in these mountains now, though tales of sightings remain. Elk that once dwelt in these hills were killed off before 1800. Can man's view of his fellows change, too? Perhaps even the fireflies will all go away, maybe eaten by some other continent's introduced bird or bat desiring a light meal.

That would be a shame, not to see lightning bugs in the evening, flickering high in the beautiful chestnut trees.

After a day of recovery all around we felt more at ease. Aunt Peggy had not traveled well, and for weeks did nothing but sit on the porch and watch for birds. Pierre sat erect and alert by her side, holding back his temptation to chase squirrels.

I had a delivery to make.

I pondered whether I should keep all the salt myself and sell it and keep the profit. Salt was valuable, and hog killing time was coming. But I didn't really consider such a thing. I still had some money from my Nassau trip, and there was a matter of honoring my word to Tyrone, who had never shorted me. I made plans for the trip to visit Zeke and his clan.

I borrowed horses and a wagon from Mr. Haywood and drove the salt casks to Xanadu. As I drew near the house where I had shared that magical week with Isabella, a feeling of apprehension came over me. I wondered what I would find there, and how I would be received.

Cassie saw me first. She ducked back into the house and Zeke appeared.

"Hello, Mister Jonathan. It is very good to see you again!"

We exchanged greetings and news of the Haywoods. "And how are you weathering the war, Zeke?"

That man, still a slave in name under those laws, had become the closest thing to a Diocletian possible in America. Like that former slave, he had lived a life that brought him to a state close to king in this little valley, and he was a good king.

In his master's name and with "Gentleman's" money he had purchased families of slaves from the low country. Workers could be bought at low prices from desperate plantation owners, some with no more plantation. Here the field workers would have a stable home.

He mostly bought entire families, and was even able to purchase Cassie's younger sister Charity and her husband Plato. Plato had not run to the Federals but had stayed to live with his wife, to face whatever life brought them. And it had brought them Xanadu, where in time she bore four boys and finally a girl named Flora.

The farm Zeke managed was tucked off the side of a hollow, or "holler" as they're known up here. A winding wagon trail led to the hidden valley with its creek, fields, orchard, view, and my sacred memories. Unless you were from that area you couldn't know it was there. They paid the sheriff in produce, ham and honey, and he let them be.

Zeke's little valley was busy and prosperous. Many black people lived there then, perhaps eighty, and the fields were producing well. There was corn and tobacco of course, which brought in cash when money was worth something, and they had increased the production of pigs, or hogs as they called them.

The gardens of Xanadu were mostly "tilled" by hogs in the winter where they rooted up the ground and left it ready for harrowing. The animals were transferred to pens for breeding. The November slaughtering and curing gave them meat for sale and to eat the rest of the year. Excess shoats were sold and traded to neighboring farms.

There were several Jersey cows on the farm. Calves were sold, and they had begun making cheese for sale or trade. Honey was harvested from bee gums, chicks were raised and traded. Unlike the Low Country, food was not wanting in their little valley.

I arrived in that golden time of year. Corn was being picked and shucked and dried for later, and the second harvest of beans was coming in, along with winter squashes and pumpkins, potatoes and tomatoes.

For all people in the region there was a danger of roving bands of deserters. Zeke told me of the problems they faced from them. The farm had dogs about, and the farmers were armed. The most common problem was crops being stolen. They shared the farm's bounty with some deserters and helped them along their ways to their homes.

Mostly, strangers never found the valley of Xanadu.

On surrounding properties homes had been invaded, vacant

properties ransacked. There were some robberies on the roadways. I was fortunate not to have encountered anyone between Green Mountain Meadows and Xanadu, but it was only four miles and Zeke said the friendly sheriff patrolled the area when he was available.

Local law enforcement was mostly older men unfit for military service or injured soldiers reassigned for the Home Guard. They were sometimes overwhelmed by the numbers of outlaws, and some of the Guards were indistinguishable from the raiders, who were not above stealing from empty homes or unwatched fields.

Zeke took me through the house past the desk he was obviously working from, with ledgers and invoices and receipts in neat trays beside his blotter and pen. We walked out to the back porch, and again I was held by the view of the rich fields and misty mountains in the distance.

Zeke was as welcoming as ever, and Cassie again brought the tea. I presented her with a Belgian handkerchief and the last of the bottles of perfume from Nassau, which she shyly accepted before disappearing back into the house.

I told Zeke of Isabella's death.

Sometimes one needs to share an important event with someone you don't know well. In doing so the ubiquity of the challenges and tragedies of life can be understood and absorbed by humanity. By speaking to another I am speaking to all. And all understand, and speak to me.

Zeke was silent as I told him my story. We smoked, and after a long silence I spoke again.

"I wanted to marry her. I wanted to build a life with her. I never told her of my hope for us. And she died. She died."

Zeke closed his eyes, and drew on his pipe, tobacco embers glowing.

He took the stem from his lips and turned his eyes to me. And instead of commiserating, he spoke the words that freed me.

"Forgive yourself."

Forgive myself.

"Forgive yourself."

* * *

My great uncle's words hung in the air. He looked at me to emphasize Zeke's command.

I bade him goodnight and left him to the care of Mrs. McKay.

I checked the departing train schedule for the next evening. I must return to academia and to my own life.

The next morning was Sunday. I packed my clothes and left them in the care of the hostess of my rooming house. I listened to the bells from churches as I walked to the old folk's home and wondered if any of those bells had been secreted during the Civil War, and brought out later to chime the peace.

Uncle Jon's fellow tenants had attended a service in the dining room led by Hiram, and it was breaking up as I entered. Hiram left to perform his assistant duties at the local Methodist church for the main morning service.

Most of the old men were in wheelchairs and seemed to be sleeping, or dead even. Uncle Jonathan was one of the only ones who could still walk on his own, though Mrs. McKay and the other attendants were very watchful and caring of all.

As the room cleared, Uncle Jon and I walked about the house for his exercise. He showed me his room, which he had shared with his friend from Tennessee, but Mr. Adams had passed away the day before.

I realized the limits of my time with my uncle and my need to hear the rest of his story. And he wanted to share it with me.

We passed through the linoleum-floored halls to the parlor again and left the urine-smelling dormitory area to the room of light and flowers. The windows were open, and sweet cool air was a blessing.

Mrs. McKay brought Uncle Jon some pills, which he duly swallowed. Then he drank the rest of the glass of water and began the end of his tale.

*   *   *

64

WITNESS OF DISTANT SHADES

Jenny and her family joined in light work around the farm that the holiday estate was now becoming, more to distract themselves from the outside political world than to actually do productive work. But Mr. Haywood began to enjoy working the garden, seeing the value of his own labor produce food. His documents and books rested.

I suppose you can spend your life reliving all your efforts, the what-might-have-beens. Or you can get up, see where you are and begin again each day. That is what he did.

Days were hot, and the nights even in those high mountains were often warm. Jenny would go out in the day with her servant, and sometimes in the evening to see the moon, the stars.

She would get letters from Martin from time to time, the first of them following her from Charleston, the others often arriving in a bundle.

He would write of camp conditions more than battles, always putting a positive light on their situation, and ending with "My enduring love will ensure my return to you, my beloved."

True to my promise to Martin at their secret wedding, I watched for her safety and monitored her room. If she slipped out, sometimes alone in the mourning of her own lost life, I would watch her as she strolled through the fruit trees, in and out of the shade. I envied far away Martin who still held her love.

One day in September we learned Atlanta had fallen.

The shadows of war and a fear of even more intimate invasion were constant. And there were other shadows, moving in the night.

Sometimes after supper I would sit at the top of the orchard beneath a large dogwood tree and contemplate what I had seen over the previous four years, and the colors of the sky.

Dogwoods are naturally an understory tree, but the people who planted the orchard left one at the top of the rise free from shade of larger trees and it had grown tall and domed. One evening I sat on the bench under the tree. I could see down the rows of the fruit trees below. I sometimes witnessed distant shades, suggestions of creatures prowling about and then slipping into the forest wilderness.

The harvest was mostly in, though there were bushels of late apples still clinging to some branches, and the pears had yet to be picked. I wrapped a blanket about me and dozed in the moon shade, waking from time to time as one of the dogs from the house came to snuff my hand, or to see a furtive shadow of a fox or a cat or raccoon scuttle on the edge of the orchard. Maybe a bear?

A chill was in the air, though nothing like the cool of a Boston autumn or even winter in these southern mountains. The moon was bright; the stars were outshone by that etched blue-white disk. It cast shadows on the grass from the trees. I drank in that cool blue glow. I refreshed the flame and drew again on my pipe, and watched a 'possum quietly rustle and amble through the grove. Then I dozed.

When I woke again the moon was lowering. I supposed it was after two in the morning, maybe three. I pulled up the blanket and considered returning to the house or the barn so as not to disturb anyone. The last clouds had scudded away, and the hard moonlight created an effect of a hundred shining canopies of apple trees, a sparkling heaven above.

I located the North Star. I thought about my future. Should I follow that star to a new life? Or return to claim what I could of my old one?

I looked down and clearly saw two figures with sacks glancing about and moving to a row of apples, Winesaps I believe. They pulled some of the nearly ripe fruit from the trees. It was mystical: bright moonlight, stark shadows and quiet chirping of late-night insects.

The shapes were like thieving brownies in the bluish mist.

I gathered my wrap and crept to the edge of the field. Still in shadow, I held my place and watched them collect their harvest and silently edge into the forest.

I followed, not thinking to bring my knife or my revolver.

396

I JONATHAN

The mountain forest at night is a wonder, so different from the swampy lands around Charleston. There are shadows unnoticed in the day that bring forth the essence of the primeval. Bears live here. Maybe even a big cat. What else, I wondered? I had heard tales.

I followed the two apple thieves at a distance. Occasionally when I was less careful, they would hear something behind and turn. I froze. They did not see me in the shadows, but they were unsettled.

They turned and continued, I gently pursued.

Half a league onward.

We walked along a creek, its waters rippling and sluicing across rocks and banks. I felt a camaraderie with these hungry reivers, all of us traversing the dark byways of creation in the night, treading in small spots of light cast through the leaves by the face of the gibbous moon. I was a comrade unbeknownst to them, of course.

I scented smoke, soft and fragrant evidence of fire. I heard the men I was stalking greet someone and was shocked by a prod in my back by what must have been a bayonet.

"Who the hell are you?" queried a rough voice behind me. I was at a loss.

"Lookie here. We got us a new one!"

Alright, I was not expecting this, though I don't know why not. The men peered around me for others who might be with me, then looked me up and down. They searched my clothing for documents and weapons. My French revolver was in my sack back at the Haywood house with my knife and most of my money. I wondered that I would venture so far without a weapon. One of the bearded searchers found my talisman of the last remaining silver dollar from Ricardo's jacket, and the key.

The man glanced at my coin put it in his pocket. He studied the key.

"If I were you, I wouldn't keep it," I told him. "It's bad luck." He eyed me, and looked at the key again. "The previous owner shot himself." He flipped it back to me.

"Federal or Confederate?"

"Neither" I answered. This elicited a chuckle from two of the growing group and a guffaw from one. "Yeah. Us too." I suppose I was not threatening. Still they took me as prisoner, at least for the night.

We all walked to the firelight where I saw a cave, a few men, a distillation device. Some were in partial uniforms with all insignia removed. Some were more interested in the new stranger than others. Some were asleep, as all decent men should be at this time of night. What did that make me? Never mind, I know.

The one who took my coin handed me a crude earthen jug of a liquid he had apparently been sipping. I sniffed it, and determined it was not overt poison, at least not one I had refused before. I took a sip, and then drank deep. Why not? I had paid a silver dollar for something.

The others assumed an air of acceptance; I was another of their shifting band.

The taste of the liquid was of grain spirits, and I must admit that it was welcome. I gave a furtive glance around, and drank again. In the distance I heard a quiet fiddle play a slow Welsh air. It was nearly dawn, and after a long walk in the shadows and my day's work I was tired. I bundled into my blanket and slept next to the fire.

I awoke in the late dawn, still tired. Men were awake and moving. One rather large fellow sat on a split log by the fire, cradling a tin cup of something hot, and stared at me. A large Bowie knife was stuck into the log beside him.

He had on a blue uniform jacket with telltale threads on his sleeve where there had once been sergeant's stripes. He hadn't shaved in at least two weeks. His dark stare was unnerving.

"Good morning," I said dully. The jug from last night must have fallen on my head at some point; at least I felt something had hit me in the head and the stomach. My mouth tasted gray and dusty.

The large sergeant was not friendly. "What are you doing here?"

I grasped my head briefly and looked for water. "Not sure. I'm not a soldier."

"I can tell," grunted the sergeant.

I saw others in different states of wakefulness. Some men were cooking breakfast, and it looked surprisingly good. There was enough to share, and they did.

We ate apples, rice, potatoes and parched corn. These deserters were mostly gracious and friendly with their food. Some mushrooms gathered from the woods, some blueberries, tubers of some sort, dried meat – mutton I think, likely stolen from a mountain farm, and salted pork, or maybe something else.

Here was a community I could identify with. These lost men of no nation had lost their worlds, yet still longed for them, or for something.

Two men strolled into camp, one carrying two rifles and one carrying a deer over his shoulders. It had been field dressed and still seeped blood. He laid down the animal and some of his campmates immediately drew their knives and fell to butchering it. As the hunter in his gory red uniform turned his bright sky-blue eyes to me he became a re-animated spectre from the field of Secessionville. I lived again the vision of sky reflected in the eyes of the fallen soldier, and Billy Smith telling me what a shame and waste it all was.

That memory, from hundreds of miles away.

One man further back in the cave was lying against the wall, his arm bandaged. He wore a Confederate jacket and was staring at me.

He looked familiar, and as I moved toward him I at last recognized him as the Irish workman of my first week in Charleston, the one who left me a bottle of sympathy that night a war ago.

"Hello, Denis."

His expression was solemn and sad, and his face was pasty white. He seemed to have difficulty focusing his eyes. He recognized me, I think, and with faint breath he told me his story and what had left him there in that cave with a bloody and swelling arm.

"We were starving. We left the regiment in Tennessee and took to the hills when we realized there was no winning the war."

Denis and two others from his platoon decided that after three years of winning, losing, marching and freezing they had had enough. In the last skirmish they could see that the men on the other side were well-fed and had warm cloaks. Their own force was living day-to-day on a handful of parched rice, limited to six cartridges, still in their summer uniforms and fighting in ice-crusted clay mud.

The officer was a drunk and had spent the last week in a warm farmhouse while his men shivered in rotting tents without enough blankets.

On the line in that little battle when they were told to charge, most stayed in their ditches. When their sergeant yelled at them to move, several rose against him and struck him, maybe killing him. That is when Denis and some other played-out soldiers fled the field. There was no hope there.

"We hid in the mountains. Some people gave us food. We kept moving east and found summer houses that were deserted. We sometimes found food in their cellars.

"We found one small house with a full root cellar – onions, potatoes, yams, beets, winter squash. A storm had damaged the house. We started a fire in the fireplace using some wood from the house to cook, and Jake lit the rest of the house and burned it all down, just for fun.

"The root cellar was ruined except where a bushel of sweet potatoes was piled. We dug into that and it was like a pudding. We ate some of it, enough to keep from starving."

They had eaten stolen yams baked in the embers of someone's burned house. I wondered if the house might have belonged to Brother Fox.

His eyes seemed to grow large as he spoke. It looked as if he was in deep and constant pain from his wound.

"When the weather warmed, we just took food from gardens. We kept moving because the Home Guard was looking for deserters, and so were the sheriffs.

"We slept in barns, or corncribs or in caves like this. We met others like us and we sometimes traveled together. We met Yankees who had also deserted, and some of them joined us. Some would break off and leave for their homes.

"I was with one group of six, mostly in Yankee uniform, and we went to the home of a wealthy man from Charleston named Johnstone. I knew this man from before joining the army.

"We approached his house and asked for food. They had just finished dinner, but said they would feed us anyway. I did some work for his family years ago when I lived in Charleston and didn't want him to see me like this, so I stayed out on the porch while the others went inside.

"The servants were ordered to bring them bacon and eggs, bread and gravy, corn pudding.

"When they were done with the food, Jake stood up and he shot Mr. Johnstone!

"Mr. Johnstone was suspicious earlier and sent his son to get his shotgun, and when the son heard the shot that boy ran into the room and let both barrels go at the group. We didn't expect any gunplay.

400

"We didn't want to hurt anybody! Just that one man Jake, the mean one. We were happy to get some food, not to hurt anyone!" Denis became more emotional and began breathing fast. "Jake did this." His eyes teared.

"That shotgun hit two fellows. When Mr. Johnstone was shot, he pulled a revolver out of his vest and returned fire. He hit several of us including me, standing by the doorway.

"Teddy was shot in both legs, and I hear they found Ned wounded out in the back yard the next day. Mr. Johnstone's son shot him in the head and buried him right there!"

Denis's face looked sickly and he sweated. He grasped his right arm and stared into the dark of the cave. I looked at his right hand and it was black. Gangrene. I had seen it after Secessionville, and in the hospitals in Charleston and Wilmington. There was no hope for him.

"Denis, do you want me to write someone for you?"

He didn't answer, but whimpered, more from moral regret than pain it seemed.

I could do little for him in his state, in that locale, in my condition. I sat with him for a while and spoke to him, told of my travel to Nassau, anything that could be distracting from his approaching fate.

His breathing quickened, and he became more feverish. There were no doctors here.

I stood and found a bottle of corn distillate, the finest liquor available within reach and returned to him. I took a long draw from that bottle and placed it in his hand, returning the favor he had done me four years earlier. I covered him with a blanket and left him in as much comfort as I could.

I had known Denis for a total of maybe five hours in my lifetime, and for that brief time he was my friend.

My stomach tightened and my vision became distorted, reddish. I stalked from camp.

65

GLITTERING ENCHANTMENT

I wandered far that morning on a trail that led eventually to the great road, the one that led to Buncombe Turnpike. From a hillside I looked through the trees at the road's broad plank surface where hogs were being driven to feed Southern troops, or perhaps just away from invading Federals.

Among the herding livestock were travelers going in each direction. The wealthier on horseback were traveling south; the poorer in ragged clothes with bags hefted on their backs were heading north to Asheville, or even to Tennessee. The road ended in Greeneville, the Tennessee one, already occupied by Federal troops. There it joined other ways to the west or to the north. Home.

I sat and rested on a pine log felled by lightning strike, not caring if the sap or charcoal clung to my trousers.

I was free enough to join the deserters and refugees fleeing north. All I had of value was back at Jenny's house: money from my Nassau venture, Tyrone's gold piece, my French revolver. In my pocket I had Ricardo's bane, reminder of his frustrated life.

The sun was just past meridian. I could walk back to the Haywood house and collect my money, my knife and gun, and return here the next day to the turnpike, a way to Tennessee and northward. I would have a long walk, spending my money to get back to Massachusetts. Then what?

Where was my home now?

The house I grew up in had been lost; my mother's parents had died, as had my own parents. What did I have in Boston?

402

Memories?

I turned back up the trail to the deserter camp.

Dappled spots of sunlight danced along the ground with the slight breezes above the canopy.

I came to the creek and paused. I was not yet ready to return to Green Mountain Meadows. I felt on the cusp of something, two worlds, a past and a future. The water flowed around a step stone, where the path crossed the brook, or the stream crossed the trail. An intersection of two ways.

I turned and followed the water toward its source.

My feet stumbled for maybe a half hour, until I saw a Wonder of nature.

My primitive ancestors in ancient Europe could have seen this sight. Elements of the scene are not extraordinary, but in concert they produced a miracle, dazzling and dynamic, and revelating something sublime.

An aura of enchantment was about this place.

The creek splashed from an elevated horizon. Water fell perhaps five feet from a granite shelf polished smooth with eons of wear, down into a natural basin of stone with white crystal stones in its rim.

A beam of sunlight pierced the forest canopy. Its shaft shot the pure pool with a constantly glittering movement of reflection – silver flashes.

A mist arose from the fall, illuminated by the sunbeam. The cloudlet created a spectrum, a miraculous miniature rainbow moving with the water's sparkles.

If some Greek village lad hunting boars in the hills of Macedon or Thessaly happened upon this pool, hypnotic in its playful sounds, he would whisper a prayer to the gods. And what if there had been a young maiden bathing in its glow, with rainbow halo about her head from beams of Apollo's chariot? How could the youth not believe he had encountered a water nymph and fall on his face in prayer to Zeus, or perhaps Aphrodite? Would he ask a boon and consider himself blessed?

I felt magic. I let it permeate me. A "Fountain of Truth?"

Thoughts of the past years cascaded into my mind, my rationalizations of the universe, of what could be, of what different people of my life knew for sure, right or wrong.

What was that Welshman in the Wilmington house of pleasure trying to say to me?

There was no nymph, and I was not in a state to appreciate even a wanton local girl, though a party of hungry Bacchae with tormentuous withes might have been appropriate.

Perhaps what I needed here were the musings of a saint, or a sage.

I paused to observe the miracle. I walked carefully to the edge of that glory of nature, fearing to break the spell, and looked into the sparkling waters.

I saw a flashing reflection, myself broken into a thousand images. Changing. My hand reached into the shallow depths and startled a spirit! A crawdad.

The water was cool, cold.

The spring that fed this small creek was a few score yards uphill where it bloomed from the earth as pure as anything beneath heaven.

I cupped my hand and lifted it to my lips and tasted, then drank.

The sweet liquid was nectar of the earth. In it I found a refreshment beyond satisfaction of my thirst. I washed my mouth in the water, and looked around me. Peace beyond my hope. My Hope.

Oh, lost Isabella.

I dipped again into the pool and sought cleansing of my heart.

I felt the sadness, the bile of sad Ricardo washed clean from my mouth, and my mind. And his sad essence fled me forever.

Visions of death and human rot were chased from my mind as I stood by the glittering surface and its rainbow aura.

I delighted in the flecks of sunlight in the shade, the birdsong music to my revelation.

A rustle in the woods drew my attention and I saw a shape, a bear about twenty yards distant. He was black against the dark laurel bushes around him. He was looking at me, and as he did, he stood tall on his hind legs and displayed a white blaze on his chest.

We stared at each other for no less than two minutes, and then the beast nodded twice, fell to four legs again and slowly left me.

I watched him go, and there was silence, except for woodland sounds and the soft chuckle of the waterfall.

I recalled Zeke saying, "Forgive yourself."

I had made a promise to myself to marry Isabella and make her the happiest I could, and build a life together with that sweet woman. That dream was dead, as dead as the woman I still grieved.

And I believed she knew I loved her.

I gazed into the shallow depths of the sparkling pool, and accepted that there was a promise I had made.

Fealty to honor and oaths is not by any means a uniquely Southern trait. But among all the vowing and pledging I had heard in my time in Charleston I equated it with the good Southerners I had known.

Amid others' pledges of allegiance to flags, loyalty to regiments and leaders, everlasting love, to defending property and sacred honor, I had promised Martin one thing at William's graveside, and earlier in that little grotto in Charleston.

Standing beside him and his new wife, with Reverend Poste reading scripture, I had promised to look after Jenny.

I pulled Ricardo's key from my pocket and determined I would not end my life in fatal despair as he had.

I let go that cursed metal, and it dropped into the holy pool, its curse undone. It crossed the shimmering surface and found a natural crevice at the bottom. And it was gone.

A burden lifted from me. The weight of my lost life with Isabella slipped from my shoulders.

I turned from my chamber of grief and stepped into my new future.

66

FULL LADLE

I left the miracle pool with purpose now. I followed the freshet from its source down the hillside and through miles of forest into the sunshine.

On my return to Green Mountain Meadows that afternoon, Jenny held a letter from Martin's commander, Major Goggin. A battle had occurred the previous month. The name of the action suggested peace and beauty: Belle Grove. It was also called Cedar Creek, and we learned more about it later.

Near the small town of Strasburg in northern Virginia the Confederate forces, many who had been in the field for three years like Martin, surprised a much larger force of Union troops early one foggy morning. The attack drove the Federals from their camp while they were cooking breakfast – without their weapons and some without their clothes. The Southern troops were so near starvation that many paused in the captured Federal camp to eat. The commander ordered the "fatal halt," as it became known, to reorganize the troops and let his men have a meal instead of continuing the pursuit.

That pause gave their enemy time to re-form. With the impetus of a dynamic ride from Union Cavalry General Philip Sheridan, the Federal forces rallied. What had been an astounding Confederate victory became a devastating defeat and retreat.

Union casualties were about fifty-five hundred. Southern losses were about three thousand, including a lieutenant from Charleston named Martin Tenate.

I JONATHAN

You may know the rest of my story, or most of it.

I returned to the mountain house and stayed there with the Haywoods over that winter of '64-'65, doing for them and keeping them safe from roving bands of deserters.

We heard of the evacuation of Charleston, which put Mrs. Haywood into a shocked depression that never left her. Then the surrenders of Lee, then Johnston, and of the last battle, a Confederate victory in southern Texas. War Secretary General Breckenridge escaped to Cuba and England. And finally the news of the Confederate raider Shenandoah, sailing into Liverpool after its circumnavigation of the world: the surrender to creditors in Britain the last active Confederate force on earth.

The war was over, the South defeated, leaving Jenny's mother heartsick. She died that winter.

Roving bands continued to be a problem even after the war. I never had to shoot anyone, but four men showed up one morning. Mr. Haywood, the servants, the dogs and I stood them down. Jenny's father had his shotgun, his man Coffee a Navy revolver, and I had my French pistol. We met them in the field before the house. They were armed with Enfield and Springfield rifles, but were mostly just hungry. No one wanted a fight. In the end we gave them one of our four horses – the gelding – and a bag of biscuits and bacon. We got their oath that they would not return. They were more in need of a way home than of anything we owned.

After a year or so I was recognized as the man of the house, and with her father's blessing Jenny and I agreed to marry. I felt we could salvage the rest of our lives together.

She was heartbroken and would never see me as a substitute for Martin Tenate, but as someone who had proven himself honest and sincere, someone who would protect her. And we grew to love each other.

There were not many big society weddings anymore. Most of the planter families who hadn't emigrated to Brazil, Mexico or California were either impoverished (by their standards), in mourning without marriageable children, or not willing for an opulent display – which would have been in poor taste. Some from plantation gentry married partners from the lower classes, like me.

We learned there was to be a big camp revival meeting near

Spartanburg, South Carolina, and we decided to join scores of other couples who would be married there.

The family and many neighbors traveled down the turnpike for the meeting. Thousands came from all around.

Camp meetings are fun, and I recommend you attend one if you can. You can meet nice Christian girls there, too.

Jenny and I arrived with Festus and her new husband Ned, a good man from Zeke's farm. We set up camp and went to the first night of preaching. Smells of frying onions and woodsmoke filled the air as we walked toward the stage where we were to be married.

Jenny looked at me kindly, though I know she remembered that night in the Charleston grotto when she married Martin. He was gone, and the grand society wedding she had expected since she was a little girl would forever be denied her.

I would make myself the best husband for her I could, and she knew that.

Religious camp meetings were growing in popularity around the country and especially in the despondent South, the Midwest and rural North. They were events where women, many widowed, could bring their surviving children for a week of praying and socializing, and entertainment by traveling gospel singing groups. And perhaps one would meet a good Christian man for a new husband.

Sermons were led by preachers who drew strong medicine from the prophecies of an earlier Testament, some perhaps taking some liberties with the message of Christ. At the center of the meeting would be a charismatic leader, a speaker, a healer. The practice of laying on of hands let this preacher channel the Power of the Lord into the bodies of women, many of whom welcomed a gentle masculine touch, an assurance that the universe was led by a Force that would help them heal wounds and sores of our imperfect world. Women, children, and some men recently returned from the distant fields of battle found comfort in the breath and touch of these preachers.

There were two stages at this meeting. One held a choir now in full voices as they sang "Come Ye Sinners, Poor and Needy." Such a message was the balm needed now for a nation of proud Americans who had lost so much.

I JONATHAN

Come, ye sinners, poor and needy
Weak and wounded, sick and sore
Jesus ready, stands to save you
Full of pity, love and power

The other stage had preaching ministers, often in boisterous voice.

It was a place of revival, song and healing. Here was a message all needed to hear, and even that pagan Welshman in the Wilmington house of pleasure declaiming a Godless world would have welcomed that soothing message. He might have returned to infidelity in his own time, but at this camp he would have prayed. And sung, of course.

Come, ye weary, heavy-laden
Lost and ruined by the fall
If you tarry 'til you're better
You will never come at all

On the other stage was a beaming preacher, a vigorous man of perhaps thirty-five years, old enough to be a veteran of the late unpleasantness. His hair and beard flowed over a long white overshirt he wore as a robe, as he called on all to come to Glory and take the hand of the Savior. I thought Jesus might have looked much like this speaker.

His words were of redemption and rebirth. "Let your old self fall away! Take up the Cross as your banner, and love your enemy as yourself!"

He raised his hands in invocation and called on the congregation to do the same.

He raised only one hand, as he had but one. He was a veteran of battle, now a man of peace.

And I recognized this man.

I knew he had a stigma on his palm. He had pierced his hand and sliced the back of his wrist that evening of the plantation party near Charleston. The night when I had developed an alibi story for the young lovers Martin and Jenny, first met Pierre the poodle, where I saw the ebony King of Ethiopia washing pots in the kitchen.

This was Kit, who beneath the great oak had sworn never to put blade to his hair or face until the South had won final victory, who was prepared to vow not to court women or bathe. Thankfully,

409

the Honored William had proposed a more reasonable oath that night.

Kit had passed through the fire.

Of the three of them, he survived.

We saw him later that night bracketed by two young women obviously impressed by his oratory, his wound, his pious righteousness.

When he recognized us, he beamed and left his two escorts at their cook fire and took us aside. He told us of his journey.

He had found Religion. This was not the do-gooding of the Wesleyan, nor the gilded ritual of the Roman Catholics, nor the self-satisfaction of the Anglicans, nor the petulant pedantry of the Calvinists in their Scottish and New England forms. This was a fiery religion, a dipper full of the burning blood of Jesus, which he had learned to drink, relish and revere.

Kit was worn, wounded, in pain and loss. His family had lost their plantation shortly after the war, and he was at a low in his life, perhaps even lower than my own had been at one time.

One of his cousins had brought him to a camp meeting after the war in the Low Country. As he listened, he submitted to the forceful prayers of one of these men of the Pentecost. He heard words that had been translated by poets of an ancient English or Scottish king. The phrases became a mix of rhythm and emotion and command, and he felt about him an experience of a brightening, dazzling light.

Kit joined others walking trails through shaded forests of trees to where that speaker, standing in a heavenly beam of sun in a shallow of the flowing river embraced each supplicant and dipped them into cleansing waters. Cold river waves covered his own upturned face while light from the sky grew into a bright and formless glow. He fell into a faint, swaddled into an aura of warmth, of liquid salvation and joy, and a heavenly chorus rose to fill his senses.

Instead of breaking his oath, he shed that life and was reborn.

When his eyes opened again he found himself lying on a comforter spread in a shaded glade surrounded by women and girls all dressed in white, caressing him and singing gentle hymns. Tears filled his eyes, and his sight was colored by happy luminescence on the gentle faces of a loving feminine choir about him.

One white-clad woman leaned close to him and spoke in a

low, clear voice: "Welcome, Brother. Welcome to the Community of Christ."

He moved his hand from the gentle fingers of a soft grip and touched his face. He was shaven, and his chin was smooth as a river stone. His hair was cropped close, nearly tonsured. He felt much as Samson may have felt, yet he was not fearful. The gentle voices continued their lilting songs. A snowy pair of hands lifted a cup to his lips. Scent of steam from the tea, soothing sounds of women, glorious radiance and other temporal comforts made him weep.

"Read to me from the book, Sister," he said. And she read:

> *The Lord is my shepherd. I shall not want...*
> *He maketh me to lie down in green pastures:*
> *He leadeth me beside the still waters.*

He had shed his comrades' world of pain and battle, the bitter world of heartache and disappointment, the land of the Oaken Three, of Patriotic Duty. Duty to an abstract government whose purpose was to use the heroic idealism of youth to forward the goals of the venal wealthy.

Is it not always so?

He had passed through a cruel and hateful world into this one of light, the world of the love of God and Man. A communion of joy, based on the words of a stern yet loving Father, and his gentler Son.

> *He restoreth my soul:*
> *He leadeth me in the paths of righteousness*
> *For his name's sake...*

We listened to him that day, years after his renaissance experience. He had grown new hair, and had become a traveling preacher. Eventually I think he married and settled in Missouri, and had six children who lived into adulthood.

He didn't use his old name. Kit was known as Brother Christopher. He was truly changed.

I've heard it said that people don't change, but I know for a fact that people do. Not all people, and not always for the better.

In his case, religion saved his soul and his life.

411

67

AN EASY REST

We built a new life in the mountains with my money, and with funds Father Haywood received from the deeply discounted sale of his Charleston properties

I took up my architecture studies again and began a business designing houses and barns for people around the area. Even today you might see one or two farmhouses with Charleston-styled piazzas, or a bit of Rococo detail and a hipped French Provincial roof where you would not expect one.

I stayed in touch with Zeke until he passed, and then with his family and Cassie's niece young Flora.

Aunt Peggy left us for her reward in her time, as did the loyal Pierre. The dog had fathered several litters of poodle mixes before he got feeble, and there were always dogs about the place.

Two years after our wedding Jenny and I had a daughter, and then another. Little Daisy died of typhus when she was only eight years old, that sweet child. May grew into a strong woman. She had seen tragedy at an early age and had a clear view of life. She married a lawyer from Raleigh.

He would be your Great Uncle Brewster.

People from my old life in Charleston would sometimes come by.

One late spring day in 1872 a fine carriage driven by a smartly dressed coachman came up, and from it alighted a prosperous looking Charles Gallard.

I last saw Charles as he was heading toward Richmond with

his fireworks.

"Mr. Vander, you look well!"

I sent the carriage and driver to the stable, and Festus brought him into the kitchen to eat.

Charles and I went to the porch where Jenny and Daisy were shelling peas, and we had luncheon brought out.

We shared stories of our lives, our two little girls, and heard what was happening in Charleston. Charles was helping to engineer reconstruction of the city and modernize its shipyards.

"Charles, what went wrong with your rocket that you were going to send into the Presidential Mansion? I never heard that it was attacked."

Charles raised that eyebrow he had shown me those years ago at the telegraph office.

"Well," he began, "Jon, that rocket was never meant to hurt anyone."

Then he told me the most amazing story.

Everyone had heard of the Battle of the Crater in July of 1864, an attempt by Pennsylvania troops from coal country to undermine the Confederate line. They had placed dynamite beneath it and blew a hole in it. The explosion caused more confusion than injuries, and when Federal troops poured into the hole, they became fixed targets for the Confederate forces in what was described as a "turkey shoot."

Charles was ordered to secretly bring his rockets into battle, to demonstrate Southern versus Northern unorthodoxy.

He prepared his rocket. He set the timers, primed the fuse, and aimed it carefully toward Washington. Three generals and their staff watched the rocket blast into the sky.

The device's large propulsive charge roared and flared it nearly beyond sight. The timer tripped the inner tube's charge, and that inner rocket shot up, up.

And according to Charles, it never came down.

I recalled that we had discussed moons and gravities, and the orbital properties of heavenly bodies on our Nassau trip. It was all theory to me. Charles claimed that his rocket's velocity was so great that it became another moon, smaller, but eternally circling the earth, a Confederate satellite orbiting forever, perhaps longer than people will remember the Southern Republic.

Another time a delegation of three sweet old ladies arrived at our place, their skirts sounding the rustle of female infantry. They had found my name on a list of "Defenders of Fort Sumter," which I never was.

They had each lost a son or a husband in the service of the Confederate government, and true to their love for them, their organization worked to honor their memories. They did this by placing statues and monuments about the South, establishing gravesites and having medals struck to present to Confederate heroes – which I certainly was not.

They were so kind and gentle and sincere, and Jenny welcomed them into the house. I was going to tell them of the mistake, but Jenny, in her devotion to all she knew and honored from that national tragedy, gave me a look that precluded any protest or explanation.

They found my name on the list from that cold morning I had returned from fighting the fire on Fort Sumter, exhausted and with a growing toothache. So, besides the cookies, tea and the blue ribbon I was given that morning in 1863, thirty-two years later these Daughters of the South awarded this noncombatant Boston Yankee a medal for being a Confederate hero!

My friend Edward from my childhood in Boston came to visit.

He had not gone to war but became a lawyer, had done well and entered into politics, eventually becoming mayor of one of the towns near Boston, maybe Newton.

Anyway, he had never been to the mountains of North Carolina and greatly enjoyed his tour. He had some word about the family of my father's widow.

My step-mother had indeed returned to New Jersey with the liquid remains of my father's estate. Her older daughter, that temptress Fanny, had married well to someone connected with a university in Medford and had two children. Edward had met her at some mayoral event, and she told him that she always expected that I would return to try to claim my inheritance.

The war disrupted many plans, not least ones within the heart.

"Laura married rather suddenly when she was sixteen, as I

telegraphed you," he said. "She and her husband, a young account representative at a machine company moved to Hartford, Connecticut, had a daughter, then two sons.

"She came to see me once and had a message for you if I were ever to see you. She wanted me to ask you to forgive her."

It took me a moment to digest this information. I had forgiven and forgotten Laura long since. That girl with the warm hands and inquisitive mind was a child when I knew her, just learning about the world, as was I. She remembered our adolescent promise and had a regret.

"I have long ago forgiven her," I told him. "We were just children."

Years later after our daughter May moved away, a stranger came up to the house, and I'll be darned if it wasn't Martin!

Well, it wasn't Martin, his name was William, naturally, but he looked just like Martin. He was younger than Martin would have been then. His last name was Tinnett.

Jenny was breathless, tearful, the dear woman. We invited him in, and we made tea. We were using China tea by that time, a special variety new to us, Jasmine.

The young man told his story. He had been born in Maryland and grew up in a small town near Baltimore. Not until he had gone away to school did he learn that his father, who had only one leg "from the war," was originally from Charleston.

He learned that his father served in the Confederate Army, and was wounded and captured at the Battle of Cedar Creek in October of 1864. He was taken to Baltimore to a hospital and eventually healed as well as most one-legged men could in those days, but would not return to his fiancée, as he termed Jenny, as less a man than he had been. He allowed the story of his death to be reported and never sought to correct it.

Martin met a woman who was serving as a nurse and married her. He changed the spelling of his name and eventually took over the operations of her family's dry goods business.

His wound never completely healed despite the best care he could receive. Eventually it became infected again. When he died, he had left in his will that William was to visit Jonathan Vander of Charleston.

It had taken a bit of research, but finally he had located the property the Haywoods owned in North Carolina.

William had been directed to return an item I had loaned his father, and the young man brought forth the silver dollar I had given Martin so many years before in that nuptial grotto. It was pierced with a hole, creating an amulet of currency and promise, which he had worn around his neck through his marches and battles.

Jenny was mostly in a breathless state during Mr. Tinnett's visit. Her eyes would drift from this handsome young man, so like her fiancée – no, her lost husband. I imagine she was recalling their days of youth and courtship, perhaps a hurried night of love before his farewell on an early train and perhaps of the life they had planned. Then her glowing eyes would snap back to the young man, his warm smile and easy conversation with me. He had come to thank me, but had brought to Jenny the long-buried memory of might-have-been glory.

A cherished memory can sleep for years, for decades, and awaken with the force of a gale.

Martin had promised in the secret wedding ceremony that he would give Jenny the best life in his power, and to him that finally meant that he would not let her live her life with a cripple.

When William drove away, we never discussed him or Martin again. But I know she thought of him sometimes. And he had been my friend too.

Martin, that man of privilege and manner and obligation, through his son, at last repaid me with the very coin I gave him. And with his example of moral honesty and loyalty, and grace.

And with his most cherished heart's desire, my wife.

Jenny and I shared more than three decades together. We had our troubles, and we had each other and could survive life's storms.

Jenny's father, the gentle man, created a new life and found satisfaction, if never again wealth. He enjoyed his little farm, his apple trees, playing with his grandchildren and seeing one of them well-married.

Father Haywood passed at the age of ninety having seen the world he had grown up in lost, yet creating another in these mountains. We found him beneath the bower of a blooming apple tree he had planted, a mournful son of Pierre crouching beside him as petals of the blossoms gently drifted down upon his calm and smiling face.

Jenny had begun to have her health problems in the late 1890s. She became slow in step, yet could smile that beautiful smile I had seen so many years ago while singing those lovely Stephen Foster airs at the plantation party.

My Jenny, the mother of my children, lived to see the new 20th Century. She died in 1902, just shy of sixty years old, still pretty, still joyous and gay, even sweetly singing songs on her bed before her passing, made easier with tincture of opium. I thank God for that.

She had lived a fairytale life until the folly of politics took away her prince and her world. I was there to lift her up, if not to the height she expected, at least to where she could fulfill some of her promise. She was a good wife, a strong partner. My beloved.

Yet I had had another beloved.

Not Laura, the excitable child with whom I had first shared a forbidden thrill in my youth, but the one I had determined to marry while on that rocking blockade-running boat and on the train from Wilmington. When I drew near Charleston again I had had a goal, a destination for my life, a promise made to myself and my universe, and had hoped to make to her.

I never got to speak the words to her and have lived a life of regret buried deep in myself where no one could see it, least of all my wonderful Jenny.

Isabella, that soul who fled from this world more nearly eight decades ago, never heard my dedication of love to her. She never saw what a loving and giving husband I could be.

When she died, I could not even find her grave to put her name on it. So I did the only thing in my power to grant her the greatest honor I could.

She wasn't able to hear me ask her to take my name, so I took hers.

Three months after the death of my beloved Jenny I had the county judge change my name to Isabella Jonathan Vander, and that is the "I" in my initials. I didn't care what people thought, and I still don't. I wear it proudly.

I have arranged that it be carved on my headstone when I finally lay again next to my loving wife Jenny.

I want my name to be displayed as "I. Jonathan Vander." It is a small thing; it is a private thing. See that it is done for me.

Jenny knew and loved Isabella as well, and always knew I did. The three of us will rest easy together.

* * *

That was all of his story he told me.

I knew that in his life Uncle Jonathan had designed houses where families lived, where children played.

He told me that when America went to war again, this time against Spain, he had been sad that the nation had forgotten what the 1860s war had taught his generation.

Again, when the nation sent its troops to France to fight the Kaiser, he spoke out and was shouted down amid the flags waving and bands playing.

He became withdrawn, secluded himself in his aging mountain home with his dogs and his books, his drawings and his memories.

He tended his garden and was friends with the descendants of the slaves managed by his friend Zeke, and they revered him for a generation. The next generation of Zeke's people cared for him out of tradition, and the next never knew who he really was and how he had been friends with their ancient patriarch. Except for Cassie's niece Flora, he was forgotten. Finally he was invited to the home where I found him.

I never mentioned the growing effort to draw America into the current war, but he was aware enough to know. Again another generation was being led by parades, flags and stirring music into killing other young men so like themselves.

He was tired, and it was late, and I bade him good night.

So, I returned to Chapel Hill and my studies, and my work with the professors and students. Another year passed, and I was notified of his decline.

I visited him again once more, though by then he was in his last hours.

I JONATHAN

He laid in his bed sunken and wan, his fingers thin and turning blue, his breath just a whisper. He was unaware of my presence, perhaps already in another place. I regretted he was not able to see me then, perhaps to give me just a smile of recognition.

Sometimes the best communication is not verbal.

When he passed, Cousin Alice came. She and I went to his old home, vacant for four years.

I really didn't remember much about the place from my childhood other than the smell of the hemlocks and pines, the wonderful view, and the warm smells of cooking and canning. No activities there like that for a long time.

I walked about the sunny property and through the old orchard, now gone to ruin from neglect. In the "champagne air" I heard many bird songs I had never known before. Wildflowers bloomed everywhere, and I found large dew-beaded webs between huge trees, with jewels of large spiders suspended in the middle of each.

Nature had decorated the property with songs and flowers and gems and light.

We had brought Uncle Jonathan's box of effects from his room, and Alice invited me to review them with her.

We found a few old letters from Charleston, a tin-type photo of a little girl in a white pinafore, a formal portrait photo of his wife Jenny with his older daughter May on her wedding day, and a folded piece of sheet music for the song "When Stars Are In The Quiet Skies."

When the box was empty, Alice lifted it and thought it was too heavy, and sure enough there was a false bottom in that box. When we pried it out, we found an 1856 silver dollar pierced to allow it to be worn as a necklace. Also inside was a scrap of white cotton cloth with a faded floral print in blue and black, and a bronze military-style medal.

On the medal is inscribed "Deo Vindice." Vengeful God.

* * *

419

Gloria, who I hoped would become my wife, has left me for good and is promised to another man.

I've done my best to recreate the story my great-great uncle told me. I'll work on this more when I return from service.

I decided to enlist. I joined the army where I am to report next week and perhaps see more of the world. HOO-HAH!

I hope that Great Uncle Jonathan would have forgiven me.

-Ralph J. Bennett

616 Simpson Street, Apt. 2B
Greensboro
North Carolina 27401
October 28, 2008

Publisher
Fountain City Publishing Company
P.O. Box 18477
Knoxville, TN 37918

Dear Mr. Scott,

My parents recently passed away and while going through their belongings I found a box of items from my mother's older brother Ralph.

I have looked through these papers and they're still legible and I think they may be worth publishing some time. I've shown them to book publishers in Greensboro and Winston-Salem but they have no interest in doing the work it would take to prepare them for the press.

I found your name and address from a friend who reads historical fiction, from from some editions of novels your company had published, and thought this might be the best category for this work.

Please look at these and see if you think this is worth pursuing and let me know. At this point I don't care about royalties or money from the story. I just hope it will someday be in print, even in a small way, in memory of my mother and her love for her brother who I never met.

He was a student at UNC until he joined the service and was killed in the war. World War 2.

Thank you. Sincerely,

Jane Bennett Taylor

BIBLIOGRAPHY FOR I JONATHAN

A Diary from Dixie
Mary Boykin Chesnut

Charleston at War, The Photographic Record 1860-1865
Jack Thomson

Gate of Hell, Campaign for Charleston Harbor, 1863
Stephen R. Wise

The Siege of Charleston 1861-1865
E. Milby Burton

Allegiance, Fort Sumter, Charleston, and the Beginning of the Civil War
David Detzer

The Bombardment of Charleston, 1863-1865
W. Chris Phelps

Secessionville, Assault on Charleston
Patrick Brennan

The Plain People of the Confederacy
Bell Irvin Wiley

Heroines of Dixie: Spring of High Hopes, and Winter of Desperation
Katharine M. Jones, Ed.

The Pocket Book of Civil War Weapons, From Small Arms to Siege Artillery
Angus Konstam

Civil War Soldiers, Their Expectations and Their Experiences
Reid Mitchell

From the Fields of Fire and Glory, Letters of the Civil War
Rod Gragg

A Treasury of Civil War Tales
Webb Garrison

Mr. Lincoln's High-Tech War
Thomas B. Allen & Roger MacBride Allen

Tales of the South Carolina Low Country, and Slave Ghost Stories
Nancy Rhyne

Tales of Edisto
Nell S. Graydon

Excerpts from: The Charge of the Light Brigade by Alfred, Lord Tennyson
The Bingen on the Rhine by Caroline Sheridan Norton
Bivouac of the Dead by Theodore O'Hara
Somebody's Darling by Marie Ravenal de la Coste
When Stars are in the Quiet Skies by Edward Bulwer-Lytton
Open Thy Lattice Love by Stephen Foster

Blue Roots, African-American Folk Magic of the Gullah People
Roger Pinckney

Letters from Lee's Army
Susan Leigh Blackford & Charles Minor Blackford

The H. L. Hunley, The Secret Hope of the Confederacy
Tom Chaffin

Blockade Runners of the Confederacy
Hamilton Cochran

Blockade – The Civil War at Sea
Robert Carse

Lifeline of the Confederacy, Blockade Running During the Civil War
Stephen R. Wise

Rebel Cornbread and Yankee Coffee, Authentic Civil War Cooking and Camaraderie
Garry Fisher

The American Frugal Housewife
Mrs. Child

Siege Train, The Journal of a Confederate Artilleryman in the Defense of Charleston
Major Edward Manigault, Warren Ripley Ed.

Enlisted For The War, The Struggles of the Gallant 24th Regiment, S.C. Volunteers,
Infantry, 1861-1865
Eugene W. Jones Jr.

This Republic of Suffering, Death and the American Civil War
Drew Gilpin Faust

Don't Know Much About the Civil War
Kenneth C. Davis

The Confederate Reader
Richard B. Harwell Ed.

Breckinridge, Statesman, Soldier, Symbol
William C. Davis

Photographer Under Fire, The Story of George S. Cook
Jack C. Ramsay, Jr.

Lowell Offering, Writings by New England Mill Women 1840-1845
Benita Eisler

Days and Ways in Old Boston
William S. Rossiter

Black Charlestonians, A Social History 1822-1885
Bernard E. Powers Jr.

American Jewry in the Civil War
Bertram W. Korn

The Jewish Confederates
Robert N. Rosen

Flat Rock of the Old Time: Letters from the Mountains to the Lowcountry, 1837–1939
Robert B. Cuthbert Ed.

Germans of Charleston, Richmond and New Orleans during the Civil War Period 1850-1870
Andrea Mehrlander

The United Methodist Hymnal
Hymnal Revision Committee 1989

Nave's Topical Bible
Orville J. Nave

Webster's New International Dictionary of the English Language (Unabridged)
2nd Edition 1952

WEBSITES
civilwartalk.com
south-carolina-plantations.com
lowcountryafricana.
next1000.com/family/EC/slavenames.html
chroniclingamerica.loc.gov
(This site scans scores of newspapers for subjects in American history)

Wikipedia has been a wonderful resource for hundreds of bits of information as well as timelines and suggestions for further reading.

While researching Civil War rockets I found a reference on a website of Burke Davis's "Our Incredible Civil War," where I read of the concept of putting a satellite into orbit as part of a Confederate Army missile bombardment demonstration on Washington, D.C. Not my idea, but too good not to use.

ACKNOWLEDGEMENTS

All work begins with an idea, an inspiration. Mine was a visit to Fort Sumter.

When I was a young boy with a biography assignment, my father suggested a person whose story had inspired him in his life, Robert E. Lee. Since that time I have read, studied, and tried to reconcile the goodness of Southerners about me with the obvious problem of fighting against their native country in defense of an indefensible way of life. This book, in its way, is my attempt to unwind that knot.

On a visit to Charleston I became fascinated with the story of Fort Sumter. I read historical newspapers about it and many books. While researching I learned that I had an ancestor in Charleston during part of the Civil War. He makes a cameo appearance in my story.

On a later visit to the Holy City I took an historic tour with the late author Jack Thomson as a guide. I told him I was considering writing a book, and he told me to give him a credit, so here it is. Thank you and rest in peace, Mr. Thomson.

After years of postponing my writing, I finally began organizing my notes and thoughts. As I completed chapters I would send some to friends and family for feedback, and I am grateful to my sister Amy Scott and to Molly McMillan for their kindness.

When the manuscript was completed in its first form I called upon Amy once again, my childhood Florida friend Rick Crary, my new friend from the Low Country Patricia Benton, and Stephen Scruggs for an African American perspective on the story. All had good feedback and suggestions.

Despite my careful review of the story, I was told that it still required editing when my sister Nancy Millar read it, so I took advantage of her professional abilities and saw that she was right. Later my wife Mary Leidig revised the editing once again.

Finally, the manuscript was passed to other friends and Civil War writers from whom I asked an honest review. My heartfelt thanks go to them: Dr. Milton Russell of the University of Tennessee, Steve Dean of the Civil War Round Table in Knoxville, Meg Groeling, author and writer for Emerging Civil War of California, Prof. Caroline Janney, Director, University of Virginia John L. Nau III Center for Civil War History, and author Jack Neely of Knoxville.

Others who gave me advice and encouragement include my good friend Scot Danforth of University of Tennessee Press, Brent Minchey of Celtic Cat Publishing, and from my childhood, Sandy Reisner, who sat next to me in ninth grade and read a short story I wrote. She told me she thought I could write well.

For these friends and family, I am in their debt, and to some I give them warning that I may press their favor again in my next project.

George William Brock Scott was born in Stuart, Florida, and lives in Knoxville, Tennessee. He and his wife Mary Leidig have two sons, Gideon and Daniel.